# SUN CIRCLE

*To J. B. Salmond*

Neil Miller Gunn (1891–1973) was born in Dunbeath, Caithness, one of the nine children of 'bookish' Isabella Miller, ambitious for her sons, and James Gunn, a fishing skipper of local renown. At thirteen, Neil was sent away to live with a married sister in Galloway. At fifteen, he went to London as a boy clerk in the Civil Service. In 1911, he began 26 years as an excise officer, many of them at whisky distilleries in the Highlands and Islands. When the Great War broke out, two of his brothers were killed and one died later of war-related injuries. Gunn was particularly close to his brother John, who was badly gassed, and in later years John's war experiences were incorporated into *Highland River*. In 1921, Gunn married Jessie Frew, called 'Daisy' for her golden hair. Tragically, their only child was still-born.

Gunn's duties in Inverness (1923–1937) left ample time for writing and for activity as a leader in Scottish Nationalist politics. The first of his 21 novels, *The Grey Coast*, appeared in 1926. The fourth, *Morning Tide* (1930), was a Book Society choice in 1931. In 1937, the acclaim won by his seventh, the prize-winning *Highland River*, encouraged him to resign his excise post and write full-time.

Notable among his other novels are *The Green Isle of the Great Deep* (1944), *The Well at the World's End* (1951), *Bloodhunt* (1952), and four epic recreations of Highland history, with *Sun Circle* (1933) for ancient times, *Butcher's Broom* (1934) for the Clearances, the hugely successful *The Silver Darlings* (1941), and from modern times *The Drinking Well* (1946). Gunn also published short stories, essays and plays. His last book, *The Atom of Delight* (1956), is an autobiography which reflects his lifelong and Zen-like fascination with the elusive spirit of life, wisdom, and delight.

Gunn's wife died in 1963, and he lived alone in the Black Isle until his death in January, 1973. Since then, his standing as one of Scotland's great novelists has grown even more firmly established, and the Neil Gunn International Fellowship was founded in his honour.

Neil M. Gunn

# *SUN CIRCLE*

*Introduced by J.B. Pick*

CANONGATE
CLASSICS
66

First published in 1933 by The Porpoise Press
and Faber and Faber Ltd. First published as a
Canongate Classic in 1996 by Canongate Books
Ltd, 14 High Street, Edinburgh EHI ITE.

The publishers gratefully acknowledge general sub-
sidy from the Scottish Arts Council towards the
Canongate Classics series and a specific grant
towards the publication of this title.

Set in 10pt Plantin by Palimpsest Book Production
Limited, Polmont, Stirlingshire. Printed and bound
in Finland by WSOY.

*British Library Cataloguing in Publication Data*
A catalogue record for this book is available
from the British Library.

ISBN 0 86241 587 X

# Introduction

*Sun Circle*, first published in 1933, is a violent story thick with sexual tension; but it is more than that. Through a harsh, intense account of invasion, betrayal and defeat, Neil Gunn struggles with problems which he could face only by placing them in a remote and secret time and in the privacy of imaginative fiction.

The book is a passionate confrontation with the humiliations suffered by the people of the Highlands throughout history, against which his pride and sense of personal integrity revolted. It delves down to the psychological roots of evil and violence, and embodies also a hypersensitive examination of the temptations to cruelty that one form of intellectual/aesthetic detachment can bring. Aniel, favoured disciple of the Druidic Master can be seen as, in this sense, a version of Neil Gunn himself.

Gunn was born in 1891, son of the skipper of a fishing boat at a time when the industry still flourished and the local community pulsed with life. He left home at the age of thirteen, returning as an exciseman in 1922. The psychological shock was deep and bitter: familiar harbours were deserted, fleets gone, his father dead, the economy ruined, the world gone sour. He strove in his first two novels to show what he felt to be the truth about contemporary Highland life: *The Grey Coast* (1926) is a claustrophobic tale of a girl trapped in a narrow, oppressive world; in *The Lost Glen* (1932), which shakes with emotional disillusionment, the Highlands are seen as a spiritual cul de sac.

It was not until Gunn found both inner refreshment and commercial success through a return to boyhood in *Morning Tide*, (1931, written after *The Lost Glen*, although published before it) that he gained the fortitude to confront and transcend the problems which troubled him. He undertook a series of novels on Highland history, and began at the beginning with Caithness in a period so sparsely documented that its wildness, depth and distance set his imagination alight, and set it free.

There may be some doubt as to the exact period envisaged. Columba's conversion of the northern part of what is now Scotland (which probably meant little more than the acceptance of Christianity by a few rulers) took place in the 6th Century, while the Norse raids and eventual occupation of the Orkneys and Caithness are generally attributed to the 9th. That's a sizeable gap, and whether the pagan Druidic religion was as enduring and refined as is shown here, and whether the Christian missionary priest would be so isolated, there is now no means of telling. Gunn read all the material available to him at the time of writing and in these matters imagination has its own authority.

In the story, the coast is threatened by Norse reivers, who sack, burn, loot, and bear off captives into slavery wherever they land. The folk of the place are, we are told, 'a dark, intricate people, loving music and fun'. The tribes owe loose allegiance to a far-off King but operate in self-contained communities, each under its own chief.

Alongside the tribe of the Ravens live, hidden and elusive in their low round houses like green mounds, the aboriginal 'Finlags', 'a dwarfish race' who speak 'the old language', and are neither to be trusted nor understood, for they move with their own lore in secret ways, like cunning moles, but more dangerous.

South of the Ravens are the Logenmen, wary to the point of hostility, who seize the opportunity of Viking assault to raid the Ravens' cattle. This is one of many references forward to what Gunn saw as the tragedy of Scottish history – internal feuding which lets in the external enemy, and makes full cultural development impossible.

As always with Gunn, concern is not simply with physical and psychological conflict, but with fundamental spiritual currents which move within and work through history. This intense metaphysical preoccupation disconcerts some readers, yet the emotional drive of the tale is so strong that if it is accepted as it runs, spiritual and physical form a unity which burns in the mind, while the intuitive mingling of history with thought and legend acquires a hallucinatory force.

The tribe of the Ravens is nominally Christian. The missionary priest Molrua has taken up residence on their land. Yet the ancient Grove with its dark trees and standing stones remains peopled by the Master of the old religion and his pupils. Drust, chief of the Ravens, accepts his wife's Christianity yet resents her rigorous zeal and assumption of right as a slur on his manhood, at one point breaking out with, 'There would never be peace in this accursed place until she was riding their backs as they crawled to the Christian priest.'

Molrua instructs the people that they cannot serve both God and Mammon, that the rites and sacrifices of the Grove are evil; but their minds move more deviously than he can guess. To worship both God and Mammon was 'for them not only simple, but wise and needful'. 'There are hidden, evil things and dark spirits whom we must defeat if we are to be Christians . . . But Molrua does not know what the Master knows.'

It is characteristic of Gunn's method that despite the passionate intensity of his emotional commitment to the story, he is concerned always to hold the balance; the spiritual conflict is not prejudged but held in the mind as a whole. Molrua and the Master each represents his religion at its purest – Molrua, Christianity in its vital flowering and the Master, the old religion at its most refined, one rising and one falling on the tide of history.

The old religion shows its harshest face in the priest Gilbrude, who dislikes the Master's breadth and tolerance, and we ourselves participate in the hypnotic exaltation of human sacrifice. In the same way, Drust's wife Silis brings to mind the history of Scottish religious fanaticism as the comment is made, 'For one could so work for the conversion of others that the sway of authority thereby engendered tended to puff up the mind in its lust for power, and God's name was used for terror, and Christ's name as a threat.'

Molrua himself presents the Christian story 'in all its newness and strange and terrible beauty, so strange and beautiful that it had the air about it still of the incredible. And because the incredible was true, the heart rose in surprise and gladness.' Molrua's mind is shown in its own beauty as he watches the Norsemen move about below him: 'Under the morning it was a strange thing to see men so behave. Their limbs and their weapons stirred like the legs of great spiders . . . Strange to watch their dark antics in the fresh light of so clear a morning. Strange that those creatures should be God's creatures, too . . .'

The Master makes few appearances but each appearance is of profound significance in the story. Whether Gunn's portrayal of a late-pagan priest is valid cannot be known, but it is entirely authentic to his own perceptions of a way through the terrors and humiliations of the world. The Master's achievement is to have reached the point of 'the dividing of forces with no gain and no loss, and no question of reward beyond the reward of being there.' The Master and Molrua have both along their separate roads arrived at a condition close to selflessness. What emerges, then, is the convergence of the way of the saint (Molrua, through prayer, fasting, and faith) and the sage (the Master, through meditation, insight and detachment).

Gunn's own struggle at the time was to move beyond the bitterness of emotional identification with the sufferings of his people, and to lift himself out of the tyranny of mood, seeing both personal events and the events of history from a point of balance within his own circle of light.

For this reason the passionate spiritual wrestling of the artist-intellectual Aniel, and his relationships with the wildly veering Breeta, and with Nessa, the chief's daughter, are crucial to the meaning of the book. That gives the reader an initial problem, for the first section deals almost exclusively with this bout of sexual intensity in such over-ripe and highly-charged language – 'a face whose skin was so alive that it seemed to palpitate' – that mind evades it as simply too much. Moods change as swiftly as a rabbit twisting in mid-leap, and we grow weary trying to keep pace.

And then there is that inimical flavour in Aniel's cat-and-mouse play with Breeta, a kind of detachment close to cruelty which disquiets and disturbs. The Master's teaching requires detachment, but as an aid to understanding, with no taint of cruelty or malevolence. No, Aniel is not easy company, but he is entirely alive. In the same way, Breeta's fleeting squalls and sudden flights can try the patience, but her vigorous reality can't be doubted.

What saves Aniel is his acute awareness. He knows he must liberate himself from the desire for psychic power, and he knows that the Master sees through him and through his temptations. A momentary experience of that state of luminous contemplation which frees the spirit lives as an essential memory in the depths of his mind. For he learns, as we learn, that the Master's teaching is in the end straight and simple: *see clearly*. No one can see clearly if malevolence infects the vision.

Gunn was wrestling with the question of whether wisdom is possible for an artist of Aniel's kind, and with the way of salvation for a 'maker' at a time of violence and destruction: 'Aniel was a maker and a maker can retreat from what evil he has done, or from what evil has come upon him, to the happy solitude of his own creation, and yet have a cunning understanding of that evil.'

And one of the evils that the author himself grows to understand – which he explored more thoroughly ten years later in *The Green Isle of the Great Deep* – is that those human beings who are of genuine value in the world are not the conquerors, the men of power, but those who endure and create, for the ruler 'lives . . . on the blood and the flesh of the people'.

Indeed his hatred for the destroyers and controllers is so great that the one failure of balance in *Sun Circle* is the author's refusal to view the Norsemen with the same objectivity as the other diverse peoples he portrays. They are seen as a destructive force without moral value. There is no rejoicing in their stoic resolution and sardonic courage in the face of death that we find in Linklater's novel from the same period, *Men of Ness*. *Sun Circle* was written before Hitler came to power and before the nature of Nazi philosophy was widely known, yet the Vikings move with a peculiarly 'Aryan' arrogance and sense of superior might, while their leader Haakon, backed and manipulated by his cynical adviser Sweyn, takes on the prophetic aspect of some blonde *gauleiter* of the Hitler Youth. The Norsemen are described as 'strangers and hostile not merely to the folk of that glen but to the earth and the air so that their very echo was an outrage'. No condemnation could be more complete. Occasionally, indeed, you feel the writer's temptation to subvert history by allowing the Ravens to destroy these invaders, but his integrity as a story-teller forbids it.

We are carried through *Sun Circle* by the relentless headlong current of the tale, yet remain continually aware of the powerful personal presence of the author, not only through style, the electric emotional charge of the writing, but in an atmosphere of dark tension, illuminated by flashes of lightning – 'the truth', he writes, 'is a flash of intuition which is a flash of lightning'. As a result, running through the entire book is an unpredictable swirl of uncanny and dangerous insight. For Gunn goes farther than exploring the history of his people and the nature of religion, farther than seeking psychological liberation for himself, he confronts explicitly the malignant cruelty that is part of 'all Beyond', that terrible ambiguity at the heart of life.

*Sun Circle* not only comes close to being a great novel, it acquires as it moves some legendary quality, bringing vividly home the essential nature of legend itself, as well as the permanent nature of Man, who requires it. If we cannot, like the Master in facing that malignant cruelty, catch 'the balanced moment of all-seeing', we can at least appreciate that 'You did not understand truth; you *saw* it.' Occasionally as we read we see it ourselves. Indeed, no reader who enters deeply into this book will emerge unaffected.

J.B. Pick

# The Outline

AT the third hour after noon the sun was still asleep in the summer sky. The moors and forests of the Northland lay under it and in glittering barren places the heat wavered and danced, turning veins of quartz to veins of fire. Beyond the mainland the blue of the sea was more intense than the blue of the sky, and the Islands of the Orcades lay at anchor like fabled ships: long shapes, with clean prows to the west, with sheer sides, not riding the sea but crouching to it with that odd menace which, like tenderness, is for ever at the heart of strength. All adventuring races have been drawn by them. Thither the Roman came, rounding northward to Ultima Thule. Before the Roman, a conquering race had here built its wonder towers and struck southward for a kingdom. And through this summer day across the eastern sea comes the ghostly echoing of master craftsmen hammering the smooth planks of the longships of the Vikings against yet another – and perhaps final – invasion.

Westward from the Orcades the sea recedes, rounding great headlands, netting vivid islets offshore, green over the white sand, brown over the tangle, and at last, released, blue to the Arctic; but caught back again by the tides and divided by the precipices of the nor'-west, where it throws wheels of light, arrows of light, restless under the intense windless sky, mouthing the rocks in a vague spume, until the coastline turning south draws its waters from all that leashed uneasy strength of the North to what has been in all ages the mystery of the West.

Here the islands that lie to the horizon are no longer like ships. The mainland dreams out to them and beyond them to where all the dead live, young and comely, with the hue of the foxglove in a woman's cheek. There is as little twilight in Land-of-the-Young as in the Isles of the Blest. There is indeed no twilight, death being but the sunset through which one sails on the last adventure of all.

To the long gaze the blue of the sea here loses the deep brilliance of the North, grows at moments cloudy like a memory of sightless eyes or the flicker of a pale robe. When at nightfall the Orcades lift anchor and their long shapes head outward, these Western Isles settle down, draw their sea-curtains about them, and close their doors. Sightless eyes are older than Homer, and the flicker of a pale robe is a passing presence whose face may not be seen.

Love and music, treacherous passion and story, gaiety and an ear for sorrow, gather at night-time within the little doors where women still go on working and singing, in this world of their own.

Out of the North come grey shapes and long seas and men, the North which is worn smooth by austere winds that have searched out all the faults and cleansed them with the dry fine sand that eternity filters through time. So that the bone itself is bitten hard as a blade, and the galley that comes grating in the night or flashing its dipping oars and breastplates in the sun, is a shape of terror and death and the glory of man is pagan and invincible.

All down the West the islands lie to the sea under this hot summer sky inviting and unprotected, and the long gaze narrows with foreknowledge of their certain rape.

Narrows and lingers a moment on one last island of all, where men, robed and cowled like women, their backs to the pagan West, are meditating the triumph of the light of Christ. And that island, too, shall be raped.

Lingers over this latest mystery, this new religion that tames kings and warriors into the mildness of women, that is not crushed but only made fertile by rape and, held by a speculative quietude, turns inland.

But between mountains the sea is forgotten, its far bright horizons vanish, and the scored earth rises against the sight.

Through forests and deep valleys narrow tracks divide and disappear. For the first time unseen danger touches the body. The touch firms, the danger moves noiselessly and parallel, until in the hush of the hot noon it holds the sick heart in the hollow of its suspense. The crushing of undergrowth by wolf or wild-boar is the relief of music. Open fighting is the song of strength, and death is acknowledged in the glory of a shout. But the Unseen that at any moment may put out a hand, that may draw living bodies within the jungle of primordial nightmare, must be propitiated by the sacrifice of one for the many, with incantation and priestly rite. The mind gropes out to the meaning of this. The body pauses, listening. The senses hear the unuttered cry, see shapes behind shapes, and movements that invisibly withdraw as they are stared at. The instincts grow needle-fine as the leaves of the pine forest, and as dark-plumed and profound. The wind of emotion stirs them and, sloughing stark fear, they rush to a dance in a sunny valley. The golden light banks up its wave of ecstasy. Love bites swift and fierce, tumbling into the shadow. Out of seedtime comes harvest – and sacrifice once more.

Until the land is passed over and the sea is caught again far in the south-east; and there, too, are islands. Above all places this rockbound coast is spacious and full of light, and has one of its islands set for a holy beacon to cast out darkness by the memory of a Certain One who also had been sacrificed for all.

And so northward at last on a face-line that is for ever vigilant, with headlands like drawn brows. Before the eye reaches the Orcades once more, it turns for rest into a sea valley, and in a little glade comes upon a young woman playing with a child. The outline gathers about them, wavers, and disappears.

I

THE young woman is not the mother of the child; she is indeed a virgin, and the play in the tree-shadow is a gay frolic. She laughs and shudders. Her teeth flash and bite. The naked little body of the boy doubles up over her butting head. He has the advantage over her and compels the assault, which at the helpless peak of his enjoyment he utterly repels.

Under the still heat of the summer day his laughter rises through its gurgling infection to a shrill over-excitement. The scream warns and yet works upon her. The shadows of the outer birch leaves fleck her ardent sun-brown face, as the dark eyes dart and flash. The dress of grey-brown wool caught over her right shoulder creases upward as she writhes back to dive forward once more. Her bare legs hiss against each other and beat the cool grass. Her lips wrinkle from a growl as the skin of her face draws sleek and her ears flatten. She is playing in the forest and has movements within her older than the child can know. Yet they touch him, too, and in a final paroxysm of mirth his eyes close and he pushes the very thought of her from him.

Balancing, she hesitates, watching the naked little body as it sways screaming. Its helplessness may topple over at any moment. Her legs lie still. Her look grows steady.

As the screams subside, the child eyes open half fearful, half expectant on a face that is now detached and piercing into him. All the fun has gone and there is left an inhuman curiosity. The heat has drained the last flicker of his energy. Her eyes suddenly terrify him, and he begins to whimper, curled fingers groping blindly. In a flash she snatches him to her body, crushing that cruel moment of penetration. His groping fingers weigh down the loose dress beneath her left breast upon which his mouth lands, crushing for the nipple. Her back snicks as though a rib had pierced her heart and, with her breath yet in her teeth, she shoves the child from her. At that moment she becomes aware that she is being watched.

Her eyes, which had dilated, gather to gleaming points on the child's face while her skin darkens all over. She brings the laugh back and gurgles teasingly before lifting her head at careless hazard.

He is standing above her, looking down a green alley, a smile on his face. It is a friendly smile, with that odd mockery a young man may allow himself when, unseen, he has been watching a young woman and has all the advantage. Then smiling still, if now a shade darkly before her full regard, his lips moved and he turned and went slowly up out of sight among the trees.

The effect upon her was to make her speak to the child quite sensibly and capably, to behave indeed outwardly with a pleasant deliberation that was in striking contrast to her previous woodland frenzy. Inwardly, however, her heart was racing at a giddy speed and her mind was groping to remember personal attitudes of that frenzy while a hand kept lifting upward her dress at the left shoulder.

The child began whimpering peevishly, and she took him on her knees. But he would not sit content any longer, and turning to her body groped for it, crying out.

'Are you tired, my little sweetheart?' And she drew him against her so that his mouth was sleepily smothered. All the time, however, her eyes did not waver from their round thought. The child felt this lack of real sympathy and would not be pacified. Besides being tired and sleepy, he was hungry. 'Hush!' she said, and locking both her arms round the naked body, she laid her cheek against the head with its fair silky hair, and began rocking gently, crooning a sad melody that was like the wine of time in a dark place. Perhaps because it was of love, which has its earthen vessels with lips to pour, or broken lips to draw a darker wine from wandering feet. Her stare deepened dewily, gathering intense points of light. The child wriggled with all his might, crying lustily. He was not to be put off. The trick of the song exasperated him. The young woman rocked the more vehemently, crooned the louder, until the words themselves broke through, liquid words of such intimacy that they flowed inward from lives beyond lives beyond lives, until her ache drowned in their soft surge.

But the child, making sure of his hold on this brand-new and sufficiently wayward world, would have none of it. And at last she held him from her, demanding sharply, 'What is it?'

He kicked her stomach. From his grasping hands she threw back her hair. His screams maddened her all in a moment. 'What are you crying for?' She rolled him within her hands.

His rage was now justified and became complete.

'You rascal!' she cried with hypocritical friendliness, getting to her feet. 'You little rascal!' The fierceness of his screams tightened all her flesh. She pressed his face between her breasts. 'Hush!' She walked out from the tree shade to the little river path, and suddenly stood terrified before the presence of a man bearing down on her.

Her instincts urged her to flight even while they made motion impossible. She felt herself flying away in urgent bits that all fluttered back upon her as the small old man moved quietly towards her within a robe which swathed him to the heels. 'Hush!' she hissed, 'hush! hush!' and when at last she must look up, he was standing before her with a faint smile. The smile, however, scarcely touched his eyes, before which her body and her desires stood clear, not because the eyes were piercing, but because they were vague as the grey-green of glass that the sea has worn on a shore, and had, in their steadiness, a sight other than natural sight. His hair was grey-bleached and his beard was of the same colour, but thin and uncut. His face, brown as the bottom of a nut tipped out of its cluster, had the grained smoothness of such great age that it seemed to have gone small and round. A short peeled wand hung from his right hand, and from his neck a green stone the size of a lapwing's egg against which a thin gold serpent opened its jaws. Yet the whole was unobtrusive and vague as the eyes, which were like the eyes of an idol.

Breeta started at the voice which came clear and quiet

with neither thinness nor huskiness in it, as though it
issued from somewhere behind the throat, as the sight
from behind the eyes.

'Breeta,' she answered.

His still silence drew from her, 'Rineh my mother and
my father Murruch.' And then the choking words, 'Rineh
of the wolf.'

The child had stopped screaming. As though he had
asked her, she told him it was the son of Silis and of
Drust, who was the chief in that place. Her mother was
nursing him.

'He is fair,' he said, and continued to look at the child,
whose round eyes stared back. There was silence for a little.
He put his hand gently on the child's head, which was near
the girl's head. Then, after looking at the girl, he turned
his back on them and took the path by the stream towards
Drust's residence which was called the Tower.

As she went her way her legs shook violently under her.
She could not get his eyes from before her. Indeed, fear
was only now realising itself. He was the oldest of all
men and yet he was nameless. She had only once in
her life seen him before, and yet every hidden thing
in her life was in his power. He had command over
what prostrated her. All dread and inimical things were
compliant before him. And he went back until time was
lost. The well of fear was his drinking-place; from the
tree of good and evil he had cut and peeled the wand
he carried. Her gorge surged up round and sickly and
suffocating.

'What's the matter?' asked her mother, taking the child
from her.

She did not answer, but stood trembling in the gloom
of the room.

'Are you sick? Or have you seen a wraith?'

'I saw – the Master,' she answered at last.

The mother, with her lined forehead and overjutting hair-
ends, remained quite still, looking back at her. 'Where?'

The hushed note released the tension in the girl, so that
she weakly sat down on the wooden bench and leant her
shoulders against the cool stone wall. Her breast heaved.

Through the pallor which had caught her skin burned her black eyes. From her temples she pushed weightily her black hair.

'I was coming up by the wood path. Donan was screaming. I lifted my head – and there he was coming down on me. He made no noise.' Her hands fell.

'What did you do?'

'What could I? The child was screaming. When I looked up – his eyes. I never saw such eyes. Have you – ever seen them?'

'Yes.'

'Where?' asked the daughter, and she curiously watched her mother who had turned her head to a thought at a distance.

'Never mind. Did he speak to you?'

'Yes. He asked me who I was.' Because her mother, too, was now in this, the daughter was regaining confidence. 'I told him.'

'What did you say?'

'I said I was your daughter.'

'And he knew?'

'Yes . . . Why wouldn't he know?'

'Did he ask about the child?'

'Yes. I told him. He said, "He's fair," in a queer way and put his hand on Donan's head. Donan had stopped crying. He's quiet yet.'

'He's even asleep.'

The daughter looked at the mother, who was standing at mid-floor, the child against her breast.

'What are you thinking of, Mother?' Relief was bubbling up in the place of her fear already. She was now watching her parent closely.

'I was wondering,' replied her mother at length, 'what was bringing him over here.' She spoke with a curious mild fatalism. With a cloth and a loose shawl she wrapped the child and laid him in his cradle, which was a rectangular box on two curved feet.

The daughter's mouth fell open a little, and she, too, attended to something far away.

'Do you mean – there is something coming upon us?'

'He would be going to the Tower? ... Did you see anyone else before him?'

The girl stooped and picked something from between her toes, saying, 'I saw Aniel – going up the brae.'

'Aniel – son of Taran the bard? ... Yes, he would have gone before to announce him.' The mother nodded to herself. The daughter began to watch her again.

'Tell me, Mother; what do you think it is?'

'How should I know?'

'Perhaps the Northmen – who come from the sea?' suggested the daughter, putting Aniel out of her mind.

'Perhaps,' said the mother.

'What would they do?'

'They would kill us all,' said the mother.

'All?'

'Yes, me and your father and your brothers – but they might spare you.'

The daughter looked at her.

The mother looked back and their faces fixed in the gloom; then the mother turned towards the smouldering fire which filled the chamber with its acrid smell, the draught from the door lifting the smoke towards a hole in the roof. The walls were of unmortared stone rounded slightly at the corners and with shelved recesses for cupboards. The bed against the south gable was raised off the ground, and was shielded at the back and at both ends by wooden frames. There were two ground beds, divided by a partition, against the back wall, the one to the south fitting into the corner behind the head of the main bed. The dresser consisted of uprights with two broad shelves between, both holding domestic utensils, mostly of wood. Pegs were driven irregularly into the walls, from which hung cloth, skins, hunting-weapons, an iron sickle, a flail, rush-plaited baskets, with one high-pegged shelf suggesting, from its odds and ends of metal, the more important property of a head of the house. Two three-legged stools stood on the floor, and a rude bench stretched against the north gable.

Light came into this room from a narrow window and the smoke-hole in the roof. By the window hung a skin that could cover it. For the men this was a retreat rather than a dwelling, and so its contrast affected their minds. The warmth, the tainted air, the dim light, the face of the woman who ruled it, held their own dominion; and there was weather and a time when the warmth grew fuggy and comfortable; when an itch of happiness came to the skin, and friendly faces listened and laughed round a fire that burned with a sparkle in frost or smouldered hot to the heart in cold misty rain.

Breeta got up, restless under the look her mother had given her when she had said the Northmen might spare her. Her mind had the vivid reactions of a child's to a forest tale of shaggy-armed beasts squeezing the body. Only this was the sea, the green, cold, eel-armed sea.

She drew up at a yard or two and stood quite still. The mother looked at her back and her eyes grew narrow and full of deadly intimacy. The girl turned round. Complete woman knowledge went between them. A weak fluttering showed at the girl's throat and she withdrew her mind from her mother's by lifting her head a little as it turned away, for she had spirit and the violence of rejection.

The mother liked that spirit, even though it now clouded her expression. The girl went towards the door.

'Are you going to the Tower?'

'Yes.' Breeta hesitated.

'He will be there,' said the mother.

'What will he be wanting there?' Breeta's voice was now low and petulant.

'Once long ago he came – and three nights after came the sea-pirates – and I escaped to the woods. I was alone, and in the dark I gave birth to you. The smell of the blood brought in a wolf.' The mother, who had said so much deliberately, stopped, for she knew her daughter had the story.

'Do you think it will be like that again?'

'Not for me!'

The mother's harsh sniff thickened the barrier between them. There was something in the humour that was terrible. 'Better comb your hair,' added the mother, 'and make yourself tidy;' then she turned to the wall-corner

on her left, which was boarded in and contained some
cooking-pots and grain-grinding and weaving gear.

From the keeping-place above the smaller of the two
floor beds Breeta took down a large-toothed bone comb,
and in a slow almost sullen way began dressing her hair.
When the comb stuck, she caught the hair above it and
then tugged the comb violently. The knot gave way with a
crackle. 'Do you think', she said, 'he is at the Tower about
the fighting – or what?'

'Maybe about both,' replied her mother.

'The chief is a Christian.'

'Are we not all Christians?'

The girl knew she was on dangerous ground. The life in
her black hair made it crinkle and stand up at the ends when
the comb passed through. What she dared not express at the
back of her mind was as black as her hair and as rebellious
and potent. When Aniel crossed over her mind, she threw
her head back with the gesture of one rising from a river.

'I don't know,' she mumbled.

'What don't you know?' her mother dared her, turning
a look.

'Bodies have been eaten by the wolves,' mumbled her
daughter defiantly and put the comb back in the keeping-
place. Then she sat down on the low cross-beam of the front
of her bed and began to twist her hair in the way the men
twisted a rush rope. Now her eyes seemed to crackle.

'You will be quiet,' said her mother. But though the tone
commanded, it did not threaten. It was in a way as though
they were both tormented because they dare not speak what
haunted their minds. The mother's lined face had gathered,
as she had looked over her shoulder, a haggard air, though
she was no more than forty. Her wisps and ends were in
contrast now to her daughter's plaited smoothness over the
fire of stinging youth.

Breeta got up. 'I'll go.' Without looking at her mother,
she turned to the door. Her mother, who was a smouldering woman when there was something on her mind, let
her go.

But part way to the Tower, Breeta hesitated. She was
in terror lest she meet the Master again. And besides . . .

she turned suddenly up the green alley where Aniel had disappeared, and began climbing. In a short time the brae smoothed out and the trees thinned, and presently she was on the edge of a wide moor. From the moor the round top of the fort or Tower could just be seen, and nearly a mile beyond it the rising floor of the sea. The line was the line of the river, and on either side of it the land rose at times steeply, but over all with the effect of two slow uprising wings. Beyond the wing on her right the far fluent curves of blue mountains descended to the sea.

The sloping lands were fertile, and showed green serpentine patches of grain with tree clumps here and there and rough pasturage.

Directly inland the ground still uprose, but very slowly, so that the effect was of a great heather moor flattening downward again beyond the horizon. But to either side of this moor were wooded valleys, that on her left containing Breeta's home, where hazel and birch and rowan trees grew, and alder and fir and now and then a twisted oak. Leftward still, and inland from her valley, a flank of the uprising earth was covered with an ancient pine forest, the eye lifting from its green-blue to a solitary mountain-top that was small and plump like a purple-ripe nipple to the sky.

Breeta moved away from her home, crossing the lower part of the moor and going on towards the crest of the next valley, which was shallower than her own and with fewer inhabitants. She stood among the first leafy bushes and her eyes travelled over all they could see, and finally came to rest on a round fort set back in this glen and commanding it from a rocky spur. Morbet, Drust's grim brother, held sway there. Far beyond this glen's horizon was a hollow of wooded land, a grove of trees, with grey upstanding stones. She had once seen it in the distance, but she had never gone there. No one went there – except at night on secret and unnamable business.

This coming of the Master from that Grove had disturbed her deeply, so that all the hidden fears of her mind heaved, came alive, and slid against one another invisibly like adders in a pit. The stories of childhood with the terror of animals in woods had always had the vivid reality of happenings in a circle of light. Even if the wood were dark, the darkness could be seen through in a way that in itself was a horror. And each action was caught not merely as a whole but, infinitely more dreadful, in detail after detail. Thus she had once overheard her mother telling a woman (who had just been delivered by the wayside) of the birth of Breeta. There had been the fight, the killing, the wrecking of the houses – and her laboured flight to the pine forest. The picture was the dark forest circle – and the approaching green eyes of the wolf; and then through what followed flashed her mother's face with its ridged flesh and burning eyes. For her mother had got beyond fear: she had been fierce and cunning, and after the birth had thrown to the brute what, snarling, it had dragged away. The whole thing she saw, for the details of animal birth made an experience that, though common, never lost its fascination and friendliness.

As she stood watching between the trees, however, it was something other than such stories that disturbed her. What had happened to her mother at her own birth had been understandable. Earth and woods and animals and human beings were natural. It was the powers that lay beyond them. . . . They said that when the Man of God first came down the glen he called the Master a sorcerer. He said that he had dealings with a devil-king called Satan who was chief throughout all the world of evil. The Man of God made witches and demons more real than ever. Yet was it deeper even than that, so that Breeta walked away lest the final thing be named in her own mind and so be evoked against her.

A natural heart-hunger turned her inland where her own glen penetrated far up into the moor and flattened into a shallow of green pasturage thinning out into hill grass and short sweet heather. Here in the summertime men and boys and young women, and old women too, attended the flocks which they had driven from home with the first strong growth. A few of the men at a time went hunting through the forest, sometimes being away for days, carrying old weapons and new weapons they had made in the long winter nights. The others kept watch, not only over the flocks, but against the suddenness of enemies. And though a fight against raiders was a rare thing, hardly happening more than once in a generation, yet the tradition of it was strong, and men were still alive who told of the raid in which most of the watchers had been killed and every beast driven away; to be followed by the White Winter of the Single Deaths, that made a cycle of stories whereby all the ways of tragedy were traced out so that there was hardly anything that the human mind in its extremity could do or could not do but was known. When an old man, womanless, started on this cycle (which ran through many winter nights) all the listening bodies were curved to boulders in the stream of his voice. But mostly the stories were of adventure, with boasting and sly laughter and some tumult thrown in.

This warm tumult drew Breeta now – away from the Master and the chief and the Northmen and that laugh of her mother – from fear and eel-arms – from the Christ who was another chief – a white chief, so that she had sometimes thought of him in her mind as the Chief of the White Winter. All these hunted and haunted her. And she wanted now the happy comfort of human warmth. A quiver of desire set her body poised. A lizard on her feet would have made her jump. She stepped lightly and quickly between some cakes of fire-turf spread in the sun. When she came to the trench, out of a part of which they had been cut, she moved to the right, looking for a narrow place to leap across – when suddenly her body drew up as if it had been stung to the heart, and her hands went like claws to her breast. The horrible instant brought a squawk from her throat.

Aniel's dress was the colour of the bank of sundried turf against which he sat, and his face was pale as the tree-stump that showed a ghostly visage here and there on the moor. When the watching stillness of his features broke in a smile, it was to the girl as if the whole moor had come to life, quivering into focus within the corners of her eyes. Before that dreadful magic she recoiled, unable in a moment to realise the simple, but embarrassing, truth.

Very embarrassing in another moment. And in still another she could almost have preferred Moor-face. Her hands dropped. The violence of her heart weakened her.

'Did I give you a fright?'

She needed to sit down. She wanted to go away. She could not move.

'Anyone coming?' he asked.

She looked automatically around her.

'Jump down,' he invited. 'I'm waiting on the Master. Jump down.' He got cautiously to his feet and looked around. There was no one visible anywhere. 'Come on down and see my wonders,' he urged her gaily. 'Come on.'

'I've got to go . . .'

'Where? Where were you going?' His voice had some of the clear searching quality of the Master's.

'I was going to – to—'

'You know you haven't to go. I was watching you.' Something in his face peered round corners a trifle inhuman and magical. After all, a dizzying moment might easily mistake his face for Moor-face. And his smile was focussed and entrancing, but beckoning rather than urgent. Quick and attractive, yet retreating; and – 'Come on!' he said.

She did not know what to do. Her breast was still heaving, half turned away. All at once she recoiled from a cool grip on her ankle. He cleverly manipulated her balance, and as she rolled over the bank he caught her. She struggled violently from his hold, but 'Hush!' he said, in the voice of a boyish conspirator, hands merely protective and friendly. Pressing down her shoulders, he listened, then cautiously put his head up again, withdrawing his hands and leaving her entirely to herself.

After a time he crouched down with a low chuckle. 'Not a living thing to be seen. What luck!' She was sitting still, looking straight in front of her. Her face that had gone pale with fear was now rich warm. A bird behaved like this after the first captive flutter. Her skin, indeed, seemed ready to rise into flight. And in a moment she would have to fly to break her indecision. Aniel chattered, netting her, drawing her deeper within the conspiracy.

'You would never guess what I was doing here. No one

knows. And you mustn't tell. You won't? Promise me.' He had been twelve and she eleven when they had first gone to the shielings. 'Remember. Remember we were out in a peat bank like this and I hid and wriggled my face round a corner at you and you got an awful fright?'

'Yes,' she murmured.

'And the black serpents on my face – you got such a fright!' He laughed, and though the sound was low it was deliciously clear. It had, too, an infectious excitement – an excitement far warmer than anything she would have found at the shielings. And she knew it, knew it so deeply that she was tongue-tied and felt her lithe body awkward.

'You got such a fright,' he said, '– *as big a fright as you got just now!* . . . Tell me.' His voice had lowered. 'Did you think I was Rhos?'

'I don't know,' she murmured, after the quickening had left her eyes.

Rhos was the spirit of the moor. And when you were alone you could stare at his face and not see it – and then suddenly see it – or see it in the very moment of moving your eyes away – and then not catch it again, but feel it at your back or lying hid behind moving heath-points on a near horizon or at a slant to your side.

'Hst!' he said suddenly, thrusting out an arm, shoving her behind him. She gripped it. 'I thought I saw him – there.' He pointed at a corner. In the tense silence he heard her quickened breathing. 'Come on,' he whispered, catching her hand. She hung back. 'Come on.' He drew her gently a few paces and pointed again. On a gleaming black slab in front of them, obviously newly prepared, was the image of a snake with its head lifting out of its coil.

Her fingers crushed his. Slowly he turned his head and looked at her. Neither of them was tall, and she was just about his own height. Both were slim-bodied and dark. But whereas he was poised easily on the moment, she had grown rigid. He noted the slightly opened mouth, the tips of teeth, the sensitive nostrils that flexed, the clear bone of the nose, the black eyebrows arched over the brown-black eyes, and the ridged meeting of her emotions in her brows. These lines in her brows had a concentrated, almost violent, intensity.

All this he observed distinctly and with an increasing interest, so that when she turned to him she surprised a look that had something in it of the idol-eyes of his Master. She recoiled from this instantly, and yet, before her body could answer, his features had run into a friendly smile, so that she hardly knew what she had seen in front of this new knowledge that it was he who had made the snake and that his dramatic 'Hst!' had been a cheat.

She turned from him – and drew up with an intake of breath that quivered to a little moan. Right in front of her was a five-legged starfish figure cut so cunningly in the black surface that it gave an impression of movement, of revolving away on its legs like a wheel. She knew the symbol in stone and some of its awful powers. As she stared, the whole bank in front began to move. She felt dizzy and swayed, lifting an arm to shield her eyes.

'Breeta.'

'No!' she cried. She was terrified at all this. He was playing with her. His eyes had been like the Master's. She threw him away violently. 'No!' Her elbows stuck out. She began running down the trench, he after her, their bare feet splashing the water which trickled over a gravelly base. For this hag in the moor had been cut by water, and in places it was deep enough to hide them entirely, but sometimes their heads bobbed above the surface.

Her terror increased as she heard him behind. He caught her up and, getting hold, bore her to the runnel. They rolled in the water. 'Don't shout!' He crushed his hand over her mouth. He pinned her under him. His face had lost all its elusive gaiety. It was human and fiercely angry. She flashed up at him. He withdrew his hand from her mouth. 'What on earth did you do that for? Are you mad?' he asked, threateningly. He got off her entirely. In a moment everything had been changed. She knew now she could go.

He stood erect and peered over the edge of the bank. He stayed still so long that a new fear was born in her. Dumbly she waited, squeezing the water from her hair.

He sat down and moodily stared before him. 'Why did you behave like that?' he asked in the clear voice that could be so cold.

She did not answer, her brows drooping.

'You knew I would do you no harm. You knew I was having a game. What on earth was the sense in shouting like you – so that *everything* could hear you?'

He was netting her again.

'I wanted to show you – what no one else has seen. I was glad when I saw you coming. I wanted to show you my images. I thought –' Through the pause he let the cold note die in the distance. The melody was over.

'I didn't –' she muttered.

He waited. 'What didn't you?'

'I didn't,' she muttered, her breath petulant.

'Didn't you?' His voice had no emphasis. She felt its distrust. But she had nothing to say. A hand kept squeezing and tugging her wet skirt. Her eyes were brilliant.

'Oh, well.' He blew a slow breath that emptied his lungs and the adventure.

She was poking her fingers now into the soft peat, her head lowered. He regarded her sideways. One corner of his mouth moved and his expression quickened.

'How could I know that you would think so little of my images?' he asked quietly. 'I should have known. However . . .' He arose. 'You're not coming up to see them again? There's one you haven't seen. You might like it.'

She did not move.

'Good-bye, Breeta.' As he looked down at the smooth nape of her neck and the rich warmth on the side of her face, his eyelids lowered. He stooped, caught her hand firmly, stood up again turning his back to her, then started off dragging her after him. When they had gone a few yards, he paused, turned round, and laughed.

She did not know where to look. Her eyes glistened, but there were no tears on her face.

All at once his full merriment came back upon him. He tugged her arm impatiently. 'Come on! Keep your head down.' He made her run. Their bare feet pelted the water up their legs; their bodies bumped; they drew up; they held their quick breathing to listen. 'Isn't it a hidden place!' he whispered. She was staring at the snake. He laughed softly. 'You are frightened of it yet!'

This delighted him now. He was the wizard, the sorcerer. She would never have seen image drawings like these before. She was where demons were made. At any moment something might stretch out! . . .

'The serpent', he said calmly, 'is the sign of Rhos. When Rhos wants to become invisible and glide nearer, he turns into a serpent. People have been found dead on the moor, with two tiny tooth-marks on their skin. Now all this trench also glides like a serpent and we at this moment are inside Rhos's belly.'

This was not only blasphemy: it was an invitation to destruction. If Rhos did not come this minute, he would come sometime when one was alone. . . . She involuntarily drew back. 'Watch out!' he cried. She swung round – to stare at the five-legged wheel. 'I thought you were going to put your shoulders into it.' He regarded his handiwork a moment. 'That's the best one ever I did. Don't you feel it's going to move? And that break in the line there – and there – as if the two legs had knees . . . like it, isn't it?' He looked at her sideways. 'Breeta,' he said, sudden low warning in his voice, 'do you feel the serpent behind is going to bite you in the neck?' She wheeled round, a harsh exclamation breaking from her. 'You caught him just in time,' he nodded. Breathing in quick little gasps, she faced him full. He half turned away, smiling. 'Come here and see this one,' he invited. She did not move – and refused her hand. 'What's the matter?' he asked, looking directly at her with bright open innocence.

She was near breaking-point.

He withdrew his glance and backed close to her. 'Breeta,' he said, feeling for her arm and running his hand down it until he got a grip on her wrist, 'you don't understand all this. No one understands *everything* – except the Master. Some day I will tell you all about –' He hesitated again, then lifted his voice from its intimate note, giving her wrist at the same time a jerk, 'Come on,' and dragged her after him.

In a pace or two he pulled up, facing her. 'I wish you would be friendly,' he said, perversely shy. 'I watched you – down through the trees – with the child.'

'You're good at watching,' she gulped.

He laughed abruptly. Her colour deepened more than it had done that day.

'Maybe you're worth watching.'

She brought her eyes to his face – and away.

'Well, I was watching you down there,' he said. 'And I came up here, watching you all the way.'

This time her quick look searched.

'You were so much in my head that . . . turn round!'

She would not turn for a moment, ears and eyes going sleek. Then she warily faced round.

On the upright black surface was drawn the outline of a woman in profile. It was a stiff drawing, with none of the life there was in the serpent or the star-symbol. Around it were trial face-profiles, each with a deep finger-hole for eye. As she gazed, Breeta had no sense of this being an effort at representation of herself. The bank was a mask to the dark dreadful forces behind. Half-faces like demon faces about that stiff-skirted figure. She had an acute sensation of the hidden things approaching. She mistrusted, she feared, she hated. She grew pale.

'Don't you like it?'

'No.'

'I meant that', he explained distinctly, 'to be an image of you.'

She looked at him with terror.

'What are you frightened of?' he asked, his voice very clear.

She began to breathe quickly again and edged away. He thought to himself, If I suddenly shout, 'Look out!' she'll scream. The temptation to shout grew strong, made him feel reckless. He was disappointed in her. She was very respectable. No different from any of the rest. He began to despise her, to feel angry. She obviously was desperately upset at getting mixed up with the image! He understood it all quite well. She certainly would make a Christian of any man! And he had been so full of what he had done! Could have danced over the moor's edge!

The detached look came into his eyes. She became conscious of it. The only thing to do was to take to her heels in mad flight. Her breast asked for the relief of that flight. She began to walk slowly away.

'Breeta!'

She took to her heels. This time she had a fair start of him and she could run. He had no idea why he leapt after her, but even his vindictive feelings went to his toes. He was physically swifter and stronger than she was, but not very much. Mentally, however, he was an arrow, so that he could, when strung up, outleap himself. He brought her down in the full rush of their flight. But whereas on the former occasion she was troubled, this time her desire for escape was sheer. So she fought him fiercely, with small gasping cries. Their bodies wriggled and mixed and crushed. He got his arms over hers, round them, pinning them in. Her knees were merciless. He flattened them out. They both grew hot. His mouth landed on her face. He flattened his teeth against her flesh, pressing them in. In a final thrust, all her body surged up – and fell back hot and spent. He removed his mouth, his eyes burning. As his head drew back . . . it jerked as if clutched from behind. She felt the clutch in his body and looked up into his face. Her eyes flashed to the edge of the bank – and met the eyes of the Master.

Aniel got slowly to his feet, brushing the water and crushed peat from his skirt. He had not yet looked up. His features were pale and twisted in a thin painful smile. When at last he raised his eyes, the Master was gone. He stood a moment staring straight before him, then climbed the bank and disappeared.

2

For a time Breeta crouched so intently that she did not breathe. The expression that had come over Aniel's face had been more awful than that in the Master's expressionless eyes. He had forgotten her on the instant and had moved slowly like one convicted, with white strained smile and nervous hands.

She drew to her feet and peered over the bank. The Master had Aniel on his left, and they were bearing away to pass on the inland side of Morbet's Tower and so over the moor's rim to the Grove. She could see they were not talking. Aniel was half a head taller, and seemed in his kilt to be an overgrown boy beside the ageless figure whose robe swathed him to the heels.

She began to claw fistfuls of heather and peat, small whimpering noises starting from her throat. Her hands tore the heather, dug deep into the black peat.

The figures were growing smaller as they receded, smaller and more lonely. The awful silence of the sun-bright afternoon spread its vastness around them.

Her emotions stung her sight. The soft peat came squirting out between her fingers. She cast a look about her, and listened to the trench, her eyes glistening in a face whose skin was so alive that it seemed to palpitate.

She slowly slid down into the trench. When she thrust herself up again, they were far away. She watched until they disappeared. The whole moor was empty. Its secret life came towards her. She climbed out of the trench at once, and turned to the Tower in her own glen.

She was quiet now and moved evenly, not once looking round or to the side. Before emerging from the belt of trees into the open space around the Tower, she hesitated. She did not want to go near the Tower buildings. She felt very tired. She could lie down on the ground. Her hands clutched at a tree; she became very nervous, clutching jerkily. Small moaning sounds choked in her nostrils. Then she was staring before her – and walking round towards the entrance.

The ancient part of Drust's residence was a high circular building that dominated the lower glen. Its massive wall was twelve feet thick and had but one narrow entrance. In front of this huge tower and pointing at the sea was a tongue of land that fell sheer to the river on the right hand and less steeply to river-level on the left. Within the wall that rimmed it were several wooden erections, the principal one, some thirty feet long, being the chief's hall.

As Breeta entered the enclosure she was aware not so much of an increased as of an orderly activity. There was, too, an invisible excitement. Mergit, a serving girl, saw her, and after glancing round came running up, whispering, 'Oh, Breeta!'

'What is it?'

'The Old Man was here.' Her excitement hung on that for a moment, then she added quickly, 'The mistress was asking for you. She said you should have been here before this.'

'What's wrong?'

'Drust's brother, Morbet, is with him,' she whispered, glancing towards the hall. 'When the Old Man came in, I – I let the eggs fall.' She was speaking and listening at the same time. All at once she was gone, and Breeta saw the chief's wife in the entrance to the round fort. She was not so old as Breeta's own mother, but much taller and golden-haired, and of a high even countenance in which there were small commanding lines.

As Breeta went up to her, she asked, 'What's kept you?' Her face did not change. Her voice had a different intonation from any other, even from her husband's. She came from the south country and wore a green dress embroidered with gold threads, a string of green beads round her throat, and a thrice-coiled gold band about her left forearm.

'I was nursing Donan,' Breeta answered.

'Is not your mother well?'

'Yes. But she told me to take him out in the sun. So I – I took him.'

Silis, wife of Drust, lifted her look from the girl's face. Her blue eyes caught some of the glitter of the green beads. As though she had forgotten Breeta and got entangled again in her own brooding thought, she turned and, stooping, re-entered the fortress.

Breeta followed her. About midway in the twelve-foot wall and to the right was a guard-chamber wherein two men were busily occupied. The younger looked at Breeta

and winked as she passed. She hit the door cheek and
stumbled after her mistress.

The interior of this ancient stronghold was circular, the
wall rising to a great height. Through a small doorway one
entered upon a stone stairway leading to a gallery which
circled the building inside the wall until a second stairway
led to a second gallery, the flagged roof of the first being
the floor of the second. There were five such galleries, with
narrow windows opening on the interior. The top of the
wall was the outlook tower. For the first eight feet from
the ground the wall, however, was solid, except for two
inbuilt chambers, one of which was used as a retreat by
Silis – for private devotional purposes, it was said. This
circular stronghold was unroofed, so that daylight flooded
the interior, which, apart from movables, had an unused
fireplace, a well, and two narrow lean-to rooms, roofed on
wooden uprights.

This circular drystone structure had a legendary age
before the outhouses had been thought of. No one but
the Master, it was said, could tell its entire history or who
had constructed it, although Drust's chief adviser, the bard
Taran, father of Aniel, could recite the generations before
Drust for hundreds of years.

As Breeta entered the stronghold, a golden girl looked
up at her over a mass of wool dyed a lovely sky-clear blue.
She was seated at a bench, and her hands kept teasing the
wool as she looked.

Breeta always got the same slight shock when she
encountered Nessa, the daughter of Silis. It was like coming
against a brighter light than the sight was accustomed to,
light gathered in a girl with eyes sky-blue and wanton-quick
and imperious. Her skin was so fair that it gave back the
light and, when her red-wet mouth opened, her teeth
glistened out of pink gums. The pink of her gums held
the transparency of all her flesh, and once when she had
cut a gum the thread of spreading blood had remained in
Breeta's mind for long enough.

Actually Nessa's face was fair, with regular clear features
and long golden hair, but in it also was a knowledge of
this power over Breeta, and in and about it was the desire

to extend the power beyond Breeta. This living attractive quality, however, she could veil in a moment with the imperious air she borrowed from her mother, and with which she could so perfectly dissemble.

She now dropped her look from Breeta and attended to her task. Her mother drew up, still under her secret thought, which had clearly little to do with the existence of Breeta. After Breeta had waited for a little, she slipped quietly to the bench beside Nessa.

Silis went to her private room, but immediately came out again, stood for a moment looking at the girls, who were both quietly industrious, and, on the point of saying something, maintained silence and passed out.

Nessa looked at Breeta and smiled, but did not speak, though her face was alive with curiosity. She stopped working, however, the better to listen. At last a voice was heard outside. 'That's father,' Nessa said, her lips closing in a small private nod. The voices outside receded. 'They've gone into the hall.' She got up.

'Don't go!' pleaded Breeta.

Nessa raised her eyebrows. 'Why not?'

'They might – catch you.'

'Catch me?' There was an imperious moment. Then Nessa relented before Breeta's discomfort. She smiled, stretching her eighteen-year-old body and sticking out a sandalled foot. She brought herself together and with composure walked out of the fort.

Breeta adored her, though she was over a year younger than herself. Everything in her nature desired to placate Nessa, to run like a stream toward her feet. It was not altogether the sun-smit beauty in such contrast to her own raven flesh, not wholly the tribal importance of what was due to the household of the chief, but something underlying both as of a dark restraint paying tribute to freedom, the tribute her dark tribe paid to leadership or to the Sun.

A small flake of stone hit her right hand and she jumped, glancing about her and upward. No one was visible, though she knew in a moment that someone was having a game with her. As she got busy, a chuckle came down the wall. Looking up, she saw the black-bearded face of Lys leaning over the high edge. 'Don't you be putting stones in the wool!' She shook her head, smiling. He cupped his mouth: 'That blue will fairly lay him by the heels!' 'Who?' she asked. 'Ha!' he answered, 'who were you with on the moor? You think I didn't see you!'

Her sense was put to flight. She did not lift her head. When, unable to bear the silence any longer, she did glance up, the wall was blank.

Because one could not see the hag in the moor from the top of the fort, Lys had merely been teasing her. It was the sort of thing an old man did to a young girl, and Lys was fifty and the father of a grown family. But men of that age and older were young in spirit, and it was fine to make a young girl blush.

'Breeta, what was he like? Uh?'

She wanted to say, 'I thought you saw him?' but she was nervous even of looking up.

'Tell me this, anyway: *did the Old Man catch you?*' It was no more than a fearful whisper, but her shoulders winced, her head drooped, her fingers got entangled in the wool. The excitement rose to her throat in a horrid way.

There came down a dry knowing comment.

Breeta's mind became a black twisted gallery of images dominated by the raked face of Aniel. She crushed it beneath her, teasing the wool, feeling for the daylight which in here somehow had gone shadowy and cool.

'Breeta!' Obviously Lys was going to the outer edge of the wall, spying all round, and then coming back. She refused to look up. She felt invisible preparations going on all around her. What was Lys doing up there? Banter always spilled from him when he was alert, though he was full of sly humour and good nature at most times. Little boys loved him in a familiar way, and he would, when they teased him, dive after them and, poking a thumb between his fingers, pretend to have snicked off a certain part of their body.

Breeta had an urge to get up, but an obscure fear held her. She had not been told to do this work, but she knew that Silis had wanted her for some particular purpose. The curious endurance of her race kept her busy. Lys tried to interest her once more, but then gave it up or got busy elsewhere. She could hear now and then the hollow grinding of stone against stone. Every corner was being cleaned up and put in a proper state of repair. From the outermost point of the enclosure came the intermittent *clank-clank* of a hammer, a sound she had not heard for many a day. It would be Goan, the smith, shaping iron.

Goan was a kinsman of the chief, an old warrior, held in high esteem. He could make iron out of earth, the men said, but it was a difficult process, and no other one could do it now but his son. Moreover, it was a particular kind of earth and not to be found anywhere in this glen. It was easier to trade skins and oil, and when Drust last year had gone to the court of the great chief who was now king over all the country, with his stronghold by the Broad River, he had also carried with him some gold taken from the Bleak Strath, and on his return journey brought home many weapons and iron implements. His eldest son, who was one year younger than Nessa, was left at the court.

Through the daylight alertness of all this, with its suggestion of desperate things impending, ran the black trench of the moor, that wound like a serpent and was hollow as the belly of Rhos. From that last desperate heave against Aniel, her body had fallen and melted as if she had fainted.

The terrifying ecstasy surged over her, so that her face was hot as Nessa entered hurriedly and took her place at the bench.

Nessa did not speak, lifting an ever-watchful eye on the door. But presently she whispered, 'What excitement! Mother does not know what she wants, and father appeared to be giving in again – but mother knew he wasn't!'

Clearly Nessa considered this great fun and loved its excitement.

'What's wrong?' asked Breeta.

Nessa looked directly at her. 'Don't you know?'

'I know the Master was here.'

'The Old Man!' Nessa smiled. 'You're even frighened of his name!' She lifted a lump of wool and thumped it down before her. 'Aren't you?' Her look was sidelong and critical.

'Are you not?'

'Me? I'm a Christian – like mother!' replied Nessa.

'I'm a Christian, too.'

'Of course,' said Nessa. 'We all are.' Her mouth was a twisting red, her eyes flickered. 'I think I'll dance,' she said. 'You go to the entrance and watch for mother.'

'No,' said Breeta, 'you mustn't.'

Nessa was amused, and crushed the wool. She looked directly at Breeta. 'Mother very nearly caught me getting this.' She looked and listened, then dived down her breast and produced a small penannular brooch of bone or ivory. 'Lovely, isn't it?' She was excited.

Breeta stared at it. 'Where did you get it?'

Nessa leaned forward, now vividly mysterious. 'Do you know a young man, the servant of the Master, with strange eyes that – that – you know – he's dark and slim – do you know him?'

'Is it – Aniel?'

'Aniel. Aniel.' She tried the name. 'Do you know him?' She was now looking curiously at Breeta, whose colour had receded, and whose throat was nervous. 'Tell me, who is he?'

'He's learning with the Master.'

'Oh, is he? You mean he's a pupil? I thought so!' She could scarcely repress her voice. 'A pupil of a Wizard!' she whispered, '– of Antichrist!'

Breeta seemed to grow paler still. But Nessa was delighted with herself now. 'I happened to meet him as he came to the gate. He wanted to see father alone for a minute. So I took him to the hall. I knew it was something important – so I went outside. When he came out I asked him if he had got on all right, and he said he had. He was nervous, so I looked at him. Have you ever really looked at his eyes? – no? Then I looked down at his fingers and they were turning over and over – this.' And she regarded the brooch on her palm, but in the same moment, hearing a noise, she quickly sent it to its hiding-place, whispering a sharp warning. As her mother came in, both girls were busy.

'Breeta,' said Silis, 'you will tell your mother to come here tonight with Donan.'

As Silis entered her stone chamber, Breeta arose and without a word passed out of the fort, Nessa looking after her with a puzzled expression. All at once Nessa got to her feet and noiselessly followed, overtaking Breeta on the path that led down through the trees.

'Anything wrong with you, Breeta?'

'No.'

'Tell me what it is?'

'It's nothing,' said Breeta.

'Tell me.'

Breeta looked about her with a strained smile, and Nessa saw that for the first time she had lost hold over her friend. Breeta wanted to get away from her.

'Is it about the brooch?' she asked.

'Oh, no.'

'You won't mention that to anyone? He gave it to me, of course, because' – she looked about her. 'I'd better get back.' Her tone had suddenly grown cool. 'Remember, say nothing about it.'

'Who was I going to say it to?'

'I have offended you, I'm afraid,' said Nessa, with something of her mother's air. She smiled, and left her.

As Breeta went down through the trees, Nessa's uplifted head and secret smile were in her mind. All at once she saw Nessa clearly for the first time. Nessa was aloof from her, did not require her – used her, and went her golden way, with intimacy only for her own affairs. That bright image, with its back to her, faded, and Breeta went on towards her home.

As she entered she saw her little brother crouching by the fire, roasting mussels.

'Where's mother?' she asked.

He looked up at her and said nothing, obviously having expected more of a greeting. He had been at the summer herdings for his first season, and still had all the wide world round his boy's mind.

His mother darkened the doorway: 'What is it?'

'They're wanting you at the Tower with Donan tonight.'

'What for?'

'I don't know,' said Breeta indifferently. She stood looking at her brother.

'Surely you must know.'

'I don't.'

Her mother eyed her sharply. 'What's wrong with you?'

'With me?' Breeta raised her brows. Her brother, Col, looked up at her, then lowered his black lashes. The brine from the mussels was sizzling noisily on the firestone and the valves were beginning to open.

'Did any of them say anything to you?' demanded her mother.

'No. The stranger, Silis, told me to tell you.'

'The stranger! Is that a way to speak?'

Col, who had been delicately turning one mussel with a piece of stick, unluckily pushed it over the inner edge of the stone into the fire and exclaimed sharply. In the same moment, however, he hooked it out deftly, together with some red embers and a flare of sparks. His mother, startled, went up to him and slapped the side of his head, adding, 'We'll have none of your bothy ways here, remember that!'

Col lowered his arm guard and retrieved the mussel, but jumped as his fingers got stung by the hot shell.

The jump made his mother jump. 'Get out of here!' she cried. He covered up. 'Go on!'

'I want my mussels,' he whined.

'No, nor mussels. Go on!' She cuffed him. He whined long enough to make it possible to grab all three mussels. Then he cleared out, giving two notes of a defiant laugh beyond the doorstep.

'I'll make you laugh, you rascal!' called his mother loudly. Then she paused, looking at Breeta, who had started aimlessly for the door. 'Where are you going?'

'Nowhere,' said Breeta.

'What's wrong with you?' demanded her mother strongly.

'There is nothing wrong with me.'

'There is – whatever it is. Did anything happen at the Tower? Did –?' She stopped.

'I don't know if anything happened or not. I spoke to no one except Nessa. She says they're all excited.'

'About what?'

'She didn't say.'

'Couldn't you have asked her? Surely you have a tongue in your head?'

Breeta was exasperatingly silent, edged nearer the door and, while her mother was questioning again, went out.

Her mother was at the door in a moment. 'Breeta, come here!'

Breeta hesitated.

'Come in!'

'What is it?'

'Come in, I tell you.'

'But what is it?'

'Come in!' shrilled her mother.

Breeta hesitated still another moment, then walked away from the house. When she had gone a little way a chuckle pulled her up. Col had broken back the bivalve and bit the lobe of flesh clean into his mouth. He was chewing it under a tree, richly moved. 'It's good,' he said, eyeing Breeta.

'When did you come down?' she asked.

'Today,' he answered. As she did not think much of this humour, he asked, 'What's wrong with Mother?'

'I don't know.'

'You look', said Col, 'as if you couldn't help it!'

This sly wit made her gaze at him, and she saw that the days at the shielings had broadened him and given him secret knowledge. At thirteen he was sliding into the world of men. Already he could smile to himself knowingly. This disturbed her.

'What are you looking at?' he asked.

'When are you going back?'

'Soon.' He levered the second mussel apart. 'Would you like a bit?'

'Did you bring anything down?'

'Cheese and a little butter. And little thanks I got. I also had something for the Tower.'

'What?'

He became mysteriously preoccupied with the mussel.

She moved away a pace, but paused to ask, 'How is Annir?' Annir, a girl of her own age, was her particular friend.

'She's having the greatest time.'

'Is she? Do you like being up there?'

'Don't I? It's great!' She hung a moment indefinitely. He looked about him with a minimum movement of head.

'Did you hear what's going to happen?'

'No.'

'The Northmen are coming.' His eyes, slyly fixed on her, glittered.

'What do you know about that?' she asked at last.

'More than you. They landed at Harst last week and there was a great fight. You didn't know that?'

'No.'

'People were killed and houses burnt. The Northmen chased them, but one chased too far and the Harst men got him alive.'

She waited, but at last had to ask, 'What did they do to him?'

'They didn't do anything but take him away.' He said this with a queer secretive smile that fascinated her.

'Why?'

'I don't know,' he said, and added, busy with the third mussel, 'they haven't killed him,' holding his breath over the mussel, '– yet.'

'Where is he?' she asked.

But his head was bent over his task with sly mysterious reticence.

She went nearer. Her voice became friendly. 'I won't tell anyone. I promise.' She placated him still further.

He looked at her with watchful, half-fearful caution; then glanced on either hand – and down.

'Tell me,' she whispered.

As his head came up, glittering challenge shone in his eyes – 'The Grove.'

She remained so still that his importance made him smile; but all at once he jumped at the mere noise of an animal in the brae face above.

Breeta sat down beside him, breathing heavily, the penannular brooch forgotten.

'Who told you?' she asked.

'No one,' he countered. 'And don't you say it.'

They were in a moment friendly, and any challenge between them had gone.

'The Master was up there today.'

'Was he?' said Col. 'Did you see him?'

'He spoke to me.'

Col looked at her. 'What –?'

She shook her head.

'It will be coming off,' he muttered.

She looked at Col. He turned his face away. They were both excited. Rooting a pebble out of the earth by the tree trunk, he flung it along the grass.

'If the Northmen come,' Breeta said, 'we shall all be killed.'

'They only kill', said Col, 'men and boys and old women. They don't kill girls.'

She sat as if entranced, and after a little got up and went towards the Tower, but at the last moment circled round within the trees towards the moor. She stared at the moor and at the skyline, beyond which was the Grove. Now and then she crushed her hands as she moved aimlessly within the trees – to look out upon the moor once more. Presently she found herself again before the Tower, and walked over the clearing quietly.

As she entered the fort Nessa looked up at her with a curious expression, which Breeta, taking her place again, avoided. Silis came out of her chamber and, ignoring both the girls, passed outside.

Nessa did not speak. Breeta's face was drained of expression. Nessa yawned. 'I'm tired to death of this,' she said to herself, and got up. She wore the same cloth as her mother, a string of white beads, a silver bracelet, and sandals. She stretched herself until her legs showed above the knees. Then, breathing more composedly, she took out the brooch, and sticking it over her right breast let the beads fall beside it. The combination was agreeable. She smiled and looked sidelong at Breeta, who never raised her head.

'Did you tell your mother to come up, Breeta?'

'Yes.'

Nessa grew restless. She was so bored that her eyes shone. The sun was going down and the fort was a prison. She walked out with a calmness that left her importance on the air. When, later, she came back, she found Breeta sitting in exactly the same position, doing the same thing. In Breeta's passive attitude there was a curious power, so that Nessa immediately felt restless again.

'Your mother has come,' she said.

Breeta worked a little longer at the wool, then got up.

'Where are you going?'

'Home,' replied Breeta.

'But the wool isn't ready.'

'No,' said Breeta, standing still. Nessa secretly watched her, but did not speak. Breeta turned towards the entrance.

'Breeta!'

Breeta passed out, and without turning her head went homeward.

As she crossed the threshold, her brother looked guiltily up from the shell-well in the inner corner of the house. Relief spread over his face at seeing it was only his sister.

'What are you doing?' she asked.

He laughed and stowed the shellfish in a small rush basket. 'The salt water has dried up, anyway,' he said.

'Where are you taking them?'

'To the shielings.'

'Won't it be dark before you get there?'

'What do I care?' He spoke with an air of bravado. 'I'm off.' As if she had made the night threaten him.

'Col.' He watched her finger her dress nervously. 'I'll come with you.'

'But you can't!'

'Let us go.' She had not looked at him, so concentrated had she been on herself.

'But – when mother comes in the morning?'

'Come on,' she said on a quickened note, and cleared him out of the house and fixed the door.

'What went wrong with you?' he asked as they pursued their way.

'Nothing,' she answered. 'We'll go up here to the edge of the moor and miss the houses.'

The heat of the day had gone and the first of the evening hung in a cool serenity. Now and then a few leaves turned over as though the distant sea had half a mind to breathe. But only half a mind, for it requires great effort to wake out of the weakness that follows the sun's heat. Yet the very draining of physical vitality disencumbers the spirit and leaves it free to delicate influences. The skin of the spirit breathes in the sweet cool air. The leaves of the trees no longer droop over, even if they do not change their position. And above all, the tree becomes a tree itself once more.

Especially was this the case with one aged rowan whose bowl was thick and whose arms twisted out and up. The rowan may keep off evil spirits, but Breeta and Col made a detour round it. The birches, however, were shady, and their slim silver bodies and graceful arms might easily have given rise to a myth on their own account, were it not perhaps that innocent young women were more the stuff of dreams and laughter and everyday. But the hazel carries the nuts of divination and wisdom. Not that that means the hazel is only for the old. The hazel is also a boy's tree, because no other tree sends up such straight young shoots of fine tough wood. Do age and youth meet here – the wisdom that must become as a little child? True it is, anyway, that the very old and the young can laugh and play together. There is a long stretch in the middle period when it might seem that something could be made of life, something serious or responsible or bloody or inspired. But between the lovely straight shoots of youth and the final nuts of wisdom, what is there, after all, but growth of wood?

On a little green flat beyond the river, Col and Breeta caught a glimpse of the sacred well. They knew it by the grey flat stone that was its lip. It was against the rising ground, and great ferns arched their broad fronds, climbing upwards. Even as they looked, an animal like a small red dog came out of the ferns and paused, delicately taking the air. It was going towards the well to drink when it stopped abruptly, warily, as if something or someone were at the well itself. Then it slid into the ferns again, and the well was left more lonely than ever.

'Come on,' whispered Breeta.

They went on without speaking. Col had never seen an animal like that before. And there had been nothing visible at the well.

After a time Breeta asked, still with a tremor, 'What was it?'

'It was like a small dog,' said Col, who hated to seem ignorant of wood lore or of the ways of hunting before his sister. But for anything to be 'like a small dog' was haunting enough. Neither of them dared ask, 'What could it have seen?'

They had a long, long way to go yet, and their footsteps quickened. When the little red dog had gone out of Breeta's mind it remained in Col's. Sometimes, when one hunted for an animal all day long without success, a moment would come in the midst of tiredness and despair when lo! the animal was there before one. Then one grew stiff as a tree and could not move for gazing at it. There was a great number of woodland moments in Col's mind. But this of the little red dog and the sacred well was not like any of them.

Suddenly Breeta pulled him up. They both listened. There was a broken padding sound of footsteps in front. They did not hear it so much as feel it in the earth, to which Col put his ear.

'It's someone going up,' said Col, but his voice was no more than a whisper.

'But who could it be?'

'It could be anyone,' whispered Col. He went in front, stepping quickly and lightly.

They could now hear the tread in the hollow of the evening. Breeta wanted to hold Col back. She had got the dreadful feeling that the faint sounds were coming up, up through the earth beneath.

Col won to a corner and crouched; then turned his head to Breeta and beckoned her to look. She saw the back of a man walking by himself, and she knew him to be Morbet, the brother of the chief. They both sat back out of sight, and Col, plucking a grass, began to bite it. Breeta looked at his face.

'What's he going up for?' she asked.

'He takes command under the chief,' Col replied with a curious smile.

'Will he be taking the men down tonight?'

'I don't know where he will be taking them tonight.'

She gazed at him. 'He was a long time with the chief this afternoon.'

Col nodded as if he had expected that. He was shutting her out from the importance and secrecy of men's ways. She was a woman. The little red dog ran through his mind. She became still again. He saw her though he was biting the grass and looking in front of him, and his mind was bursting with the desire to tell her things. But this desire made him feel like a child, and lately something had got hold of him that made him shut out woman from certain places. No one had ever told him to do this. He was silent, and his importance before her went to his head. As he smiled, his body twisted inscrutably.

She saw all this and, though she might have cuffed his head or spanked him, the thought of doing either never touched her. Her mind faltered.

'Let us go on,' he said in a friendly, commanding voice. And she followed him. He suddenly liked his sister. 'We won't be long now. Are you getting tired?'

'Col.'

'What?'

'Perhaps I should go back?'

'Hach, never mind,' he said. 'You can go back in the morning. You could leave very early.'

She went on silently.

'Was mother going for you today?' he asked.

'No,' she replied slowly, 'it wasn't that.'

'You're not frightened of the Northmen? You needn't be frightened. We'll smash them to bits.'

'Were they saying that in the shielings?'

'Yes, and far more. Listen! do you hear the dogs?' His face grew alert, his eyes shone. 'Did you hear yon voice?

That was Garam. You can hear him over two moors.' He laughed and began to tell her how they mimicked Garam and made fun of him. He rushed into boyish shieling gossip. His hero was Bronach. 'You should see him jump! His feet go through the air – like that! He's great!' An eager itch came over his body. He suddenly wanted to run. 'I'll carry the shellfish behind me. Or could you put it under your dress?'

The glen was growing shallow and the trees small. They had left the riverside so as not to overtake Morbet and, presently breasting a rise to the right, saw the shieling lands spread before them and rising slightly to a far low horizon, north and east.

It was a wide peaceful scene in the evening light. The bothies were a cluster of beehives in the flattened centre, where the stream in this hot weather was little more than small pools fed by invisible springs. Away to the left, or west, the pine forest rolled dark to the inner mountain, whose nipple now stood up from a visible curve of breast, all in a blue-purple so deep that it seemed swathed in a drift of smoke. For Col, mystery was there and adventure and the cycle of the great hunting stories to which any summer season might add a new one (the season's minor adventures embroidering many a winter night). Far beyond that mountain were the Koorich, a pastoral people, whose shepherds were sometimes encountered on the remote verges of the forest. They were reputed to be a wandering race, and the strangest stories were told about their manner of life. Garam said that they were all small and hairy, that they ate raw flesh, not as any man would when he had to, but as a matter of choice, and that the first time he had ever seen them was when two of them were devouring a white-skinned body which he was certain was a human child. They had rushed off with it when he had appeared. Everyone pretended to believe Garam, who was small and hairy himself, and squat, and full of a childlike faith in the monstrous. But always something lingered from Garam's story, something of arrested laughter, so that Garam was called to tell his story again and again. Besides, the Koorich were near enough to certain legends, and in their hairiness they had more than a reminder of the solitary human beasts that lived in the mountains, as everyone knew. When there were no women present, Garam would go into details about the eating of the child, and even bite himself.

But no one was simple enough to believe Garam. And, in any case, where would a couple of shepherds get a little child to eat? They had most likely been skinning a lamb. But Leu, who said this, had a great admiration for the Koorich. And Leu's story was what everyone believed, for Leu had produced as evidence the Koorich's pipe.

And now a rhythm of notes, clear as a thrush's, deeper than a blackbird's, came between them and shouts from a stretch of ground below the bothies where men were competing in games. Col turned to his sister and said, 'That's Leu!'

They paused to listen, Col almost on tiptoe, his eyes shining. They knew the melody Leu played, and the scene before them, with the evening falling as a cool transparent shadow from the sunken sun, brought enchantment upon them. Col made a vow in his heart that far in the forest he, too, would crush a Koorich and take his pipe from him and practise and practise in secret until he came before them playing more wonderfully even than Leu. And the weight that was on Breeta's mind slid from it, but instead of laughing her lip began to tremble, and her eyes grew brighter than Col's. She felt more wretched than she had done that day, and wanted to lie down or go away into a lonely place.

'Isn't he good at it!' But glancing at her, Col saw her face begin to work. 'Come on!' he mumbled, moving off with a wonder that overlaid his desire to shout.

Presently, however, turning round, he saw her smiling and full of trembling fun, completely changed. She met his look with a bright challenging air that was also a veiled affection.

'Isn't it fine to be away here?' she said in a lover's voice.

'It's great!' answered Col, his chest bursting with energy.

The turf bothies were now growing bigger, the cattle

and sheep becoming something more than grey-brown and dark boulders spread about an encampment. The shouts of the young athletes could be individually distinguished. The laughter of a hidden group of girls dealing with the evening's milk in the enclosure beyond the huts came high-pitched and disturbing, so that young men's heads turned from their sports, their eyes glistened, and they made men's signals and remarks that sometimes drew abrupt mirth. The old men sat around watching the play, and talking, and sometimes calling heartily to a young man who persisted in doing his poor best with good humour and (for their benefit) an exaggerated style.

Col and Breeta came unexpectedly on the now silent Leu, sitting against a hillock of new peat, the Koorich pipe in his hands. As he looked at Breeta, his fingers moved lightly on the holes and he smiled.

His face was thin, not so much brown as dark pale, and when it smiled a simple girl's heart might very easily trip. Shyer than Aniel's face, with more of the moor and less of thought, the eyes deeper in their liquid brown, yet like Aniel's face too. Breeta said they had been listening to his playing as they came along.

He withdrew his eyes from her to the pipe and fingered it. Then he looked at her again. 'So you're up for the night?' His eyes had a deep glimmer.

'Yes,' she answered. She pushed the ground with her toes – and suddenly looked into the glimmer. 'I thought you would have had them all dancing.' She mocked the glimmer.

'There's Morbet,' interrupted Col in a quiet tone.

'What's that?' Leu's brows wrinkled perplexedly, as if Col had drawn him from his secret place.

They watched the chief's brother emerge from the stream path upon the players, who immediately stopped their sport to gaze at the approaching figure.

'Come on down,' said Col. And all three of them went towards the bothies. But when they were come near to the players, Breeta said, 'I'm going this way.' Col was watching Morbet. Leu looked at Breeta, who smiled curiously to him, swinging away towards the women. Leu then looked towards Morbet so that Col, turning, wondered what Leu saw with his intense abstracted stare. 'Let's go down and hear what they're saying,' urged Col. And Leu went with him, carrying his pipe as though it were a stick, for he had forgotten how precious it was.

Between old and young there were nearly thirty men in the group, with hair growing over their brows, medium in build and for the most part very dark. The older men had wide bushy whiskers, and their bright eyes shone out of good-humoured retreats. They had now a quiet air, and did not in any way press about Morbet, but on the contrary each kept his place with an easy confidence that was yet ready and respectful. For they knew that Morbet must carry news.

Morbet meantime mixed with them, and when he came before Taran, Aniel's father, he said that he would like to have a few words with him. At that they moved quietly out on to the moor, where they stood talking together.

Bronach, the champion athlete, said, 'Let us to it!' They knew the interruption was meant to take them away from appearing to gape on the private talk of two of their leaders. So they watched Bronach catch up the stone again, which was as big as his head, and balance it on his left palm. He was thirty years old, thin and of no more than the average height. His bearded face was lined, and his black eyes were piercing. There was a sinewy quality about him rather than a brute strength, and though this was typical of them all, Bronach had the quality to a point of quickness that was explosive. As he stood up now, right foot to the mark, a swaying rhythm set him rocking, until, quicker than eye could follow, his body whirled round within its stance, left foot landing where right had been, and the stone described its perfect arch beyond the farthest peg. Throwing from the left hand was his handicap against most of the younger men, who now took up the contest with a heightened gaiety, because they were so conscious of the two on the moor.

Of these two, Taran presently came and beckoned to the older men, who followed him with quiet demeanour to where Morbet was.

The laughter beyond the bothies had ceased, and

women's faces could be seen peeping over the turf wall of the large enclosure, or round the sides of the bothies. They were like fascinated creatures watching a conference of alien beings, their isolated heads having, too, something gnomish or of the wild.

Breeta had been the centre of a group drawing from her all the gossip of the Tower. Now heads nodded and looked towards the men. They were full of a hidden silence that was the more revealed when they spoke, the older ones seeming to carry within them a profound and awful knowledge, the very old sucking their breath with sighing emphasis. But excited glances passed between the young, who had never seen death mow a long swath, and who certainly had not envisaged death as a personal enemy. Of these, Breeta was the most excited. When a bent old woman turned away with her burden to the bothy muttering, 'Oov-oov!' Breeta laughed silently, her eyes flashing. This vitality drew all the girls about her. Breeta, who could be kind and smiling and on occasion moody, was like a swaying snake. They all liked her in this mood. At such a moment Breeta felt herself more potent than Nessa, who had always walked upon her heart like a sun; whose brightness had been to her for loveliness; whose petulance had been command. Two or three of her intimates, taking her by the arms, indulged the privilege of leading her away upward on to the moor.

But, glancing back, Breeta said, 'They are breaking up.' They watched the men drift to the stone-pitch, leaving Morbet and Taran still in conference. After a time these two parted, and Morbet started back down the glen. Breeta said she must see what was happening, then pulled up and in the strangest manner eyed her companions. 'Do you know where they'll be going tonight?' They were dumb. 'If they are going' – she swayed – 'if they are going – that way' – and she nodded towards the horizon beyond which lay the Grove – 'what about following them – in the dark?' The queer hectic fire in her face fascinated them. They whitened a little. She laughed. And at that moment there came a ghostly whistling across the moor from the direction of the forest.

It was also heard by the men at the stone-pitch, and in no time the disquietening silence of the encampment became a world of tumult. Boys started away towards the forest, shouting and rushing and tripping one another. Young men walked and ran with them. Little girls danced behind, screaming shrilly. And no one enjoyed the fun more than the dogs, great strong brutes that snapped and barked and doubled. Soon their figures were stretched out in a straggling line over the moor, and the long-faced cattle gazed at them, the lean-legged sheep rounded themselves up to gaze at them, and the old men and women gazed also. For the hunters had returned and tonight there would be high carnival.

There was no high carnival that night, however. The game was handed over to the women to be flayed, and Taran talked to the hunters. Three of the hunters had not yet returned, having some time back struck the rare spoor of a bear.

It was high summer eve, and the blue dimness of twilight had merged into the dusk of early night. Boys began to subdue their voices, and if a dog barked he was listened to. The air was magical. Here and there youth lingered about the little doorways of the bothies. All the women were inside. Now and then a man appeared and wandered mysteriously into the moor. The expectancy had an undernote of dread. Young men slipped away also in twos and threes. The voices of the old women shrilled to the young boys to come inside and go to sleep. 'It's high time!' they said in scolding tones, as if concealing from themselves what was on their minds. But the boys knew.

Breeta and two or three of her friends were together in the turf cabin of the little old woman whom they loved. This old woman could cast their fortunes and tell them strange stories, and use words of the old forgotten language in referring to certain parts of the body and to acts of love and generation. These words would make the girls nearly die of laughing as they swayed and nudged one another. Her withered old face would smile benignly, as she would nod, saying, 'You may laugh as you like, but that's the truth.' Then they would pester her to tell them more.

And Grannybeg would sometimes warm herself by telling them secret things and relating strange happenings.

When a woman is married and without a child, what does she do? Ah, well, listen. Then Grannybeg tells them of the woman's journey, and of the stone she will come to at the end of her journey, and how that stone has hollows worn in it, and what she will do to that stone and to the hollows, until the girls feel an itch running on spiders' legs over their bodies, and their bodies grow rich to the skin with warm blood, and they are all plump and wary and full of spluttering mirth. Yet Grannybeg so describes the journey in the dark and the half-dark, with the Stones watching, and awful dark bodies in the trees watching with hidden eyes, that they dare not laugh aloud. But their inner merriment glimmers red and their voices hush soft as kisses. 'Be full of fun if you like, oh yes, but when it comes to your own time, ah, then we'll see!' But none of them could believe it would ever come to her time, and so they renew their pressure on Grannybeg to give them details of the physical acts that are done at the stone. But that she will not do. Then they beg her at least to show them the little stone she keeps, the green pebble that is like a flattened egg with a hole in the middle of it. Grannybeg will not show them that either. But always she promises she will help them with it – when their need arises.

All this they love because of the something unlawful and terrifying and tempting about it, with a secretiveness that enriches and lingers – lingers even into the sunlight where it reaches for knowledge in a slow red shy stare.

Now tonight, because there was no light in the bothy – with the reason for that and for all the men going out to the moor – their gathering was stranger and more exciting than ever before. They sat near the open doorway, their black hair back from their foreheads, their eyes alive in the dim afterlight from moor and sky. They were growing, too, more and more uncertain of Breeta, who appeared in such a reckless mood that they were thrilled. But she shocked them to fear when in a calm direct voice she asked Grannybeg where the men were going so mysteriously this night. Grannybeg's eyes lifted.

'How should I know, my honeybee?'

They all followed Grannybeg's eyes to the open door, and in that moment the silence was so complete that the encampment might have been lifted off the earth.

When they peered at Grannybeg again, her wizened old body was doubled and slightly swaying. Breeta hunched down and whispered, 'Tell us, Grannybeg.'

The other girls grew very still.

Then Grannybeg's voice caught the high inflection as she intoned, 'How should I know? How should I know?'

'I know where they are going,' said Breeta.

'Do you know? Do you know?' swayed Grannybeg.

'They are going to the Grove,' breathed Breeta.

'Oov-oov,' said Grannybeg.

'What are they going to the Grove for, Grannybeg?'

'How do I know, my honeybee? How is it that I should know? Indeed, indeed, how?'

'The Northmen,' said Breeta, tracking her, 'landed at Harst when most of the men were up at the shielings. They killed everyone at the dwellings – except the girls.'

'Ah, the day,' said Grannybeg, 'the sad, sad day. Oh, sad, sad, that day.'

'Grannybeg, hsh . . . they say they have a Northman at the Grove.'

'Child,' said Grannybeg in such a quiet voice that even her body grew still, 'what do we know of the mysteries? We know nothing. What possesses you, child, to be daring the Shrouded One? What possesses you at all?'

'Breeta, be quiet,' mumbled one of the girls.

'Hsh, Breeta,' tremored another.

'Grannybeg,' said Breeta, 'did not Molrua the preacher curse the Grove? Did he not curse all those who have anything to do with the Grove? Did not the preacher long before Molrua curse the Grove, too?'

'Child, child, will you not hold your tongue? Are you not afraid?' She peered at Breeta till her face glimmered thin as a moonbeam. 'What has come over you?' She was an eye peering into Breeta.

Breeta's face was hot and her chest was panting. Sometimes her words had come quickly as if from a choking.

She avoided Grannybeg's eye, but her mouth had a queer smiling, reckless and desperate.

'What does it mean?' she went on. 'What does it all mean? Are we Christians or – or what? The stranger Silis turned on her husband this day.'

'Breeta,' said Grannybeg, in the low honey voice, 'listen to me, for your spirit is troubled and the reason for all its troubling is in your secret heart. You are like a fire that can neither keep nor hold. There are more things in life than one thing. We are Christians, we are all Christians; that we are, yes, yes. The chief himself is a Christian, even if his proud wife Silis thinks he is also something more. But if he is more than a Christian, Breeta, he is also not less. Not less, child. He knows – of the other things. And so it is, child, that he would save the people to be better Christians. There are hidden evil things and dark spirits whom we must defeat if we are to be Christians. Does not Molrua say it himself? He says it. He says it. But Molrua does not know – what the Master knows. And who would tell him, child? Who? Who need tell him?'

Thus Grannybeg divided before them the old dark potent way, that ran in the hollows of the bone and deep into the hidden world, from the way of the preacher that lay in the sun like a green path. And they knew she was right. It was necessary that the men should go this night. It would *make sure*.

Make sure of what? Hsh! . . . Bend the head low, curl up, so that the body will lie under and be passed over. Under the whistling arrow, the hedgehog curls up in the little wood. When a dog barks, the rabbit flattens its ears and becomes as a stone in the field. Let the EYE not see. Oh, hsh, hsh – who uttered that word, him IT *will* see.

'I saw today', said Breeta, when Grannybeg had ceased, 'a beast that was like a little red dog. Col was with me. It came out from the ferns to the well – yonder. Then it seemed to see someone – and went back into the ferns.'

'Did you see anyone yourselves?' the old woman asked.

'No,' said Breeta. Grannybeg was silent. Breeta asked her, 'What does that mean?'

'It means,' said Grannybeg, 'that Molrua the preacher is among us again.'

They saw that this was right, and were strangely moved.

'What – what sort of dog was it?' asked one of the girls in a small voice.

'It was a little lovely red dog. Its hair was redder than the hair of Silis, and when it went back into the ferns not a fern moved,' said Breeta. With the others listening to her, Breeta was soothed and lifted on to an arch a little above them. But the arch was thin as a bubble. She smiled.

Then Grannybeg's hand reached over. It was wrinkled and bony, and the fingers that closed on Breeta's hot wrist were death cold. Breeta's heart leapt back within her. Grannybeg's eyes were moonbright and divining.

'Hush, my child, quieten you, quieten –'

'No!' screamed Breeta, and leaping up rushed at the door against which she smashed her left shoulder and, rebounding outside, began running, crying, 'No! no!' and then crying it madly within her, weeping, her mind all blotted out – 'no! no!' running, she did not know where.

What had been gathering within her all day had at last burst upon her. With Nessa she had been quiet. With her brother she had heard the old sweet music. Out of the music she had looked at Leu. Among the girls she had found herself growing daring and exciting. All the time her blood had been rising within her. Now it had burst over like a fountain and drenched her and blinded her eyes.

Breath rasping through a harsh throat, she at last pulled up and turned towards the settlement, hands pressing her chest. The bothies were dark and silent. The whole world was silent and immensely wide. All at once a small witchlike figure was coming towards her without sound. Breeta screamed and, turning once more, made blindly into the moor. A thin screech pursued her. Sickening sounds came from Breeta's open mouth as she stumbled and sped. But the swifter she went the more the screech was in her ear. The terrible little witch was gaining on her. (They had all known that Grannybeg could turn into a witch! They had known it!) She could feel the hand not far from her, just behind her, coming up . . . Her body pitched forward.

She dug into the earth, squawking, crushing her eyes – 'No! no!' her inside heaving in sick fear.

But no fingers clawed her shoulders and, facing round at last, she saw nothing. A dog's mournful howl rose on the night, the foresignal of death. Even while she sat up, her body leant back, her hands pushing against the heath, pushing her away by inches. She got to her feet and began stumbling sideways, looking back at the distant basin of blackness that must be the encampment. Holding her breath, she stood still. The dog bayed again. Another dog answered. The mournfulness of the howling was more terrible than death itself. No gleam of light shone from the bothies. Death was abroad.

She had never been out alone in the night before. She could have crawled now to Grannybeg's skirts and clung to her feet. She could have become abject in submission . . . The urge to crawl to Grannybeg's skirts began to get the better of her. She started back, and was at once aware of a dark figure coming towards her, but no longer the small witchlike figure. The first dog could not stop his howling. It had got the better of him. It got the better of the night. It rolled the path for Death to Breeta's feet. She started running into the moor silently, and only when she stumbled did her throat give way. Her skin had gone quite cold. Her body had grown light; it was without purpose, and sickness was a feather in its throat. Only one hot spot remained, and that was in her left shoulder. It began to burn, to throw hot roots downwards. All it needed was an overtaking hand to grasp it and tear it out roots and all. That's what it was there for – waiting . . . Without any feeling of impact with the ground, she lay still.

She became aware of herself waiting again, waiting intolerably . . . She lifted her head and looked behind. There was nothing, no one.

She sat up. It was as dark now as it would be. Northward the far horizon was green. Out of that green it came to her, as out of watchful green eyes, that this was midsummer night. Midsummer night! She saw the figure coming along the moor towards her. She could not move. It came slowly but directly. It paused – and came on. The pause was too much. She was on her knees, and all at once she was screaming, 'No! no!' her voice thick with terror, her hands writhing and knotting. The figure stopped dead. 'No, no, leave me! Oh, leave me! Leave me!' Her screams tore over harsh sobs. The figure did not move. 'Go away!'

A thin whisper, unearthly clear, 'Breeta.'

'No! no!'

The figure advanced.

She writhed in a paroxysm of terror, screaming abjectly.

The figure stopped, and from it came in a low sweet whistle the rhythm of notes that Leu had played. The whistling was a ghostly echo, it was a mockery, it was a last deception and enchantment. She was done for. Already a fainting weakness came into her madness. And now the figure was upon her, had caught her shoulder at the burning place, was down beside her in the heath, arms round her, voice hushing, drawing her close, pressing her face against a breast. She let go, and her blood ebbed away on a sudden strange confidence. Her body gave a spasmodic shiver. She gripped, pressed her face into the breast, muttering, 'Leu! Leu!' and fainted into sleep.

For a time the figure lay with her in his arms. There was a vague scent out of her hair and, when his face touched it, the skin was so tickled that he pressed his mouth and nose firmly into the dark mass and breathed in the smell of the body itself, which had something familiar about it and disturbing. He lifted his head and cast about him with a wary urgency. But the green light was watchful. He stared and threw a glance at the stars, remote and slow-wheeling to let in the dawn. The dawn! He turned to the girl and drowned his mouth again, felt her along his legs and body. He lifted his mouth and slowly sat up, looking at her pale face in the nightlight. A cruel tenderness crept along his flesh. To have her, living and yet dead, was to laugh at Orion's sword. Her hair was black mystery. Her helplessness. . . . O, hidden sun!

Sun was hidden. In the shadow of the empty world necromancy spread its bed. But already, already Sun was gathering his majesty about him for his awful uprising on midsummer morning.

Midsummer night yet, though, with pulse tracking pulse along the grey-dark moor, with rebellion on tiptoe waiting for the reckless laugh, the low chuckle that mocks Orion's sword and chokes its mouth with that which it devours.

He lifted his eyes from her face and from the soft fall of her body. There was a pulse in his throat. 'Leu!' she had called. The beating in his throat choked him. His indecision was a torment. Sun! He must go. He must go at once. He breathed heavily. At that moment he fancied she moved.

He went still as the bog, then set his fingers over her face. They touched only her hair as they at last withdrew. He got to his feet, lifted her in his arms, and glanced about like one searching for a place to hide his prey. His eyes steadied on the moor's crest.

At last in a heathy hollow near that crest he stretched her out and stretched himself beside her. But this lying was a deceit. Her ghostly face had the aspect of death. His hand went under a small breast and his ear to her mouth. She was alive with the faint thresh of sleep that follows poisoned exhaustion. Only if the mind turned upon her to devour, would she awake in fear.

Yet he was exhausted himself from her weight, and all at once gave up his mind and lay beside her. 'Leu!' she had called. So it was Leu, was it? Leu was the one! Leu, that pipe-player! His mind cleared, and into it came a sharp cruel temptation. Before it could touch her, however, he turned and walked away, his head falling down the other side of the night.

The night moved round on the slow wheel of the stars. While the sky had yet the afterlight of the sun in the north-west, it had already the forelight of the dawn in the north-east. All the north, indeed, was thin with this light from a sun in the abyss, and the rim of the world was clear as the crest of a precipice. The far sharp cry of a moorbird was its sound. Its colour was blue, quivering to green. Its spires uprose in white light. And now its time was not night, but morning. The change went over the moor in a cold shudder. The moor itself and all its bodies turned grey. The greyness spread like a trance of death. Each grass, each heath point, shivered separately and stood still.

The greyness centred in Breeta's face until it grew paler than the exposed dead roots of a bogpine at her back. From the world's shiver her knees crept up for warmth. Curled, she lay still.

The moor waited, silent and flat.

Breeta's eyes opened and caught this waiting. Before she knew where she was, her whole being was intensely alert. Her eyeballs roved. Feigning death, she was safe; but, moving, what might not spring on her? The peaty soil was black, the moss grey-green. The grasses were bent over, the heath points straight. The world's body was low against her face, which slowly turned over and tilted up – and looked warily around. Her elbows quivered to her side; her teeth chittered.

She listened as she trembled and pushed her head up, now ready to leap. For she had lost a sound, a cry. A rosy light caught the nipple of the distant mountain. A bird from a valley tree sang across the morning. And all at once there was birdsong in the sky, interwoven and invisible, weaving down. The grey was silver. The trance of death was the shiver of ecstasy. And – the cry again!

She crouched back, flurrying the heath, eyes staring over bared teeth. Nothing moved about her. She cast round and round, straight-armed, pushing fists into the heather. She became aware where she was as if someone had spoken, and, fascinated by the near crest, crept towards it.

She saw first the rising arc of the sun, and then below it and before it she saw leaping reddish-yellow tongues of flame. Against the distant blood-red sun, the flames leapt no farther away than the dark Grove. They flickered and shot, forked and fell, without sound. Against the oncoming sun, their dance was unreal and small and terrible. As the sun rose their little tongues rose.

Once more the cry; and though the fire was small in that waste in that dawn, it drew every living nerve to it as to a burning heart. The cry had risen out of the flames, springing to the sky, and, its peak reached, fell away into the sun. The cry had been a piercing scream, but it also had been a defiant spear. Before Breeta's eyes the Grove began to sway. It came alive with swaying bodies. The air swayed.

It was swayed by a chant from the swaying bodies moving
sunways in a river. This music possessed her with terror;
a music she had never heard, and yet, hearing, knew. She
could not close her eyes, which grew hard as stone and let
the flames come near. Too near. She choked. She fell down.
She was delivered into mortal weakness. Within her own
circle she quivered, quivered to hand-gripping. She rolled
over, got up, and started running home across the moor.

At first she went blindly, beyond caring what leapt on
her, making whimpering, gasping cries. But soon she
choked back these sounds and crouched her shoulders
with the cunning of the hunted. Out of its cold sheath
her body bounded with increasing power and with great
speed. She overtook the young morning wind with her wet
lips. Her shoulders squared; head up, she gave herself to it
like a hind – and swung outward when she saw the top of
the round fort in the smaller valley as if it had been alive.
As probably it was – with men's eyes. Men like Lys. She
only went the faster, and in time struck in from the moor
to the fringe of trees in whose shelter she threw herself
down exhausted. But soon she raised her head, looking
round at the watching tree trunks, then got to her feet and
noiselessly passed out to the fringe, by the side of which
she trotted evenly. She took care not to be seen from the
top of Drust's fort, and at last came into the trees above
her own home.

In this refuge she paused, her breath easing, her whole
body gathering comfort as if she licked it. A thrush sang
over her. Small coloured birds cried *pink! pink!* and flitted.
The world was still ghostly thin. The leaves rustled and
sighed. Without a sound a great brown hare hopped out
of the wood, sat up, and looked at her.

Its small pointed head with tall pointed ears was witchlike. Its prominent eyes were round and full of uncanny
watchfulness. It knew Breeta was there, and yet neither
wanted to go away nor to stay, but sat in an intermediate
stage weaving one country to another. It wove Breeta into
the far country. It had the air of ever going and taking
Breeta with it. Breeta got lightheaded and entranced, she
stared so hard without breathing. The brown of its fur was

unbelievably real and so soft that a breath of wind divided
it. The eye was alive. The nostrils suddenly wrinkled and
smoothed, in a way human and inhuman. It drooped,
watching Breeta; touched grass and lifted its head with a
jerk. Breeta leaned back. The hare hopped away – and sat
up again. It was the witch woman!

'No! no!' cried Breeta harshly.

The hare hesitated an instant more, then suddenly
flattened its ears and took to its heels. But, as if it had
changed its mind again, it stopped and sat up on the moor.
It now looked three times as big as it did before.

Breeta plunged down through the trees, the witch of last
night going with her. She struggled from the dark memory.
Her home loomed upon her. She ran to the door, fumbled
with the fastening, squeezed through, crushed the door
shut, and stood panting. There was no sound of pursuit.

The house was very empty. She stepped noiselessly,
afraid of the beds. The pale light from the small window
fell on a dark head. Its wan face . . . was it a face? She
had to make sure. With sick terror she approached – the
hollow grinding-stone! She stumbled from it, threw herself
into her bed, and pulled the rustling skin over her.

The air under the skin grew close and warm about her
curled body. Her open eyes saw tiny flicking suns. She shut
her eyes and saw pointed yellow flames. The lights died
into the darkness of night. The noisy beat passed out of
her blood. She breathed heavily so that her head could not
hear anything. She smothered herself in her warm breath.
There was no sound in all the world but the singing of
birds. The clear singing of birds that was of an unearthly
sweetness and the farthest singing was beyond the edge of
the world. . . .

She hid under the skin. . . .

Footsteps put a circle three times round the house, a
sunwise circle of soft padding sound. Breeta lay at its
core, curled in a circle of her own. But when the door
crunched open, her heart raced out of the foreknowing of
sleep. Two men came in, and the air that came with them
carried swiftly beneath her covering the aromatic smell of
burning wood. The new kindling. All fires had been put out

last night, in house and bothy – everywhere. Now Fire had been born again. On the earthen floor their feet slithered to silence by the stone hearth. There the fire was built up, and what had been missing in the room was now no longer missing.

During this time no word was spoken. At last her elder brother sat on the edge of his bed. Her father turned to the family bed. There was a moment's silence before his voice came:

'Is no one here?'

She drew back the skin from her head. Her father was a strange figure between night and the spectral morning.

'No,' Breeta answered. 'Mother had to go to the Tower – with Donan.'

'Why?'

'I don't know,' answered Breeta.

Her father stood unmoving, then without a word got into bed.

Breeta listened to the breathing of the two men and curled up again behind it. The spearing yellow flames had come into the room, but she was safe from them now, safe from fear, safe from everything except a vague dreadful concern that was beyond in the day, this day, next day. . . .

She wondered if her father knew she had gone to the shielings. She had fled into the dark from the shielings – but no, she smothered her face. She dared not remember. Something terrible and – she did not know what. . . . All her flesh gathered into little convulsive knots. The bird-singing was ringing across the morning. The hare sat up and looked back at her. . . . She had mastery over Leu, could draw him, use him like a brother. But . . . but. . . . She held her lungs until they nearly burst. Then letting her breath go, she followed it, her head falling over.

The light came from the little window in blue spectral shafts. The breathing of the three bodies could be heard in a stillness waiting for something to move.

## CHAPTER TWO

DURING the forenoon of that same morning most of the able-bodied men set out from the shielings for the Tower Glen. The old men and women saw them off with blessings, but the young women, in a little group by themselves, waved and giggled, whereat the young men waved back and now and then out of a boisterous humour slapped and tripped one another. They were followed by young boys like Col, until the time came when the boys were ordered back 'to protect the flocks and the old'. The ordering was a flattery, and the boys turned in embarrassment, their hearts bursting. One overgrown boy followed still; but a man said, 'You'd better go back, too:' and he blushed and went.

The men kept on their way, glances full of excitement, laughing and restive. 'Mind who you're pushing,' threatened Garam. 'Ho-hok!' crowed a hidden voice. 'I'll ho-hok you!' said Garam. 'That's right, Garam; don't stand any of their nonsense.' 'Neither I will,' said Garam. The young men charged one of their number into Garam's back. 'Will you stop that?' roared Garam. 'It wasn't me!' pleaded the young man. 'I'll make you all laugh', said Garam, 'out of the crooked side of your mouths.' 'Quite right, Garam,' agreed the young men.

They made Garam their butt. The Northmen, they said, were such experts with their sharp iron axes that in one blow they could split a man in two from the crown of his head to the place between his legs. 'Between your legs! In that case I could do more good split', said Garam, 'than you could do whole!' The conversation then became such that their mouths grew luscious. Garam, encouraged by his contemporaries, exploited young men's ignorance in broad terms. When he got a sally home, his eyes glimmered and his feet staggered jauntily. A squat, knotty tree of a man. They all loved him. Their hearts were uplifted with their heads, and their bodies went lightly against the unknown. Their eyes flashed with good humour and friendliness. A small dark people, all the more homogeneous because of an odd mouse-fair head rising here and there.

Drust, awaiting them in his hall, gnawed moodily at the hair he sucked from the right corner of his upper lip. His eyes were blue with a hard glint that brought the danger to the surface. Normally it was a good-humoured face, the cheeks emerging smooth and ruddy from the golden-red beard, the brow low and broad, the eyes set wide and not deeply, the teeth uncrowded, rather large, and the colour of dull ivory. Returning early that morning, he had wrapped himself and gone to sleep on skins on the floor. He had slept through the first entrance of his wife. But less than an hour ago she had come in with a platter of boiled grain and milk – and the inevitable question about last night. Because he had been expecting the question – had slept where he did in order to avoid it – it instantly angered him, and there had been a scene. He was now gnawing over the fierce things he had said. She was beside herself over the affair at the Grove. That was the truth. There would never be peace in this accursed place until she was riding their backs as they crawled to the Christian priest. He had walked to the doorway and actually seen the priest, Molrua, leave the enclosure, so that there had been a secret conclave in her stone chamber already! His blood was still hot. This place wasn't good enough for Silis. Nor the folk. Nothing. But if the Northmen got a footing, by her God, she might be glad of it as it was!

Silis came in at his back. 'The missionary, Molrua, has been here.' Her tone was clear and cold, but conciliatory, though in using the word missionary instead of the common word priest, she conveyed the idea of a high mission and a whole new world of religious thought. 'He is going to speak to the men when they come down.'

Drust made no move.

'He expects you to lead them to his hill,' she concluded. 'That's his message.'

'Do you mean', said her husband, turning round, 'that that is his order?'

'It is no order,' said Silis. 'He expects you.' She faced him calmly, tall as himself, and with a quickening in her face that would have made its beauty warm had it not hardened the bone.

He bit the lip itself.

'You would think', he muttered, 'that I was a piece on a board.'

'No one plays on the board here.'

'Oh! That's what they do where you come from! This is a savage place. They don't play anything here.'

'They play at circles – with stones,' she said, lifting the wooden platter.

Her quiet tone, with its edged meaning, infuriated him. She always made him speak more than she did, leaving his intemperance to gnaw his conscience in quietude and madden him the more. But he was also a chief. Since, however, their son had gone to the court of the king, her importance had most subtly increased, an outward manifestation being a Christian air of delicate forbearance. She could imply, too, with the fall of her breath the difference between one mode of life and another. She could make him feel with her lashes that the man who was once a gay, clean-shaven, promising leader was turning into a whiskered country boor, while the centre of civilisation in their country of the several kingdoms was ever shifting farther south.

All this, indeed, had been growing on her these last few years. She was now the mother of a family, and scheming for power. But he wanted things to slide on in the old way, with plenty of time for hunting. Year by year he loved the forest more, and he could sleep anywhere. The rough kindly ways of the people grew into his liking. Little by little he had become less concerned with his personal appearance. And the more he set himself to his background, the more she withdrew from it and him. He missed his son. He loved his daughter. Between Nessa and the baby, Donan, there had been no family.

Now the advent of Donan, unexpected and preceded by strange portents, was mixed up in an odd fashion with the story of Drust's infatuation for the Black Hind of the woods. Some thought that the coming of Donan would soften Silis and make her agreeable to her husband. Perhaps Drust himself thought that by her Christian prayers she had won a gift that would bring back the golden weather of their early days of great love. Perhaps at times she thought so herself, for her eyes had been seen to shine softly in a daydream. But there had been no such effect. On the contrary, she had come from childbirth with her body thinner, the bone firmer in her face, and something behind her eyes that Drust always saw when he was not looking at her, but what it was he did not try to reason because at once his mind became dull and angry.

Her nature was proud; how proud, only he, Drust, knew; knew why, for example, she had never got over the evening several years before when she had heard of the first fair-haired child born in the inland village of Finlag.

This story had had a deep attraction for the Tower Glen people themselves; and all the more so because one of those concerned was the little old man, named Bardan, with the high blue cap, who came amongst them now and then.

Bardan was one of the tribe of little folk who inhabited the Finlag dwellings that were so many green mounds gathered together. A dwarfish race, with flattened noses broad at the base, with big mouths and big ears and shiny dark eyes. They were a clever, quirky folk, kindly or malevolent, but never to be understood because of some hidden loyalty to something no one knew, so that when offended they withdrew into themselves and out of sight.

Half Bardan's language was the old language, and he made odd verses of poetry on anyone or anything. When he appeared, the children always flocked about him, laughing and dancing and sometimes teasing him, for they thought him a little queer in the head. 'Make poetry on that blackbird,' they would say. And looking at the bird with his twinkling eyes, Bardan would hunch his shoulders and raise an arm:

> 'I see a blackbird on a tree
> Singing a little song to me.
> He sings a little song to me
> Sitting on a hazel tree.'

This always entranced the children, who danced and shouted:

> 'I see a blackbird on a tree
> Singing a little song to me . . .'

Then they would wrinkle their foreheads and cry, 'What comes after that?'

Now Bardan had a daughter whose mother had died in giving her birth, so that the girl had grown up with her father. She, too, was said to be light in the head like her father, and ran wild and whistled the birds and knew where the beasts hid. She could break out of undergrowth or tall bracken like a hind.

Well, this girl, who in the old language was called the Black Hind, for she was clean made in leg and body, was once lost in the forest for half a moon. This coincided with the time that Drust with a small company was also in the forest. And the story went that Drust, who had got separated from his companions in an eager stalk, had followed his quarry into a thicket where, seeing a sudden movement, he had let off an arrow. Great was his surprise at a woman's scream and the sudden outrush of the terrified Black Hind herself all but naked. They had stared at each other, then he had run her to earth, for the arrow had gone through the flesh of her leg and soon crippled her. Otherwise, of course, he would never have caught her. Her leg, indeed, was in a terrible condition when he came to examine it, for in the race the arrow had hit against trees and lacerated the wound so that the flesh was all but severed.

When Drust and his companions went stalking in the forest, they always made trysting-places where at appointed times they would all meet, for it was easy enough to stray from one another. Two waited at the first tryst for him, and the other three went on to a place one day distant. But at none of the appointed places did Drust appear.

The men kept travelling from tryst to tryst, shouting as they went. They were frightened to go home without him. And not until many days, when they all came back to the starting-place, prepared to raise the whole glen, did they find Drust sitting awaiting them, with a strange expression on his face, for all the world as if he had been 'beyond'. All he told them was a story of how he had been lured away towards the mountain by a hind, and how, when he had wounded it, he had fallen out of his senses. They did not believe this, particularly when he bound them with a certain look to speak of his absence to no one. Only much later had details come out or been invented. But how Drust had nursed and kept the Black Hind, for the better part of a fortnight, became a curious and tender story in the minds of the young, though there were those who said that the whole affair had been far beneath his dignity, and the insult of a brute to his queenly wife. But, all in all, such is the strangeness of human nature, that of the things that Drust ever did, none gathered about it such warmth for him in the people's minds as this episode of the forest. It mellowed, too, through time, and what at first might have been objectionable got smoothed and coloured, until it was the most moving thought of all.

Perhaps the unconscious veil to all this was in the face of Silis now, as she lifted the platter and, while going, yet hesitated, hardly even regarding the face of her husband, which had no trick of coldness, so subtle could her coldness be. Nessa came panting into the room – but immediately pulled up before her mother, who demanded in her level voice what was wrong.

'It's Taran,' said Nessa. 'He asked me to tell you', and she looked at her father, 'that the men are at hand.'

Her father nodded, 'I'm coming;' and turned away from them both as if to busy himself. Silis hesitated still, then followed the chastened Nessa.

Drust had really nothing to do, and took a turn about the empty room, troubled not so much with thought as with thought's rebellion. The craving came upon him to clear out and go to the forest. Beyond the wall Taran was waiting for him, and said:

'The men are down below.'

'I hear them,' Drust answered.

Taran lifted his eyes from his chief's face, which was warmly constrained.

'Well?' pursued Drust.

'Are you going to speak to them first or –'

'Or what?'

'Molrua has arrived this morning,' remarked Taran simply. 'I think he is expecting us.'

'What makes you think so?' asked Drust as simply.

'I think – it was arranged,' said Taran, whose eyes had grey in them. In stature he was smaller than Drust, and leaner, and his head was dark and long. There was great intelligence in his face, which had a natural gravity, and a voice that was slow and cool. His voice, when repeating the old verses, caught a legendary tone so expressive that no one had ever interrupted him. Many bards are fiery and given to boasting, but Taran was not one of these. Yet was there the deep note of boasting when he spoke of the heroes and battles of the past; in the quietness it was a booming, stirring note, with a strange and lingering excitement.

Drust could not question him further lest his wife's order be exposed, so he asked, 'Do you advise that?'

Taran appeared to reflect. 'Yes.'

When they came down to the river level, the men who were standing about, or leaning against the hill, stopped talking. Drust and Taran went ahead and crossed the tributary from the Little Glen near where it entered the main stream. A large knoll now rose out of the river flat on their left hand, and as they went towards it they saw the hooded figure of Molrua descend its green side, for on the flat top of this knoll he had built himself a small round stone dwelling. There he had dispensed the sacraments and baptised in time past, but now he had other business.

As Drust and Taran with the men behind were drawing nigh, Molrua raised his hand silently over them, then let it fall and greeted Drust with a smile, saying, 'God be with you.' And his smile rose up over all the men, too.

'And with you,' replied Drust calmly.

For a little the natural kindness that was at the heart of

Molrua broke in hesitation. He looked like one who was glad to see them and glad to welcome them, but had no easy words for his human affection.

Then he stepped up the hill a pace, so that he was raised over them, and pushed back from his head the hood of his brown cloak.

All the faces there looked towards his face, which now was calm and open, the brow broad and bare, the bleached hair receding to a thick mass, with ruddy traces still behind the ears. While he took the Gospels from their hide casing, he said in a voice dealing in treasure, 'I will read to you the word of God.'

The Latin words he intoned so that the sound of them, though without meaning, moved the spirit like the long roll of a wave, or of wind dying away in a forest. And as the wave falls but to rise again, and the wind passes but to come more strongly, so his voice rose in authority, falling but to lift and go against and over them with increasing power.

What he said in Latin he then said again in their own tongue, and because he had translated it thus many times to himself, the words came without stumbling and had the deepness as of magic added to them.

And all this he did, not appealing to them as he went, nor yet calling to their humble understanding to follow him, but with reverence placing before them the mystery of Christ and the miracle of His death and the salvation of His words. Like one completing a holy office, he closed the illuminated page, and stood looking over them in a deep silence.

Then he spoke to them:

*No man can serve two masters: for either he will hate the one, and love the other; or else he will hold to the one, and despise the other. Ye cannot serve God and mammon.*

And as Molrua spoke, Drust knew that he had been told of the gathering at the Grove, and he knew also that he had been told by Silis. Drust could see this in the mind of Molrua and, although he thought he was the only one who saw it, yet this was not so, for all the men there, who knew how it was with Silis, saw it as clearly. There came into the manner in which Molrua spoke a high urgency as he strove to divide the way before Christ from the way after. His spirit struggled to fling the lightning that divides darkness from vision. He was compassionate. He pleaded. Christ had come to save the world from darkness. Christ was the Son of God, the one God who had made the world and who had made the stars, who was before the world was, who was today, and who was for ever. All the little gods and signs and portents, the images and beliefs and stones, the groves and trees and wells, were but the aids man had made for himself while he had been searching through all the ages of the world for this one God. And now the one God had been found and had been proclaimed to them by his Son, Jesus. There was no longer any doubt. The truth had been found and was fixed for all time. How glorious it was that this was so. How it made their minds free so that they rose like birds and sang for gladness, sang in the daylight, in the air, within the trees, upon the grass, sang their songs of love and kindness – under the Sun, *which God had also created*.

As his ecstasy came upon him, the light stood about Molrua and in his face. The story of Christ was bright and new as the sunlight, and like the sunlight made the earth new and bright. Nay, it was newer and brighter than the sunlight. The sunlight would be no more than sunlight without it. There would be no quickening, no joy, no peace. Christ ran through the sunlight, quickening and radiant. The sunlight was God's smile at the end of Christ's journey, and in the same moment Christ was with God.

Now not only Drust and Taran, but the men also, saw that Molrua was profoundly moved, and was not taking the Sun from them by cunning and giving the Sun to his God. And there was one figure, too, who had come down the Little Glen with Morbet's men, who also saw that Molrua was not thinking in his heart to damage the Sungod. That figure was Aniel, who hung on the outskirts, not having known of the coming of the Christian priest.

And Molrua's ecstasy began to work upon all. At first

their minds had been dark against those who had been
bearing tales to Molrua, for they would have wished
Molrua to know nothing. They would have wished that
for two reasons, and the first was that they would not
willingly have hurt Molrua, or indeed any gentle creature,
for their hearts were soft and kind where affection moved;
and the second was that they wished to guard from Molrua
all knowledge of the secret life, so that they themselves
might have both lives, and thus fulfil all the desires within
them. To worship both God and mammon was for them
not only simple, but wise and needful, for mammon has
little meaning in a communal life as simple as Christ's, but
much meaning belonging to the earth and the blood and
to impulses as old as time. God was over and beyond the
earth; but there was the earth and the darkness beneath,
of which God and Molrua need know little and need be
told less. Take no heed of the morrow. They took none.
Give to the poor. They gave.

But such division of the mind was what Molrua strove
against and, striving, made them feel uneasy of their secret
darkness in the light. For to Molrua, why should not one
accept the blessed gift of God? Why? What madness it was
even to endanger the gift. Such madness, O my people,
my children! Do you not see the madness and the danger?
It was as if one came and offered you not only herds and
flocks and houses, sea-vessels and riches, everything that
the heart can desire, with freedom from danger and the
peace of your enemies, not only these, perishable at the best
and for the short time of a life, but – Heaven itself, Paradise,
the lovely glens of Paradise, and not for a little time, but
for all eternity. Ah, not only that! Hardly even that at all.
Listen to me. Listen! Does not your heart swell up within
you when you think of that last journey of Christ? Would
you not gladly have saved Him if you could? Children, I
would have let myself be nailed to the tree for His sake. I
would. I would. But – He let Himself be nailed to the tree
for my sake and for your sakes. Ah, shame it was! Shame
on us! Shame! Shame! Molrua bowed his head and prayed
for a little, prayed that we be forgiven, as though Christ had
been crucified but yesterday amongst them.

Much meditation in a lonely retreat had worked its marvel upon him. Although his spirit was wrought up, yet such was its nature that even when he cried out his voice penetrated with sweetness. The story of Jesus, and of His crucifixion and of His rising from the dead, was as a story told for the first time, in all its newness and strange and terrible beauty, so strange and beautiful that it had the air about it still of the incredible. And, because the incredible was true, the heart rose in surprise and gladness. And lo! the sunlight had the light of Christ, for it was quick with an inner brightness, and went through the leaves of the trees, and ascended with the birds, and shone in their falling music. The earth itself was changed with the magic of Christ's presence. Everywhere. Everywhere.

A calmness came on Molrua out of his short prayer. His duty remained to him.

So for those who did not believe in Christ, for those who turned from Him and refused His way of salvation and denied God the Father, there was only the one place left, and that place was Hell. There are never more than two ways: the way upward to Heaven, and the way downward to Hell. And no man can go both ways, just as no man can serve two masters. Ye cannot serve God and mammon. You cannot walk down Hell's way and hope to reach Paradise. Walking down Hell's way you reach – Hell.

Then Molrua spoke to them of Hell.

His face was now stern and avenging; the pity at his heart at moments made his aspect terrible; his voice travelled a great distance.

The terrors of Hell, the tortures of the damned, the thirst unquenched in the burning that never consumed.

And even that was nothing – nothing, I tell you, nothing, compared with the treachery that gnawed the heart, the treachery to that One who had hung on the tree, the shining One who had been crucified, the treachery, O my children, the treachery to Christ.

There could never be forgiveness for that, never; at the core of Hell's eternal torture the bitterness would gnaw.

Consider the laws you live under. There is the law of hospitality to strangers, there is the law of justice, but your last law of all is to be valiant. In the barbarity of the old creed, what happened to the one who was not valiant? Your heathen teachers consigned him on death to the marshes and vapours of their hell. But if that happened to one lacking in courage, what happened to the treacherous? What could happen to him? What could be done to him that would be sufficient?

Christ was their leader. They knew of Him because he, Molrua, and others, had told them. Christ had laid it upon them that they tell one another. They knew now. There was no going back. He who followed the old ways, knowing the way of Christ, was damned. You cannot follow the druid, the wizard, the sorcerer, and follow Christ. If you are with the druid, you are against Christ. If you follow heathen practices, you deny Christ. You cannot serve mammon and God, the druid and Christ.

A movement, so slight that it was like a breath of dark air, went over the faces of the men. It may have been no more than the flicker of many eyelids, or response to the catch in the breath of little groups of women who now stood beyond the men, or to the drawing nearer to Molrua of Silis and her daughter Nessa, with Breeta's mother carrying Donan, and Breeta herself self-consciously behind.

Molrua having made these matters clear, began expounding to them the teaching of Christ. Here once more his spirit rose, for in this morning of Christ's rule it was more inspiring to speak of life than of death, of reward than of punishment. And Christ's ways were so full of mercy that you had only to trust Him and believe, and your evil was forgiven you. Nothing was held against you. And no one could take this gift from you. That was its crowning wonder. If your fellowmen outlawed you or scourged you or mocked you, still was Paradise yours – if you believed. No king, no druid, no clan, no earthly power, had dominion over your after-life. Christ would save you in the teeth of all the persecution of the world – if only you believed in Him. This was the new freedom, the freedom of the individual soul, walking in the light towards eternal glory.

And believing in Christ, you followed His teaching, His way of charity and kindness, of peace and goodwill, doing good to them that hate you, turning your cheek to your enemies. . . .

Molrua's ecstasy came upon him again, but now a thin red thread of agony wound round his cry. For if all these men stood defenceless before the Northmen, what would happen to them and to their children? What would happen to their women? Molrua knew what would happen. He knew. He battled with his knowledge. He strove before them and under God. The way of Christ had been the way of thorns. The way of Christ on earth had been death. Who were we to expect less? Yet the way of Christ was simple and lovely, could all men but see it. All men. But all men could not see it. . . . O God, wilt thou not pass this cup from our lips? In his red pleading, Molrua extended his hands to God and raised his face, and cried in a loud voice:

*A furore Normanorum libera nos, Domine.*

His agony was complete, and yet in the heart of that moment like a far echo was the echo of Christ's agony in the garden. And because of that comparison of himself with Christ, he felt instantly abashed, and bowing his head stepped down to the level of the men and stood for a little in silence. Then lifting an arm, he blessed them in a strange quiet voice, and, turning, moved slowly up the hill, veiling his head with the hood of his cloak.

Drust and Taran turned away and began walking down the path by the stream. Their eyes were straight before them, and they did not speak to each other. In the face of Drust his blood kindled, but Taran's face was pale, and the men who came a little distance behind them thought that these two were going towards the sea by arrangement. And presently it came into the minds of the two that they were going towards the sea, so they held on.

The men from the Little Glen, with Morbet and Erl at their head, came after Drust's men, and Aniel, who was one of the last, glanced over his shoulder at the Tower women. They were not twenty paces from him, and Nessa returned his look before her lashes fell and her face gathered a smile, not so much in movement as in colour. It was a recognition so reserved that it shut off a warmth which he did not credit, yet which had a curious exhilarating effect upon him. Breeta, however, did not look at him at all. And of a sudden he decided she was pale and cold and ordinary, with nothing in her of the uncertain, of the daring, of the love of danger, of fun, of wild loveliness. And all at once he was angry with her, and disliked her, and the veiled glance from Nessa twisted his mind with a laugh.

For Molrua had moved him. Molrua's picture of Christ had taken on ghostly flesh there in the sunlight. For a moment Aniel had seen Christ so clearly that he could have drawn Him with cross and thorn. And Molrua's eloquence had had a strange sweet quality. His own father, Taran, could make the passions mount and swing in fervour, so that the body wanted to arise and strike and behave valiantly. But Molrua moved the heart to a new sorrow, made it tender, and its tenderness lovely, and its weakness unyielding. Until the time came when his face had grown challenging and revengeful and he had condemned – condemned the Master. For a moment even then, Aniel had doubted, there in the clear sunlight, until his mind turned inward to the Master whom he loved.

And now he knew that of all those moving off, the two who were least under the influence of Molrua were Nessa and himself. Probably she had not been moved at all, and her meek listening had been a deceit! The thought of this made the queer laugh mount to his head. He had regretted giving her the penannular brooch, for it had not been meant for her, and had taken a long time to fashion, but now in a reckless mood he was pleased, very pleased!

He looked at those along with him and in front. But no one had eyes for him at all. He was the emissary of the Master. The secret laugh touched his face. Perhaps they were half afraid of him. Already he had observed little boys dodge him and run away. No one spoke.

'Where are we going?' he asked a young man beside him.

'I don't know,' said the young man.

'I think we're going to the beach,' said an older man politely.

They were all prepared to speak politely and calmly, hiding that which disturbed them. They began, indeed, making remarks in quiet voices about normal things, one asking a question and another answering.

Aniel did not speak again during the walk towards the beach, and in that time his body grew cool and his estrangement from those about him secret and complete. But he would not go back now, even if he had not had to report to the Master. By the time he stood by the sea-edge the strength of the mood woven by Molrua upon them was clear to him. One here and there let his eyes pass over him with that lack of sight which denied him, which had, indeed, hidden in it something more active than denial. Their minds, satisfied and wearied from the fierce excitements of the Grove, had been at once soothed and troubled by Molrua, and were now darkly resentful to that which had glutted them. Or if not to *that* – then to the presence of one who reminded them of it. Aniel understood the thought that made them wonder how he could have listened to the denunciation of the Master with such unconcern, and a resentment cold and thin as the edge of Drust's sword clove his own mind, but his mind met together and healed behind the edge, so that his lightheartedness became more close-knit than ever.

Drust's eyes beckoned him and he went across with an open expression. Morbet and Erl and his father, Taran, were standing with the chief, whose face was still congested. Aniel looked at it and smiled modestly, waiting.

Drust regarded him steadily. Aniel lowered his lids without altering his expression.

Drust turned to Taran. 'He has great spirit, this son of yours!'

'He had enough spirit once', said Taran, 'to take his own road.'

'But what has happened to it now you don't know?'

Taran was silent. And in the silence, Drust turned to Aniel. Drust's half-smiling face stung Aniel who said:

> 'My father is dumb to be Bard
> To the great chief Drust of the Ravens,
> The Ravens that wait for their masters
> To come in from the sea in the longships,
> The Northmen that harry and kill
> And spare not women nor children,
> The Ravens will kneel down before them
> And turn round their cheeks to the axes,
> Dumb as my father the Bard
> Before the great chief of the Ravens.'

Aniel spoke the lines as though he were repeating them from memory. In such a manner might a pupil say them to his master, or a son to his mother. Yet his tone, his slowness, his suggestion of volume, were most subtly imitative of his father's grand manner. And in the last line there was a ghostly emphasis on 'great chief' that, if not satire, brought a momentary hardening to Aniel's eye, a glint that was as uncertain as Drust's initial doubt of him. Then he smiled very slightly, waiting.

More blood gathered in Drust's face; then the right corner of his mouth went up, wrinkling his face. The wrinkles spread. He laughed, jerking up his head. He laughed his wife Silis out of him, he laughed the priest Molrua out of him, and all that was black through congestion he laughed out of him. Hands coming up pushed nothing back, and the man emerged. His laughter went round the beach like swallows. The beach cried under his crunching feet.

'Their masters, eh?'

'Master is a word that comes easily to me,' murmured Aniel.

'You stick up for your master, don't you?'

Then Aniel raised his eyes and met the chief's eyes and said, 'I do,' with no trace of a smile whatsoever.

Drust held the look strongly. At last he said, 'I believe you,' and his lips met and his eyes glittered. Slowly the glitter passed to a shining mirth. He turned to Taran. 'Is the darkness in your face anger or fatherly pride?'

'A father—'

'You've fathered better than you know!' interrupted Drust. 'Hell's horn!' He slapped Aniel on the shoulder.

Drust was not often demonstrative. Everyone there responded and breathed happily. Laughter found its undereddy. Drust addressed them:

'Every man will see that his weapons are ready. The Northmen have landed without warning and killed and burned. No place has been prepared for them. But we are to be prepared. And by our fathers we'll see to it that they get more than they give.' Then he raised the Raven cry, and Taran responded thunderously. Whereat everyone shouted, 'The flesh off the bone!' and cheered loudly. Excitement found its tumult. The young men hit each other in boisterous sport.

Drust held council with his principal men. Whereafter there started goings and comings, of eager youths, of darting boys, of animated solid men, until the foreshore became a hive, with the broad valley behind it for hunting-ground.

So the happy afternoon wore on, the sun clear in the sky and the sea plashing lazily the long curved shingle of the bay guarded by its sea-rocks on either hand.

As the sun declined, the excitement settled to a contentment that was friendly and quick-eyed. Far as the sight could roam the sea glittered emptily. The horizon was a thin line, very remote. At hand the green water came towards the shore, curling a foot high before falling over and drawing back, the shingle rumbling in a slow sigh. At the foot of the precipice away to the right were shelving rocks, from which a boy's cry rose now and then, shrill and cavernous as he landed or just failed to land a small fish. To the left was the flat of the river mouth, and beyond, at the root of the headland and backed by a steep green slope, was a very old village, so old that with its containing wall it looked like a huge flattened mound, out of which the roof of each cottage or chamber lifted a humped back. Wailing cries came from the common roof, upon which an old woman sat rocking a child. Other bodies moved also, and one face of a bent man with white beard looked spectral, so steadily was it turned upon the life on the beach, where men and youths were grinding flints, polishing edges, boring holes, thonging shafts, laughing and talking. Apart from weapons which from time to time Drust had brought back with him from the south land, there was little iron to be had. Most cunningly, Goan the smith had cut down some leaf-shaped swords into spearpoints not larger than a man's finger. They were so made that they could be socketed firmly. But there were not many of them and, though they were coveted, yet there were men who proclaimed that they preferred the flint. This was the careless boast, but it excited them to excel, and they were a knacky people and cocked their heads at their craft like artists. Indeed, it was clear that they loved working together like this under a common impulse. It gave rein to all their social instincts, their gossip, their boasting, their story-telling, their singing. Boasting, indeed, was an art as difficult and nearly as delicately developed as their story-telling. It was the vehicle for their lighthearted gaieties. A man boasted, conscious of his fine exaggerations, and could carry out the comedy to an uproarious or (the audience knowing their man and prompting accordingly) to an angry end. Let me show you how to do that! And while the next strove and strove, the rest egged him on in ever-watchful mirth. This gave to their sports and crafts a desire for excellence and finish. While always behind them stood the community's traditions, which meant the feats of the heroes, and these Time, the prince of boasters, exaggerated to his own measure.

The jest of the boast produces by reaction the jest of satire, and the extremes of both are farce and tragedy. There are always in all times only the few great players. But one like Bronach, who excelled in manly sport, never boasted. He was to others the secret boast, and boys followed him at a distance or said to one another of a sudden, 'Look, there's Bronach!' and watched where he would go.

There was a group of some thirty men and youths squatting on the beach, with boys shouting and playing behind them on this calm evening by the sea. Presently a small boat appeared off the headland to the left, and in a little while two more were observed about the rocks on the right. The spring tide was at low ebb, and some said they had seen the wafer of the new moon before it had set, and jested of chance and luck. The boats were coasting after crabs and shellfish and visiting certain rock-cracks for lobsters. They fished lines, with hooks variously made, but mostly of bone, and caught large-mouthed, red rock-cod or blue-backed lithe. Around the rocks on the right, too, was a wide cove with a clear sandy bottom leading into it where flounders could be speared. In this cove Drust's sea-boat was secured. It could carry twenty persons on a long journey. It had been the marriage gift of Silis, and as an emblem bound her not only to her husband but to her south-land home. This boat, too, had the legends of boats before it, but they were legends of the forebears of Drust rather than of the people. And there was one story of a great fight in which two hundred boats as big as Drust's took part. Some of the defeated enemy made the shore and took to the mountains, where they lived and were a terror to the shepherds and to women left alone in houses, until there came the day when they descended upon a shieling and carried off five young girls. Throughout the land the young men banded themselves together and hunted the robbers. There were mysterious deaths and deeds of great fierceness. But none of the girls was ever seen, except the one whom an ancestor of Bronach brought home with him. This first Bronach had long been given up for dead, when one day he arrived there on the shingle in a small hide boat and stepped ashore with this girl. She was a small beautiful girl with jet-black hair and wild eyes. But Bronach would never tell what had happened or what he had done, though it was clear that the first child the girl had could not be Bronach's child. Bronach, who had always been a quiet man, then became quieter than ever. The girl gave him a large family, but it was said by some that she was afraid of her husband and by others that she worshipped him. He became a man of leading in the community and the chief of that time entrusted him with power. In his old age he became very severe.

But what was said of the Bronachs would take a long time to tell. For some families had more history than others, and though for the most part they lived as a community, sharing in common, yet each family was jealous of its own tree. Each family, too, had its secret name which referred to the misdeeds of some of its dead, and often the raising of these names caused strife. But only the young or the violent-without-sense would raise heat enough to spill blood. For mostly they were a social pastoral people, lifting, above their private distinctions or dissensions, the chief's emblem of the Raven, which sometimes among themselves they called the Blackbird.

Yet if the idea of honour is in the act of boasting, as also humour and comedy, let it be said that there is, too, the fierce sense that in the last extremity makes the individual save himself by flying like a hunter or snarling at bay.

On this evening the mood of the people was clear as the sky and curled over like the sea-wave. It was a happy mood, with sparkles in its hollows and froth on its crest. There was also in it the benign slow movement of the water which is a movement full of memory, and will alter as the fates decide. . . . The waves would smash. The Northmen would come. . . . But now the lazy curl-over on the shingle and the receding sound as of wind in a patch of ripe grain.

Bronach got up and held his iron-tipped spear in his hand. The wood was white from its polishing with the skin-stone, and kept slipping to and fro through his fingers as he felt for its balance. Then his hand closed and rose above his ear. His body drew taut, his head setting to the spear, which kept pricking the air until it quivered to the final still moment of the thrust, when to those about him Bronach's eyes seemed to fix on a living enemy. His poise drew to an intent fierceness through which the left shoulder thrust slowly forward. All watching him held their breath. The children stopped as they drew near. Then quicker than the flick of an eyelash the spear shot forward a foot and checked. But such was the explosive energy in the thrust that his bare heels ground the stones noisily at the check. Then he lowered the spear, weighing it thoughtfully, and turned to Taran, into whose hand he dropped it, waiting, without speaking, for an opinion.

Taran handled the spear, ran his fingers along it, nodded at the perfect socket and, balancing it, smiled. The spear was like Bronach himself. Taran handed it to the men beside him, and soon there was a group about it. It was Aniel who handed it back to Bronach after a minute's intent inspection, saying, 'It's finely finished.'

He felt a trifle shy of Bronach and, after hesitating a little, turned away, the image of a more deadly spearhead before his inner eye. Goan had followed too closely the shape of the arrow flint.

The boys started shouting and running to meet a little round-hatted figure. 'There's Bardan from Finlag,' the men laughed. And Taran said, 'I was waiting for him. The Finlags are never in a great hurry.'

But the children, dancing about Bardan, had almost brought him to a standstill. 'Make poetry!' they demanded.

He threatened them. They screamed with delight. They pushed one another in on him. He raised his long birch stick, shoulders crouched, feet making little stamping runs.

> 'If you will not leave me,
> You will be drowned in the salt sea;
> And if you are drowned in the salt sea,
> You will no more be.'

They cheered. He had made poetry. 'Tell us who made the sea salt?' one boy demanded.

'Ah, you rogue!' said Bardan. Whereupon all the other boys took up the cry. But he now forced his way through them, waving his stick and turning round sharply when a daring one tugged him behind. Ultimate desire was centred in plucking off his hat. By the time he reached Taran, he was very angry.

This anger, however, everyone saw he had largely assumed in order to be in stronger countenance before Taran.

It was hard enough for one Finlag to get into the presence of the great without a score being made fools of. Not that there was anything like a score altogether, for the Finlags were a dying race, yes. There were, indeed, only a few old useless fellows like himself at Finlag; the others, such as they were, were hunting or pasturing, and he could not get at them in a day. They would come in good time. Trust him for that! Word had been sent. When are the pirates coming, anyway? demanded Bardan, lifting his bright eyes to the empty sea, cunning in their innocence.

'Where are Leuch and Poison and Tanag?'

'Where would they be, but away for days in the mountains? Is it sitting at the house you would expect them to be?'

'What are they doing in the mountains?'

'They are beyond the mountains, if you would like to know, getting more gold in the Bleak Strath. They want to give this gold to Drust, the chief, and they expect for presents two iron swords, two small knives, and the hook that cuts grain.'

'They're not expecting much,' said Taran.

'They are not,' said Bardan, 'considering the risks they are running every minute of the day.' And then he described the human beast he had seen himself a week ago. The hair grew out of his nose in two tails. He had one eye at the root of that nose and it would burn you up to look at it. He made a roaring noise and his mouth gnashed *gyable-gyab* – like that! That was as sure as may the shafts of Bel strike him dead on the spot, and his bright eyes concentrated warily on Taran.

'And when will they be with the gold?' asked Taran.

'Who can tell that? But if they are alive – and may Bel protect their ways in his sunlight, and may the demons of the night miss them in the passing – if they are alive they may return in a few days, but in plenty of time, rest you assured, before the chief himself takes his sea-way to the Broad River.'

'If they are already gone –'

'Do you not believe me?' interrupted Bardan.

'Very well,' said Taran. 'You have sent word to the pastures, and many men will be here tomorrow – without fail.'

'How can I say how many there will be? There will be as many men as there will be.'

'The number will be seen. And now will some of you see that Bardan is given fish and shellfish? And if you will honour my house on your way back, there will be food for us all.' And Taran smiled kindly at Bardan, whose eyes twinkled with pleasure, for he had got through his interview very well and would boast of it when he got back. Some of the younger men thereupon led Bardan towards the rocks where they would get him his gifts, and the boys came behind.

'Make a poem on a young woman,' said one of the youths.

'I will that,' said Bardan, for he was now in great feather. And when he had made his poem all the young men laughed excitedly, and turning on the small boys told them to clear off and not be listening.

'Why is the sea salt?' piped a voice behind.

'All right. Tell them why the sea is salt, Bardan, and then they'll go.'

'Long, long ago', said Bardan, crouching on his stick, 'there was no sea in it at all. At that time there was nobody in the world but giants. And the giants were so big that they could put one foot over a mountain and leave one foot behind. When they wanted a drink they let the river run into their mouths, one after the other, so that the river never got a great distance at the best of times. Well, in a year of years, didn't a great star fall out of the skies into the place where the sea is now? He was a huge fellow, this star, as big as twenty, yes and a hundred mountains, and he burned with a terrible fierce heat. So that all the land began to get dried up, and the grass withered, and no grain grew. The cattle and sheep became thin and had not the pith to breed, and so they lay down and died. At that the giants themselves became frightened, and prayed to Bel and offered their greatest sacrifices. But Bel would not help them because, he said, if a giant couldn't help himself, what use was it for anyone to be a giant at all? Besides, the star had said things to Bel, and it was Bel himself who had thrown him out of the skies. And that in itself was a strange thing. But

I won't wait there now, for meantime the giants gathered all the great rocks they could and threw them at the star. Anyone can see the rocks along the shore to this day. And that proves the story is true, because otherwise how would the rocks be there? But the star did not shift for the rocks. Not him. When one hit him in the side, he threw back a wicked stream of sparks, so that some of the giants got great burns on them. Now among the giants there was one little giant, and they all got angry at him because he wasn't even in the way. And some were for throwing him at the star, they were so mad at not knowing what to do next. Then the little giant, who had been sitting thinking, called all the big giants together. "I'll tell you what you should do," said the little giant. And then he told them. Some laughed, but some grew more angry than ever, for no two people see a thing in the same way. However, those who laughed said that as everything had been tried they might as well try the little giant's plan, too. It would at least make the star mad, and that itself would be something. So after a time, when they were all full up with the river and their bellies round – like that, they came to within a certain distance of the star and began streaming the water at him. And when one had emptied himself he strode to the river and filled up again. At first the star was mad, and hissed and sizzled and nearly drowned them in steam, but he could not send sparks. So the giants kept streaming. The star got madder and retreated before them a little. They followed, spouting great curves of water – sss – like that. The star went farther. They stood on the rocks and spouted and spouted. Until at last the star had to go off the earth altogether. And so where the star had been was now the great water that the giants had made. And that's why it is salt to this day.'

The boys roared with laughter at this, and as they jumped away one very little boy asked, 'But how is it salt?' And then a bigger boy behind him, imitating a giant, said, 'That's how!' And the little boy, wiping the back of his neck, began to cry. At this they played the game of Giants and Stars as long as they were able.

Aniel, passing them, smiled to himself. But when they saw Aniel leaving the beach alone, they ran farther off shouting louder than ever. The men saw him leave also; but now there was no animosity against him in any mind. Instead they gave him laughing praise upon the way he had scored over his father and released Drust (for in releasing Drust he had released them also). Oh! (they agreed) he had the ready wit. Yes, he was more than the mere son of his father. Was it not well known, moreover, that the Master preferred him before all the others? A clever lad, worth the watching. There, he's off. It's not often anyone from *there* comes over. But then . . . who is so certain that the Northmen are coming? (*Hsh, who could know but the Master?*) How? (*Be quiet, you!*) Then after a time a man from the Little Glen said in a low voice, 'Did you hear about the witch on the moor?' 'When?' 'Last night – and then again in the grey dawn – *at the very time.*' Who saw? . . . It was the beginning of the legend of Breeta.

The hush of evening came upon them and their minds grew quiet and alert, and at last Molrua, the Christian priest, sank down through the glimmer on the water and the glimmer on their thought without sign.

As Aniel went up by the river he came within sight of the flat-topped knoll whereon Molrua had his dwelling. What the Christian priest had said entered his mind again, and he became excited as with an odd fear. This he smiled at, for he had been buoyed up ever since he had extemporised his poetry for Drust. What secret elation that had given him, for clear as clear could be he saw the delicate but powerful thing he had done. For a moment he had looked nakedly at their thoughts, and then with word-sorcery both released and changed them. He might not have the power of his father, but his penetration was finer and clearer. This clarity had given even a keener elation than that which came when he made a perfect image. So that there was pleasure in lingering with the men, and their company had warmed him confidently in a way that it had never done before. It was as though all at once he grew into man's estate and took his place amongst men – but with a secret power of his own.

The knoll was now on his right hand, and, as he glanced towards its crest, he was startled by a sound in the river to his left, whence Molrua came towards him bearing a jar of water.

Aniel's heart went into his throat, and he was going past without sign, when Molrua said to him:

'And what's your name?'

'Aniel.'

'Who is your father?'

'Taran.'

'Taran the Bard.' Molrua's face was quiet and tender, and full of a strange humility. He was like one who had come through fire, and all that had been thick with self in him had been burned to the clearness of glass. For rather would one be crucified upside down than appear to suffer in the way Christ had suffered.

'I like your face,' said Molrua.

Aniel quickened, and his eyes flashed in avoidance.

'You must come to see me some time alone.'

Aniel did not answer.

'Will you come now, Aniel?'

'I am – late,' stammered Aniel.

'Very well.' He put a hand on Aniel's head. 'God be with you, my son.'

'And with you, Father,' muttered Aniel and walked away, and as he walked his feet felt so light that they nearly tripped him. His response had been the response of the weakling, of deceit, cried his mind, gripping him within. His ears grew hot. He gulped and hissed breath through his teeth, laughing silently; while all the time he felt the priest going up the hill with water that was cool and clear as his spirit.

It had been his intention to pass near the Tower, for the praise from Drust had moved him, and he felt that if he met him again there would be further talk. Shyly, he did not really desire this, yet vanity likes the gaiety of importance. Now, however, he turned up the Little Glen. This was the shortest way. Furthermore, if he had gone by the Tower there was a chance that he might have seen Nessa and her hair . . . in the trees before him, looking at him. . . . Breeta came across his thought, veiling it. . . . He put them both aside, and as he went up the Little Glen,

in the clear evening, he gave his thought to the picture of
Molrua on the hillside and himself outside that picture,
looking on. The picture had been with him at the shore,
with the power of division that vision gives. The clear light
came cool and sweet about his spirit. And yet because of
that division which was like a flaw extending to the core
of time, his elation was troubled.

Before he entered the Grove, he came on the Master
sitting on a turf bank. The small body was like a part of
the bank, an outcrop of the ancient earth. The face was so
old that its beginning was lost in the ages. The skin was
the colour and texture of a scraped sheepskin that, drying
in the sun, had been forgotten. And blindness veiled the
eyes as from the sun. When the eyes were steady for a
long time they looked quite blind, but when they shifted
and focussed, the breast had the melting sensation of
transparence before them. Nor did turning away help, for
their look was apprehended in the spine.

Now to Aniel there were three persons in the Master.
First, there was the person whom all the people feared.
To them he was terrifying and mysterious and silent as
a god. They feared him more than any god, for he was
midway between the Above and the Beneath, the Far and
the Near; he divided the kingdoms of life and death, and
made balance of payments between one and the other in
goods and in souls.

Second, there was the person whom Aniel knew. This
person was withdrawn out of the first, like a son withdrawn
out of the father, and spoke to Aniel simply of the things in
life and the way of life. Yet in so speaking he did not become
familiar to Aniel. On the contrary, he raised in Aniel such
a glow of clarity – as if the voice were verily within Aniel
himself – that Aniel yearned towards him in affection and
homage. For, beyond what the Master said to him, lay the
vast dominion of the spirit yet to be apprehended of the
novice.

The third person was this dominion of the spirit. Already
Aniel caught glimpses of it, often in moments of tranced
vision after just leaving the Master, and frequently, too, in
his image work. These were moments of intense happiness.

Occasionally they passed into periods of abstraction, when his bent for picture-making exercised itself of its own will. And the picture he saw was of the Master abstracting himself from the second person, or son, and withdrawing as a ghost, withdrawing and going afar off, his true spirit, his final self, his holy ghost, going further into regions of stillness, until he came to the centre, and there he stood with eternity about him in a circle of light.

He now said to Aniel, 'Sit down and tell me.'

'I come from the shore where they are getting their weapons ready.' Aniel was often nervous when starting to speak to the Master, but this vanity soon passed. 'When the men from the two glens met, Drust and Taran led them towards the Christian priest, who must have arrived in the early morning from his far retreat.'

The Master waited. Aniel answered, 'I know it was a far retreat because I asked afterwards, and also he was like one who had meditated alone for a long time.'

Aniel then said, 'He moved the men. He was very – They turned to the sea, saying nothing to one another. They were disturbed.'

'You relieved them?'

Aniel's body twisted sensitively.

'Tell me,' said the Master, 'were you moved yourself by what the Christian said?'

Aniel watched his own fingers plucking the grass. 'No,' he said.

Then he became confused, for the Master knew he had been moved, knew that if he had not been moved he would not have seen between Drust and his desire. And he had to see.

Aniel therefore rose out of his confusion. 'He said many things. What Christians have to do. To give to the poor without letting it be known. To turn your other cheek to your enemies. But chiefly he said that you cannot serve God and mammon.'

The Master's voice had a clear quality that isolated each word so that all its meaning emerged. The effect was vivid on the listener's mind. Yet there was no effort in it, as though it came of itself out of an immense memory. The eyes faintly cleared at the mention of mammon. Then the voice was within Aniel's head. 'When a man believes in something outside himself and is ready to be sacrificed for it, then that man becomes a force among even a strange people, and in time his god becomes their god, even as they become his brethren. Why should that be? Why does a man run after the new god? There are many reasons. Take this one of earthly power. The druids got earthly power. Over long ages they kept this power, until in the end they became more concerned about keeping it than about anything else. The Christian religion has no concern with temporal power. It is concerned to save the spirits of the people. And it preaches, not enslavement to earthly power, but the freedom of the individual spirit to find its own way to the pleasant plain of Paradise. It lifts up the gentler virtues, it speaks of tenderness and charity, of a merciful God, who will give everything if only you believe in him. Like something that is too good to be true, it attracts the man caught in his dark net. As a new faith the Christian will thus become very widespread and strong. It, too, may last thousands of years. It, too, may get caught in the tangle of temporal power and decline, and again a new faith come in its place. What that new faith may be like, and what the faith beyond that, no one may say. But I know that, beyond what we have arrived at, nothing really new can ever come to the mind of man, unless the mind itself enlarge and gain the knowledge that is beyond life and, when it does that, it will no more be man but god. It will know what life is, where it comes from and whither it goes and, more than that, why it comes and why it goes. Until that time, the human mind can know no certainty beyond what we know, nor can it ever be better trained to stand between and hold the dividing of forces than we have trained it. Of that only can we be sure. Nor is that the illusion of knowledge that comes from long meditation and desire. For we have tested it, and in the final loneliness have faced the malignant cruelty that is part of all Beyond; facing that, we have caught the balanced moment of all-seeing that is our moment of serenity. For all faiths and all unfaiths have their moments of serenity. But inasmuch as ours is not a simple belief, but an intense and prolonged striving to get at the dividing of forces, with no gain and no loss, with no question of reward beyond the reward of being there, therefore may we feel that it possesses human loneliness in its naked form. You yourself get glimpses of this, so far only in your image-making. Time will divide the image from the making, and then you will cleave through and stand on the edge between the Two Forces of the world. Does all this interest you, Aniel?'

'Yes,' said Aniel.

Presently the Master went on, and his voice now was quieter than ever, as if it came out of the heart of the evening and had the light on it that was fine and remote as the light beyond the horizon.

'Take no heed of the morrow. What heed have our people ever taken of the morrow? Give to the poor. They give. But they do not give as Christ would have them give. Christ said to give secretly, and god who sees all will reward openly. Christ has to offer reward. But here there is no reward, and anyone being rewarded by man or god for giving to the poor would grow hot with shame. A young hunter comes with a piece of flesh to an old woman. She blesses him and he goes away laughing. There is neither openness nor secrecy about it. It is on the pleasant side of nature, and its emblem is mirth. By giving to the old woman you have defeated the malignant, and smile in your strength, and your heart grows warm and your youth invincible. What sort of people, then, did Christ live amongst that he had to tell them to give to the poor, and who his God that would reward them openly if they did it secretly? You see, then, that they must be a people, different from us, who have made a new god for themselves. And this Christ, who was the son of their God, they offered up as a sacrifice, nailing him to a tree and letting him hang there until he died. It was a strange thing to do, and has in it the thought of a savage people about a remarkable man.'

They sat silent for a long time.

'What is it you remember?' enquired the Master.

And Aniel answered, 'I remember the light.'

'There was that light, then, about the Christian?'

The Master sat like a stone. 'In the centre of the circle of light.'

Aniel felt that he had overheard the thought, and was startled and embarrassed. But the moment passed, and he was lifted into a higher moment where his body grew as cool and his thought as clear as the water in Molrua's jar.

Even as he experienced this, he knew that the Master was withdrawn from him, and very quietly he got up and went towards the Grove. On the little winding path within the trees the shadows were strong and full. The light was departing. Bel, the life-giver, the giver of light. The Master's thought was so fine that it was an edge lifting upward to a dividing ridge. In his presence fever was stilled and thought became transparent, and the very skin of the body was cleansed.

The moor opened again before him, with an upstanding Stone like an eternal finger. Then more Stones like an eternal hand. The hand was the grey colour that the ages distil out of passion, with knowledge winning to an awful stillness and power.

He had a small round hut, not unlike Molrua's, where he dwelt alone. There were other huts, and from one of them came a man's voice in an ancient rhythm to the plucking of a five-stringed harp. The reiteration of the simple theme was maddeningly sweet. Aniel lay on his back. The low music might have formed of itself in the heart of the evening. It meant nothing. It was intolerable. Aniel came completely under its sway, his features drawing thin, his eyes shining. His breath began to hiss the melody through his teeth until his chest choked with the insurging air and his skin ran over cold. But in the hollow of exhaustion the melody still sailed. The world was an immense sea, and life was no more than a note of music, on the crest, in the hollow. And the rhythm, the lost rhythm . . . he tried to fight it back from him, to win the Master's detachment, to stand with the Stones. But he was young, and, defeated, followed the music.

## CHAPTER THREE

THE afternoon of the following day, Breeta left her home
to go to the Tower. The excitement and mirth of the men
in the glen made her feel restless. They were full of fun and
jokes, and fights were common among the boys. There had
also been a fierce night fight between two of the men which
kept everyone talking and on the alert and full of the desire
to excel. For nothing is more thrilling than a fight, and the
thought that oneself may be at it any moment keeps the
eyes bright and laughing. They measured and admired one
another, and life was sweet and expectant.

Breeta, going towards the Tower, felt her discontent
increase, and turning from her path went up through the
trees towards the moor. Even as she did so, there came
from above the notes of Leu's pipe. It was the same melody
he had played at the shielings – and the same as had been
whistled on the dark moor.

Such a flurry took her heart as weakened her. She leaned
against a tree. The night moor, that had secretly haunted
her, terrified her now. She could not go on; she would turn
back, escape. For the moment, however, she was too weak
to do anything. And, when she was able to go back, she
went on.

Leu, his shoulder against a tree, looked at her and
dropped his pipe. And in that instant she knew, with
a dreadful certainty, that it had not been Leu who had
followed her into the moor and held her in his arms as she
had fainted.

His look, narrowing, caught some of her intensity. He
took two slow steps towards her.

'Did I frighten you?'

Her face flashed away – and in upon the moor saw Aniel
leap out of the hag where he had his images and come

towards them – not directly, but bearing on the Tower. Leu followed her glance and, when he turned to her again, saw that she had shrunk back among the trees. He advanced now with seeking, challenging eyes.

'You look upset.'

'Do I?' Her manner was strange.

'What's wrong?'

'Nothing. I must be off.'

His look caught an intense nervous concentration.

'Breeta.'

'I'm off.'

He caught her arm.

'Let me go.'

'Wait—'

'No!' She wrenched her arm free.

Fire leapt into his dark face. But she swept from him down the way she had come. When she reached the burnside, she went along towards the Tower, not knowing how she went or why. All the world around her was interlaced like dark roots, and the small clear space that was herself had to go warily, with its heart ready to bolt. Even the Tower, though she dreaded it, was yet a haven. Just as she was leaving the trees for the clear space, she knew that Aniel was watching her on her left. But she did not look, and one low note of a whistle quickened her feet.

As she entered the enclosure, she encountered Nessa hanging on doubt. She smiled at Breeta, examining her expression. Breeta did not respond, but kept on towards the fort.

Nessa stopped her. 'Anything up?'

'No,' said Breeta, and went on again, hearing Nessa's soft laugh. She could not help looking back from the door of the fort and, as she did so, Nessa waved to her and went out of the enclosure.

Her mother was not inside the fort. Breeta fancied she saw the movement of a head in the private stone chamber. As she was going away, something flicked past her face and, looking up, she saw the bearded Lys grinning upon her. He winked and nodded his head in the most lovable way, as if he were aching for company and the stories that made the skin rich.

Something in his rough friendliness gave her confidence and, smiling back, she left the fort, knowing as she continued towards and round the hall, that Lys was watching her. She found her mother with Donan in her lap sitting on the southern side of a small outhouse, her body rocking slightly to the quiet rhythm of her lullaby, lank wisps over her lined brow and staring eyes. For a moment something withdrawn to bone-hardness in her mother's attitude made Breeta's step hesitate. Her mother turned her eyes and looked at her penetratingly, as though Breeta were a stranger, and then asked in a normal voice about domestic affairs.

'You take the child,' she said, 'and I'll go down myself for a little. If she asks where I am you can tell her.'

'Where is she?'

'About somewhere.' She handed Donan over.

'Has everything been quiet?'

'Too quiet,' replied her mother, her laconic tone showing that her mind was still preoccupied. Then she walked away.

When Donan saw her go he began to whimper. The more Breeta coaxed, the more he whimpered. There was no doubt of the child's fondness for her mother. Breeta, sitting down, began to sway and croon. The whimper rose to a cry. Breeta held on hypnotically, but she knew that the crying might be heard in the hall, and her unease was communicated to the child. Goan, the smith, paused on the way to his forge. He was a big, brown-bearded, round-headed man, and made such a stooping face before Donan that the child stopped crying in sheer affright. 'That's the brave little fellow!' boomed Goan. Whereat Donan turned his face and buried it in Breeta's breast.

'I'll take him for a little walk,' said Breeta, getting up; and, humming a quick gay tune, she danced the body as she swung from toe to toe around the hall, through a window of which thick male voices reached her, for Drust was entertaining a former enemy who, with four of his followers, had come of his own accord to discuss the cause of the home seaboard against the dreaded invasions of the Northmen.

As Breeta went on, she kept humming; and Donan, interested by the change of scene and amused by the dancing motion, stopped whimpering. Breeta was so concentrated on what she was doing that she appeared to look neither to right nor left, but held steadily on by the moor-edge of the trees. Presently she sat down and began to play with the child on the edge of the shadow. She had seen no one.

Where had Nessa gone? And Aniel? Her laughter was quick and exciting. Donan responded. Donan gave himself over to the mounting sport, tried to make his eyes follow the head that was too quick for him, thrusting and tickling before he could avoid or clutch it. In his rich mirth, she caught him to her and began rocking him and crooning into his head, upon which her mouth pressed as she stared at the moor.

An uncanny sensation beset her, like the memory of one who had been in the arms of a dark demon or god. And – that divine feeling when she had swooned and been lost in the night – with whom? *with what?* A demon that had taken Leu's shape?

Donan did not like the croon. He wanted fun. She crushed him against her. He rebelled. She suddenly got up with him and turned from the moor down through the trees, and before she had gone many paces came on Aniel and Nessa standing together. For all that she expected it, surprise shocked her, so that she stood for a moment gazing at them. Then she went hurriedly past, seeing their arrested bodies with the faces looking at her in an odd smile as she went blindly on until the stream pulled her up.

Her mother found her there as she returned from her home. Breeta explained that the child had been cross. Her mother, angered by her moody expression, scolded her. 'You'll come with me to the Tower now.'

'I'll come in a little,' said Breeta, and turned towards her home. Her mother called after her; then, taking a firm hold of the child, muttered and went to the Tower.

Breeta followed in a little while, her body upright and reserved, her bare feet quiet on the grass. As she passed beneath the trees where Aniel and Nessa might still be, she looked straight in front of her, hot light in her eyes. Presently, not wishing to approach the Tower by the direct path, she went up through the trees, lingered a little on the edge of the clearing, then approached the enclosure. As she entered, the four strangers appeared accompanied by Drust. Their leader was a brown-haired man, like Goan the smith, with gathered brows, a strong chin, and hard eyes. Two were physically related to him, but the fourth was a tall dark man, with the keen reserved manner of an adviser. Their ponies were brought forward by one of Drust's men and they mounted. All five had an air of restraint, which showed itself as the leader and Drust gave the salutation of farewell. Whereupon Drust re-entered his hall, Morbet and Taran glancing up at him.

'What do you make of it?' he asked Taran bluntly.

'They have at least found out how we stand.'

'Exactly! The rest was to blind us. They knew we were waiting a raid and could not give them men. Why, then, come and ask? Because they were expecting a raid themselves? But the whole of the coasts of the sea will be expecting raids!'

'I did not like him', observed Morbet, 'when he said, "So you won't help us?"'

Drust wheeled. 'It made me boil!'

'You controlled yourself well,' said Taran.

'Curse them!' said Drust, and started walking. 'They are brewing something. I don't like them. I never did like them.' He paused. 'I wish the bloody sea-reavers would come and be done.'

'What if they don't come?' said Morbet, who was a plain-spoken man.

'They'll come,' said Taran.

'How do you know?' asked Morbet.

Drust stood and looked at Taran, who answered after a time, 'How do we all know?'

'We all know,' replied Morbet, 'because the Old Man said so.'

'Well?' waited Taran.

'How does he know?' asked Morbet.

There was a curious silence.

'They'll come. It's in my bones,' said Drust.

'I should like to know how he knows,' said Morbet.

'Do you believe him?' asked Drust.

'Yes,' replied Morbet simply.

'Well – what?—'

'I should like to know,' said Morbet, and Drust saw that his brother's expression was growing hard and battle-dour.

'Did anyone watch which way they went?' asked Taran.

'Which way could they go, but back?' Drust enquired.

'I know,' said Taran. 'Lys would see them in any case, no doubt.'

'What do you mean?' Then Drust went to the door and called.

Breeta heard him inside the fort. Silis came out of her chamber and, pausing before Breeta, asked, 'Where's Nessa?'

Breeta looked self-conscious. 'I saw her out there,' she said.

Silis considered her expression. 'Was she alone?'

'Yes,' said Breeta, but she had hesitated a little.

Silis hesitated also, but only said, 'Go and tell her to come in at once.'

Breeta went along the wood to where she had seen Aniel and Nessa. But they were no longer there. She stood listening so closely that she heard her heart . . . which leapt as she swung round. Nessa was smiling at her with a strange bright look. 'Who are you looking for?'

'You,' said Breeta. 'Your mother wants you at once.'

The smile died, and Nessa's expression narrowed to a little ridge above her nose. The colouring of her skin was a warm conspiracy beneath this annoyance.

'How did she know I was here?'

'I told her,' said Breeta.

'What right had you to tell her?' flashed Nessa instantly.

Breeta's dark eyes flashed in response, but the excitement made her body awkward and she swallowed nervously.

'I never thought you could be so mean!' said Nessa

intensely, the soft red of her girlhood flaming into the blaze of the woman.

'I only said you were here.' Breeta's brows netted.

'Did you say I was alone?'

'Yes.'

Nessa's lips remained slightly apart as she looked at Breeta, then the blaze died down and the girl came out again. 'Why didn't you say so at once?' Her manner was disarming, her voice friendly.

Breeta had got control of her excitement and stood quite still, unsmiling.

'Mother would be furious, as you know.' Nessa went on explaining, with an inner smile of happiness. It came out in her voice. She took Breeta's hand. 'You forgive me, don't you?'

Breeta withdrew her hand. 'It's all right,' she said. Her face was pale and controlled, her eyes dark and full of fire. She did not look at Nessa.

'Breeta,' said Nessa, 'you look splendid!'

Breeta turned her head and met Nessa's eyes. When the look broke, a faint excitement touched Breeta. Nessa went up to her, put her arms round her, and kissed her.

Breeta stood back from the embrace. Nessa laughed.

'I must go, or mother will pitch her flints. She doesn't really want me for anything. She's afraid I may have ridden away with the four men! Breeta,' – her voice dropped intimately.

Breeta waited.

'Stay here. And if Aniel comes back, come and tell me.'

Breeta did not move, did not answer.

'I love you,' said Nessa, and went away strangely smiling.

Breeta knew she need not go to the Tower again that night. Her duty was at home. Her father and brother would eat in the evening. She had the flesh in the pot. So she had better go down. She waited some time, however, before she actually went. And when she was down, her mind returned again and again to the trees.

A couple of the older men put their heads round the

door asking for her father. She told them he had not come up yet from the sea. For he was a keen fisherman and had, amongst other things, invented a pliable wicker net, bag-shaped, which was a deadly trap for salmon at the narrow tail-ends of some river pools. Then a girl of her own age came in and, following her, a couple of young men looking for Breeta's brother. They asked so many questions as to his whereabouts that laughter found tongue in the room. The girls held more than their own in the word-strife, Breeta entering upon a reckless defiant mood that excited them all. For it was only with individuals like Nessa and Aniel that she felt uncertain, and was accordingly often dumb or even moody. The bolder of the two young men, with a swagger, threatened her. 'When you cannot answer, you can only hit!' she scorned. 'I'll do more than hit,' he replied, and, lunging, caught her. By a deft motion, however, she eluded his grasp and, as he swung round off his balance, gave him a back-thrust that set him sitting on the floor. He reddened under the laughter, and leaping to his feet went straight for her. She conquered her instinct to dodge, and blazed at him. He locked his arms about her. Breeta wrestled fiercely, her voice angry and intense. He lifted her off her feet and began carrying her to her bed.

'Look out, here's someone coming!' cried Mellig sharply.

The young man stopped.

Breeta broke from him. 'You wolf!' she flashed, her eyes all fire. 'Out you go! Both of you!'

They were going off rather sheepishly, but when Balla found that there was no one coming, he hesitated.

'Come on away!' urged Den, his companion.

'No, by the Stones,' swore Balla, whose body was hitching and swaying in a youthful swagger. It was the greatest wrestle he had ever had. 'I'm going back.'

His companion held him by the arm, without much difficulty. 'Come on. Her father will be here any minute.'

'Oh, well – her father.' Balla was persuaded. But when they had gone some distance, he stopped. 'Did you know where I was carrying her?'

'To her bed.'

Balla's eyes brightened queerly. His chest filled and his throat thickened.

'What would you have done?' asked Den.

'Huh!' smiled Balla. His friend laughed softly. Balla's thought sank so far into him that he became silent, and walking on forgot his friend. Then he sat down with an odd exclamation, and presently, out of a shining silence, said, 'It was great, yon. Let us go back.'

'No.'

Balla looked at him. 'You're frightened. You're a calf.'

'I'm not.'

'Why didn't you catch Meelig?'

'Because – because if anyone *did* come. . . .'

'Huh!'

'I'm not a calf,' said Den levelly.

Balla laughed fondly. Den grew white with anger.

'I'm going back anyway,' said Balla, and moved off as if Den did not exist. But when he was out of sight he slipped into the trees, for his legs had begun to tremble. Her flashing face and eyes were burning him up. 'You wolf!' He smiled like a fool and breathed deeply.

But the encounter had no such weakening effect on Breeta. On the contrary, her anger held, and not even the amber of Meelig's honey eyes could all at once seduce her to softness. But anger leads to a hard brightness and, when Meelig hinted at her own difficulties with Den, both girls started laughing and were soon on the friendliest terms.

Later her father and brother came in, bringing two men with them. Out of the pot she lifted the lump of meat on to a shallow wooden platter, and then filled four bowls with the broth. The men started on the meat and drank the soup as it grew cold. Because of the guests, Breeta put a round of oaten bread on the dresser before them. They ate the meat in a rich noisy fellowship, sucking their fingers, and laughing over events. Often these men had but one meal a day, and so the goodness of the food could be seen bringing a glow to their skins. The older guest began to tease Breeta out of courtesy, and asked when it was coming off. 'You'll be the sweetest tune ever anyone played.' This was a delicate reference to Leu. Her lashes fell as she smiled. With her father present, she could offer no retort. The man watched her turn away and admiration made his skin even richer, though all in all he preferred girls stouter.

Breeta left them to their talk. Outside the sunlight was thinning and the air was clean. Before the men had come in, she had washed herself and done her hair. Now she went down to a river pool and washed her feet and legs. When she came back to the path, she felt more confident than she had done since the Master first came upon her with Donan. Buried in this confidence was a heartening hostility. To what, she did not know, but it was there, invigorating as a challenge. As she went along the path she saw Balla coming towards her, saw him stop and then come uncertainly on. In a moment she knew that he was consumed with awkwardness, and became so alert and reserved that her beauty was like a whip. Balla grinned, stood, stuttered. She looked at him, saw him, and went on.

Balla also went on, hurriedly and slowly, but mostly hurriedly, trying to escape from the fool that gnashed his teeth.

Breeta went up through the trees, smiling and well content. As in the case of the men with their food, her skin also grew rich and glowed, but with a certain reserve as out of the cool water. When she arrived at the place where she had left Nessa, she glanced about her as if someone were looking at her, took a step forward, and saw Aniel dead still against a tree.

His eyes were watching her with smiling curiosity; watched how she accepted his presence; and kept watching when she turned away her head. Her face grew hot and anger mounted to her forehead. She was not in a mood to be dominated, and the weakening tremble that went over her legs gave her face a quick intolerance. Her eyes caught the flash of the wild and, moving away, she said, 'I'll tell Nessa you're here.'

'Breeta.'

But she went on. In a moment he had caught her. She faced him, breathing rapidly. Before her agitation, his eyes wandered away politely. Her anger increased. He smiled. 'I have made a new image,' he said. 'Would you like to see it?'

'No.'

'Oh. I thought you would. It's the image of your friend – your friend Rhos – you know, as he is *at night*.'

Her jaw fell; her eyes stared. He did not look at her, appearing to reflect, amused.

'Perhaps you would tell Nessa. I'd like someone to see it.' And his eyes lifted to hers, held them a moment, and dropped. Involuntarily she started back from him, then turned and walked away quickly. She was going through the gateway of the enclosure before she realised quite where she was. As she entered the fort, Nessa appeared in the doorway from the staircase and questioned Breeta with her eyes. Breeta nodded, whereupon, with a glance at her mother's chamber, Nessa wandered idly out. Breeta sat down beside her mother, who began to ask her about the two guests, and whether they had eaten well, and if the soup was tasty. They spoke in whispers, for the child Donan was asleep, and Silis was in her room.

As Breeta left the fort she met Nessa, who remarked, 'I thought you said he was here.'

'He was.'

'Where?'

'Over there.'

'But I've been there and I saw only a man with a pipe.'

Breeta was silent.

'Who was that?' asked Nessa.

'Leu.'

'He may have frightened Aniel away,' Nessa thought. As she lifted her chin, her throat was white and tender. Her bosom was mature under a brown gold-woven dress, and her hair in the evening light had deep rich colours. The thoughtful groove over her nose gave her girlhood a certain imperious conviction. She hesitated what to do. 'Good night,' said Breeta, and turned from her. Nessa looked after her, the groove deepening; her eyes flashed, then she walked into the enclosure, to overhear Lys say to her father, 'No sign.' Her father repeated the words, and the groove over his nose grew black.

The following day there was still no sign. Eleven men came from Finlag. The boys followed them, laughing at and mocking the dwarfish figures; but Bardan, who was at their head, repelled the boys strongly and complained fiercely about their conduct to Taran. All that evening the boys and youths tried to get glimpses of the little men, who were quartered in the winter enclosure for the cattle.

Every now and then the little men thrust spiteful malignant faces over the enclosure wall, and then the boys ran away laughing excitedly, because they were really afraid of these faces.

Next day there was still no sign. The excitement had so moderated that here and there was a spirt of opinion that nothing was going to happen at all. They were wasting their time. A few of the younger men were secretly resolving to slip back to the shielings for an evening's sport. A rumour had started, too, that the shielings were going to be raided by some of the roundhead clan from Logen. Taran said it was nonsense, but that evening he went to Drust.

Drust swore slowly and emphatically.

'Someone must have thought of it', said Taran, 'after hearing the Logenmen were here. That's all that's in it.'

Upon their uneasiness Aniel entered. The two men looked silently at him as at a god's messenger.

'I have to say secretly', began Aniel, 'that the Logenmen are arming, like you, to meet the Northmen. If, however, the Northmen should pass their creek by, and attack yours, and defeat you, then it would be a great loss if your flocks also fell into the Northmen's hands. While you are engaged with the Northmen, the Logenmen may therefore decide to fall upon your shielings in force and remove your flocks to their own distant pastures.'

The two men stared at Aniel.

'Say all that again,' ordered Drust grimly, 'and say it slow.'

Aniel did so. When the irony had at last penetrated, Drust remained quite still as before a surpassing wonder. Then he nodded, and a gust of breath broke on an oath. Within a minute the extraordinary impudence of the message had him beside himself. The weapons shook on the wall. All his pride emerged and fire played on the surface of his eyes.

Father and son watched him, conscious of the spirit that set his leadership apart.

When the fury had passed, Drust said almost coldly, 'We'll have to fall on them at once.'

'Chief,' said Taran, 'shall we consider the matter—'

Drust looked at him.

Taran was silent.

'May I speak?' asked Aniel.

Drust eyed him.

'I am here only to warn you. No one can say that this will certainly happen. It may have been spoken in jest.'

'In what?'

'In jest,' said Aniel.

'Do you mean you – you trumped up these words?'

'No.'

'Well, what?' roared Drust.

'The words I spoke to you were overheard. I was to tell you in order to put you on your guard. That is all my mission.'

It took Drust a little time before he nodded grimly and said, 'I see.'

'May I speak?' asked Taran.

'Well?'

'The difficulty is not the lack of being provoked. We could fall on them any time for that matter. But the going there, the fighting, and the returning, would mean days. It might even be without great results if they are watching. And the Northmen might arrive when we are gone.'

'True,' said Drust.

Taran was silent.

'Have you no more to say?' asked Drust.

'I think we should hold a council,' said Taran, 'and then you could order what to do.'

Drust looked at him, then got up without a word. Father and son passed quietly from the room. Within the trees Taran turned on his son.

'What made you speak your message as you did?'

'I told the truth.'

'You could have told it otherwise, you idiot! Trumping up your words to be clever! Was the message not desperate enough without making him mad with it? You fool!'

'I am your son,' said Aniel.

'Take that, then,' said the father, as he slapped him strongly on the face. Aniel staggered back. Having hit him once, the father wanted to hit him a second time, and before Aniel could regain his balance he did so, adding, 'And that! And—'

But Aniel avoided the third blow. They faced each other at a little distance. 'Maybe that will teach you,' said Taran, and, turning, walked down through the trees.

As he debouched on the river path, he met Bardan who was in an excited state, and cried at once, 'They have all gone home! They have all gone home!'

'Who?'

'My men.'

'How dared you let them go home?'

'They went. I couldn't stop them. They were mocked by these devils of boys. They – they—'

'You will go and bring them back. You will go and bring them back now!' roared Taran in his great voice.

'But how can I go?'

'On your feet, curse you! and the sooner you bring them back the better it will be for every one of you.'

'But – but—'

'Don't but me. If a score of you aren't here by noon tomorrow, you'll be butted out.'

'But—'

'I have spoken.'

Bardan trotted after him. 'But—' Taran pulled up, dark-faced and silent.

'I – I'll do my best. I'll go now. But if they're gone – if I can't get them – I'm not to blame.'

'You heard me?'

'Yes, but – No! no! I'm going. I'll do my best.' Bardan started away.

Taran sent a young man to gather the council, then he sat down in a quiet place to think the matter out.

It was a neat problem. If the Northmen did not come, the shielings would not be attacked. If they did come, the shielings would be attacked while the fight was in progress at the beach. A division of local forces would be fatal to either enterprise. Drust would rather desert to the Northmen than let the Logenmen have their way, out of pride. There was sense in that, too, because the flocks were more valuable than the houses. Also the Northmen would be more terrible fighters and would kill more. And if all the Ravens were with the flocks, then most surely the Logenmen would notdare attack, because they were fewer in numbers and Drust had powerful family connections. Now all this would be set in motion by the appearance of the Northmen. What if the Northmen never came? Were they always now going to be in this state of preparation? But Taran did not really speculate on these two questions, because he felt that their coming was known in the Grove, not from outside information, which might be deceitful, but by divination, which excluded all doubt. They were coming soon; but an exact time, naturally, could never be stated. Very well, taking the problem like that, would it not be wise meantime to divide the flocks, leaving one half where they were and driving the other into the Finlag country? Then tomorrow to find out the true attitude of the Logenmen in some way, and if they were working for a secret assault, to arrange that when the Northmen appeared the glens should be deserted and the Logenmen surprised and overwhelmed? But that would mean getting Drust *and his wife* to agree to desert their stronghold, which would be duly burned down. That might appear like flying before the enemy without even a fight. And Drust's pride was up. True, he would rather let anybody win than the Logenmen, but . . .

Taran settled down to it. A long experience had taught him that someone must always think a thing out. Otherwise events would be met as they arose, without preparation, without plan, and with disaster. He could generally inspire Drust with a decision. But he, Taran, must first be very sure in his own mind of what should be done.

Drust, however, had a very clear mind indeed on this affair. He would give the boatload of Northmen the surprise of their lives; smash them in bulk and individually; and, that over, gather his men and, heading along the coast, intercept the Logenmen on their return, necessarily slow,

with the herds. And then – Drust's mind was so clear that
his shoulders and fists talked as he walked the floor. He had
seen the killing mood in his brother Morbet. The treachery
of the Logenmen made the brain run mad.

Silis came in. Against her dark-brown dress her skin was
strangely pale; her manner was grave and her eyes steady.
The look of her made Drust immediately hostile.

'Molrua, the Christian father, would like to speak this
evening.'

'Who's preventing him?'

'Will you not order all to attend?'

'No.'

'Will you not attend yourself?'

'No.'

Her eyes did not waver, and in the cool light her tall
figure gathered a pale menacing beauty.

'Why?'

'Because I said no.'

'But why?'

Her even insistence raised his voice to a shout.

'Because I said *No*!'

She removed her eyes from his face to the window and
stood unmoving.

'Is not my word sufficient? Must I always be giving
reasons or getting orders or listening to Molrua? No, I
say! NO!'

'Then God means nothing to you, nor Christ and
His sacrifice?' The quiet manner, with its penetration,
maddened him.

'They mean as much to me as they do to you!' he roared.
'You think you will civilise us! And when we are humble,
you'll get all your own way. Who wants power more than
you? Who? You think I don't see through you. What do
you take me for? We're going to fight and burn and kill,
woman; and your job is to pray for us. I've had enough
of this.'

'Who do I want power for?'

'Who? Yourself and your precious family.'

'They are also your family.'

'Don't blind me with that. I know what you think of me

here, and the life and the people. You would like to go back yonder and be a ruling power. Succession through the mother! We're not good enough. All right, I'll show you. For I'm going to rule now. Do you hear? Get ready! The council meets here shortly. It will be your duty to serve us – to serve your warriors – with ale. Do you hear? Get ready!'

She turned away.

'Do you hear?' he cried, going after her.

She turned round. Into the room came the far tinkle of Molrua's bell. The sound was clear and sweet. There was peace in it and the slow rhythm of a hooded man walking; the sound rose from that man in an arch, white under the blue dome until, delicate and thin though it was, it turned the evening of the world to crystal.

Its intrusion pierced Drust. 'Do you hear?' he repeated.

'I hear it,' she said.

'I don't mean it, I mean me! You'll serve the ale here or I'll know the reason.'

'I'll serve no ale.'

'Won't you?'

'No.' She turned away.

He caught her roughly and swung her round.

'I say you will!' His face was inflamed, congested. Her eyes caught a glint of fire. They stared at each other in an intense animosity, the woman prouder, fiercer, than the man, perhaps stronger, because more reserved. The bell called from the hill of the priest's dwelling. Drust swayed on the edge of violence. He had never struck his wife; and the passion now between them was the reflex of a once mad passion of love.

Perhaps the priest's bell saved the woman, for when she turned and went out Drust cursed the bell in thick incoherent oaths and smashed what came in his way. Not that he cared whether he was a Christian or not. He could defy the old gods and the new. But his wife – something rose up in him that gnawed and maddened. By the black gods, if only he could tear her out!

When later his principal men came in, they found Drust flushed a little and full of welcome. He caught his spear from the wall and beat the boss of his hanging shield with a thunderous sound. The serving girl, Mergit, was at the door.

'The ale,' he said.

She disappeared and presently his own attendant, Brin, entered with a great jar. Drust looked from him to the door. No one else appeared. Drust's lips pressed together for a moment, then he sat down.

Drust was in his usual good humour, only perhaps a trifle more watchful and given to smiling. He applauded Taran's effort. It was very clear and intricate. What could they do without him? And, as Taran said, the Logenmen were the principal enemy, for the Northmen would go as quickly as they came and, after all, some of their dwellings were such miserable hovels that they would be the better of getting burned down. His own hall – the unimportant dwelling of an unimportant chief. Fill up the bowl again; send it round. They were getting on very well. And now you, Erl, of your wisdom.

The chief's mood made them speak with a care that the ale magnified to eloquence. Altogether it was a very earnest and interesting council meeting. Drust was obviously enjoying it more and more. He beat his shield again and had the jar refilled.

When the time came that voices rose together, Drust clove through them to a startled silence. He told them that he had expected Taran, their bard, to have stirred them not to retreat with the words of the cunning councillor, but to valour with the deathless deeds of his ancestors. Too much soft living had made them soft. Peace was a disease. And the only thing that ruled them was the voice of their women and the tinkling of a priest's bell. They were going to fly before a boatful of Northmen. They were going to let their dwellings be burnt as the homes of cowards. They were warriors, by the gods of their fathers! Even the Christ-god of the priest had let himself be nailed to a tree rather than turn tail to the enemy – one against an army, against the men and gods of the world. But we are not humble priest-gods, we are warriors! Warriors! Taran is the bard of warriors, the exciter to mighty deeds, the user of kingly language. You heard him. And his fire has passed to your heels – to make you run!

Taran rose, his face pale as the chief's was flushed.

'Taunt me, if you like. You know I was thinking of the people. I have tried to see what would be best for us all in the end. You mock me. Go on mocking me. But I tell you now, O Drust, that if you say one word of mine was meant for cowardice, then you lie, and I throw the lie in your mouth!'

Drust got to his feet with a crash of wood. 'Did you say lie, you coward?'

'I said lie.'

Drust caught up his spear.

'Swallow it!' he roared. Before his red menace the black Taran stood unwinking, his chest square set.

As the spear hand went back, from the end of the narrow board Erl cried, 'Steady, O Drust!'

The interruption was a sting that Drust instantly turned on, and with all his force he hurled the spear at Erl's head. But Erl, who had half risen, was in the same moment sitting down again, and the spear whistled through his hair and, finding wood, buried its point and quivered.

Morbet laughed a note or two and lifted the ale to his mouth. When he had drunk, he said, 'We may need them all, brother.'

Drust fixed his chair and laughed. 'Sit down, Taran. Death was never nearer you and you didn't wink. Put the bowl round, Morbet. Life is coming back into us. This is what we are going to do. We meet the Northmen as they land and cut them up. Then we set along the coast, head off the Logenmen, slaughter them to a man, and drive back the cattle. The sea fight will only put us in trim for our vengeance. Nor will that be the end of our vengeance, by the blood-gods!'

As they looked on Drust's face, enthusiasm went through them like a fire.

Taran rose up. 'I did my best, O Chief, and I do not regret it, but your way is the right way of the warrior and makes the heart sing!'

'Sing then, greathearted Taran!' cried Drust. He was

now the man they knew in the woods and in danger, and the broad simplicity came upon him that gladdened everyone. Taran delivered his poem of the valour of ancestors in a rolling voice that carried them like a river. They applauded him, eyes glowing. A divine energy thrilled them. Some of the younger men could not sit still, and two of them getting to the floor fought with shield and sword, until one stunned the other. 'No death, my heroes!' cried Drust. Fellowship grew warm and rich. Drust thundered on his shield.

Lys, who was on the tower, heard these sounds and his mouth grew dry. He thought of one long beaker of ale and grinned hairily at the man who kept him company. By the Grey One, they were having a time of it down there! They told each other stories of olden days until the Nameless Ones could be felt so near that the skin ran over cold. But another outburst from the hall warmed them again. The sea was a vast grey shield, the woods still, the mountain a dark nipple for a sky-god to suck.

The stars came out. A wind ran suddenly about the tower, like the draught from the passing of a presence from the sea. It disturbed the thatch of Breeta's home down in the glen. She stirred restlessly. Her breathing grew fitful. There was no other sound in the house, for her father was in the hall with the chief men, and her elder brother had taken the chance, with a group of other young adventurers, to repair to the shielings for a night's fun. Clearly there would be great fun with the older hands away and the girls spoiling for a song or a dance or what else more shyly or slyly offered. Besides, this very expectancy of the fight excited everyone, but particularly the girls. In fact life took on the bright smiling and the eager ways of those greeting strangers and pressing hospitality upon them. The most ordinary girl became lovely, the most backward youth a little reckless. And the young men would walk home through the early dawn and never be missed!

The thought that had been smoored in Breeta's waking mind was blown clear in sleep. The figure on the night moor was not Leu nor yet Rhos. Even in the slim cast of the advancing body with its hidden face there was a familiarity that held her breath altogether, a foreknowledge from which she could not move. The face cleared and looked at her with that pale curious smiling power before which her flesh always grew weak. Aniel. He came a step nearer and her joints melted and she began to sink. He took her in his arms. She gripped him wildly and fainted. Ages passed, and she was lying by herself, deserted. The world was a frosted sheet running from under her chin flat – flat as a moor . . . the grasses, like hairs, shivered . . . and – the cry!

She awoke in mortal terror, and, as she choked her panting breath, the far sound of a horn faded out of her ears and out of the quivering air. The grey dawnlight grew still as death. Then the whole house trembled under the blast of a horn no farther away than the Tower. It was the war horn. The Northmen were come at last.

## CHAPTER FOUR

I

CURLED up in her bed, Breeta listened to the overtones
of the horn dying away, until her throat got so dry that she
had to break her stillness by swallowing. In a moment she
was on the floor – listening again. Swiftly she broke away –
and drew up. The early light from the narrow window made
her wide eyes glisten. Her breath hissed in her nostrils. She
was like a trapped animal blazing out of her body in vivid
fear, throwing her body behind her eyes, which swung on
the door. There came the thudding of running feet and a
thunderous knocking. A voice shouted. She withdrew the
bar and Balla, spear in hand and stone axe against his body,
looked at her and asked for her elder brother.

'He went to the shielings last night.'

'Your father—'

'At the Tower all night.'

'You – alone?'

'Yes.'

His bright look broke, after revealing him. 'You go to
the shielings. Quick! Save yourself!' Awkwardness was
consumed in the young warrior. Feet came running. Here
was Leu, who also wanted to know where her brother was.
But his face was narrow and dark.

When she had answered him, he smiled in a half-twist
of his mouth, his dark eyes burning. She felt the blood
rising to her face. A voice called, 'Come on, boys!' And,
'Come on!' said Leu to Balla, and they immediately made
off, Balla giving Breeta a final wave as he did so.

She stood watching the running figures, then one or two
more came past, trotting with their heads slightly forward
and their weapons swinging.

Breeta's home was newer than the various clusters of
cottages usefully placed for the most part by the running

waters of the countryside. Her mother was a very distant kinswoman of the chief, and her father, though unrelated by blood to a ruling house, yet had a certain tradition of eldership among the dark or older races. In this respect he was somewhat like Taran the bard, who, however, boasted his descent from a 'counsellor of kings', and whose son, Aniel, could therefore fittingly be a pupil of the Master. For it was known that once upon a time the wise man, the diviner, the druid, had in certain respects even more than a king's power. These ancient days were to be remembered in glory, for their power was passing and much that had been of renown was falling into disrepute, and was known to be true only by the blood down secret and often dark ways. Further, the ancient governing greatness of their northern land was tending towards a centre ever moving south, and Christianity itself had come with its teachers and converts and orders from provincial and high kings. Not that Christianity had conquered, but it had raised the shadow, the consciousness, of hostility, and so already that which in the old days had been done naturally was now done in secret and with terrible silence. Though there would always have been silence – before the terrible gods.

Breeta was drawn to the Tower. When the last man had padded past, she shut the door, went along the path for a little way, then turned up through the trees. It was a clear lovely morning with a fresh wind from the sea. The blue of the sky had an after-dawn delicacy, brilliant overhead but filmed to the horizon by wisps of wind cloud. The birds still praised the dawn, though the sun was now clear of the sea, which, as Breeta emerged on the edge of the Tower clearing, glittered and sparkled to its far reaches.

Up here she felt safer than down in the valley, yet all at once she knew she did not want to go into the Tower. The shielings were at her back, the whole world of retreat. To be shut up in the Tower would make her feel that at any moment strange men might come and hack down the walls and capture and ravage her. She would run till she dropped dead first. Her mother had fled long ago into the forest. She, Breeta, had always feared the forest and the moor places, but she knew, too, that in desperation she could give herself to them – whatever that might mean of terror in the beginning. And somewhere, indeed, so deep in her mind that it was lost, was a sensation of terror receding invisibly before and around her. And in that deep forest or hidden moor to come suddenly upon a man playing his pipe, with Leu's face . . . or the face of Aniel, so still that the heart jumps for a sick moment. . . . She looked around the trees, listened to the wind in their leaves, and was suddenly of them. They thrilled but covered her, and as she moved round within their verge her flesh was responsive and her heart terror-light as her feet.

Voices from the Tower-top drew her up and in a moment she saw the heads and shoulders of two men and of Silis and Nessa. They were gazing seaward. Breeta drew back, and selecting her tree soon commanded the path to the shore. Along it went a group tailing off from several figures on ponies. Towards the group men were coming in from both sides. She saw one man, hurrying too rapidly down the slope that was the off bank of the river, slip and tumble. There was a splash, and a rumbling sound of laughter from the hurrying mass. This sound brought a smile that trembled into an excessive brightness in Breeta's eyes. All her flesh began to tremble. The bare heads were like a dark grove moving towards the sea, the sea upon which her uplifted look found nothing but a vacant glitter. Far as eye could reach, there was nothing. A quick shout from the Tower-top made her realise that something was being seen. She climbed precariously, and all at once, across a dip in the high coastline, a long vessel moved, curved high at prow and stern, with broad sail set. Even as it slowly disappeared, another came into sight and as slowly disappeared under the cliff-heads. Incredible shapes out of sea-beast nightmare, they so affected Breeta that she forgot her precarious position and had suddenly to clutch blindly at a tree-top which swayed and cracked. The noise attracted those on the tower and the voice of Silis called out 'Breeta!' But Breeta had crashed through a leafy cascade to the ground, along which she rolled into the wood and lay still. Again her name was called, and presently she heard the enclosure gate being rattled. At that she got to her feet, hurt in no way, and worked upward within the trees until she came to the edge of the moor. If without being seen she could cross the moor toward the Little Glen, she could command the shore from a tree-top there. Along an undulation of the heath she could avoid the top of the Tower. It was her usual way and she started. As she came by the tail-end of the hag, which wound its snake-belly into the moor, she saw two figures coming down the horizon beyond which was the Grove. Instantly she slipped to cover in the hag and then carefully lifting her head watched their approach.

They were coming at a run, and, without stopping, parted company opposite Morbet's fort, one branching off down the Little Glen, the other holding straight on; and this other Breeta was all at once certain was Aniel.

She withdrew her head slowly, and slipping up the hag a few yards found a tiny bay where she flattened against the bank. Always as Aniel came near her, her heart began to beat and to send a horrid weakening to her legs. She resented this bitterly, blaming him. Even now she was listening for him with an acuteness that cramped her heart. She would not have hid, for example, from Balla, nor yet from Leu. When actually she did hear something like his feet drawing near, she ceased to breathe. The sound stopped. He must have gone past. With slow care her head went up. The moor was empty. At once a feeling of insecurity possessed her. The moor drew in upon her. She swung round – to find Aniel standing beside her in the hag. She flattened against the bank, her splayed fingers sinking into the peat, her mouth remaining open after its screech. Then her throat moved and her flesh darkened. Hate flashed from her shifting eyes. Aniel merely kept looking at her. She turned her head away.

'Have they gone from the Tower?' he asked in a friendly tone.

'Yes.'

'I must be off.' He took a pace or two and turned. 'What are you going to do? Why aren't you in the Tower?'

'I'm all right.'

'You're not. Who knows what the end may be? Where were you going?'

'I'm all right.'

'Breeta,' he said sharply, catching her by the arm, 'you're not!'

'I am!'

'You're not!' He shook her. 'Don't you understand?'

She wrenched her arm free. He was now roused and his eyes flashed back. The challenge between them was so naked that for a time neither spoke. The panting movements of their breasts heightened the tension. His face grew ruthless in its impatience. She came into all her strength as if she flowered out of him thus exposed.

He steadied back into himself, but without lifting his eyes from her. 'I must go,' he said clearly. 'You'll wait here. I'll come back for you.' Then he leapt the bank. 'Breeta!' She looked over the bank. His brow was darkly impatient. 'Remember, you wait here. And whatever you do, don't go to the shielings.'

She said nothing.

His voice rose, slightly infuriated, 'Do you hear me?'

She did not answer. For a moment he looked as if he might come back at her, then even as he swung round he was running.

But he did not go to the Tower now, passing it on his right and heading for the sea, holding high up to the left of the valley, dipping down through a final small glade of trees, and coming up again to a green ridge set back from but overlooking the creek. There he lay down to watch the outcome of the battle, for it was of the ancient law that those in the Grove need neither pay tribute nor take part in war.

The men were now lining the beach where two or three nights ago they had amid friendly excitement been polishing their weapons. Even as Aniel looked at them, picking out the centre group that must enclose Drust and his father, the nose of the first galley appeared round the great headland to the left. It came slowly before the slight wind, so slowly that to many on the beach it seemed without end, first the tall carven prow like a questing sea-snake, then the bulwark hidden behind a row of shields like painted scales; then the square sail set nearly amidships; the round shields again side by side; and finally the upthrust stern in a stiffened lash of tail. The sail fell and now the beast had the likeness of a gigantic centipede, its belly low to the water, its legs sticking out in a row. And suddenly these legs stirred and lengthened and dipped into the sea. A second vessel followed, and when it too had cleared the headland and got to its oars, both vessels slowly swung round their prows until they steadied on the beach.

No thought of meeting the Northmen any way but in straight fight could have occurred to Drust. In this matter of fighting there was indeed a simple code of behaviour, so simple that had the Northmen landed and been greatly inferior in numbers, Drust would have felt it laid upon his honour to offer them terms rather than immediately to destroy them. For there is no glory in the slaying of the few by the many. Valour is a personal possession which the owner hands to the Keeper at the gate of death. There is no other passport to the Pleasant Plain, that Green Plain in the Isle of Heroes.

Accordingly no thought of ambush or tactical concealment occurred to these men. As the galleys saw them, so they saw the galleys, and the edge of the tide was the line between them. Nor was there as it happened great disparity in numbers, for though Drust ought to have had, by Taran's reckoning, a hundred and forty men behind him, he had barely half that number, while each galley with its ten banks of rowers and as many more warriors to relieve them, made between them a force of some eighty men.

Yet, human nature being what it is, Taran in his heart was greatly disturbed about the smallness of his force and could have wished it to be much greater than the enemy's, whereas he saw that it was likely to be less. He cursed bitterly therefore those who had not come in, naming them for cowards, even while he knew that if any were to blame it was those leaders, including himself, who had spent the night in carousal instead of in their own villages. The whole weight of this evil chance was upon

him, and if only there had been one galley – as at Harst
– he would still have been right. But now against these
Northmen, famous men of Lochlann, who were in their
prime, trained and hardened warriors, experts with the
shield, the sword, and the axe, what chance had these
homegrown, crude-weaponed bunch of his countrymen,
from old men to youths? Each would have had to be a
Drust, and weaponed like Drust, and to have had the hard
jaw of relentless Morbet. They hadn't, and they would go
down as saplings and old trees before the keen edge of the
singing axe.

His emotion worked upon Taran. His desire to bring
his own folk through this deathly menace became a fire
within him. He strode to the front and turned his back
to the approaching galleys. He threw up his arms and
called upon his countrymen to remember their fathers
and their fathers' fathers. He named the heroes. His voice
gathered the body and rhythm of a sea-wave, that broke
over them without breaking, so that they rose on it even
while it drenched them. Their faces paled and their eyes
glittered. They were an ordinary people become exalted
by the greatness that imagination for ever discovers. And
when Drust boomed a hero's name, the marrow, wherein
the name dwelt, quivered with the pride that rises from the
one to include the many, so that men become brothers and
will die for the very name's sake.

Drust began slowly to strip. As he pulled his arms out
of his jerkin and exposed the flesh of his shoulders and
back, the excitement of his men turned to a coldness on
their faces. The younger among them had never seen the
markings on Drust's body, the dark raven with outspread
wings between the shoulderblades, the three blue symbols,
and the red circle in its boat beneath his heart. There was
an intimacy in the sight that stirred them to final loyalty.
Their hidden feelings flowered before them. Their leader
was one of them, and the greatest.

Drust's body affected Taran, too, and his voice rose from
the plaint of the butchering of mothers and children to a
note of high ultimate contempt for the bloody sea-pirates
whose bones this day the ravens would pick. When he

put the war-cry of his tribe to the men before him, their answering shout swept the longships, wakened the aged in the sea-village beyond the river mouth, and startled swift pigeons from a riven sea-cliff.

But the longships came slowly on, straight for the beach, rows of oars on each side falling and lifting in a single motion. They were clearly feeling their way towards knowledge of the shore and of the enemy, and at a stone's throw from the Ravens, now strung out along the sea-line, executed a clever manoeuvre.

As a high-pitched voice rapped out an order, the starboard oars held water while the port oars swept the longships broadside on to the beach; then all oars gave way with fierce energy and both vessels leapt forward for the shallow river channel. The draught of the vessels was not over three feet and, by the time the prows grounded in the channel, the men aboard jumped into water that did not outreach their thighs, jumped too over both sides of the vessels, so that they were swarming round and forming into the thin line that gives elbow room for individual combat while the Ravens were yet rushing up to dispute their landing. From being at a very great disadvantage, the Northmen were thus in a few minutes on almost equal terms with their foes.

To stream in small numbers from the prow of a vessel on a steep beach before a waiting enemy might easily prove disastrous. But to wade through shallow water towards that enemy, now thrown into confusion and inclined accordingly to be the more headlong, is to have all your strength deployed and ready for the first shock.

The tide, too, was more than half ebbed, so that the ground, slippery with weed and slime, was smoothest to him who went most cautiously. And the seamen had been in too many fights of the kind to let enthusiasm defeat their cunning.

It was otherwise with the Ravens, whose enthusiasm would have carried them through fire. Drust and Morbet checked them on the edge of the weed, but only for each to hurl the smooth stone that fits into the palm. And even then they were too eager, too bunched, to make proper use of the deadly missile. The Norse shields took the hail for the most part in a drumming rattle, but a few of the invaders were hit and stumbled, five of them collapsing and floundering in the shallow water. At which sight the Ravens resumed their advance ardently with mighty shouts of encouragement to one another and death to the enemy.

It was indeed no moment for delay, for the Northmen, spreading out behind their great bossed coloured shields, were presenting an ever more terrifying spectacle. Yellow and black, smooth peaked helmets, axe to the body and sword in hand, they were a company of warriors of fortune, the younger instinctively moving with those by years long skilled in individual combat. They had nothing to defend but their lives, and conquest was their game and spoil their victory. Therefore, advance carefully, keep cool, pick your man as he comes and let him have it. When the sword sticks, and the shield falls, step aside for arm-room and swing the axe. The back swing can smash a head and the foreswing cleave one.

Their leader was a splendid young fellow of imperious bearing. Grizzled faces were beside him and spoke to him calmly, the battle light smiling in their eyes. He gave a shout that the moving line caught and echoed. On the water's edge they steadied to meet the dark onset.

From the beginning the result was inevitable, yet the Ravens attacked with such intensity that for minutes the double line became one and swung and shook with no emergence of superiority either way. The Northmen indeed gave a pace or two along part of their line, but largely to relieve the pressure of the onslaught and to free their arms.

Apart from their leaders, the Ravens had little iron, and though with their stone axes and flint spears they were quick-muscled and expert, yet were they lacking in that battle sense which made the eyes of the grizzled faces before them smile in cunning foreknowledge. The great shields of the Northmen, too, deceived and exasperated young men shieldless and urgent for the encounter that is face to face. The sword and the axe their quick eyes might have followed and their spears evaded, but the shield was a wall that met their thrust and in the same moment left the way open to their bodies. This indeed was precisely what happened to Balla. Sharp-pointed weapons had whistled through the air, but Balla had hung on to his favourite spear which had so often saved his skin in forest encounters. That he should stick one Northman with it he was certain. But now he was excited and eager and came face to face with his man all in a moment. There was no hunting approach, no weighing of the chances, no preparation of the fatal moment. Suddenly two eyes were meeting his at spear's length, and Balla, swift as an adder, struck. But where the eyes had been the shield now was, to receive the point and to hold it – for Balla had struck with great force, with such force that the shield had jerked backward, drawing Balla a pace forward, his right arm extended, his breast open – to the sword that thrust out and pierced his body to the backbone. The sword snicked free, the point ripping, and Balla swayed, his face agape, then clutched his stomach as he fell to writhe in the shallow water and redden it.

In a way the action was desperately easy, fatally simple. His opponent was a heavier, taller man than Balla, but not to the extent of making so certain and so quick the conclusion of a bodily encounter between them. Yet there it was as though the result were machine-made. As indeed in a fashion it was. For his opponent had the smoothness of a warrior regulated by his perfect mechanism. The clear eyes, the tempered adventurous spirit, and the mastery of iron, that were to make him, nay, that were already making him, a conqueror of the western world.

Balla had had need of something extra to balance the deficiencies in his gear. And that something extra could only have been a fighting superiority in mind or spirit. The will was not enough. Courage was not a shield. The Northman pushed the groaning body aside with a foot, while he tried to jerk the spear from his shield – and failed – even while his eyes with triumph sought the next encounter.

Now Bronach the athlete had precisely that something extra which Balla lacked. It is the incalculable quantity, out of which the ultimate mastery comes, and though an

existing machine may crush it in its single manifestation,
yet in the end it conquers and enslaves the machine itself
even while it perfects it.

Bronach's smooth-shafted, iron-tipped spear went back
and shot forward – but checked as the shield before it went
up and the face was covered. Then in the moment's rhythm
as the shield came down, the spear, that had already swung
back, shot forward all the way. It penetrated through the
eye into the skull and jangled Bronach's arm and stuck.
He tugged it fiercely and leapt from it even as a sword
lunged at him from the right. Slipping his axe, he swung it
at this new opponent who received it on his shield. Bronach
swayed from the blade-thrust, and feeling by instinct that
he was being attacked again from the side, leapt at his man
and bore him backwards into the water.

Bronach was slimmer than Balla, not so heavy, but his
muscles had the explosive power of a cat's. His fingers
curled up like claws; his forearm, in a grip, hardened to
stone. He now clung into the body, pinning the arms,
crushing it, content for a moment that they should struggle
and revolve and resolve themselves, if possible, into an
unattended combat. His opponent, a well-made man in
his prime, was amazed at the strength of this slim dark
fierce figure, and struggled to get his arms free with an
exasperation that increased to a humorous petulance, his
eyes opening wider, his throat raking the harsh sounds
of one caught unexpectedly in a maddening net. Then
Bronach saw a Northman coming at them. This is what
he had feared: the jealous watchfulness of the friend, the
brother. The Northmen were too many, too strong, for the
band that they were hewing down. Bronach drew himself
into the body, pressed his forehead into the throat, then
jerked his head against the chin, making the jaws clip
loudly, and disengaged himself so that the descending
sword shot between them. He caught the blade and leapt
to his feet, but could not hold to an edge that left blood
streaming from his palms. The Northman lunged at him.
Bronach swayed and backed. The Northman followed up
and Bronach stumbled. The Northman impetuously thrust
and slipped, sword and arm falling flat on the water.

Bronach from his knees swung at the head, smashed the face with a fist and, catching the half-unslung axe, pulled it free. But even as he straightened himself, two men were upon him. He retreated, casting a swift glance as he did so over the general encounter.

Isolated fights were splashing the shallow water, but elsewhere there seemed naught but a shouting swaying mass of Norse helmets. He caught the odd high-pitched scream of a countryman: maddened anger through a mortal wound. They were being wiped out. As the two men pursued him, he stopped, and, swaying as if to dodge, straightened and went at them, swinging his new axe as he did so. As the axe came down, it shot, to his amazement, from his slippery palms and smashed in the second man's forehead, killing him instantly.

Bronach retreated once more, and, leaving now the water, came on dry land, picking up stones as he did so and hurling them at the pursuing shield. In a few moments he had worked round behind his own men, where Taran was watching and exhorting.

For it was no part of the province of a bard to fight. His indeed was to suffer the elation of victory or the agonies of defeat. This was defeat, and Taran's agony brought the sweat of suffocation to his forehead. He had seen the swords do their work, the swords and the shields fall and the axes swing. Only in the centre did Drust and Morbet and a few more hold still together. Drust was fighting like a great warrior, and Morbet had more than the Northman's smiling light in his eyes. They were rapidly being ringed in. The young imperious leader worked at last face to face with Drust, and as he did so his eyes blazed and he shouted, 'He is mine!' Drust did not know the words, but he knew their meaning and accepted the challenge.

This prolonged the action and increased the killing. For though the Ravens were not a warlike people, yet there was that in the deeps of their minds which was intricate and close set as jealousy, and dark as hate. The riddle of their tribe was: *What is blacker than the Raven?* The answer: *Death*. When carried beyond a certain point, they fought with an intensity that lost all care of self.

Rendered weaponless, they leapt to clutch and tear. To the Northmen they were cat-savages; and, roused by this intensity, the Northmen themselves became even fiercer and more vindictive than was their way. All along the swaying moving line, death cut and pierced; the weed turned from brown to red, grew treacherous with death-throes, and bouldered with black-toothed heads. The defeat was turning to a slaughter. Taran should have called the retreat, but he was powerless while his chief lived. A Norse berserk approached the centre group. His own people slipped as they made way for his axe. The axe was a toy that he whirled invisibly. Breeta's father, tough and hardy, lunged at him, and was split in two like a boneless stalk. Another went down, the giant roaring a frenzied incantation of 'Kill! Kill!' his throat hoarse with ecstatic joy, the neck muscles whipping, the head bare and flaxen, the eyes blue and blazing in a countenance like a drunken god's. Morbet faced up to him, thrust, had his arm snapped, and blundering back against Drust so upset that warrior's guard that the young Norse leader got him in the side with his sword and Drust's shield dropped, his head bowed, and he fell to his knees and to the ground. At that a roar went up from the Northmen. It was an exhortation to death, leaping from mouth to mouth, and so the hunt started.

The Ravens knew what it meant even before Taran's great voice told them to save themselves, and some were seen rushing through the water for the far side, and some were climbing the beach, the very desire for escape becoming as vindictive and fierce as their fighting. And many were wounded but the greatest number were dead.

The surge came towards Taran, but he did not waver, for he knew that he could not live and remember this day. It was his duty to live, for who now would there be to rally the scattered men and all the women and children? But to each man a time is given and his time had now come to Taran. This he knew in a way that is beyond all other knowledge. He raised his sword.

This gesture attracted the enemy towards him and first among them was the roaring giant. The wave had all but reached Taran when Bronach, half crouching to some stones, took a flying leap at the giant and bore him to the ground. The sheer unexpectedness of this pulled them up so that they staggered and jostled one another, uttering exclamations and astonished oaths. For a little while the whirlwind at their feet so engaged their attention that even Taran was forgotten.

It was said that the Bronachs were originally of the tribe of the Cats, a great tribe to whom the Ravens had a certain blood relationship. Bronach now exhibited a fierce in-fighting quality, a clawing towards the centre or heart, a dark constricting of the will upon destruction, that, whether Cat or not, was utterly without mercy. The berserk roared, anxious only to free himself and lash out. He needed things in a world around him to hit at. Bronach clung in and choked. Bronach could tear out the throat with his teeth, and indeed was pressing as if towards that consummation, while they whirled and the berserk heaved and flailed with his legs.

Bronach had pinned the right arm, but the left was free and in its effort to tear off the attacking body was scoring blood lines across Bronach's naked back. The right, too, was fisting Bronach's hip, the fingers trying to dig into his flesh, and crushing dangerously near the weakest place in man's armour. At that moment of particular peril, indeed, Bronach retaliated by smashing inward with his kneecap between the legs, and the giant screamed and rolled with agony. At that one of the onlookers cried out and prepared to thrust at Bronach with his sword. Whereupon Taran striding forward slew the man, before five swords leapt at him and cut him down. The killing of Taran released the men from their fascination of the combat on the ground and they came at the tumbling bodies eager to dispatch the human cat, but now their leader was there and all in a moment they were regarding the combat as an exciting entertainment, calling, 'Crush him, Ric! Tear his heart out!' and using other homely sayings. And Ric was now on top, entangled still but trying to heave himself up with his left arm, conscious that if only he could get his hands together he could choke and break this black fiend's neck.

But his left arm was knuckled under him, and as his head dropped his jaws were made to clip loudly, the teeth biting through the tongue. The frenzy of madness came upon him. The lips drew back from a snarling blood-dripping mouth, but the black head was still under the chin. The giant's strength became immense. His whole body heaved up from the knees like a great beast rearing from the death menace at breast and throat. His face and muscles swelled and grew gorged with blood. His right arm tore free and his shoulders shook back and fore as his hands came clawing at the black head and his throat tried to stretch out of reach. But the teeth were at his throat, and all at once he screamed and broke into a flurry of insane action, tearing himself free blindly and staggering to his feet. Bronach, who had let his grip relax, was already wide-planted, panting, shoulders crouching. But all eyes were watching the giant who was staring at the demon before him. Blood was at his torn windpipe in a whistling froth, and before he knew what had happened to him, he choked and guttered, and as he did so he advanced, stumbled, swayed a moment, then slid to the ground, blood-drowned, his face gorging darkly, and died.

Bronach looked round the ring of eyes. His drawn blood-streaked face was the mask of an inhuman force. Its awful logic repelled the watchers so that suddenly they snarled and hated and, advancing, pierced the lithe body as it feinted and leapt. And even as, sword-spitted, it drew its last slow breath, the lips of the mask drew from the teeth, the eyes glittered in an infernal penetration of challenge and contempt, and, after the body had crumpled to the ground, remained staring still.

They cursed it with the returning of their breaths and two swords slashed and pierced it anew. They voiced a black vengeance over it. And thus encouraged, they swept forward, leaving their leader and a few of his principal men together upon the beach to take account of and acclaim their victory.

The leader, being no more than twenty-five summers, was full of a splendid elation. He was without his headgear and the increasing wind of the morning played in the fair hair thrust back from his forehead. His face was smooth, none the less boyish for the sprouting beard, and its slight flush deepened the glancing brilliance of the blue eyes. In the set and carriage of head and shoulders was the grace of born leadership, the air of mastery that discovers itself even at this supreme moment in a restraint so warm that it wove itself in and out the flesh, as if it had been left to modesty to put the finishing touch with a smile to a piece of fine workmanship.

The smile deepened as Sweyn's scarred face warmed in congratulation. That grizzled old warrior was moved to compliment. 'It is your first victory. You behaved like a brave leader. When you have proved yourself in many fights you will some day settle in a land like this – perhaps even in this land – and be a great jarl. This is what I told you of when you fled from your father and came to old Sweyn's door. What do you think of it now?'

'I like it very much,' said Haakon. 'I owe it to you.'

'Not all to me,' said Sweyn, in a mild voice, for it was said of him that he never slept indoors of a night but went out into the dark to observe the ancient practices of his religion.

'To you and to the favour of the gods,' said Haakon.

'To the gods,' said Sweyn, and looked into Haakon's eyes.

Haakon returned the look. His smile faded and a quiet acceptance informed his face, giving it a high serious air. The sunlight moved with the wind on his head and turned his eyebrows and eyelashes to a fine golden transparency.

'What should I do?' he asked, a faint perplexity on his brows.

'You should make the offering to Odin,' said Sweyn.

Haakon looked away. 'Very well,' he said, and waited, his head high.

The others remained in silence at a slight distance. The groans of the wounded ran along the ebbing tide. A great shouting came from the old roofed-in settlement beyond the river, into which some Northmen had chased a few of those who had escaped. Sweyn turned and walked towards the body of Drust, bent and examined it. 'He is not yet

dead,' he said, and catching Drust under the armpits
dragged him up on to the dry crest of the beach, where
he laid him full upon his face, the bare back exposing the
dark image of the raven.

'A sign!' said Sweyn, pointing to the bird of the vikings.
Drust groaned and moved, and as Sweyn was about to put
his foot on him, lay still.

'Time is short, Haakon,' said Sweyn, his face now hard
and eyes steady. 'He is your prize. As you came on him in
the fight, I saw that you remembered your blood-friend,
Eilif, who was caught on these coasts and sacrificed by
barbarous priests. You swore then.'

'I swore,' said Haakon, and his sword being still in his
hand he went and stood over Drust. Then with the point
of the sword he drew around the dark raven a similar figure
in red. With a foot he kept the body from moving too much
while with the sword he now cut away the ribs from the
backbone on either side and drew forth the lungs through
the openings thus made.

Red hands and red sword he raised to Odin. 'I have
avenged my friend, Eilif!' his young voice cried, offering
itself also to Odin.

Nor was Sweyn dissatisfied because Haakon had no
more to say, for he saw the whole young body itself was
a warrior's gift.

With the rites completed, Sweyn stooped, and lifting a
heavy stone threw it upon the body. 'He was a brave man',
he said, 'and a strong leader. We will raise a mound over
him.' Whereupon Haakon, laying his sword aside, also
threw a stone, as did the others, and Sweyn said that those
left in charge of the ships would complete the mound.

Now though all this had taken but a short time, already
deathly deeds were being done by those in pursuit, whose
minds were raised in exultation by the blood game.
Through the narrow dark passages of the settlement
fleeing bodies scuffled and shrieked.

On his hilltop Aniel heard these sounds and presently
saw a column of smoke arise and flatten in the growing
wind. A Northman appeared, going towards the ships,
a struggling shrieking young woman in his arms. There

would be a few young women or mothers left even at this season to look after the very old or the very young. Aniel did not wait for more. Already he had delayed too long, for his face had bit the grass when his father had been killed.

It was when he began to run that he found how excited his flesh was. During the battle he had lived outside himself, his spirit swaying and fighting on the beach, his emotions crying for victory, beseeching the god of war, imploring the flaming Sun to blind the enemy; but he had hardly heard himself, unconscious of his convulsive flesh, his earth-tearing nails, so ardently did his spirit lash the beach.

Now as he ran with staring eyes, the thin air about him rose up, up into a roofless world; it was so thin that the ground beneath partook of it. The trees breathed it in the small glade while their trunks stood still to listen. He slipped between them and climbed up again. From behind came a man's cry so terrible that it urged his feet to their toes. Emotion began to creep upon him; a pricking sensation beset his eyes, a choking urgency his throat. He should not be running away at all. He should not. His face twisted in an impotent wrath. His breathing grew harsh. The meaning of what had happened was getting full grip of him when at last he saw the little hill on which Molrua the priest abode. He hesitated but a moment, then with the added vigour that purpose gives he swung downward to the left, crossed the narrow green flat and rushed the hill, his hands clutching the steep face at every other stride. There was no sign of the priest on the flat knoll and the quietness of the little round house made Aniel stand still. He stared at the flat stone with the cross upon it, then strode quickly to the door that was always open and called, 'Are you there?' He did not add Father, did not add anything, for here was something outside his knowledge and it caught his breath. Getting no answer, he tiptoed to the door. Glancing inside, he saw the priest's kneeling body doubled over a stool. The head had fallen forward and the hands hung down to the ground, like a body that death had visited in prayer.

Aniel went into the hut; he touched the body, at the same time speaking aloud to give himself courage. The body stirred, and presently Molrua was blinking upward from his knees. 'What is it, my son?' He arose.

'The Northmen have landed and defeated us. My father and Drust and a great number have been slain. The Northmen are coming up the glen now. They will be here at once.'

Aniel spoke quickly and Molrua gazed steadfastly at him, but with the light that only half sees the outward vision.

Aniel urged him restlessly.

'I fell asleep,' said Molrua. 'I set myself to watch and pray, but I fell asleep.' His voice was quiet and gentle; there was in it a condemnation so complete that it was passionless; there was nothing that Molrua could add to his self-knowledge, nothing that man could not fail in. He smiled.

A cold shiver rayed from the nape of Aniel's neck. 'Come – at once,' he stuttered.

'So you ran to save me?' The smile caught Aniel; the eyes deepened. Aniel grew suddenly warm and awkward in the light of that humility.

'There is time yet – if we hurry.'

'God bless you, my son.' He laid a hand on Aniel's head. 'You will now save yourself. Go you.'

'Won't you come, Father?'

They went out at the door. The morning was bright with the early sun, the wind was fresh and cool, a lark sang in a sky whose blue was half veiled here and there in wisps of drawn cloud. It was a lovely morning, and the wind that cleansed was also bringing – what was it, this faint haze from the sea, this scent of . . . smoke . . . fire? Fire! It was fire! And that was a shout. Again. Again.

'They are coming, Father!'

Molrua turned towards the sea whose far horizon he could just see. Yes, they were coming. And even as they watched, three Northmen appeared over the abrupt rise in the ground beyond the meadow-flat in front of them.

'There they are!' cried Aniel under his breath, backing away at once. 'Come on!' and he slid over the inland brow of the knoll, raced down its side, and made for the Tower.

Molrua appeared not to have heard him, so concentrated was his gaze. The three Northmen, with their peaked helmets, round bodies, and busked active legs, had an odd air of unreality. As they came over the rise they paused, looking at what lay before them, then began to move about uncertainly, facing one way and then another. At last one of them, his back to Molrua, shouted and waved his sword. The other two did the same thing. Clearly they had discovered the true way and were calling their comrades.

Under the morning, it was a strange thing to see men so behave. Their limbs and their weapons stirred like the legs of great spiders. They were beings not of this world, and on the rim of it they moved in all the excitement of discovery.

Deadly and voracious they were; the prospect of death their excitement, and its reality their food. Strange to watch their dark antics in the fresh light of so clear a morning. Strange that these creatures should be God's creatures, too. Deep the mystery of God. Deep Thy mystery, O God.

Molrua turned and went into his hut. His legs were trembling a little and so he sat down on the stool over which, as he yet prayed, he had fallen asleep. Seated, he looked before him, his hands limp against the wood.

He had fallen asleep, but in a strange manner. He had been praying that God would take the cup from them, and while he had been praying his mind got linked up with that other time when he had been on the hillside and had acted like Christ in His agony. Then he had been so abashed that thereafter he had prayed with his inner sight darkened. By darkening his inner sight he closed the light against himself. There was no greater penance. In this darkness, he bowed his head, baring his neck.

But after a time the light had come about him, for to God even the darkness is clear; and the last deeps of the heart know when humility is so complete that no stain of self remains in it.

And when the heart is so purged, it grows light and the body grows light with it, and peace comes over all and stills all into that serenity which is as the waiting for the coming of a Presence. Often indeed the light had grown bright against his eyes, so bright sometimes that his eyes had been dazed a little and hurt, and his body had run over with a sweet and terrible weakness. When he had emerged from that experience, the light of day was always fresh and clear and his limbs were buoyant with movement and his mind all eager to be up and busy. Then he had done his best work. Within himself he had found a great persuasiveness. In his time, anger he had known too, and wrath, and in his wrath he had scourged many. Often he had shaken with wrath and opened before the wicked the doors of Hell. But wrath had little true power compared with this persuasiveness which comes in inspiration upon the mind, and moves it to such profound penetration that brotherly guidance is assured and joy brought forth.

Ever since he had talked to Drust and his men he had meditated and in that time had slept little. His concern had two aims: the assurance of his own acceptance with God, and the dedication of such worthiness to the service of bringing other souls to salvation. There was danger either way. For one could so work for the conversion of others that the sway of authority thereby engendered tended to puff up the mind in its lust for power, and God's name was used for terror, and Christ's name as a threat.

Now when a man had gone and lived in solitude by himself – as he, Molrua, had done in the birch glade – the peace of God and the agony of the kind Christ came upon him. There was no terror, no threat, only the aspiration to walk with God. The thorns in the way were the weaknesses of the flesh. And when the flesh was torn the wounds were bared to the light, which healed them. But out of this came such a concern with oneself, or such an unconcern and serene happiness, as made one forget the duty to the heathen who were also the children of God.

Now last night he had pondered deeply through these twin ways on what he had to do, and before the war horns had interrupted him he was in the assurance of a sweet communion. All the land opened out before him. His hill was its beating heart. His hill became (and this was his ultimate dream) a little Christian community of workers, with, if it were God's will, himself as its head.

At that he receded far within himself and became a small boy again; and the preacher that came to the place where he was born, in the distant south country, terrified him and all the other children too, so that they ran and hid, while their elders watched, and some of them mocked from behind trees. But they were frightened a little of the peaked hood he wore over his head, and of his quiet ways and of his lack of anger, so that he might easily be a strange being in disguise, finding out about them. But his father, who was the chief of that people and a known fighter, would have nothing to do with the preacher and ordered him away on pain of death. Indeed if his father had not himself been such a fearless man, he might quite well have killed the preacher, for his father loved the old ways deeply and was angered at what the preacher said. Then the preacher went away, and some mocked him as he went, and when he turned and raised his arms, the sleeves like wings falling away from them, and blessed them in the name of the Father, and of the Son, and of the Holy Ghost, a piece of rotten branch whirled against his belly, doubling him up with a suddenness that made his tormentors laugh. The desire for laughter grew. Branches were cracked and pieces nearly an arm's length hurled through the air. Desire to excel overcame any last feeling of shame, and it was he, Molrua, then a boy of thirteen, who threw the piece that caught the preacher behind the jaw and laid him stiff on the grass. It was a moment of triumph and the others shouted, when all at once his father came striding upon them. 'Is this a way to treat the stranger?' he bellowed in flaming anger. His son of thirteen boldly said, 'I did it.' 'You did!' and his father hit him so hard that he felled him to the ground, whereupon he picked up the preacher under his arm and strode home with him.

His senses returned to the preacher that night, but his mind wandered a little because he was not well nourished. Now Molrua's mother, when she heard of what her son had done to a stranger, was very vexed, for she was reasonable in her ways and kind-hearted. So that Molrua, because he

loved his mother, hated the preacher. And the preacher
stayed on, for his mother, fond of listening to talk, listened
to him. At that time his mother was with child, and it was
her fancy that the preacher be not put away, but be left to
go about the household doing menial tasks, so that no ill
might come to her child.

At first her husband looked sideways at this, but said that
as things were he did not care one way or another. And the
preacher was certainly very gentle and very obliging and
told many marvellous stories. And though the workers
smiled at him, they also thought him a being different
from themselves, one even suggesting that he was a great
chief in disguise because of the way he ate his food and of
his absentminded manners to a serving maid. Sometimes
he was very absentminded. Now Molrua (though that was
not his name then) hated him more than ever, but when
he suggested to his father that he should be sent away,
his father turned on Molrua and was angry with him,
reminding him of what he had done to a stranger. And
so his father ignored the preacher.

Now when his mother was delivered of a son, she fell
dangerously ill and was like to die. None of the skilly
women could relieve her malady. When she was nearly
dead, the preacher brought a potion out of the woods, and
when he had administered this he prayed to his God for her
life. It was a moving prayer fraught with the beseeching of
a heart that was itself full of kindness and the desire to heal
the wounds of all. He dared to ask God for the recovery of
this woman as a sign.

The recovery of his mother was the beginning of the
strange turmoils and adventures of his life. She had the
son baptised as a Christian, and at that the father went on
an expedition and was killed. Then his mother sent away
the preacher and took Molrua into her counsels, talking to
him and helping him, so that he loved her again. She also
had power over all the leading men, and one day, when
there was open jealousy, she sent Molrua on a mission.
And thus he came on a fine morning into the community
of the Christians that was by an arm of the sea.

That community became a memory always bright as it

had been on that first morning. The brightness of it had, too, the extra brightness of his conversion, having beams in it of a golden light in which everything on the earth was seen as for the first time. Scales were removed from his eyes and he forthwith saw with astonishment and joy.

Now while he prayed last night, all this – and much besides in his life that his vision encompassed rapidly – had made his communion sweet and full of assurance. And at that very moment, the war horns had racked the new day with their terrible message. His prayers had been in vain, his assurance a deceit, and his dream of the future a mockery. The strength ebbed from him. His body shivered in the cold. He was not merely unworthy of God's help; he was simply nothing, nothing. The tide of nothingness rose up over and engulfed him.

Aniel had brought him back, Aniel who Silis had said was the disciple of the druid. Back to the realisation that the Northmen were here, that they had slain and were advancing to further slaughter, and that he should save himself.

Molrua stared at the wall, his eyes wide as in a trance, his hanging hands limp against the wooden seat. They were here. It was finished.

In the centre of this impotence and, as it seemed, at a great distance, the figure of the preacher, whom he as a boy had laid low, came before him – not as he had first seen him but as he had finally left him . . . when that preacher had long been the head of the little Christian community. An old man with bleached hair and steadfast kind eyes, blessing Molrua as he departed: *'Go ye therefore, and teach all nations, baptising them in the name of the Father, and of the Son, and of the Holy Ghost; teaching them to observe all things whatsoever I have commanded you: and, lo, I am with you alway, even unto the end of the world.'*

And, lo, I am with you alway, even unto the end of the world. Molrua saw the lips of his earthly master move, and heard the words issue clearly, and saw the hand raised in benediction. Around the master was a pale light which came out from the skin on his face and from his white mantle.

A faint trembling came over Molrua. It passed and he blinked several times. His breast filled slowly with air and he shivered again before his breath came forth. Then he stood up, casting about him. The bright air of the doorway set his eyes wide, and they looked upward as if they were expecting Someone. This dazed them a moment and an unearthly hurt came to his forehead, like a hand laid there binding it. Then the hand was removed and the light was shining and very still as if Someone outside were coming up through it.

Molrua went out at the door, and before him at a few paces a Northman was standing on the grassy crest. He looked fixedly at Molrua, his knuckles standing out upon the shaft of his axe. A cut on his left temple dropped a red thread to the eyebrow. The lips were hard against the teeth.

Molrua felt the whiteness about him more than ever, as though Someone were now coming in upon his right hand. He had no fear, and as his eyes glimmered he raised his open hand. This action released the Northman. Molrua did not stir, and so the axe, descending, severed the lips while they were still blessing.

Retrieving his axe, the Northman glanced about him. He had an uneasy feeling of other presences. The strange look on the man's face had strung up all his muscles so that he had had to come at him quickly, urged from within. He eyed the gaping door of the little round house and went to it quickly. But he was in only for a moment when he glanced out again and from side to side. Then he ransacked the interior, tearing down, and kicking over and breaking a jar and spilling the water upon his feet. In that simple dwelling the most valuable thing was the hide case with its copy of the Gospels. There was neither gold nor silver. Even the carved head of the bachall or staff was innocent of metal ornament.

At the door again, the Northman glanced about him, glanced at the vellum pages of the scriptures in his hands and threw them from him. It was altogether a queer place this, and quite possibly he had killed one of the terrible magicians who offered up sacrifices with black rites.

He strode away, but at the crest had to look over his shoulder. There was no one there, nothing but the dead body and a leaf of that which he had thrown from him moving in the wind.

2

The Northman ran down the hill. His disappointment at having found nothing was balanced by an odd feeling of successful escape. He was a man set firmly in his prime, and his eyes, that were a very light blue, had an acquisitive hard quickness. One of his fellows on the path by the stream shouted to him. He gave them a wave but did not go towards them. A large body were coming over the crest at the end of the meadow-flat. He turned away from them all around the base of the knoll.

He knew what they would think of him, their admiration for his fearless odd behaviour, tempered by envy at the thought of the things which he would be sure to get. For he always found objects of unusual workmanship in wood and gold and silver and jade, and had a celebrated collection of curiously shaped bronze knives in the farmhouse that was an ancestral possession. Even the interior of that home itself was a wonder of carved wood. Men often gathered there and talked, for this Magnus was hospitable and loved sly jokes as he worked with his knife or edged a tool.

To be with the main body was to acquire nothing unusual. It was sheer bad luck that this magician's hill had given him nothing. But somewhere about it there must be a hidden store; and there really was no danger, for the natives would now be running for their lives, taking all their precious things with them. Time was short for the lucky chance.

And there must be a lucky chance, for the story was strong that somewhere in these parts was a valley of gold, where nuggets as big as a robin's egg were picked up in the bed of the stream. Black painted savages like these could not understand the value of gold. They probably used it for door clasps or cheese presses. It would be exciting to come on a cheese press of solid gold!

He eyed the top of the fort on the rise beyond the smaller stream. The heads that moved there had doubtless been watching him. But the capturing of the fort would take time and would require all their efforts. He knew the sort of building it was. Not the wooden walls of old Norway! If, however, they did capture it, they would get the finest haul of all. His eyes glittered greedily. He would fight for his share of that too – but in good time. Crossing the green flat on his right, he went up among the trees and pursued his way until he was moving above the off bank of the stream that came down the Little Glen. The hillside grew steeper and more difficult, but presently he saw upstream, and on the opposite bank where it lay back to an easy slope, a group of small houses. There was considerable commotion, bodies crying and moving hurriedly.

Magnus dropped down the hillside, and as he came out on the footpath surprised two men hurrying in his direction. They stopped, amazed, and at once took to the hillside he had left. He crossed the stream and was entering the trees when a stone whizzed past his ear. This angered him and from shelter he turned round. But nothing moved or gave sign. A stone crashed in the branches overhead. He withdrew, but now going very carefully. A half-dozen of them might even attack him. And clearly he could not do much against the houses single-handed, not anyway until most of the more active had gone. But he would at least see where they were going; so much might be credited to him later for useful information.

He was now moving with light feet, wary and listening. Trees hemmed him in and certainly would prevent the full swing of an axe. Trees were good for ambush. They were all infernally good stone-throwers. Beyond this slope of trees he had seen a moor. It might be as well to get to the edge of it.

When the trees were thinning out he drew up at the glimpse of a body threading towards him. It was the girl Breeta hurrying with such blind concern that she nearly ran into him. The shock gripped her. He was himself rather shocked, for terror gave her beauty a vivid almost horrible quality as though her flesh were being crushed. He saw her tongue. The attraction of this moved him strongly. Excitement swelled his chest and he panted through his nostrils; his acquisitive look flickered on her great dark eyes. Ornaments of gold and silver are pleasant to own and to handle, but a living ornament of this sort would be an individual triumph. She would be an immediate triumph too! At his first step her body stumbled awkwardly back upon itself, half turned, screeching, then in an instant, as if consciousness had flashed to its toes, was rushing at full speed into the moor, given to stumbling still, the legs uncertain, and to screaming at each stumble.

Her screams might have been heard at the Tower, if the attention of those within that stronghold had not been bent on more desperate needs.

Aniel, when he had fled from the Christian's hill, should have gone direct with the news of the conflict to the Grove. But he could not pass the Tower, lest of those escaping none might bring the fatal tidings, each believing that some other would do so, each desperate to save his own blood and gear.

When he came by the enclosure, heads were watching him from the Tower-top: Silis and Nessa, the bearded Lys, old Talorg the bright-browed, and Erp of the one arm with his keen young face. Although they could not see the shore, they must by this time certainly have seen the Northmen on the river flat and have known that the result was defeat. But did they know how desperate? The face of Silis had a pale flash in its terrible restraint. Nessa's mouth was open in a breathless pause; the men waited.

'Our men have nearly all been killed,' cried Aniel. 'The Northmen are coming.'

'Where is Drust, your chief?' asked Silis.

'Drust is dead,' answered Aniel.

For a minute Silis was silent, then as though she were alone, she cried, 'Drust is dead. Drust my chief is dead. He is dead.' Her loud harsh voice made them shiver. Her face was an instrument on which the past played. Her young love for Drust in the golden days. The love that burned in her so fiercely that when, in these later years, she was driven to deny it, it had ingrown, tortuous and tormented, seeking consolation in power, in the Christian religion that humbles the spirit and makes all mortal love as dust, in that very humbling which makes pride a poisoned dagger. And now Drust was dead. What is Christ's religion when your love lies dead? What is power? And what are your offspring but wandering shadows?

All their flesh grew cold in that woman's cry, and in the silence thereafter the high terror of the meaning of life became as a mirror to death.

Aniel broke the silence, even though no more should be said, but he was excited by her.

'Morbet is dead too – and Taran my father.'

He caught the echo, 'and Taran my father,' within a lonely place in his mind. The meaning was writ upon him. Like Drust, his father was dead.

Those on the wall looked at him and looked away. No one kept looking at him except Nessa, and her face had the bright startled expression of one looking at a snake. The snake may have been in her own mind, or in her mother's cry, or in death.

'Are they many?' called Talorg.

'Yes,' answered Aniel, 'more than half a hundred of them are coming. There's still time to get away.'

Silis was gazing in a dread concentration down the valley. Talorg, turning towards her, followed her gaze. They all stood looking in the same direction. Aniel judged that they were watching the Christian's hill. The Northmen could be there now. In another moment he saw by the tenseness of those on the wall that something was about to happen. The excitement of waiting without seeing induced a faint sickening weakness. He could not take his eyes from Silis's face, and presently a groan starting in her nostrils dribbled brokenly from her mouth. 'O God of the Christians!' she muttered, and her head fell over arms that clutched the wall.

'There is still time to fly,' said Talorg to her in a quiet voice.

She made no answer.

'We cannot hold against an army – not for very long,' said Talorg.

She raised her head and looked at him. Her magnificence flamed.

'You may go. I am prepared to defend my home alone.'

'It was not so meant, lady.'

She gazed at him. 'If we are not enough to hold it, it is death to stay.'

'I prefer death,' said Talorg, with a ghost of a smile.

Her magnificence deepened.

'Though I could have wished', added Talorg, 'that *you* would have accepted the better chance of life. Who now will lead the Ravens?'

'I will lead them', said Silis, '*now*.'

Talorg bowed before her, then turned to address Lys. Aniel had never quite seen the meaning of Talorg's behaviour before. He was always a courteous man, disliking quarrels, and for that many thought him soft. But Aniel saw now that he was not soft at all. He was nearly sixty and had been too slow at any time to be a great fighter, but he was going to fight calmly now, with a queer sort of impersonal courage. His brow was pale and smooth as a man's thought in the dusk. As a little boy Aniel remembered playing pranks on him. One of their games was for a boy to meet him and say solemnly, 'How do you do?' To this Talorg would reply in his characteristic manner. When Talorg had passed, the rest would come out of hiding and say, 'I am very well, thank you, and how are you, my little man?' with mimic voice and gesture; which always led to shouting and a mannered war dance.

Now Erp of the one arm cried, 'There they are!' Moving round to the point of the enclosure, where Drust's stone carried the bird emblem, Aniel saw many Northmen come over the sharp rise beyond the river flat. He stood watching them for a time, fascinated. Their shouts had an intrusive quality that was hard and destructive. They were strangers and hostile not merely to the folk of that glen but to the earth and to the air, so that their very echo was an outrage.

As Aniel came back, the voice of Goan, the smith, was loud and commanding in the enclosure.

'Where are you going?' called Talorg.

'Back to the Grove,' answered Aniel.

'Very good,' said Talorg. 'It looks as though we shall need all the help we can get.'

Aniel so understood that he could not speak.

When at a few paces he looked up again, Nessa was the only one watching him. A curious expression came into her face that was like the beginning of a smile, or a restraint that momentarily glistened, with a movement of the head backward and a drawing away of herself in invitation and denial. The whole subtle gesture flowered out of her flesh and made his feet stumble, his heart beat strongly and warmth flow over him. Then she nearly turned away – and he turned away entirely.

Lack of sleep and the emotional stresses of the last few days induced this bodily weakness that could flush easily or had even experienced that nausea of expectation when Molrua the Christian had been killed – for Silis could have seen nothing less.

His father was dead. His father, the man who had been a man when he first saw him. He could hardly feel that at all. Perhaps that explained why Nessa had not cried out when he had told of her father's death. Perhaps she would have cried out if her mother had not. (*Drust is dead!*)

Nessa had shown a fine courage, a fine restraint. Like one of the heroic maidens of legend, stronger even than her mother, silent when her mother had faced the fates. Or . . .? A vague doubt rose in him. He could not understand. For there was something – there was something – that made him hot.

As he walked away into the trees, Nessa's face in its withdrawing gleam was upon the plane of his mind which was pale with his father's death. And at last he stood looking unseeingly at the moor before him. Not even yet had his father's death become intimate. If he shut out everything else and said, 'My Father!' and let the surge come over him, he would sit down and weep. Nessa's face . . . and the death of her father. The withdrawing gleam that was invitation's denial. That she could have taken it like that!

Once, when his mother had died, he had been overcome with grief, had gone away into the moor to be alone; and when there had started drawing. The intense pleasure of that drawing! The joy that was sin. The denial of the secret gleam as he had walked home and let grief take his features – until, in the death room again, grief convulsed him.

Perhaps Nessa would be overcome when she . . . His mind came to a pause and the paleness spread completely over it. The death of his father began to come up like a sea haar. Inaction beset him. He was being shrouded. A woman's scream constricted his heart to a flat beat. He stared at Breeta being chased by the Northman, and not until she had leapt into the trench did he start running.

He ran very lightly and with great speed, the small straight-bladed bronze dagger, drawn from within his belt, flashing past his right hip. Breeta's shouts directed him and he did not take to the trench until he was over them.

The Northman had her pinned down. Her eyes caught Aniel as he leapt. Aniel stabbed the Northman between the shoulders with such fierceness that the blade was going in for the third time before the Northman reared from Breeta's body on to his left side, surged up, and fell on his back. Breeta scrambled to her feet and flattened against the bank. They both remained looking down at the death struggles, at the pale acquisitive eyes, whose light of sheer astonishment dulled to understanding; heard the strange oaths until they guttered in red froth. The Northman ignored them. He heaved. Caught like this, Odin, O Odin! His head rolled. A spout of blood came from his mouth. The whole body choked and the head fell slowly over.

Crushing back against the bank, Breeta crept past the body. She was panting heavily. Aniel went up to her and they stared at each other.

Aniel was now far beyond the exercise of any outward mannerism. His face was completely drained. It was blank and yet strangely concentrated on the girl before him, hunting it did not know what. In her face was the same tenseness, but with a flickering shutter of fearfulness, or

watchfulness, ready to descend; until she saw that Aniel,
like a boy, was searching her out. Her face stilled; shyness
was lost in the light of her eyes. When his arms went round
her, she found that he was trembling. She caught his body
strongly and pressed it against her breast. 'I'm tired,' he
said. They lay down. He kissed her. Their kisses grew long
and fevered. Their bodies gathered a wild energy. It swept
them from the dreadful deeds of that morning. Ecstasy
came upon them. And with death at their feet, the ecstasy
in its consummation was unflawed by care or thought.

### 3

Breeta had risen and was peering over the edge of the
bank towards the Tower, whence the crying of voices
reached her, but no life moved on the moor. At any
moment, however, Northmen might come out of the
trees. They would be pressing up the Little Glen towards
Morbet's stronghold. Her mother was in the Tower. Her
mother once had laughed at what the sea-raiders would
do. Anxiety quickened within her, but not at all for
Morbet's stronghold, hardly even for the Tower. She
instinctively turned and looked down at Aniel, and found
his eyes open.

Her colour deepened as she turned her head away at
once. 'Do you hear?' Her words were a small gulp.

He got up and scanned the moor, putting out his hand
at the same time and laying hold of her arm. He drew her
beside him and they both looked away. His fingers went
down her arm and caught her hand and pressed it. She
knew from the way he did this that he was thinking more
about it than about anything else. Swaying back a little
she was able to glance at him sideways and observed a
movement in his throat. The same movement immediately
took place in her own throat, and at that moment she knew
that he was even shyer than she was. She began to tremble
with happiness. He faced round and looked at her. It was a
sweet terrible ordeal. He caught both her hands and kissed
her. It was a quiet gentle kiss. She found she could not
look at his eyes. Her happiness became too great for her.

She looked away, trembling, her heart unable to master the emotion that was so exquisite as to be half pain.

He let her go and busied himself. Taking his knife out of the peat, he began cleaning it. He had killed the Northman and saved Breeta. The goodness of having done this quietened his emotion, but it also strengthened it. He felt responsible towards Breeta; this suffused him with a grave pleasure. He cleaned the blood from the knife with a smiling care. Then he put his knife back beneath his belt and turned to the dead man.

'Let us go,' said Breeta urgently. She could not look at the body with its staring eyes, its cut temple, and beard and breast heavy with darkening ooze.

Aniel, kneeling, took the Northman's knife and axe. Then he hesitated. Breeta looked at him. He closed the Northman's eyes. 'May you find your own raiding ground,' he murmured, with a queer smile.

Breeta warmed. She knew what Aniel meant from his tone. He was pretending to be grateful to the Northman. She turned away and Aniel followed.

'Why did you say that?' she had to ask.

'Don't you wish him well?'

She made no answer.

'Tell me,' he pressed.

'You haven't told me why you said it,' she answered.

'Breeta.'

'Yes.'

'Don't you wish him well?'

'You haven't told me,' she answered, moving on in front of him.

He looked at her legs and ankles, then he looked at the dark dampness of the peat along her back, and gave a small laugh.

'What are you laughing at?' she asked, half turning.

'Something I saw,' he answered.

She tried to look across her shoulder at herself, then glanced back at him. He was smiling with a flash of the old teasing manner. She walked on.

'Breeta.'

She paid no attention. Her head drooped a little.

He caught her up. 'Breeta,' he said, softly, urgently. His fingers ran down her arm. 'Breeta!' He had to get in front to see her face. She was smiling. He charged her against the bank and, as she swung to her balance again, caught and kissed her.

At this their shyness dropped from them a little, and gaiety took its place. The distant shouts from the Tower were a sort of hectic applause, centring them in themselves. They were moving quickly, but with occasional lagging moments, as when their ears listened, and their thoughts were for the world of disaster around them, but even when they worked up an anxious moment, when his brows met, with a man's seriousness, they were but acting their respective parts, conscious at the quick only of the body standing so close.

'What was that?' she cried. Listening, he heard only her breathing, and the sound of it secretly caught his senses.

'What?' he asked.

'It sounded – I don't know,' and she held her breath.

He looked at her. Her brows were knitted; her lips parted and her breath came out. He was not interested in what she heard; but he couldn't yet make fun of her. He wanted to tease and laugh. A great light merriment was mounting in him, like froth from a happiness too deep. There was something also within him continuously desiring to flash about her, to touch and flash from her, to hold and leave go. In its pleasant exhaustion his body went nimbly as if under the influence of a heady drug. The death of his father was very remote from him now.

'Here', he said at last, 'we'll have to go carefully.'

The deep hag was growing shallow and a little way in front was no more than a slight hollow in which grass grew more profusely than heath. He had already hid the Northman's axe, and now he hid the knife.

'Where are you going?' she asked.

'To the Grove,' he said, but did not look at her at once. When he did look she was half turned away, with the startled expression still in her brows.

'Will you come with me?' he asked, watching her.

She turned full face and looked at him. He lowered his

eyes with a chuckle, but did not care for the sound of it himself. He would like to tease her. It would hurt her. All at once this artificial mood passed from him.

'Breeta, listen to me.' He sat down on his heels. She crouched also, for his words were winning and friendly. 'I should have been at the Grove by this time. But that does not greatly matter, for the Northmen will be held up at the Tower for a long time. Besides, I had to warn them at the Tower. And I also went off my way to warn Molrua the Christian. I shouldn't have done that, but – I liked him.' His words were now very simple and direct. Her love for this mood could be seen stirring with her blood.

'What did he do?' she asked.

'He would not come. He had been praying to his god all night – and had fallen asleep. "I set myself to watch and pray – but fell asleep," he said. I cannot tell you how he said it.'

She looked at him and her eyes grew dark. 'What happened to him?'

'I think he was killed,' he said. 'It must have been by the man who nearly – had you.'

Her face stilled.

'Listen, Breeta. I'll have to go to the Grove. We'll crawl on yet for a bit together, and then I'll leave you. You'll lie close until I come back.'

'You'll come back?'

'Yes, I'll come back. You would like me to, wouldn't you?'

She did not answer, and because of his wanton question there were sudden tears in her eyes. He spoke her name gently and drew her to him. His voice broke in a soft breath of laughter, mocking her lowered lids. A tear fell on his hand. A great tenderness invaded his tiredness. He lay back, drawing her with him. 'We're safe here. I won't go at all,' he said.

Because he so understood her that he did not mind her tears, neither did she mind them. This suddenly was a new and terrifying pleasure. It could not last long. She wanted to lay hold of it, of him, but she was frightened. For there was something finally about him that was beyond her, something not of knowledge so much as of a hidden taste, something that she feared. It had always placed her at a disadvantage with him. And only once had she been her forgetful fierce self – just after he had delivered her from the terror of the Northman.

And *that* now. . . . He was caressing her, caressing her hair. She rose in rebellion against herself and clasped him. She was hot with shame against herself and clung close into him. She tried to get away from herself and pressed her forehead hard against his throat. She nearly choked him.

'Breeta!' he remonstrated.

She became fierce as a beast. He gripped her chin and tore her face away. 'Breeta!' She was sobbing. She turned from him and hid herself. He put his hand on her shoulder. She threw it off. With the luxury of tiredness, he lay back, watching her. At any moment she might leap to her feet and make off. She would certainly do that very soon – if he did nothing. He waited. At the first straightening of her shoulders, he leant over her. She started away. They fought. His mood grew earnest and impatient. Out of the male need to dominate, he had to down her. His strength came back to him from a painfully pumping heart. But a madness seemed to have seized her. She was trying to tear herself from him and had no longer any knowledge of what she was rightly doing. Their legs intertwisted and strained. He forced his body at her. They panted and grew hot; their faces crushed damply. Her head held from him but he got at it and ultimately pinned her mouth. It moaned against his, and her strength went from her.

Immediately she lay still, he lay still with her. 'You're strong,' he muttered, breathing like a spent athlete. She turned her face down between her arms. They lay side by side for some time saying nothing. His mind was free and pleasant. It was a strange morning for playing truant! He should have rushed to the Grove. Every means for gathering men in defence would have to be considered. There were those at the shielings. The Logenmen – had the Logenmen attacked? It was high time he was going. The necessity for going excited him as he lay still, with this girl beside him. It was, however, like something exciting

him in a dream; they were withdrawn to its hidden centre
and lay safe; a delicious treachery.

He got on his elbow and looked at her. Feeling his
passion move in him again, he said at once, in a quiet
voice, 'I'm going, Breeta.'

She stirred, but only to bury her head deeper.

He drew the hair from the back of her neck and touched
the skin with his teeth. On his feet, he looked about him.
The moor was still blank, but he knew that men must be
approaching it from many sides. On all fours he started
off. She did not follow him. From a little distance he called
softly but commandingly, then started on again. She was
now following him. In a little while he got to his feet and
stooping slightly in the moor fold went on rapidly. At last
he threw himself down and waited till she came up.

'Do you remember this place?' He saw her expression
quicken and she looked at him despite herself. 'You
thought', he said, 'that I was Leu that night.'

Her expression burned and she hung her head. Her
dumbness made her flesh rich. He laughed, 'Have you
thought all along that it was Leu?'

'No.'

'Who told you it was me?'

'No one.'

'Was it me?'

She did not answer and her brows gathered.

'It's only my fun. I must be off. No one will find you
here. I'll be back as soon as I can. Goodbye, Breeta' –
he leaned to her – 'my little pasture,' and he was gone,
leaving the air in a small eddy of delight.

She watched the place where he went over the crest,
then drew back and stared across the moor. Her dumb
expression gathered a faint smile. Quickly the smile became
self-conscious and she glanced about her. Then she lay
down and was overcome by her experiences. Her eyes
grew brilliant; she poked her fingers into the peat; she
looked steadily and glanced quickly; the delicious unrest
went over her body and made her think about it. The wind
was cool and came about her legs. It was still early morning
and the larks were singing over the moor. The wind ran in

the grasses and moved the heath points. She was – she was
– oh, she was – she couldn't – she couldn't tell him. Her love
overcame her. She beat her brow into the grass and clung to
the moor. She was a dumb fool. What would he think – she
behaved – oh, she behaved – In this dumb way she spent
her love, until the desire to see him conquered her, and she
crawled up to the moor crest. Far away she saw his body
approaching the trees. Its slim moving shape struck to her
heart. The Grove was a hostile darkness waiting to swallow
him. Not until that moment did she realise how fierce was
her need. Her body emptied, her need became a pain, her
fingers closed to fists, and cruelty ran along her fear like a
knife-edge. She hated the Grove. She feared and hated it.
She crawled back and curled up under a moor root. But
as she lay, a smile formed deep in her pale brown features
and dark brown eyes; and she had the story of all time for
confidence. A cry came across the moor from the Tower.
Her mind ran along the cry to find her mother. Her father
would have been at the sea fight. Like two threads, they
converged on her heart. A blind hand came up and drew
them quietly away. But she had to close her eyes.


4

Aniel was thinking of her too as he approached the Grove,
but only in such a way as to make him think more of
himself. That a youth should kill a man and win a woman
– his first man and his first woman – all in a morning,
is something for his legs to put into their stride and for
his head to balance. The knowledge of it, however, can
be conveniently placed behind the mind, where the true
sources of strength have their secret place. As he looked
at the Grove, his eyes held an enigmatic light, and could
not keep from smiling. Those there could now think what
they liked, or say what they liked: both would be for
the innocent front of the mind to tackle. He staggered
an odd step, mostly from a weariness not unpleasantly
lightheaded, but also a little from the pride that likes its
manliness a trifle drunk. Breeta's quick lynxlike body . . .
Suddenly he veiled his expression, for he saw over against

the Stones the Master and Gilbrude talking together, and heard Gilbrude's voice raised harshly.

He feared Gilbrude and had hoped to meet only the Master. Gilbrude was taller than the Master, with cut hair, a long grey beard, rounded shoulders, bushy eyebrows, and grey-green suspecting fanatic eyes. The Master was gentle and wide-minded. Gilbrude was the narrow hard priest, who would not abate a jot in the ritual of learning and divination and sacrifice. He worshipped his gods and hated the Christians whom he would gladly have exterminated, or, if not gladly, at least for the honour of his gods with solemn ritual and due prophecy – and grim satisfaction.

It was Gilbrude's opinion, indeed, that the religion of their fathers had been betrayed by worldly chiefs and weak druids who allowed innovations and did not enforce discipline and punishment. It was as necessary to divine by the movement of the disembowelled entrails today as it had been a thousand years ago. And not merely to divine and to propitiate, but to undergo the very experience for its own sake. A chief won honour from killing another chief, not because the other chief was thereby dead, but because he had killed him. The feeling of the dark mystery of life, of death, blood and the earth, the black womb of the earth and the blazing eyes of the sky, was being sicklied over until life at its root, at its conception, in its seed, was diseased by a cancer that would in time wipe its tribes from the sun and leave of them only a savage memory. Had not their organisation been weakening for generations? Had it not been losing power over the people? Were they not worshipping almost by stealth? Could not anyone see that complete disrepute was at hand and the end not far distant?

The Master was the head, but Gilbrude was next to him, and Gilbrude was for strong measures. They could yet wipe out the Christians and bring the free-thinkers to account. And, with their power strongly rooted once more, they could work towards the central unifying authority they had held of old over the chiefs of that northern land, long before the fair-haired people came at all. The Christian power was seeping in from the south, and the north was losing its own cohesion without gaining any benefits from whatever new systems were being built up. If indeed any were being built up at all, which he, Gilbrude, doubted.

Much of which he had been repeating to the Master, not as new gospel, but as a perverse way of implying that, as for him, he did not greatly care how the fight went.

'But if we are defeated and the Northmen come with their barbarian ways, would not that be an end of us all?' suggested the Master.

'It would at least be a rapid end,' said Gilbrude. And he added, 'Only, as you know well, they may defeat us, but they won't stay. They'll kill and get what they can and clear off. Then – we should do something. It's our only hope. It's the only hope for the people. As it is, the old peoples, who were here from the beginning, are they not dying out already? Why? Because they are a simple people, fond of playing at games and making music and laughing. They are simple and feckless and will be damned,' said Gilbrude.

'Do you mean they deserve to be damned?'

'Well,' said Gilbrude, and closed his mouth.

'I think it's more difficult than that,' said the Master.

'If there was no difficulty, there would be no need for talk. You're either going to rule or you're not.'

The Master was silent.

The silence drew Gilbrude to its core, where rule was like a small dark force set before truth. Truth grew and expanded like a wheel of light.

'Have you changed – do you no longer believe – certain things?' challenged Gilbrude harshly.

'Do you believe all things?' asked the Master.

'I do,' said Gilbrude. 'I do!' His whole manner was growing inflamed and accusatory.

'You believe even in the practices of a thousand years ago?'

Gilbrude's face darkened.

The Master waited.

Then Gilbrude, his voice thick, his eyes burning through his eyebrows, said, 'I do!'

The Master regarded him, the sparsely bearded face calm as stone, the eyes like worn glass.

'You *know* I'm right,' said Gilbrude, now with the low harsh eagerness of one who has committed himself. 'Would there not be many who would follow me? I know there would. I *know* them. Besides that, it is in the heart of every one of us. There is not a living thing that I could not make quake with dread – or tremble with delight – and you know it.'

'Yes,' said the Master.

'Well?' cried Gilbrude.

As that challenge hung in the air, they saw Aniel approach. The young man's face was full of tidings, which he related immediately he reached them, telling them of the death of Drust and of Morbet and of Taran his father. As he mentioned his father, no special emotion touched his features, which looked exhausted but calm, the eyes open and frank. 'Most of the Ravens have been killed. The rest tried to get away. Some were caught. The sea-village was reaved and set on fire. They are burning before them. They have now reached the Tower. Silis, the wife of Drust, and Talorg and a handful of men are holding it – but for how long no one knows, for there will be half a hundred Northmen attacking them there by this time.'

Lifting his piercing look from Aniel's face, Gilbrude snorted with a wild humour. 'It seems as if it was going to be a rapid end all right!' He looked dangerous.

'They killed the Christian on his hill,' said Aniel calmly.

Gilbrude's mouth closed, then curled open. He threw a look under his brow at the Master and said, 'We are losing all our leaders.'

But the Master seemed lost in thought. His calmness at that moment exasperated Gilbrude. There was a restraint and dignity about the little man that made his disciples worship him, for the dignity had all the simplicity of kindness. They feared his clarity, but only in so far as everyone fears truth. In selfless moments, truth is the most exciting conjecture of all.

Gilbrude and Aniel both became conscious of waiting for him. Without speaking, he moved away. The grey of his cloak was darker than the grey of the Stones, whose tall shapes stood at attention as he passed. He was lost for a little, then he appeared going up the rising heath.

Gilbrude muttered ironically. Aniel began to drift to the huts, when Gilbrude asked him sharply, 'Where are you going?'

'I'm a bit tired.'

'Tired? A young fellow like you tired!' Gilbrude knew that Aniel was favoured by the Master. He had, besides, the same sort of blank innocence! He was going to ask him about certain verses, but turned away, wondering why they bothered about such as Aniel at all.

That was probably what was wrong. Time was when sons of the chiefs were taught here. This had been the centre, the brain. Justice, religion, learning. The Master should have been the great judge; he himself the great priest; and such as Aniel but apprentice versifiers. And now – seven of them all told, with not one noble novice among the lot! And the Master – weak. Gilbrude's thought grew dark and vengeful. Its habit indeed was to run in subterranean channels. Often, rounding a black earth rock, it stood and gnawed itself. Schemes beset it. Orgies of power deployed before it. Blood is the food, and fertility the force. Life rose up – and looked at the Sun. Around and above were the gods. And when the gods pressed, life retreated until he, Gilbrude, had it all around him, a great stream, swaying and chanting; until he, Gilbrude, fed the gods, and the gods withdrew.

The Master had travelled in many lands. He had knowledge of all things, of strange tongues, of plants, of healing, of the movements of the stars, of occult divinations, of beasts, and his eyes had the power to drain the mind they looked at. Yet he was weak. He got lost in contemplations. He could not organise. He cared little for power. He was old, he was done. That is the truth, thought Gilbrude, leaning against a Stone and staring at the place where he fed the gods.

But finally, behind all, *Did the Master believe?* Gilbrude looked about him, and stared at the same place again. Did he believe in the gods? Were they still real to him – or were they being abstracted and only the ghosts left in the shape of meanings and parables and legends? Because of his excessive age, were the gods really become phantoms? In these intense moments of abstraction did he actually sometimes die and send his wraith into other worlds?

What was it about the small body, the smooth still face and grey eyes, that remained in the mind so that one novice had been overheard to call him a god?

Was he a god?

The question infuriated Gilbrude. In every way the Master was the opposite of what a god should be; and yet there was something about him that had the still awfulness of a god. The last of the gods, come to destroy them, no doubt.

The fierce inner life moved intolerantly in Gilbrude. And now there was hope. The Northmen had won. Drust and the leaders were dead. When the Northmen left, the dispossessed would be gathered. The Christian was dead. Did the Christian help them to win their battle? Had he not, on the contrary, been the means of their defeat by the way he had denied the ancient gods? That would be put strongly to them! A new leader would be ordained. And the Master, become too old at last. . . .

As Gilbrude built up his dream of power, and of the restoration of the ancient faith, Aniel in his round cell was thinking also of the Master. If it wasn't for the Master he would quietly slip away to where he had left Breeta. He might fear Gilbrude, but he would not care what he might say. But the Master . . . He sat on his stool and in a short time his face grew still as the Master's own. No clear thought came into his head, yet his spirit was bathed in luminous air. This air had the stillness, too, of far timeless origins, like memories of summer childhood or of the childhood of the world. Its place had the freshness of new grass, and at a distance the loveliness of high hanging banks of green leaves, held by the silence that follows bird-singing. But the greenery came as it were only on a wave, and faded again into the air, and the air faded until only a condition of rest was left, of infinite quietism, where even the inner ear no longer listened. And all this was suspended like a round globe, buoyed up by some

profound knowledge of himself that had come out of this
morning . . . this morning, and in a hollow of the morning
she was lying.

He lifted a slate pencil and began drawing a face on
the smooth stone board. He discarded the pencil, and
restlessly handled some small unfinished carvings. He put
all these from him and stood at mid floor. His face was
fine and worn, the eyes large with a hot weariness in them.
Whenever he moved there was an exhausting anxiety in
his breast like something that would not dissolve or was
dissolving in warm flushings. He was afraid he would be
told to do something that would prevent his return to the
moor. That was what the anxiety was, and all at once he
walked quietly out at the door.

The Master and Gilbrude and Fael stood at a little
distance, and Fael was talking excitedly. Two faces were
watching them from the trees. As Aniel drifted past, he
obeyed the Master's look and approached. Fael's story
was that the Logenmen had attacked the shielings. The
night before there had been merriment and dancing, and
many had lain down to sleep in the long enclosure where
the new-cut bog-grass was. No one believed that anything
was going to happen – and did not know of the enemy's
approach until the dogs woke them, when it was mostly
too late. Many had been killed, and the cattle and sheep
were even now being driven across country to the land of
the Logenmen. Fael was only a year older than Aniel, and
what he had seen had excited him very much. Every now
and then, indeed, his eyes glinted with some special horror,
but what it was he kept to himself.

The Master's face held a weary sadness. Clearly the
killing of so many fine men affected him with a lassitude
that made even the need for speech seem vain. Yet when
he spoke there was no trace of this in his voice, which was
clear and ordered.

'The Ravens have now to gather to the defence of their
stronghold and save those who are in it. Someone must
see that this is done.' He looked at Fael and then at Aniel.
Before Fael could speak, Aniel said: 'Yes, Master. Those
who fled from the shore will have gone towards the shielings

or into the forest, and those from the shielings will now be coming down. I could go over the moor and meet them. I might also go to the Finlags, who are good with arrows. I could take all that side, if Fael would take this.'

Fael readily agreed.

The Master looked at Gilbrude. 'Say what is in your mind.'

'Are we safe ourselves here?' asked Gilbrude.

'I do not know,' said the Master. 'But it would seem safer for us if the Northmen were attacked elsewhere than here. Would it not?'

'Yes,' said Gilbrude, and then stood with closed mouth and eyebrows lowering over his eyes. He had something further to say.

'Go you,' said the Master to Fael and Aniel.

As Aniel walked away he wished he could have assured the Master that there was nothing in the world he would not do for his safety and the safety of the Grove.

This bred a feeling in him that he was leaving the Grove for good. It was like a dark home, and now he was walking away from it to the light of open days. His very excitement at seeing Breeta in a few minutes was part of this removal, part of its certainty. Already its hold was loosening; already he loved it, had no feeling against even the memory tests which had always irked him. It was a magical circle where those who acquired curious knowledge were not troubled by friends and relations. More than that, the friends and relations looked upon the Grove and its inhabitants with awe. Their exaggerated belief in black mystery and fearful hidden transactions with the gods was something to smile at. Gilbrude encouraged their belief, for he was cunning and fierce. In a way, too, he believed so fiercely himself that occasionally to that which one had done many times would all at once be added an emotion that made the skin creep. Often, too, on a dark night, there were mysterious sounds not only in Gilbrude's own cell but in the open space in the Grove, and more particularly at the place of sacrifice within the Stones. Demons, gods, sacrifices. Gathering new herbs with the Master, as the leaves were bursting from the trees, made one strong against demons.

And one could always stay them, even mislead them, and a charm or rune from the Master was infallible.

It had been a good place, where now and then in his drawing and carving he had known a loneliness of delight that was intimate and sweet, like the scent of a flower, and all that the scent meant, inhaled slowly. There had been a secrecy about that, stirring hidden emotions, and the cool softness of the flower would be on the mouth. Sometimes, too, one got into such a state of remoteness that the most curious shapes came up under the hands. Once he had shown a drawing of an evil spirit to Fael, who had cried out suddenly. The more he had daringly drawn spirits of that sort, the less he had feared them. And one day in an awful secrecy he had tried to draw the Sungod. That had been wrong. He had trembled with fear and had washed it out with haste. But the temptation remained.

Gilbrude had been against all this but the Master was for it. And after the Master had talked long with Gilbrude, Gilbrude said nothing. Aniel imagined that the Master had said to Gilbrude that work of this kind would be a new and terrifying manifestation. That would have been quite enough for Gilbrude. But the Master loved to see things drawn well for their own sake. The most exciting experience had been the learning how to produce different dyes. There were many women in the glens who could make dyes, and one man who could tattoo them on the body. Tattooing was a secret craft. There was a process of initiation, and pride in the visible attainment of manhood.

Now all that was well enough, but a trifle ancient for Aniel, who wanted the dyes as colours for his own use. The endless verses he had to learn got muddled; but his colours became ever more bright, especially one luminous yellow. Over against it he had produced a lovely purple from the dog-whelk.

Then had come that amazing secret time of walking with the Sungod. It had drawn him dawn after dawn from the Grove. Never had he so profoundly believed in his religion, never had he known such ecstasy. He walked with his body cleansed to the coolness of flower-stalks, and at first with the unaspiring quietude of the flower-head, sensitive to the wind, easily set ashiver. But more and more without this humility, flashing now with the sun's arrows and, before he knew what he was doing, hunting at last with the god himself, until he came to know the god's perfect body and swift features and sunbright hair and skin.

One early morning when he had crossed the moor to see how his god moved about the sleeping houses, he had come on a scraped skin pinned to a door. Its grey surface attracted him like a witch-face. It would take paint. Quietly he stole to the door and removed the skin, and where it had been he drew the outline of a half-sun above the horizon.

While he worked in secret on the skin, the wildest talk ran through the glen, for that one should steal from another was so unusual that it dropped out of mind, while in any case the proof of an unearthly visitation was in the awful symbol on the door; until at last Garam, the owner of the skin, was affected and could not sleep, and so contact had to be arranged with the Grove.

Aniel knew nothing of this, though he had sometimes chuckled to himself at the thought of Garam's amazement. Probably he would think he had been visited by the chief of the devils! Then one quiet evening, while he was absorbed in his painting, the door behind him darkened, and the Master was standing there.

The Master had that sudden appearance of a god himself. Aniel began to tremble, the enormity of what he had been trying to do rushing down upon him. The Sungod's face in profile, the sun yellow, the kingly purple in a wind wave, but all with a stiffness that would not break to the life of the hunting god whom he knew, until in the end the stiffness itself had gathered a certain terror, not without its awful attraction.

'There was a skin', said the Master, 'stolen from one Garam who, because he thinks he was visited by a demon, has nearly gone out of his mind. They brought him to me last night.'

Aniel's head drooped.

'There is one god whom we worship as the giver of life.' There was an austerity in the tone that condemned utterly. The Master might encourage drawings and certain religious symbols had to be cut on stones, but between these aids and usages and the effort at incarnating the Sungod himself was the gulf between true worship and idolatry. There was finally something native to the Master that found itself in pure thought or perfect communion rather than in material images. At that moment Aniel knew how much the Master also loved the Sungod.

He tore down the skin and with his knife began scraping it. He worked feverishly. When he looked up again the Master was gone.

AS ANIEL now went his way from the Grove, the feeling that he was leaving it for good strengthened in him. He turned near the moor crest and looked back. The foliaged trees were dark, and he saw one small figure move away from the Stones. Something stirred profoundly in his heart and he went over the crest and came where he had left Breeta and found her sleeping.

As he looked down at her, a small smile warmed his face, and his eyelids flickered in an odd calculating way as if he wondered how he might wake her. Her head was tilted back a little, drawing taut the clear line of throat and chin, and her mouth was open sufficiently to show the tips of her upper teeth and to let her breath thresh easily. The skin of her face was smooth and her lashes lay dark on her cheeks. It was all at once very like a child's face and utterly defenceless. Its defencelessness could rouse pity. This aspect of her face he had never seen before and even as it made him awkward it touched him with a strange elation. His eyes ran along her body and along her bare legs to her peat-stained feet. Her toes were mute, those on the under foot being turned away from him.

He came back to her face, his own expression grown deeper and more concentrated. Very quietly he got down and touched her, leaf to leaf. She quivered and her eyes flashed open, her head and breast in the same instant jerking back with a startled cry. She had violently pushed him from her, before she realised where she was and who this was. Then in another flash her eyes lost their fear and

she said 'Oh' on a half-shy note that was half a moan, and
her lashes fell and she held to him. It took him a little while
to still her tumult, and during that time he repeated softly,
as though it was the greatest joke, 'Did I frighten you?' He
caressed her shoulders. 'I didn't really frighten you?' He
drew her closer and their love grew warm and hot.

When they were at last sitting together, he said to her:
'Breeta, I have got to go quickly and find the men to defend
the Tower.' He told her all that had happened at the shore
and at the shielings. She looked at his face; it was open and
friendly. It was a comradely face and there was nothing
hidden in it. She turned her eyes away because it affected
her so much.

'Do you know what happened to my father?' she asked.

'No,' he said. 'It was difficult to make out single ones.
I saw that Drust and Morbet were killed and—'

As he stopped she looked at him. He did not want to
mention the death of his father – lest it interfere with their
happiness. This, he saw, was mean and treacherous, and
with a crinkling of his brows he added, 'and Taran my
father.'

Her breath drew in sharply. He faced her and saw the fall
of her hands between them. The look in her eyes absolved
him. They saw each other for a moment. The shy restraint
that held her, he loved. He showed this and then turned
away, 'Come on.'

They went inland over the crest of the moor until the
lower reaches of the glen were shut out and the flat hollow
of the shielings was not yet visible. There they were in an
empty world. They had not spoken since they started, and
Aniel now drew up and, looking about him, sank slowly to
the ground.

'What is it?' she asked.

'Feel that,' he said, putting his hand on his stomach. She
looked concerned. 'Do you feel anything?'

'No,' she answered.

'I thought not,' he said, with a sad air.

'What . . .?'

'There's nothing.' He shook his head. 'I'm so hungry.'

She looked – and laughed.

'How are you?' he asked.

She felt herself. He felt her, too, and nodded. 'Same thing.'

She was overcome with mirth.

'It's no laughing matter,' he said. 'I've eaten nothing since bread and water at noon yesterday.'

She looked about her as though she might conjure bread out of the moor.

'Now,' he said in the same odd fashion, 'we take a bee's line that way. Clearly none are coming towards the Grove. Both sides would avoid it, they fear us so much. Are you frightened of me, Breeta?'

'Yes,' she replied.

'What are you frightened of?'

'You.'

'Breeta.'

'Yes.'

'Say, Yes, Aniel.'

'Yes, Aniel.' It was the first time she had used his name, and colour touched her cheeks. Her glance had an avoiding sparkle.

'This is the most serious and terrible thing that has ever happened to us. The men we knew are dead; the young men like Balla and Bronach and Leu. That has been at the back of my mind all the time.'

'Yes,' she murmured.

He looked at her.

'Yes, Aniel,' she said bravely.

'There's nothing I can do. I'm not a leader. This morning has been very sweet. If I have lost time – we could not help it. But now – I'll have to do what I can. Do you feel that we have spent too much time on ourselves?'

'Yes,' she said.

He looked at her. But she had spoken in a low voice and would not repeat his name.

'When we get down to the glen, we may have to separate. That's what I had to say. You understand?'

She looked at him. 'Yes – Aniel.'

'You lovely one,' he said, and got to his feet.

They went quickly. Once he stumbled and she caught

his hand. 'It's the hunger,' he smiled. He held on to her hand, and this made them feel like children, so that sometimes they laughed and swung each other. The tragedy of the morning was behind their least action and made it pleasant and irresponsible. They began at last, however, to hear their laughter like the excitement that rises from a tremulous terror. And that made their mutual feeling sharp as pain. Once a spasm of emotion towards her companion so overcame Breeta that she weakened and stumbled. She picked herself up. 'It's the hunger,' she smiled. He looked at her. Through the dazed light on her face her whole being cried to him, and they embraced wildly, her voice repeating his name over and over. After that they went on without speaking until they came to the glen path.

'There's someone coming,' he said; and presently round the trees a man appeared, naked to the waist, blood down cheek and shoulder. He pulled up, eyeing Aniel, then came on, with the quick fugitive air of one who has seen and done desperate things.

'How many of you got away?' Aniel asked.

'A few.'

'Tell me.'

The man looked at Aniel, his eyes feverishly bright, and asked: 'What's happened?'

Aniel told him of the shore fight, the dead, and the Tower besieged. 'We need everyone we can get.'

The man looked questioningly.

'To fight the Northmen at the Tower,' explained Aniel.

'How many Northmen?'

'Fifty, maybe.'

The man laughed and looked past Aniel, who suddenly remembered Breeta. When he turned round there was no one to be seen. She had vanished. The man was now edging past him.

'Where are you going?'

'Home.'

'What for?'

'Things.'

'But we must get together. We must save the Tower.'

'Yes,' said the man. And then he turned round and ran on. It was his single gust of terrible laughter that left Aniel standing still.

Presently three more appeared. Aniel stopped them and again asked for tidings; then told them his news.

'Quick, boys,' said one of them, 'we must save all we can,' and they rushed on.

Aniel saw the logic of this, which was less awful than the first man's laugh. Those who had escaped were going to make sure of themselves, and gather what they could towards that end. To defend the Tower was impossible. It was everyone for himself now. A few broken men and the women and children, hiding in the forest, hunting and killing, until the danger was past. The fierceness in the man's laugh had been the fierceness of the beast, with cunning added. Aniel saw that his own attitude to the Tower was the gentle one of the student. It withered in this primal fierceness. The Tower and all inside it were doomed.

There came at times an odd quality of detachment to Aniel's emotions. It was the mind working behind the emotions, as it did when he was drawing images conceived in emotional heat. He saw now quite clearly that the Tower was doomed. The man's laugh was right. Its harsh sarcasm was the note of a profound instinctive knowing. Very well. His skin ran cool, his mouth closed, and the sharpness of the hawk caught his features. It was a youthful pride, but it was fierce, too, and intolerant. He went towards the shielings and presently came on a man named Sharag who had been a friend of Aniel's own father. He was sitting by the stream and was weak from loss of blood. Aniel washed the wound and made a pad of moss for it, and bound it with a strip of cloth. As he did this, Sharag told him all that had happened. There had been a shambles in the cattle enclosure of young men and women sleeping off the dance. He named some of the young men. One of them was Breeta's elder brother. Sharag was affected very much and spoke in a gasping way – partly from weakness, and partly from the memory that left his eyes staring. There were grey hairs in his black beard, and his head was matted from a shallow cut. He had heard of the defeat on the shore, and of the death of Drust. But he had not heard of the death of Aniel's father, Taran.

He looked at Aniel almost wonderingly. 'Do you tell me that?' There was a great simplicity in the man, for he was physically strong and his nature was kind. He removed his eyes only when he began to think of Aniel's loss.

'What's to be done now?' asked Aniel.

'Gather all the things we can – what else? . . . When I saw what was happening, I ran from the shielings and sent our dogs to drive the beasts into the forest. That's what drove the Logenmen from the killing and why so many of us live. They headed off most of the beasts for they had their own dogs, and our dogs left the beasts to fight them. It was a battle of the dogs. The moor became a place of terrible roaring fights. The Logenmen went mad, shouting at the dogs and lashing them. But those on horseback rounded up the beasts, though many by this time had gone into the forest. Then in the mad noise the beasts began running this way and that, and at last straight over the moor northward. The Logenmen rode after them and with a dog or two turned them. By this time they were thinking only of the cattle and the sheep, and when at last they had got the beasts going in their own direction they followed them.'

Aniel saw the picture and heard the tumult. 'How did you get your own wound?' he asked.

'I got it from one of two Logenmen,' said Sharag. 'I killed one with the other finally.'

Aniel quickened. 'What's to be done now?' he asked again.

'Some have gone to find the beasts in the forest, and some are down here to save what they can from the Northmen. Before night, all who can will meet at the first trysting-place in the forest and settle there what's to be done.'

'What of those in the Tower?' Aniel asked.

Sharag sat looking before him, stone-eyed.

'We cannot leave them there to be killed,' Aniel urged. 'How many Northmen?'

'Two score, perhaps,' answered Aniel.

Sharag said in a monotonous voice, 'Drust is dead, and Morbet, and Taran your father.'

'But what of Silis?'

'Her chief is dead,' said Sharag. The great wives of story sacrificed themselves over the bodies of their chiefs. His tone was fatal.

'We won't do anything now,' said Aniel; 'I see that. But tonight, when we see how we stand, surely we'll try something. We can hardly let them die there.' His eagerness of tone caught an edge. This attitude of Sharag's touched something hostile in him. He rebelled against it. Sharag said nothing. 'I'm going,' said Aniel.

Sharag's eyes turned at last.

'I'm going to the Finlags – to get help there. I may bring some of them to the meeting-place tonight.'

Sharag appeared not to understand.

'The Master', said Aniel almost coldly, 'told me that was what I had to do. So you can expect me. Don't let the pad slip.' Then he went down into the stream and crossed it.

As he began to climb up through the trees on the opposing slope he changed his course, swinging leftwards along the face and coming finally towards a rounded tree-clad eminence which commanded a lower reach of the glen, with the Tower above the stream.

Many a time the defences of the old fort had been discussed. Against any band of ordinary marauders it had proved itself in living history, but against trained warriors like the Northmen, with time to set about reducing it and no one molesting them, could it stand? There were legends of unsuccessful sieges lasting many days. But this enemy was as no other, and Aniel's curiosity became acute.

When at last he came in sight of it he thought the worst had happened, for smoke drifted over and around it. But the more he looked the better he saw that the circular fort itself was still intact, though the enclosure was in ruins. Drust's hall was gone. Smoke was drifting from where it had stood. Clearly, too, stacks of wood had been thrust against the doorway of the fort, for a cloudy column rose there. The enclosure wall had been breached in two places and the old gateway was completely gone.

He could see Northmen moving about, and he could see movement on the Tower wall. An anxious pride beset him. He remembered Silis and Talorg and Erp of the one hand; and Goan the smith, you could rely on it, had got inside at the last moment, and with Lys would be hurling boulders on the heads of any who dared approach the one small door. Nessa's face and hair gleamed a golden note in the smoke, as though the smoke drifted in his own mind. And in the same moment he thought to himself, Have they arrows? And he decided that they might have had a few – but not many. How foolish! With arrows they would not only never be taken but they would kill the enemy. Arrows made him think of the Finlags. His body got the shiver of inspiration. A group of the Finlags, crawling up through the trees, and then discharging a volley of their sharp flint-tipped arrows! Those beautiful deadly 'fairy' arrows!

But arrows were not for war, they were for animals. What warrior ever went to his rest with arrows? He could understand the pride, but how foolish here and now! What did it matter *how* you killed them *now*? With the women there, and the leaders dead, kill them in any fashion. Kill them for killing's sake – they deserve it – gods of our people! A love of his own people and of this their place came upon him with an intensity he had never before known.

He saw the Northmen gather in a dark mass. They were holding council. He waited, and presently most of them broke away, some walking quickly up the stream, others disappearing towards the Little Glen, while those who remained spread themselves about the fort.

The meaning of this manoeuvre was immediately clear to Aniel, as though he had heard them say, 'We cannot take this place without time; so let us gather what we can before the stuff disappears.' They needed fresh food and grain and animals. The women would be clearing the stuff away. Women. Slaves. Gold. Everything. Some of the Northmen broke into a trot. They had been held up overlong.

Aniel remembered the shieling men he had met. They would be caught! Running, stumbling, falling, he made back to where he had left Sharag. The bitter logic of the defeated came home to him at last.

With the exception of the man who had laughed, those
he had previously met, and several others, were with Sharag
when he broke across the stream. They were resting by their
burdens. 'The Northmen are coming up the glen, running,'
he panted. 'Get over the stream and make straight for the
forest. Quick!'

They immediately became active, casting glances down
the path, and, reshouldering their gear, crossed the stream.

Then Aniel remembered Breeta.

'Come on with us,' cried Sharag, looking back at him
standing in so strange a way.

Aniel started down the glen. The stealthy movement of
his figure affected them oddly, as though its action towards
the enemy carried mysterious power.

Aniel kept within the trees above the path. There was
no movement about the first little cluster of houses. Nor
about the second. But he could hear cries now from round
the next bend. He climbed higher, and in a little while
saw at least a dozen Northmen about the Eesg village.
Beyond, smoke rose out of the trees. That was Breeta's
home on fire.

A high witchlike screeching ascended from the Eesg
settlement. Several bedridden persons were there. The
women and children must have been cleared out by the
early fugitives from the shore. All at once a grown girl ran
amok screaming in a frenzied way. She was the half-daft
one who would never be separated from her grandmother.
It was said that once, when she had been drinking at a
well, a serpent had got into her belly, because ever since
she was always drinking. Aniel watched the Northmen
deal with her. As a prize she was obviously anyone's
joke. Their shouts, full of a coarse good humour, were
suddenly increased after one of them had been bitten by
the girl.

Aniel turned away, climbing still higher. Wherever Breeta
was, she could not be in that glen now – unless they had
already got her. There remained the moor. He was so
preoccupied that he all but ran into two Northmen.

Indeed for a moment he glared at them, and only when
they came at him did he break back. As his excitement

mounted, his exhaustion increased but in a way that somehow made him run more nimbly, slipping round trees, falling, rolling, his heart pumping painfully, a sickening tremble in the flesh above his knees. His knowledge of the wood helped him, and breaking at last on to a path he slanted down for the stream at full speed.

As he came out on the flat one or two Northmen, already prospecting beyond the Eesg village, saw him and tried to head him off, while the two behind shouted their encouragement. His trembling weakness now was such that he could hardly feel the ground skimming under his toes. It was marvellous to him even as he ran that he did not pitch headlong. He had only to go crashing by the shoulder and that was the end of him. He could feel the crash coming – but he had first to gain the stepping-stones. And he gained them and took them in a mad flawless run. As he went gasping beyond the bank, he was aware of his luck, for the last three stones had been blurred by eye-film.

The Northman behind him had overstepped himself and smashed his shoulder in a pitch to the stones. The others helped him out. Looking over his shoulder as he gained the trees, Aniel saw one of them spring to the bank.

Hope came into Aniel's heart. If only he could keep going! He tore at the steep hillside, pulling himself up, gasping, not listening. But strive as he liked, all his movements slowed down. On the first fall back of the ground he stopped, and through the harsh tearing of his breath heard the movement of a climbing body.

But he could not go farther, he could not move another step. He drew his knife. The concentration of his instincts narrowed his brows, made his eyes glisten. The cat-student. He might have satisfied even Gilbrude at the moment as an evocation of the Grove, of its darker spirit, hunted but fierce, and at last ready to slash back.

The footsteps came on, not – as he had thought – from below, but rather towards his left, and, as he waited, Breeta emerged and stood before him.

He gazed at her. His eyes ran slowly all over her, legs, skirt, breast, throat, the face taut in its gaze back, rather a fierce lynxlike child's face, with a deep fire, however, in the black eyes. The fire watched him. He smiled to it, sank slowly down, and lay back at full stretch.

He was not unconscious, and he enjoyed the feeling of his body ebbing from him, but particularly he gave in to the luxury of her nursing, which was gentle in a wild way as if she were imploring him or had discovered something not precious so much as passionately desired. He closed his eyes, aware the action was more than half a trick, for at first she did not quite know how to handle him but now she lay alongside him, and made queer panting sounds, and pushed the hair from his forehead, and set her hands to his face, and caught him, burying her mouth in his breast where his name was smothered in a heat he felt.

His weakness spread. It flushed hot to his eyes. In a moment there was the sting of tears. But they were not tears for his own life: they were tears for death, for all that had happened, for the dead. He huddled down, so that his head came below hers and he hid it, his chin catching in her dress and pressing it down. Her breast rose and fell against his mouth and nostrils. She grew suddenly quiet for she felt the wet sting at her heart. He grew still also, and in a very short time she perceived that he was fast asleep.

For a little, her hearing grew extremely acute, and once, when the Northmen on the other side of the river set up a sudden halloo, she drew him to her as if he were a child. Her face, too, though fearful, was strengthened in cunning. She glanced and listened and looked at his head and loved his warm mouth. But it was all unsafe. And safety she must have now.

She loosened her hold very gently and covered her breast. His head fell away, the mouth open. 'Aniel!' she whispered. But there was no response. For a moment she looked strongly at the face with its rather delicate pale-brown skin, its fine features, with something of nobility in the forehead, of that taste which she always feared. His hair, which she had pushed back, was dark and thick and rumpled, clearly hair used to the comb. She could hardly believe her fortune. The trees played in the wind. Her eyes were drawn up one tree and transfixed by two eyes staring down. Tufted ears, bearded chin, and the face of a cat, with the black-spotted yard-long body crouching in a fork. Breeta's face became tense and expressionless as the face of the lynx. Her whole body tautened and crouched. Her lips met and parted in a flash of teeth as she spat at the brute. Their eyes held a moment longer, and then the lynx withdrew.

There came a noise now of stones rumbling in the stream, and somewhere along in the wood a distinct heavy trampling. She whispered in his ear, she shook him, and finally shook him strongly. 'Leave me,' he muttered petulantly, his eyes shut. She persevered. 'Don't care!' he muttered. She was distressed by the time he came to his senses, and even then he wandered away with her half asleep. She supported him with one arm, and in the other carried a small parcel. 'Do here,' he mumbled. But she kept him going, persuading him like a child. He leaned heavily on her and did not look at her. When at last she was leading him into a thicket, he resisted, saying, 'To the Finlags,' and held upward, walking as though in his sleep. They came to a tumbling trickle of water, and got down on all fours and drank. They looked at each other with the water dripping from their hair and noses, and leant over and met – and drew back.

'I could sleep for a million years,' he said.

She smiled and got up.

He remained on all fours gazing at the water, then slid over.

'But whether it's sleep or the weakness of hunger, I don't know.'

'Are you hungry?' she asked.

'I'm so hungry', he said, 'that I don't know.'

There was an amusing seriousness in his voice that she saw was meant to hide his real weakness. He was far more awake, too, than he pretended to be. She produced her small parcel, which was a straw packet containing hard cakes of bread stuck together by a great thickness of soft cheese. She handed him the bread. He looked at it and looked at the thickness of soft cheese. He took it and bit off a mouthful. The water had prepared his mouth, and when the bread got chewed up, with the cheese amongst it, the whole had a caressing divine flavour.

'You left me to get this,' he mumbled, not looking at her. 'It's very good.'

'Col took down the cheese the other day; it's fresh,' she said, and kept her smile to herself, for she saw that he was awkward before her – for the first time.

'You should have told me you were going,' he said, and then took another mouthful.

'I hadn't time.'

'Did you see what nearly happened to me?'

'I did. I was hunting for you on this side – and then saw them running after you.'

'It was no smiling matter.'

'No,' she said.

He glanced at her sharply.

'No, Aniel.'

He tore away another hunk. 'The truth is,' he said thickly, 'when I saw the Northmen coming I went back over yonder and hunted for you. If I had slipped when I was running, you would have been the cause of my death. So I accept your bread.'

'You are very kind to me,' she said humbly.

That made him worse than ever. Under his awkwardness her mind was light and quick. It was a very gay feeling, because he had nearly always made her dumb.

'Won't you eat yourself?' he asked.

'I'm not hungry.'

'Why?'

'I'm just not hungry.'

'Eat that.'

'I can't.'

'Eat it.' He frowned.

She meekly took the piece of bread. She certainly needed food, but she couldn't eat. There was an odd excitement in her throat that went against food. She broke off a piece of bread and began slowly chewing it. He was now wolfing his bannock, the jaws working in a way that made the muscles tired so that he had to rest them now and then. His whole attitude was very matter-of-fact. But she knew, too, that while it was real it was also overdone – in the nature of an elaborate game. He was making up for his escape, his weakness, his tears, his sleep. He would probably like to snap at her! Her own meekness was an even more elaborate deceit. She loved it. But he caught her smiling.

'What are you smiling at?'

She appeared embarrassed.

'Tell me. What are you smiling at?' His tone was hard, and somehow, in spite of herself, even though she knew it meant nothing, it hurt her. She wasn't smiling at anything.

'Weren't you?' he said elaborately.

'No.'

He did not look at her. He rested his jaws and then went and drank. 'That's good bread,' he said, sitting down to it again.

She felt miserable, almost near tears, all in a moment! She was tired, that was the truth. He was unkind. It was madness to feel like this. He would despise her. Just when she had felt equal to him, too, within understanding distance of that taste! Her eyes filled. She quietly turned her head away and began plucking the dry moss idly. But she heard the movement of his head towards her.

'Breeta.'

She could not face him.

He gave a small chuckle of understanding. It humiliated her. He ate noisily.

Presently she heard something coming towards them with the crushing movement of a wounded animal, but she could not turn to Aniel. Nor did he speak to her though he was now dead still. Like that they waited, until a dark head thrust through the leaves on the other side of the watercourse. The body lay spent, the head fixed on the water. Then the head lifted, exposing a face that suddenly saw and held them. It was the face of Leu.

For a moment the face had a hypnotic power, not so much because of its drawn pale expression, that gave it a ghostliness of agony, as of the eyes that directed upon them a dark intensity wherein recognition narrowed to tiny points of light.

Aniel called his name and in no time was beside him.

Leu was wounded. He wanted to drink. Aniel said he

must see the wound, but Leu said abruptly he wanted to drink. He called sharply through clenched teeth when Aniel lifted him and set him to the water. He drank slowly. 'That will do,' said Aniel, lifting his head away. Leu protested, but Aniel now was firm. There were three flesh wounds, none of them fatally deep. Obviously a lot of blood had been lost, and there was an increasing throbbing pain shooting to the fork of the leg. Aniel had a fair knowledge of herbs for cuts, and now he told Leu to lie at ease until he gathered something that would clean and stop the wounds. When he returned, Breeta and Leu were talking together. He washed and padded and bound the wounds. 'Is that easier?' It certainly was cooler. Leu smiled.

'Eat some of this,' said Aniel.

'In a little,' said Leu, and dominated them with the knowledge in his eyes. It was clear that he could not be moved from there.

'I'll tell you what I was going to do,' said Aniel, speaking more than he meant to. 'I was going to the Finlags. I was going to get a band of them to come with me to the first trysting-place in the forest where all are to gather tonight. Somehow we must relieve the Tower. Let me see. If I go now, I could send help back for you or – or I could come back myself. You see –'

'Send help back,' said Leu. 'We'll be all right. You must get them together – if you're going to do anything.' It sounded a slow goodnatured speech. Aniel, nearly flushing, nodded quickly.

'Right,' he said briskly. 'But I'll see.' He did not look at Breeta. 'I'd better go at once.'

'Do,' said Leu. 'And send little old Poison if you can.'

Aniel looked at him. Leu's lips parted. 'Tell him I've got my music pipe. I lost a lot of pith going for it.' Then his lips met in a twinge of pain. 'All right.' Sweat stood on his forehead.

Aniel got up. 'It's a long journey, but I'll do my best.' And with that he started off.

Leu had made him feel extraordinarily awkward. Hardly ever had a human being done that to him before. Leu was so sure of himself, with his veiled infernal knowledge. What

did it mean? That he had seen Breeta and himself together
and wanted to imply something? Perhaps. But that was
not what gave Leu his assurance. Leu was a sensitive and
often a timid fellow. But he was now like a man who held
death's secret.

Aniel went hurriedly, so that he had not too much time
for thought. Soon he did not think at all, though his mind,
after its kind, was surprised every now and then at its game
of picture-making. The only two people in the picture were
Breeta and Leu. His mind, for example, would conjure
the picture of himself lying back and Breeta nursing him.
But when his mind lost that conscious picture and began
picture-making on its own, he would suddenly observe that
the man whom Breeta was nursing was Leu. And she did
it in the same way. Leu's pain, for example, increased.
He would cry out with it. Breeta's concern for him would
redouble. Leu would hang on to her in his pain. Aniel
grew hot.

Aniel remembered that strange night on the moor when
she had clung to him, calling, 'Leu!'

He set himself to a trot, for the food had filled the empty
hollow of weakness, and in the afternoon came in sight of
the Finlag settlement.

In a shallow upland clearing were a colony of round
green mounds, some of them stuck together. From the
wood behind a youth might race and jump on top of
them. From that wood Leu had said he had often listened
to music coming from the green mounds. As Aniel stood
silent, gazing at the strange scene, an old black dog came
barking towards him. At that a head popped up out of a
green roof, whistled the dog, and popped down again. It
was a startling apparition, but Aniel felt at once that it
meant his coming had been advised. The mounds were
withdrawn from him and watchful and ominous. The old
dog continued to bark. Some pups came tumbling forth.
These were the black dogs that the glen dogs hated, and
killed when they could. Bardan came out of a little door
in the side of a mound without his headgear, so apparently
great was his astonishment.

Bardan's welcome was ingratiating and his dark eyes

were everywhere. He never ceased chattering as he drew Aniel to his house. They entered through the little door to a chamber whose floor was below the level of the ground. At first the light was dim, and it took Aniel a little time to make out the body of a small stout old woman whose dark eyes were watching him closely. Bardan addressed her in a quick way that Aniel could not follow. The words indeed were the old words of which he knew only a few – the few they had learned as boys, and might still use when referring to certain parts and acts of the body. Its old-fashioned rich mirth was lost on Aniel today. Indeed it was with a queer sense of shock he realised that here was a tongue folk used solemnly and courteously.

The old lady handed him a small wooden bowl of milk and a piece of dark bread. Her manner was free, and yet had a certain timid kindness. When the light from the roof opening struck her face, it showed pale, even slightly yellow, and very broad. Her nose looked as if it had been flattened, and her eyes were beady bright. She had gold rings in her ears and on her fingers, which bore out what many said, namely, that the little folk were better workers of gold and silver than of cloth, and had their hordes hidden under trees on which they had put a spell. This spell was enough to change into another shape any human being who disturbed it. Once, from behind her back, two child eyes flashed at Aniel like the terror-timid eyes of a fawn.

The milk had the sweet richness of deer's milk – the deer which only the black dogs could round up.

Bardan went on talking to his guest about anything and everything except the thing that mattered, so that it was with a dazed effort that Aniel said at last: 'Have you heard of the great battle on the beach?'

'What battle was that?'

'The Northmen landed early this morning and defeated us. Drust is dead and Morbet, and nearly all the men.'

'Are you telling me that?' cried Bardan in an appalled whisper. The woman made a curious sound in her nostrils and her body rocked quietly.

'Didn't you hear?'

'How could we hear? Who was to tell us? Some are in

the gold strath for Drust – ah, that he is no more! ah-h! –
some are at the summer grazings, many are with the arrows,
hunting. Drust, you say, and Morbet? Ah! And all the large
men of the Great Glen! Didn't I know them? Didn't I go
among them? Wouldn't they cry, "Here's Bardan – let us
get him to make a poem?" And the little boys? Tell me,
what's happened to the children?'

'Some of them were killed, but—'

'My sorrow, is it that way? The little ones who would be
saying to Bardan, "Make a poem on that tree," or ah-ah
– it is hard to believe, the wicked strange people there
are on the top of the world. My dear, is it not the hard
thing to believe that the little ones are no more? Never
again shall I go down the glen with my little birch bowls
and my whistles and my knick-knacks. And sometimes
they would have great stones of flint for me which they
would pick up on the seashore, and they would say, "I'll
give you all this flint for one elf arrow." For they liked
the little arrows better than anything I had. And I would
point out to them that the arrow was small and sharp so
that it would go in between the bristles, and in between
the bone-joints, and when the word was said on it, that
then it always found the heart even though it was aimed
at the tail. Ah-ah, to think of it. . . .'

And while Bardan went on, the little old woman rocked
gently, appeared not to look at Aniel, and when he had
finished the bread and milk she offered him more.

Aniel thanked her and said he would take no more. He
remained standing. 'I have come here', he said, 'to get some
of your men to go with me to the first trysting-place in the
forest tonight.'

In the little house he was an upright spear. Bardan's
mouth fell slowly open. 'What would that be for?'

'Because the Northmen have landed, because they will
destroy this country and all of us and you, and we must
meet to see what is to be done.'

'But – but they're away from home. Some of them may
be in tomorrow. I'll tell them when they come. Where
exactly did you say they must go?'

'Tomorrow will be too late. They must come tonight.'

'But who said this? Who ordered – who—?' groped Bardan, with courteous confusion.

Aniel spoke quietly. 'I am Aniel, the son of Taran the bard, who was killed fighting this morning.'

'Killed, you say? Taran!' Bardan's whisper lifted to an intoned grief. It affected Aniel; Bardan said such cunningly fine things about Taran. Aniel was not deceived, and yet he was moved nearly to tears. These little people had a curious sort of minor music that could draw sighs from trees. It was the music the women of the glen sometimes sang to their children in the gloaming. When a man would listen to this music, he would have the feeling of a child pressing against his breast, pressing it into his heart, or he could feel how a woman would have her breasts drawn wrinkling into her heart from the music and the pressure put on her arms. But that would be only in the early part of the listening. When that first feeling was at its height, the music would suddenly be clear and fine as light on still trees at a distance. It would have the sound of wind in trees, too, when the trees listen to themselves in the pale light of no sun. It would recede into the forest and come upon grey-green glades where the head is bowed and no one is near, no one and nothing, save the invisible whose pointed ears are alert, but whose footfall is quieter than the drift of sleep, until there would be no feeling left at all – only listening. Nor would the mind even dream of the Pleasant Plain, or if it did would shrink from it in order to keep its own intimacy, to be withdrawn in delight of the treasure that was now round the heart. For there is a secret here that neither the lovely dead nor the swift gods know. It is the immortality of life, the young heart against the mother heart, and its music sets a man brooding or walking in defiance, and the memory of it can in a lonely place make him shout with defiance and laugh, for he knows the challenge of his own creation against the immortality of the jealous gods.

The mind of the Finlags had this cunning, and it carried through their music to the work of their hands and to their spoken words. The big people thought them deceitful, and at times despised them with a certain amount of fear. Aniel was sure that Bardan had heard of the fight, that the Finlags would accordingly have driven off their beasts, and would now be beyond finding. Yet, knowing all that, he was deeply moved by Bardan's grief for the death of Taran his father. And when the little old woman uttered every now and then her low half-choked cry, it became unbearable.

'Will none of you come with me?' he cried.

'Who can?' intoned Bardan. 'Only the old are left and the children.'

'Can't I go for them?'

'But where? But where? And what use would they be against the great Northmen?'

'So you refuse?' said Aniel, looking at neither of them, but with a quiver in his throat – a quiver of anger.

'No, no. But how . . .?'

'I am come from the Grove.'

Bardan gazed at him.

'The Master sent me.'

Bardan broke upon humble profuse talk. He would go himself and get some of them. Yes, he would go, though it took him days.

'There will have to be a dozen at the trysting-place tonight,' said Aniel, turning away. 'That is all.'

Bardan followed him up into the daylight where Aniel remembered Leu. He told Bardan of the wounded man and his request for old Poison. But Poison was away with the cattle. Aniel regarded Bardan with the steady expression of the Master. 'Some of you will fetch the wounded man here at once and nurse him to health. If all that is not done . . .' He withdrew his gaze from Bardan and lifted it to the sky. Like that he stood some time, then walked away into the trees.

But even as he went he was conscious that he was being watched. And there was something within him, too, that made him feel he had been ineffective. He should have threatened more fiercely. How was he ever going to get the men now? And who would assist Leu – and Breeta? He would go back again and tell Bardan properly. As he swithered, a woman appeared before him. She was little and dark, and though she had come from the trees by impulse, her look was steady and grave. Her face indeed had a strange beauty. Her nose was broad, her eyes were set to a delicate slant, her cheeks were smooth and full. Her face was like a comely mask to an inner wildness or fire. She reached hardly to his shoulder and she was a woman in her prime. Aniel was dumb. She did not look at him so much as watch him. And all at once her voice startled him, 'Is Drust dead?'

'Yes,' he answered, fascinated. The mask tautened, grew so taut that the cheekbones went white and a sound escaped from the nostrils like the squeak of a mouse. At that a little boy came running out from the trees and, clinging to his mother, glared at Aniel. His hair was mouse-coloured, and his nose was not very flat at the base. All in a flash it entered Aniel's mind that this was Drust's son, and that the woman was the Black Hind with whom Drust had stayed in the forest. Before he could look at her again, she was gone. He stood for a moment, then blindly followed after her. It took him some time to catch her up and he knew he would never have caught her had it not been for the child.

She blazed back at his intrusion. Without looking at her, he said with a clear humility, his breath choking him now and then, 'Drust was killed and Morbet and Taran my father. A great number were killed. The old were burnt in their houses. And the hall of Drust is destroyed and the fort surrounded. In the end they will destroy us all. I came hoping to get some of your men to join our men and to avenge the dead. We –' He stopped, conscious of her eyes. 'Bardan says your men are days away. Tell me, can you get a few of them to come to the first tryst in the forest tonight?' And he looked at her, adding, 'The Master sent me.'

Her eyes shifted from him to the forest. He had to follow that look, and when he turned to her again she was moving away.

'There's another thing,' he said, not following her. 'Leu, the pipe-player, is lying wounded by the Oorish burn. He asked me to send Poison to him.'

She had stopped, without turning round. Now she moved on again.

'Will you send him?' he called.

She looked at him over her shoulder. The blaze had a brilliant agony. Then she ran out of sight. Listening, he caught the high intense sounds of that agony. The little boy began to whimper. The whimpering died away in the trees.

The story of Drust's forest love shook its leaves in his mind. He started walking about the settlement. Once or twice he called aloud. But even Bardan was gone now. There would be old and young hiding in the dwellings, but what good were they? The story of Drust's forest love obsessed him. There was nothing more he could do. He started back to where he had left Breeta and Leu.

The thin veils were spreading in the sky and the wind was rising. It was a long journey and his mind had in it now a high pervasive tragedy. It linked him to Breeta and to their morning on the moor, brought a strange loveliness to their relations. He no longer feared her with Leu, and yet she could be – had not the Northman very nearly had her? But his mind would see no picture beyond her fighting body. It could see that, fierce and lynxlike. She was more intense than he was, more sure, and more splendid. His admiration grew, and his picture was of Breeta and himself offering homage to that small dark woman of the Finlags and her small son. He looked at the swaying trees and at rocky outcrops, seeing them not at all and then seeing them intently, until his walking through them was a walking through himself. This maze of the mind was pierced by a far cry that pulled him up. Then he started running.

The picture he came upon was certainly arresting. Leu, shouting in a mortal agony, seemed to be attacked by one of the Finlags who hung to him, while Breeta, her clothing torn low from her breast, stood above them, slightly bent, panting in a dreadful fascination. Undiscovered, Aniel drew up within a few yards. Leu threw out his arms, then crushed the Finlag and screamed, his teeth grinding and biting, his head rolling and butting in a maddened way. It was a ferocious spectacle, and not until the Finlag got his fingers at Leu's throat did the struggle subside. But even as he looked, Aniel saw that the fingers were pressing against and not gripping the throat, while as Leu's strength ebbed there arose from the Finlag the small crooning sound of a woman suckling her baby to sleep. Finally Leu was sent entirely to sleep, his head falling over with an expression of congested exhaustion. Still humming his rhythm, the Finlag examined Leu's face, then withdrew his hands, and turned to Breeta – and saw Aniel, and immediately crouched, alert and suspicious.

'What's happened?' asked Aniel.

Swinging round, Breeta stared at him. Plainly she had been in the fight herself and had not yet collected her wits. Or was it deeper than that? for all at once she sank to the ground and buried her face, leaving nothing moving but her shoulders.

'Dead,' said the Finlag.

'How?'

'Poison.'

Instinctively Aniel put his hand to the fork of his leg. The Finlag nodded. Aniel went and looked at Leu, then turned to the Finlag who was a man past the prime of life, very hairy, with broad nostrils and quick eyes. 'How did you come here?'

'She sent me.'

'Who?'

'Her.' And he nodded back to the Finlag settlement.

'What's your name?'

'Poison,' he said, with a self-conscious expression.

Aniel gazed at him. 'You must have come quickly.'

The watchful eyes glittered.

'Let us bury him,' said Aniel thoughtfully. They found a place in a fold of the rising bank where it was not a difficult matter to break down the overhanging earth. When they had stretched Leu out, Aniel said the burial talk over him. It was the first time he had thus judged the dead, and his praise of Leu made it certain that that young warrior would miss the marshes of hell and go straight to the Pleasant Plain that is Paradise. Aniel himself was uplifted by his oration, and the power that moved in him made him glow. Leu was not only a warrior, but a musician. Out of the sounds of trees, the singing of birds, the speaking of quiet seas, the racing of light and shadow, out of the breasts of women, the fun of children, the swaying of strong men, he selected his notes and his rhythms and created new shapes all in tribute to the gods. And his shapes were so strong that they haunted the earthborn and so lovely that the gods must delight in them. Aniel had never improvised like this before. And the truth of what he said (with Breeta watching and listening) so overcame him that, though his head had been uplifted, he uplifted also his arms and spread his fingers wide to the wind-hazed blue of the evening sky.

Some of the radiance of that sky came about him as though his Sungod had hesitated behind his chariot to look back on this slim youth held to the earth only by his feet. From the fold of her body Breeta's face had lifted and, as she watched, she saw the squatting Finlag stretch over Leu and steal from him his pipe. Catching her eyes, he flashed his challenge. The wind came in a rush and all the leaves flickered and rustled, each a piece of light that broke and flew away and yet remained, gleams on the earth's body, stirring under its Master, the Sun . . . *swish-h-h*! and all the gleams were in a green flame, swept upward, poised – and flickering back to where Aniel dropped his arms and the Finlag crouched unmoving.

Without a word or look for his companions, Aniel set about breaking the lip of earth over the body. The Finlag, retiring out of sight, came back with a ramming stick (and without the pipe). When Leu was buried, Aniel turned to Breeta. She was gazing past him in a stare within which the Finlag focussed himself, scowling threateningly at her over his shoulder as he slipped noiselessly away.

Aniel's voice had the quiet clearness that follows exaltation as he sat down beside her and asked what had happened. His whole manner was simple and friendly.

She would not speak at first but he prompted her and at last she told him of Leu's increasing agony, how he rolled with pain and cried out. Clearly she had been terribly distressed, not knowing what to do. Nothing she could do was any use. Leu held on to her. He begged her to – to say to him – something. He implored her. He tried to—

She choked. Aniel said, 'I know; he wanted you to say you loved him. He knew he was dying. It would have made death pleasant – if you had said it. It would have helped him against the pain.' He paused. 'Did you say it?'

'No,' she cried, 'I couldn't,' and she flung herself on the ground, sobbing wildly, 'I couldn't,' and clawed the earth.

Aniel looked around. The Finlag was gone. Desire to recall him spired and fell. He leant over and kissed her neck.

'No, no!' she cried, and wrestled with the meaning of Leu's awful agony. Her breasts came out from the torn cloth.

The sight of her thus writhing on the ground moved his passion. He put his arm round her and drew her close. She struggled violently from him and then as violently clung to him. 'I couldn't.'

'You couldn't,' he said, soothing her. He got the smell of her hair and her skin. His body that had thinned in exaltation now grew rich and golden. But his passion did not whip itself up because of the exaltation still in him. Life grew lazy and lovely and kind. He murmured her name. He soothed and crushed and released her. Life was a flood in which the body bathed.

'We are curled here like adders on a bank,' he said at last, smiling to her evasive eyes.

He saw that she could not be quite at peace; saw, for example, that she could suddenly have stooped at his mouth and leapt away; that she had to do something; or, doing nothing, must evade him. Their bodies *were* like adders on a bank; they were like, too, the bodies of furry animals playing on a bank – going back, back into time, until there was nothing but themselves and the bank and the green leaves – tall, up under the sky – and the fanning wind. No responsibility; no dark duties; only the light, and the curled warm bodies. This ecstasy of curled warm bodies that could touch and stretch and lie over and gaze and smile . . . had not the Master once said that he could be an animal, even a tree ? This then was what he meant! Not with a woman, not for example with Breeta here! – Aniel's wrist fell limp across her breast – but the Master by himself, all by himself. An animal! At this vision of the Master, the smile gurgled into Aniel's throat.

'What are you laughing at?' she asked suspiciously.

'Listen. The Master – don't start like that – for you have no idea what he is really like. I worship him. I wish', he said lazily, 'you could worship him too.'

She moved restlessly.

'I was going to say – the Master – he can enter into human bodies before this body. He can sit down and think and think, back through this morning, last night, the day before, the moon before, the year before, years and years until he is born, and then before he is born, back through the life before that in the same way, and back beyond that. But it's very difficult. I've tried it. I can go back a good bit, but I can't get into a previous life, though often and often things have happened to me which I knew in a moment had happened to me before, sometimes in this life, but often in another life – something that couldn't have happened in this life. Have you ever felt anything like that?'

'I don't know,' she mumbled.

'Smile to me, Breeta. Let what is troubling you slip away. Never mind – anything. I know. It's all waiting to jump at me too. But – but – oh, curse it, you've destroyed it! Come on then!'

She did not move.

'You're moody,' he said. 'High time we were off . . . And I felt as if you and I had crawled out of a black stream on to a bank! I was going to have told you all about it! Come on!' She did not move. 'What's troubling you now?'

'You can go yourself,' she said.

'And what'll you do?'

She was sitting up with her head turned away, pinning the torn cloth with a piece of twig.

He suddenly laughed and attacked her, and laid her out flat. Then he tickled her until she screamed and scratched. 'Well then!' she said, watching him feel his cheek. He looked at her narrowly. She edged away. 'It was Leu's pipe,' she muttered.

'Leu's pipe!' His face opened.

'Yes,' she said; 'the Finlag stole it – while you were

sending Leu to the Pleasant Plain. He stole it – and made me frightened to speak. And now Leu is gone away without it.'

'He stole it – from the dead Leu?'

'Yes.'

Aniel grew very still. 'Why were you frightened to speak?'

'He scowled at me so.'

Aniel's expression flickered. His tongue flashed between his lips, and his breath came in a gust through his nostrils. After that he sat unmoving. She watched him until she forgot herself.

'There's nothing I can do now,' he said at last.

'I wish', she fretted, 'he had his pipe.'

'There is nothing more terrible than to steal from the dead. I suppose it was too much for Poison. Leu learned tunes from him. There may have been something between them that we know nothing of.'

'I don't trust him.'

'You mean you don't trust him – now that you think about it? Are you remembering how he put Leu to sleep?'

She glanced at him with a terrified expression as though he had surprised a thought she had hardly admitted to herself.

'It's difficult, Breeta. We can do nothing more now. Many a time I have been listening to Leu. I loved his tunes. He had such cunning fingers and every note was round as a bubble.' They sat very still. He looked at her; then he caught her hand and said gravely, 'Let us get up.' She arose with him and he led her to Leu's grave. 'Say after me, Good-bye, Leu.' '*Good-bye, Leu.*' 'We both loved you.' '*We both loved you.*' 'We wish you well.' '*We wish you well,*' and she drew close to Aniel. Then Aniel said in a clear voice high into the trees, 'They will give him the best pipe in all that Land, because he will play it the best. And so he will be music to them.'

As they walked away, he knew that he had cleansed her mind. He knew also that never had she loved him as she loved him at that moment. This gave him a deep pleasure, and if there was vanity in it, then the vanity was no more than a kindness that would have broken its bread at her feet.

In the silence, as they went on, their love grew and became a great sweetness between them. 'It will be dark before we get there. Are you tired?'

'No,' she responded quickly.

Their steps hurried, and presently they were running side by side, dodging the trees, stooping, hitting into each other, and often she was a step or two ahead as though her mind were fleeter than her feet. He looked aside at her; she caught his glance and held it. His face leaned towards her; she tried to meet it, but with the running their mouths missed and their faces bumped. They both laughed. She looked inspired and lovely. Never had he seen her glow like this. What he had been going to tell her about the animals came back into his mind. It would keep. He pulled up. 'It won't take us much out of our way. I should like to get a glimpse of the glen. We must bring all the news we can. What do you think?'

She agreed at once, his words having the thrill of a conspiracy.

'Keep close!' He bore away towards the right. They went quickly and sometimes they whispered together. In this companionship there was a happiness so buoyant that she could hardly keep it under when she looked at him. The desire to express it was indeed an ache in her breast, was fierce wings to her feet.

As they approached the glen slope, he slowed up. 'No good taking any chances.' His smile was glimmering and arched and intimate. She followed now in his steps; he put a hand behind him, stopped her, and drew her forward.

They were a long distance farther inland than the Tower. The trees of the glen were indeed thinning out into bushes. The moor rose beyond, and over its farthest crest lay the Grove. On the near edge of the moor a party of Northmen were foraging. Aniel and Breeta remained very still watching them.

'I knew this would happen,' whispered Aniel. 'They're wanting fresh food – and they'll hunt till they get it. They know there must be flocks somewhere.'

'Will they have taken the Tower?'

'Don't think so. Wind is against their boats, too, and it's rising. Looks as if it's going to blow into a real storm.'

'They may have taken the Tower.'

'If the whole of them couldn't, how could a few? No. They'll have to find some other way. They're not bothering today. That's what I think.' His voice had risen confidently, had gathered a quiet note of defiance. 'Your mother is safe.'

Breeta clutched his arm. They both listened intently, and heard a thudding sound within the rustling swaying trees. They thought it came from below them. 'It's all right,' Aniel whispered, bracing himself. 'Let's get back.' Breeta cried out, and as he swung to her crouching shoulder he saw two Northmen among the trees. Her senses had been acuter than his. They were in flight before the Northmen could shout. But the next moment the whole hillside seemed alive with shouting. A javelin smashed into a tree trunk before them. Breeta was fleet as a hind. Aniel, on her heels, cried to her now and then a hoarse note of encouragement. He had all he could do to keep up with her. She screamed and swerved left. He ducked under the thrown axe. She looked over her shoulder to see if he was all right and stumbled. 'Up!' he cried. The Northman was all but upon them as they sprang away. The Northman followed the girl. Breeta was like an arrow flashing between the trees. Aniel was running parallel. Breeta swerved again, and Aniel lost her. He had instantly to swerve himself, and in another moment was being hunted. Anger spired within him. He fumbled for his knife. His anger became a flame and he forgot Breeta. When he had drawn his pursuer towards the pine forest, he dodged and circled. The enemy was a young fair man, broad-chested, with blazing blue eyes, concentrated on cornering the quarry. Aniel hated them all intensely. They both circled warily, panting. The Northman was not wary of danger but only of the dark youth's escape. Aniel saw this in his eyes, this certainty of power, of superiority. It was at once a maddening and terrible thing and, before he knew what he was doing, Aniel broke and fled. His anger at this increased, became bitterly malevolent. He was not

a fighting man, and he could have shed the Northman
had it not been for Breeta. It was the combination of
his own inadequacy and Breeta's danger that humiliated
him. It was all mixed up, too, with a sort of black horror
or fear. He was now frankly, madly flying, and broke into
a treeless tongue of land at full speed; but even as he did
so he saw Breeta, below him, disappear under the first of
the pines. Her pursuer emerged. His own pursuer shouted,
and the man lower down turned his head. Aniel flopped
in a bundle, and his enemy tripped upon him and shot
clean over, pitching by the head into the boggy ground.
In a moment Aniel was up, and heading for the pines.
He had not gone far when he knew that pursuit had been
abandoned. He lay down, gasping into the pine needles;
turned over on his back and threw his arms wide. His
eyes were wet. His body, thus spreadeagled, was a bitter
sacrifice. In the evening light the trunks were ruddy pillars,
warped and gnarled with generations of secret life. Their
knots were ingrown and fierce. Their tears were round
clear beads of resinous sweat. Out of the agony of the
birth of generations had come their strength, their assured
strength. They scarcely moved in response to the swaying of
the high dark branches. The colour of their trunks was the
reflection of blood thin-drawn in their ancient skins. They
were his citadel, his temple, the grove of his thoughts; his
malevolence, his shame, his fear – all his emotions were
there, bedded in circle upon circle, knit to the core. He
turned over on his face again. They could take him, the
pillars could approach and take him. The release of sacrifice
would complete his escape. He let his body relax, his weight
sink. . . .

A whispering ran between the pine trunks. He heard it
draw near. Overhead, the branches flung the ancient forest
song . . . gathering it from afar, bringing it forward in a
wave, swaying in ecstasy beneath its crest, hearing it pass
on and grow faint in the distance . . . only to be aware of
its gathering afar again, coming forward in a wave, nearer,
overhead. . . . The whispering between the trunks was the
whispering of human voices, but not men's voices. And
when it ceased he carefully lifted his head. At first he

could see no one, but presently he made out Breeta as she paused between two trees, intensely alert. Words fell from her mouth and another voice answered. It was the voice of the woman whom Drust had loved, and all at once she was visible. Beside this small woodland creature of the Finlags, Breeta looked tall and slim. But some emotion which they hid from each other was alive between them. It made Breeta appear terribly anxious for Aniel; it kept the Finlag silent for her lost lover. All at once Aniel was aware of a face peering at him round a near tree bole, and his heart stood still. The face withdrew. He crawled to the tree bole: the face was gone. He stood up. Breeta choked a cry. The son of Drust caught his mother's skirt and pointed to his discovery. They watched Aniel approach. Breeta was blood-flushed and could say nothing. The small woman's eyes never left him. Aniel stooped playfully to the boy. 'It was you, was it, who gave me the fright?' Then he smiled to Breeta. 'I saw you get away.' There was no taint of embarrassment in his voice. On the contrary, it sounded hard and amused. He turned to the Finlag and met her eyes and held them. 'Thank you for sending old Poison. He arrived in time to help Leu to die.' Her eyes had a hazed expression as if they had been smitten by a bluish sun-film. There was something extraordinarily tragical in their inscrutable look. They were the eyes of a woman from some far arid land, but how he felt this he did not know, though it had probably something to do with his ideas of previous existences or race memories or perhaps only something he had heard from the Master and forgotten. She did not speak. Her eyes winked slowly like a hawk's, and then were removed from him to her son. He had thought him a rather helpless little boy, but now he perceived that he was also an acute woodland sprite, and the way his head kept moving and his eyes flashing from any angle arrested the attention.

'Could you tell me', Aniel asked her, as he played with the boy's glances, 'if any of your men will be at the tryst tonight?'

'Yes.'

He looked quickly at her, then calmly said, 'Good. It's time I was off. Are you coming?' he invited her.

She remained silent.

Aniel nodded to her silence. 'Shall we go?' he said to Breeta, and started off. He was relieved to hear Breeta following him, though not until they had gone some way did he speak to her.

Hitherto he had thought he was a youth without moods. And now here he was hardly able to speak to this girl because of what had happened with the Northman. He should have been gay over their escape. They should have been friendly, walking hand in hand, laughing; more friendly even than they had been just before the Northmen were encountered. And he knew, even as he walked with her, that she could not understand him, that she must be bewildered. He cast her a sidelong glance. She had the straightforward enduring look, but instead of its being dour, it glistened. This touched his heart. His face withered slightly. Then he said, 'Those Northmen maddened me.'

She looked at him and looked away.

'I should have killed one of them.'

'You couldn't,' she said, excusing him quickly.

'Oh? Why?'

'Because—' She hesitated. She saw his meaning. She had never meant to say that he actually would not have been able to kill a Northman.

'Because what?' he pressed her.

'Because we had to get away.'

He smiled through his nostrils. After a time he said in a certain tone, 'We are always running away. We are lucky to escape. I know.'

She could make nothing of this mood. Because, however, of their relations, she endured it. During the little while she had been with the Finlag woman, something, she did not know what, had passed between them. For a moment she had even been shyer than ever she had been with Aniel, more keyed up, with a feeling of almost naked intimacy, of something unbearably desired about to be spoken or revealed. Nothing had been revealed – save this forefeeling of the emotion that had to do with their secret woman lives. As she walked now dumbly, she had for that queer girl of Drust's forest love a strange and almost sad (yet secretly glad) regard. The Finlag endured.

'Why should we run away from them, curse them?' said Aniel aloud. 'Not that I'd mind even the running away; it's the certainty that they are superior beings, that we are black brainless savages. I saw it in his eyes.' He was going to add, 'And I ran from it,' but hadn't the courage. She clutched his arm. Following her look, he saw two wolves.

They were standing still, heads reaching forward, eyes in the forest gloom reflecting light in a faint blue-green fire. Usually wolves were caught slinking away against the dead starved background of winter; rarely like this. Their stillness, caught up in the menace of those pricked ears, was suddenly terrifying. Then one lowered its head and slid away, and the other quietly followed. In a few moments they were gone, not whence they had come but onward towards the glen.

Aniel and Breeta stood looking after them into the trees. At last Aniel said, 'They have smelt the blood,' and half laughed. Breeta withdrew her hand at the sound of that laugh, but Aniel clutched it. With a wrench, she tore it free. He caught it again. They struggled. The struggle was fierce until he conquered and subdued her.

They went on without speaking. His fingers hit her arm and ran to her hand. 'Keep your eyes open for wolves,' he said solemnly. She glanced at him. He was smiling. 'I hated having to run away,' he explained. 'But now I don't mind.'

She knew he was waiting for her to say something.

'If anything had happened to you—' she began.

'Yes?' he prompted.

'Who would do anything?'

He pressed her hand. 'Good!'

Her brows wrinkled. 'I don't think—' Words were always difficult.

'You're right, Breeta, all the same. And, anyhow, wouldn't you have been sorry yourself if anything had happened to me?'

She did not answer. He stopped. 'Clear your brow,' he ordered. 'Go on, smooth it out,' he threatened.

'You killed a man – and saved me – already,' she said.

His face grew warm and awkward. 'Come on,' he said, moving off.

As she stole a glance at him, she saw that he was shy. When he met her eyes, she did not remove them. 'You witch!' he said. 'How you have delayed me this day!'

'Have I delayed you?'

An access of affection moved him to a swift happiness. He glanced round about the tree trunks. She glanced too. The light was thinning amongst the pillars and the waves of wind overhead were like waves on a sea.

'I'm not nearly so tired now as I was in the morning,' he said. 'The bread you gave me saved my life. Are you tired?'

'Not very,' she answered.

'I feel as if my body was light.'

'Yes.' She smiled quickly.

'All the same, we'll have to hurry. I'm glad about the Finlags coming. You know what I was thinking? I was thinking there's nothing like arrows. If we get the little Finlags crawling up in the trees by the Tower, and then shooting their arrows? The Northmen will never expect them and every arrow will hit.'

'Yes,' she said eagerly.

'We might yet save the Tower and everyone in it.'

Their steps hastened and sometimes they broke into a trot, but they were nearer exhaustion than they knew and once, when Breeta stumbled, he told her to lie still, and he lay down beside her, and so they rested listening to the wind and the stillness that was beneath the wind. But they rested only for a little while, and soon they were going more hurriedly than ever, close together, flitting on their bare feet between the pillars of that ancient wood.

A DOZEN men, most of them old and bearded, sat on the broken ground of the first tryst. The pale night of the northern summer was torn by the lashing black trees. The backs of the figures were bent. Earlier, a voice had spoken and a voice had answered, but as the night deepened, so had the silence between them, until the raising of human speech would have been a mortal effort against the dark gods.

This fear of the human voice increased. The air about them became the haunt of faces and forms. The trees around the clearing saw more than human eyes. Their contortions were responses to demoniac powers. Their branches tossed and clawed the sky, or flattened streaming. Their bones creaked, and sometimes the inner black foliage hissed and champed like mouths.

Far on the beach the dead bodies lay unburied and the wolves had scented their blood. The forest was alive with the prowling eyes of devouring beasts. The wind-devil lashed the trees. All nature was let loose by the angry gods. The gods were very angry. Else, why the wind? Why the rising storm, the rising wrath? If the weather had kept fair, the Northmen would have departed. Now they must stay. If their vessels were wrecked they would have to stay for ages. Who had done that? And the Logenmen. Who had put it into the heads of the Logenmen at this very time? So that nearly all the flocks had been taken and they were left desolate, driven from their land with its springing grain, their houses burned, their women and children herded northward, choking their cries in the night. What had the Ravens done to incur the wrath of the gods?

What had they done?

No voice spoke and the mind grew thin as the air that the branches lashed; clear to terror as the pale night; quivering like a held breath; aware of the incoming gods, of the demons gnashing and laughing.

At times it was enough to sacrifice a beast, a small beast like a hare or one as large as a bull, and from long long ago, when white bulls were roaming the forest, came legends of splendid garlanded occasions. But that glory was gone. And always, then as now, the sacrifice of any enemy or a criminal was a tribute of particular favour. But when the utter wrath had been incurred, when the flapping of the Black Wings was at hand, then greater than the white bull, more potent than the enemy, sweeter to the earth's black mouth than all other blood was the blood of one's own tribe out of the body of a virgin or a youth. No greater sacrifice could be made

than this. A patriarch has sacrificed his own son. But in that
there is lamentation and woe. It is the desolate obedience
that clears the mind to an arid plain. It is the injunction
of high destiny which in fulfilment turns the soil of the
heart to a burning sand. It may be necessary before the
High God, or son and father and family and tribe will all
pass into everlasting torment, but it leaves the living heart
barren in a weary land.

It is not so, however, with the free sacrifice of the youth
or of the virgin. The virgin becomes as a shaft of beauty;
her limbs flow with golden fluids; her heart is a yellow
flame passing through her eyes and her brows; death is
love's dark whisper; the knife is the sting of teeth in the
flesh; the sacrifice is a passing to the One Beyond. She
goes therefore with a smile and elated, with excitement
and trembling, with the awful fear that for ever and in all
things precedes the moment of ecstasy.

And with that sacrifice, more than with all others, is the
One who is over all well pleased and his wrath turned, and
disobedience forgotten.

Disobedience. The seeking after strange gods. That god
of the Christian, for example; who is a white pale god,
pleasant in the sun, but for such an hour as this of what
power, of what value? A puny crying god, who was himself
sacrificed. No power in him, no fierceness; no storm set
in black brows, no wind-threshing vengeance, no terror;
no sacrifices to be made to him, no appeasement, no
dark drink. What did he know of the flesh and the
vitals? And what of the cravings in the loins and in the
womb of the earth; what of portents, of dread foreknow-
ings, and of desires too terrible for thought? They nailed
him to a tree. They sacrificed him in lingering cruelty.
*To whom?*

Deep in their marrow, Christ was a make-believe, a white
shadow, and it was with a profound feeling not merely of
past guilt but of present relief that they sat bent before
terror. For this terror went deeper than its truth. It ran with
their blood as it had run with the blood of their ancestors.
It was the earth and the night and the flailing trees; it was
the stain of birth and death; it went fleet-footed with the

animals and pale with the wraiths. It was at the end of all things, like a mouth.

Sometimes one of the figures moved or turned a head. Occasionally a face stared into the trees. No word could ever be spoken now. They sat at the heart of their own terror, shielded by the foreknowledge of the virgin sacrifice. Let the terror increase. Let its shudder chill. Not until the pain has become unbearable is the knife welcomed as a sweet deliverer.

There grew in their minds a cunning opposition to the black branches that were curved like the great bones in a whale's mouth. The bones met and parted and tossed and spouted their black spume. But the jaws could not reach down to them. Nothing could come at them because of the design in their minds. And this design grew in each mind in the same way, and with the same strength, so that all their minds were one mind. And when that mind thought of the sacrifice, a faint excitation beset it so that it seemed to be within the mind also of the god, and being there, the trees were foiled and the nameless demons kept at bay.

But for how long, without the sacrifice?

*Now. . . .*

There was movement within the forest. They heard it coming. Their faces turned and, listening, they heard nothing. But it was coming, it was coming now. It was – there.

Breeta and Aniel stood within the pale rim of the circle, behind them the small dark figures of the Finlags. Aniel of the Grove, the loved one of the Master, the maker of images: Aniel come from the Grove, the Grove of sacrifice, and with him, slim and captive, the virgin Breeta, the beautiful dark girl, the fiery one, to whom the Master had spoken, upon whom he had at the beginning of their trouble laid his hand, in foreknowledge, in dedication.

No one greeted them, no one moved, and yet it was as if the ring opened to them. Aniel by a strange compulsion went forward. Breeta hesitated, caught him up, hesitated yet again, poised on flight, then swiftly was by him, pressing against his side. Aniel gripped her arm and they entered the ring.

Aniel stood looking from body to body. What had been on his tongue went from it. The dark circle was round him like a band, a band about his forehead, making him stare. Breeta uttered a strange whining sound and pressed against him. Virtue went out of his legs and he sat down, pulling Breeta with him. A sickening palpitation was in his breast. A nervousness went over him, a wave of utter exhaustion. It set his head the higher, the breath snuffling in his nostrils. Breeta's fingers were clawing at his thighs.

'I have come,' he said, but his voice was a husky whisper. He cleared his voice. 'I have come,' he cried, 'with the Finlags.'

All the faces were towards him. No one spoke.

'The Finlags – and their arrows.'

No one moved.

'I have come,' he said. 'I have come—' And his voice went from him.

The faces in the band had each upon it the pale hand of the summer night. There was light in this pallor, an eerie light to which the threshing trees added a terrible stillness. Dark sunken eyes were behind it, and around it the twisting hair of beards.

Aniel stirred himself once more.

'Are you ready?' he cried in a high thin voice.

No one answered him, but it was as though they had all answered him, 'We are ready.'

At that Aniel grew so weary that his mind became confused. Breeta's fingers were still clawing his soft flesh, but they were like the fingers of a child. He did not mind them. He was sick with weakness and wanted to lie down.

Breeta was still whining.

He grew weary of her whining. There was a voice in him like a faint curse. He sat still and his head drooped forward, but when his eyes closed the band drew nearer and he opened them to find the band at the same distance.

He stared at one figure; the others continued around him. His lethargy deepened. He had no longer the energy to speak.

The trees upreared like rooted stallions whipped by demon riders. Their mad forelegs pawed the air. He had not the energy to look up at them. Over him they strained wildly forward, reaching down – but could not reach. The arch of their backs eased; their manes tossed; they lashed uprightly. The next time they would break loose. They did not break loose.

If they broke loose they would crush the circle underfoot. There was something coming up behind them, with release in its hands. Something – Someone.

The Shrouded One who had to be appeased.

The mind of the circle began to flow through Aniel's mind, stealing his identity from him. Like theirs, it grew thin as the air and clear to terror; yet still did it retain in its forehead a heaviness of lassitude, a foreknowing of doom – the knot where the circle joined.

Breeta's whimpering grew less urgent but more continuous; her body was snuggling into him, low down. He was tired of her body. The knot pressed against his mind, irking it to a dull pain.

A beat began in the pain, the beat of hooves, hooves pawing the air, the thin air of terror.

When the pain was drawn away, his mind was a mind in the circle, but more important than other minds, because its clasp opened the circle to sacrifice. He was the young novice leading to sacrifice. The procession was conjured within him. The figures walked, himself, Breeta, the bearded men, the Finlags like black gnomes, out across the moor, to the far Stone. He saw Breeta stretched, saw her body take the knife. She did not cry out. Her eyes shone in a flash of brown gold. The ecstasy of the moment was remote and impersonal as the beginning of the world. It was within the meaning of the world, like destiny. Before its consummation, love and hate, birth and death, were accidental as a dance of flies.

The whimpering beside him had ceased.

His mind settled to a final stillness. The bearded face before him thinned into the night, only its pale watchfulness remaining, watching him – waiting for him.

The compulsion upon him grew, lifted into a clear urgency, in which there was no haste, only movement forward, out across the moor.

He got up. Breeta was up beside him, clutching at his arm. He started walking forward. The others had risen also and were walking in a line at each side. The Finlags came behind in a small noiseless group.

The trees fell behind them. In the north-west the afterglow was a delicate green, like the colour in the remembered eyes of a stranger. Watchful eyes – eyes they had seen before on the moor – without knowing their meaning. To the north-east the light was a tremoring of whiteness, rising beyond a crimson dye.

Breeta looked at Aniel and saw him upright and slim, his eyes levelly ahead. He was walking like one in a dream, and though beside her was yet so remote from her that the horizon cut him at the shoulders, and left his head moving against that northern sky. When he stumbled on the uneven surface, the shake settled him within his dream, so that he went on remoter than ever. There was something terrible in this remoteness and fateful in the dream. She wanted to cry out against it, but could not. She could not utter even his name. Her throat was a place into which she could bring no sound, as when vomit may not be brought to relieve sickness.

She stumbled and went on, looking ahead. Her steps were quick, and different from the steps of all those about her. She knew this. She was the centre. No longer could she hold Aniel's arm.

Nor could she rebel. She dared not rebel. She dared do nothing but go on. So she went on alone, with her bodyguard, and with Aniel beside her, their leader, their high priest.

Her love for Aniel brought the weakness to her throat that was like sickness. Their priest; *her priest*. All their minds were upon her, stealing her mind from her. She had rebelled against this, she had fought and whimpered to keep herself, to keep Aniel's mouth, to keep his hands, to keep the fierce crush of their strife.

But they could not be kept. They were being drained from her. Her concern was hectic and childish. And she was too tired, too tired. She was beaten down. She was too tired.

Then quietly and almost without being aware of the change, she was walking in a trance, her eyes set forward, the sickness fading from her breast. There was at first a faint sweet release in the change. All the emotions she had sent outward in desire, came back as a cool sheet and swathed her about, withdrawing her within herself, within a loneliness where she was whole. Her lips grew cold. Her head turned slowly and looked at Aniel, and she saw now that it was she who was remote from him. She saw this with the clear weariness that fades out like a withered smile on the lips.

She was now not herself but someone else; or, rather, she was herself in a legend. The women she had known in legend and shivered at; the chief's wife who slew herself upon her husband's body; the girls who were changed into swans and lived for centuries singing their sorrows on cold hungry seas; the girls stolen and encaved by giants; but, more than all the legends, the maidens who gave themselves to the dark gods for the salvation of their people. For the woman who died over her husband could be understood as her high song was understood; and the girls who were changed into swans had the bright light of the seas on their plumage, and their sorrows were sad as long-drawn waves. But the girl who went smiling to the fierce stab of the dark death, she had been to Breeta a creature of different mould from herself, a different being; someone she could never be, not even in her saddest moments, when cast out for her youthful tempers and most forlorn.

And yet here she was, with the shadow of that old Breeta somewhere within her, the shadow one sees of oneself when coming back to the valley where one was born. And these men around her – she knew them, too. They were the kind bearded men, whom she had always looked at as a little girl with a certain grave fear, whose advances and playfulness had made her feel shy, whose kindness she had loved and, grasping, had run away from. Now they were clear to her. And the instinctive fear of that little girl towards them was clear at last.

She knew them with a cold and awful insight. She knew why the little girl had run away. She knew. Even old Echd, who was stupid and dour and passionate, of whom they made fun and told stories, who was squat and thick-necked and gobbled his few words, was now the most terrible of them all. She saw that there was in him a profounder strength, a deeper everlastingness, than in any. His mind at the moment was calm and benignant; was indeed tender; his thick grubby paws would be gentle. The terribleness of this docile creature wrapped her fate about her ineffably.

There was a faint elation in being thus at their centre, knowing what moved their arms and bodies and legs like instruments. Without her, they were nothing. With her, all life gathered meaning and encompassed terror and death. There were no words in her mind obscuring the feeling of this final knowledge, just as there had been no words in her mind when as a little girl she had stared gravely at the bearded men and run from them with their gift.

The One Beyond did not enter her head; her sacrifice had no relation to marriage; the Pleasant Plain might not know her flying feet. All that was what was said solemnly in whisper; it was the grandiloquence of the men, the excuse-makers. Not even a faint suggestion of it touched her mind. She went like one hypnotised and fatally enwrapped, an excitement where the sickness had been.

This excitement, this elation, swam about her breast and made her divinely careless. A little more of it, a spouting of it to the head, and she could easily take the knife herself and plunge it in her breast. Then she would fall down into darkness. That darkness was the lure. That exquisite swooning darkness. It would be to fall asleep on the Pleasant Plain itself.

And yet now and then, on the edge of a breath, as a melting ridge along her breast, came the old anxiety, particularly when she stumbled, and the child Breeta of the glen turned over within her; but the anxiety and the pain were dulled and passed with a vanishing surge of tears behind the eyes.

The night sky overhead was a fresh blue between thin clouds wind-drawn to points, the newly washed dry blue of a garment. They had risen from the valley and the wind streamed against their bodies, hurrying to the white cauldron down in the gulf of the north. The light about them was dusky pale, and the unsheltered moor was tight-drawn against the wind. No emotion can stand long against wind, which in the end generates its own reckless emotion of fatigue. For a time it buffeted and troubled Breeta, but soon it dissipated the last chance of rebellion against her fatal mood, and her mind went streaming northward like loosened hair.

So that when in their pilgrimage a small figure stood before them, she was neither startled nor afraid. It was the Master. She regarded him with a vague curiosity, for he it was in whom all the others were summed up. She continued to regard him steadily. He approached her and looked into her face.

There was a long silence.

The Master turned to Aniel and read his face also.

'Why have you brought her?' His voice was intimate within the wind. They all heard it and heard nothing else.

Aniel could neither move nor speak.

'You have brought her,' said the Master, 'to the sacrifice.'

Because of something in his voice, no one could move or speak.

'You have brought,' said the Master, his voice falling gently, '*the virgin*.'

They all stood breathless in the wind. Breeta fell quietly to the ground.

'Take you her then,' said the Master, 'and follow me.'

Two men lifted the unconscious girl, and not until the others came pressing against Aniel did he stagger on.

Now as they went they saw a radiance in the air beyond the crest where the Grove was. They took this as a sign and were moved accordingly. They walked no longer with purpose, but as those in all the deep security of being led.

Upon the crest, the Master paused. There was truly a radiance, and it came from the Grove. To the eyes that gazed, there appeared to be a colossal fire sacrifice; but soon they saw that the Grove itself was the sacrifice, that all the Grove was on fire.

All the Grove was on fire. The tree trunks and the

branches were black skeletons writhing against swaying sheets of flame. As great yellow tongues were torn upon the air, the outer twigs and leaves ran into the heart of that furnace like molten flesh. It was too far away for sounds to reach them. And so the holocaust was set in a silence which was magical and terrible. The fire, too, had its effect as fire, as flame; monstrous and outblown, it had a greater effect than ever before. It was the sacrifice of nightmare, of a demon's dream. Tiny black demons danced across the flames.

'The Northmen,' spoke the Master.

Horror stretched out its paralysing hand. The gods would split the heavens in twain. The light about the moor was darkening.

'The Northmen.'

A shivering crept about their skins, a black hate.

'Before our gods,' said the Master, 'there they are.' His voice was clear and intense; it began where hate left off. They could have crawled beneath it; they could have licked it as a whip. Without a word, Echd lowered Breeta to the ground and slid away towards the fire. One by one the others followed him, the Finlags instinctively breaking their group formation and swiftly spreading out, their small bodies bent forward at the shoulders, each with his bow and sheaf of deadly arrows.

The Master watched them go. The Finlags were absorbed quickly by the moor. The Ravens could be followed a considerable distance in the dim light. The Master turned and looked at Aniel.

Aniel's eyes were in front. His face was pale and the wind blew his hair about. There was in his expression somewhere a dry doomed smile. His body wavered, yet persisted in keeping its front.

'I know how it happened,' said the Master.

Aniel's smile withered.

'I think I know,' said the Master, 'all that's happened.'

Aniel's head drooped and jerked up again, as though it had been hit.

'You forgot,' said the Master.

There spread about Aniel the conception of the virgin.

The outline grew vast and his mind became confused. He felt blood dripping from his head; he shook it.

'This is the end,' said the Master.

It was the end of the Grove, the end of their lives, the end of the world.

'The end,' said the Master.

It was the end. The voice began telling him of the end. The doom was final. The Grove was being burned from the face of the earth for ever. The meaning of this grew until the flesh was consumed like shivering leaves in its flame; until the blood fell not outwardly but inwardly behind the eyes, screening the eyes, darkening the earth, and the earth itself began to slip to its own black doom. The rush of this awful ending was coming through the voice, was being ordered by the voice. The Master's voice was the voice of the One Beyond. Aniel turned through his darkening frenzy. He could not see the Master. The darkness parted like a veil. There was no sign of the Master anywhere. No living thing moved about him, nor out on the moor – nothing moved – except the far-leaping flames of the Grove. Aniel blundered into the body of Breeta, looked long at it, then got down beside it and turned the face upward.

The face was cold between his hands. She could not be dead. She had fainted and needed water. That was all. Water.

But there was no water anywhere. The hags were dried up with the hot weather. Nor had he a vessel to carry water. He must carry her.

'Come, Breeta,' he said, on his knees, gathering her on to his shoulders. 'Come.' But she fell off him when he tried to stagger up. He tried again, however, and at last stood swaying with her. He stumbled as he went, drunkenly and not caring, saying to himself, 'Steady!' He had no concern for Breeta at all. She was all right. All he had got to do was to carry her. He carried her for such a long way that there was finally nothing in his mind at all but the need to go on. She was, too, by a pressure at the throat, choking him. His right foot dipped and she pitched forward by the head.

On all fours he looked at her tumbled body. Her head had got doubled up under her. He turned her over. It was a hollow piece of marshy ground and her face looked dirty and as if it had been dead for a long time. He felt the neck. It was hard, but it would be hard even if it was broken. The head fell over very easily.

She was probably dead. He had a sudden repugnance to feeling below her breast for the heart. She would be as well dead. If she wasn't dead, it would be easy enough to kill her. The idea of killing her stirred something in him. His mouth grew thin. To be done with her . . . to wipe out. . . .

The desire to kill her went round his forehead like a tightening wire. It bit inward till apprehension was keen as pain. He would kill her. Strangle her. Be done with her. Throw her away. Revulsion rose up, blinding him, thrusting him at her.

But before her throat he drew back. He set his hands clawing in the marshy ground, squeezing torn lumps until his fingers and body ached under the constriction.

Then on all fours he went casting about him; found an almost dried-up spring; thrust his face into it; and in the end brought a great sponge of sopping moss and applied it to her face and neck. With a livid fascination, he watched her recover.

He watched every motion she made, from the first opening of her eyes until she sat up. He saw memory coming back upon her, saw the startled look round for the others, and then the slow awful concentration of her eyes upon himself. His hind quarters sagged down.

She scrambled back from his slight movement and finished on her feet. But she was giddy and sat down again abruptly. Then she lifted her hands, made wiping gestures, threw her head back, gasped so that he heard her, until there moved within him the answering wild flurry of his own heart.

He was waiting now, he found, with an aching intensity. But she never looked at him again. There was one final sustained moment when her fingers seemed to be easing her temples from the burden of her hair. And then she was on her feet.

She stood looking about her, rather wildly, the wind moulding her body, and then she walked off into the moor.

## CHAPTER FIVE

THE carpenter of Haakon's longship stood cursing on the beach. Though the Northmen were easy masters of a country peopled by savages, three things eluded them: fresh food, the Tower, and sea-weather; and the carpenter couldn't see why, by the wind-breaking of the Thunderer, they hadn't been able to bring him at least some cow's hair. He hadn't control over the waves. And if everyone of them was so secretly bent on plunder that the vessels were left with insufficient man power to heave them clear of a sudden sea-rage, what in the name of Thor could they expect him to do about it? Probably these disembowelled magicians had worked up even the sea. The Northmen were a mighty race of sea-reavers. Oh yes! That explained how he couldn't get even a few hanks of decent cow's hair.

'Why didn't you bring a few with you?'

'Oh yes. Why didn't I bring my whole bloody building-yard?' And he glared at Thord lying lazily on his back. The others smiled. Thord fixed his hands behind his head and said solemnly, 'You know how Haakon dislikes the unclean mouth and how Sweyn would look at you.'

'I know', said Sigrid, the boatbuilder, 'how Sweyn will look now when he finds that the stove planking is still unfixed. And he can look', added Sigrid, 'until he's blue in the face. He always goes out at night to his religious rites. He wouldn't kill any man at night. Oh no. But I'm not wanting him to kill a man: I'm only wanting him to kill a bloody cow.'

Sigrid was a small hardy nut of a man, full of quick tempers, with winking eyes and restless hands. Because he had always to be doing something, enforced idleness irked him and so the action passed to his tongue which had quite a gift for irreverence. Many of the more irresponsible spirits found their pleasure in goading him to profanity against the gods. Sigrid had been known to take Odin's name in vain in a way that made the flesh crawl. His yard at home was the evening meeting-place of the wild spirits of the whole fjord. And what gave it its crown was the exquisite workmanship of those same restless hands. There had been the saga of his model longship, a perfect thing – the length of a man's arm. The tale of its profane adventures had been put together by a drunken skald and fathered upon Sigrid. Young men learned snatches of it and blushed when an elder or parent, coming upon their laughter, asked what the joke was about. It was a considerable joke! They rolled away, enjoying their spluttering laughter more than ever.

They could have rolled away over the sea, the wind of their profane mirth driving them on the maddest adventures. The fjord way home became an ocean, each headland a hostile outpost, every bay an encampment, until they went within their own doors quietly and spoke little.

There was not much for them – not for all of them – within their own doors. The mirth was repressed, the profanity hidden. The father was a responsible man, saying little, sometimes goodnatured and pleasant, occasionally gloomy, at rare times brooding over some private feud with a neighbour or with neighbours against neighbours – but always to the point of action, even treacherous action, but action.

For the father was at once tenant and owner and overlord of his farm. There were no tribal dues. He was the master, the Individual. The only law governing his property was the law of its disposal to his family, and as that did not come into operation until he died, it did not greatly concern him. It concerned the family, however, and some of the young men returning at night from such haunts as Sigrid's were readily enough fired by the idea of disposing of their shares to one member for cash and then – the high ocean to adventure, where mirth whistled the wave-tops and the gods' names went rolling down the dark.

And even with the older men – for at best there must ever be increasing pressure of neighbours and relatives restricting a man's elbows in a lusty community – the strength of that jealous individualism kept the lust of adventure more than half awake. Indeed it would seem but in nature that as the youthful exuberance and daring talk were subdued by the years, the need for adventure should find outlet to keep a healthy balance. Consider then the man in his prime, or in his late prime, with youth and profanity gravely surmounted, about to set out on adventure mad enough to make the gods rub their eyes. The farm lands, the sea harvests, the daily toil, the family needs, the women and the worries, all the small wearing unadventurous things left behind, and in front the whale's way to all the places of the earth, in the name of glory perhaps and of plunder certainly. The grey earth-mist rolls back from Valhalla where the heroes every day kill one another and every day are restored by Odin. Valhalla at the end!

With many a name did they sing their roaring highway, that rolling highway for drunken gods. The highway from the hungry fjord-mouths to the coasts of princes and the inland cities of kings; to the founding of Romanofs and the making of Normandy jarls for future emperors; from Sigrid's little wind-whistling yard to the ultimate domes and turrets of Stamboul. What was there to keep them back, with plunder on the way, and glory and Valhalla at the end? Acquisitive, brave, clannish, individualist, treacherous, loyal, sober, drunken, fierce lovers and fiercer swordsmen, the vices and the virtues in mass, with valour over all.

Sigrid came as the result of a lost bet. He would rather have been with his tools, for iron was his god and wood his goddess. But he was here with not a handful of plunder come his way and, worse, without the necessary cow's hair to spin a three-strand yarn to make the started planks watertight. The whole sea had beat in on a rising tide and a roaring wind and bumped the bottom planks of Haakon's ship on accursed boulders. There were no boulders on his sea slip. But they were here. By Odin, they were. And Haakon's ship was his ship. Every groove between the overlapping planks was his own handiwork. Did they think he could stuff the grooves with mud?

'Is it really hair you need?' asked Thord brightly.

'I know what you need,' growled Sigrid.

'Wait,' said Thord, taking his hands from behind his neck; 'why not take the hair off these girls?'

'Off what?' roared Sigrid.

'Off their heads, of course.'

The laughter made Sigrid flush and his eyes glitter. But his tongue came back, and Thord's rather beardless skin flushed like a virgin's.

Sigrid smiled then. 'All the same, Thord, you're a clever fellow, even if it's easy to see what your mind runs on. Talking of grooves,' and so he had his speech out with a final lewdness that drove sleep from them altogether. They got up. Yes, come on, Sigrid – to the women!

The sea pounded on the beach. The early morning light shone green through the curled crests of the oncoming waves, and sparkled in brilliance on the blown spray. The stones roared down the beach. Crest behind smoking crest to the far horizon, and overhead the sky, milky blue, and in the wind the freshness of the growing day. As they came out from the lee of Haakon's longship, they filled their breasts and looked at sea and sky.

'It's going to keep on blowing.'

'Holy Thunder,' prayed Sigrid, 'do thou cork the wind-god.'

In the dip behind the stone crest of the beach a number of the Northmen were stretched in sleep. Beyond them three Northmen were walking up and down with the gait of seamen, sometimes saying a word as they passed, but for the most part saying nothing. Their chests were round and their heads thrown back a little as if they were softly whistling or humming. The roar of the beach knit the walking bodies and the sleeping bodies to the sea and the windy sky. In the walking bodies was induced an endless rhythm that sometimes was a known melody, but as often a hypnotic wave bringing back memories of distant days.

Sigrid and the three men with him went by the cairn over the remains of Drust to the river slope where the

trussed bodies of five young men and seven girls were
lying together. A poor enough haul of slaves.

As he stood before them, Sigrid felt the edge of his knife.
'Ha, who is first for shaving?'

Eyes bulged dreadfully upon him. Two of the young men
began heaving and wrenching at their bonds.

'I think you, my dark beauty.'

'Steady,' said Thord. 'She's mine – and you know it.'

Sigrid looked at him innocently. 'What for?'

The exchanges completed, he went to another and
was stopped. 'B'Odin,' said Sigrid, 'this is an immoral
company! What difference will it make whether their hair is
on or off?' And he would not be moved on, but brandished
his knife and got to his knees: 'And now, my – well, you're
hardly a beauty, are you?'

Her narrow-browed beetling face grew narrower with
terror.

'But you have hair, and, hoaryodin, it looks tougher than
any cow's. Now—' She let out an astonishingly fierce yell.
'Hush, my pretty one.' Her yells increased, but, as his
hands came near her head, she snapped at him in a flash
of teeth that just missed.

The three onlookers laughed. The yelling started again.
'Sigrid, she'll waken the sleepers.'

'Will she?' said Sigrid, deftly turning her over on her
face and shoving her mouth in the gravel. The other
women now began to cry out and strain at their lash-
ings. 'Shut up!' roared Sigrid. 'Here, curse you, won't
one of you hold her head.' Thord obliged him. Sigrid
sat astride her back and skilfully if slowly severed the
strong hair. When her face was released, it was gravel-
crushed.

'You haven't improved yourself,' said Sigrid good-
humouredly. 'Now who's next? Don't look at me like
that, young fellow – or I'll – oh yes, I will. Here, hold
him, it's time this mat was off him, anyway – it will always
reduce our livestock.' Then he paused. 'If you don't stop
yelling,' he cried, 'I'll knife the lot of you,' and he flourished
his weapon.

It was an amusing game, for they all clearly thought

they were going to be butchered, whereas Sigrid and his
friends knew they weren't. Sigrid put them through the
most violent extremes of terror. There was one rather
fine-looking timid girl, whose breast and face developed
a dreadful hiccup of agony. Her eyes became distended,
showing great circles of white. She had a particularly
pure skin, which with the blood flush gathered a sore
raw look, the black round the eyes being like smears on
red flesh.

Sigrid, as the game grew upon him, had the others
rocking with laughter. His imitation of a magic-man
approaching the sacrifice was crude enough for complete
appeal. None of the rest of them had any such versatility.
Sigrid was unique. And the joke – that the captives believed
him – completed the fun.

Sigrid got hold of the fiercest youth, turned him on his
face, sat on his head, and raised his own fists and knife to
heaven. Whereupon he invoked imaginary gods in a stream
of gibberish that purported to be the captives' tongue.
Norse expletives dropped into it with explosive effect. In
the midst of his oration he back-heeled the near captive
who was becoming obstreperous, while his face retained
its solemn appeal.

At last he jumped up, saying, 'Hah, what do I see –
the gods are coming – my prayers are answered – behold!'
Down the glen a handful of Northmen were returning. He
stood back from the captives. 'It ees feenished,' he said
to them with a grave foreign accent. The captives were
completely forgotten, as the four went on to the fairway
laughing together.

The Northmen who arrived had only one captive, but
his smallness excited the greatest interest. 'It's an old man,'
cried one. 'Look at the grey hairs in its beard!' They all
crowded to look. Another, trying to catch the beard, had
his fingers nearly snapped off. The mouth was wide, the
ears large, the nose broad and flattened, the skin weathered
with years. It was incredible that one so little should be old!
A big Northman prodded the Finlag to see what would
happen. They prodded him with axe-shafts as they might
tease a lobster.

'He's crying!' said one at last. 'Great Odin, he's crying!'

This so thoroughly astonished them that they looked on in silence.

'No, he's not! He's whining; he's crawling for mercy! Look!'

'Leave him,' said Sigrid drawing his knife solemnly. 'Have you no mercy?' The Finlag eyed Sigrid with terror. Sigrid stood before him dangling a fistful of human hair. Then he addressed the Finlag gravely: 'Yakelyookeljumjum, cut your hoaryodin, yakelyookeljumjum, cut your hairy throat,' accompanying the speech with appropriate action. The Finlag screamed. Sigrid staggered backward so violently that he hit into Thord's stomach and upset him. The men roared with laughter. The Finlag, whose hands only were thonged, bolted from their midst. They could not give chase for laughing, but one of those who had brought him in chased strongly, though he was tired and had looked on at the sport with weary pride.

The Finlag ran with astonishing speed. The sight of his little twinkling legs doubled up the Northmen who watched. 'Go on, little one!' they yelled. 'B'Odin, he'll beat him! What fun! O god, go on!' Their throats grew hoarse. Look at big Kan! Look at his great legs! 'Go on, little fellow!'

They roused the whole camp.

When at last the Finlag was brought in, his captor was in a black humour.

Sigrid started forward, but Kan turned on him. 'Stop your silly fooling – or I'll set him at you.'

'Oh!' said Sigrid, firing at the tone.

'He's enough to settle your gaggle.'

'It would take more than the two of you to do that.'

'Would it?' said Kan, staring at Sigrid.

'It would,' said Sigrid.

Kan's stare grew stony. He took a step towards Sigrid, who kept his ground. Kan swung his fist, but Sigrid ducked and avoided the blow. Kan, being spent, grew coldly infuriated. But Haakon had come through the crowd and stood in his way.

'What's the matter?' Haakon asked.

Kan looked at him for a time and then said indifferently, 'Nothing,' and turned back to the Finlag.

'What's this?' asked Haakon, before the Finlag.

'Mine,' said Kan.

'Where did you get him?'

'I got him', said Kan, 'at the temple of the magicians,' and his mouth closed and sent his breath strongly through his nostrils. His face was set.

'Have you no more to say about it?' asked Haakon.

'Not much,' said Kan.

No one stirred.

'Will you say that much?' requested Haakon.

Kan's eyes stared before him, his cheekbones were glazed, his mouth hard. He turned away to the Finlag. Sweyn, who had come up, glanced sideways at Haakon, whose cheekbones were pink.

'Kan,' said Sweyn, 'tell us about the magicians.'

Haakon turned on Sweyn. 'I am speaking to him.' His eyes flashed.

'Very good,' said Sweyn, nodding, and seeming to step back a pace without moving.

'Kan!' said Haakon.

The bone-faced fair-haired Kan turned slowly round. His humour was growing bleaker. He looked at Haakon steadily.

'Will you tell me what happened?' commanded Haakon.

'The others can tell you,' said Kan.

'You shall!' roared Haakon, drawing his sword.

Kan felt at his side and remembered he had lost his sword. 'Will anyone give me a sword?' he asked quietly.

Haakon took a step forward and then jerked to a standstill. His fury nearly blinded him. Kan's life hung on a thread. No one gave him a sword.

'What do you want to know?' asked Kan.

Haakon settled on his heels. His sword went down. 'You heard me.'

'We were looking for cattle,' said Kan evenly. 'We came on the temple of the magicians. We saw a head on a tree. We thought we knew the head. We caught three of the magicians. We tied them to the tree. We got some gold and ivory and strange instruments. We set fire to the houses and to the trees. It was a great blaze in the wind,' said Kan. The spirt of his anger was spent.

'What happened then?' asked Haakon, his voice quiet now.

'Then we were attacked. But we could see no one. Darts whizzed past us in the bad light. They came from nowhere. One pierced through the eye of Skervald and killed him.'

'What!' cried Sigrid in a loud voice.

Kan looked at him steadily, his lips in a twist, and turned from him.

'We thought we were attacked by the spirits of that place,' said Kan. He looked at Haakon. 'We retreated.'

'I should have run,' said Haakon.

'We ran,' said Kan.

They waited, the wind in the hair of their heads, looking at Kan.

'One of the three we tied to the tree was a man with short hair and a great beard. His eyes were all fire. He spat curses at us and raised his demons against us. I smote him in the face. He broke his bonds. I killed him with my bare hands. It made me feel strange. We set fire to the whole place.'

'That should have cleansed you,' said Sweyn.

'We felt that,' said Kan. 'We were roused up. We became like madmen in a battle. Queer sounds came from that fire. High terrible sounds. Then the darts began to whizz past our faces. We could not see them. We could see no one. We believed they were Longbeard's demons. We ran from them.'

There was something of the skald in Kan's simple utterance. His grandfather had been both a skald and a fighting man of repute. Moreover, Kan was often a silent man, even morose at times, so that his words now made a vivid picture. He plainly did not care what they thought of it. He was neither boastful nor excited. A withdrawn grim movement about his mouth attracted them by its strength.

'The darts pursued us,' said Kan. 'Then we saw men appearing like the men we fought on the beach. We separated a little. In jumping into a hag, I jumped on him,' and he nodded at the Finlag. 'He wriggled under me. I smashed his ear. I – he lay still,' said Kan.

They all looked from Kan to the Finlag.

'The men who came', Kan went on, 'fought more desperately than those on the beach. The demons had got into them, but they had no weapons. Skervald was already dead. A small thick man killed Kolbjorn in a terrible way. They were many more than we were. So we fought retreating. Some darts were still falling. One got me in the shoulder, but the wound has healed, so they did not use poison. Another dart went into Sam's stomach, and before we could rescue him they had snatched his axe and killed him. At that we all grew mad, and—'

Kan paused. A light had come into his eyes. He let the light fade. As if he had been talking about nothing in particular, he concluded, 'On the way back, I saw this little fellow staggering off. So I caught him again. That's how he's here.' He lifted his eyes and looked straight at Haakon. 'The gold and the ornaments got spilled on the moor.'

'I am vexed about Skervald and Kolbjorn and Sam,' said Haakon. 'They were brave fine men. You did well, Kan, and those with you. You angered me for a moment. I withdraw that.'

Haakon's simple tone moved them all and made them look with pride at Kan.

'It's all right,' said Kan, but they saw he was pleased.

Sweyn asked, 'What are you going to do with your demon, Kan?'

'I don't know,' answered Kan.

'Do you feel he is a hostage against their gods?' Sweyn half smiled, watching Kan.

'Yes,' said Kan, looking unsmiling at Sweyn.

Sweyn contemplated the Finlag. 'He is not a demon.'

'I thought that,' said Kan. 'But they must be the defenders of the magicians' temple. They must be – something.'

Sweyn nodded. 'That's true. I'll talk with you about that again.' Sweyn was skilled in all magical rites. 'It looks as if we are not in too great favour with our own gods. It might be wise to appease them.' He spoke musingly, still looking at the Finlag. 'Something must be done.' He appeared absentminded. They knew that look in Sweyn's face. Sweyn lifted his eyes to the horizon like a seaman and stared a long time. No one spoke, but several looked at the Finlag in an odd way.

Haakon regarded Sweyn deliberately. Sweyn said to him, 'They will be more moved against us on account of their gods than for any other reason. It has troubled me how they knew we were coming. Never, except once, have they known it before.'

'Do you mean they learned from their gods?' Haakon asked.

'I do not know for certain,' said Sweyn. 'Their gods are barbarous devils, and their magicians have terrible ways of divining the future. Kan and his lads have wiped out a vipers' nest. I knew it was in this land somewhere. What their attempts at revenge may be, I do not know. But I fear them.'

'What is to fear?' asked Haakon.

'I do not know,' said Sweyn. 'As we do not know what power may be gathered against us – from all in there.'

'That is true,' said Kan, looking where they all looked.

'Are we going away empty-handed?' asked Haakon. 'We have lost – how many? – for nothing.' He felt fear and distaste of the place upon the men. Most of them had had little sleep for days. They would stand any amount of fighting, but they had no taste for magicians and demons. He had none himself. But this, his first great adventure, could not pass in half-failure.

'Listen,' said Sweyn. 'We landed here, we overthrew the forces against us, we had a great victory. All this country, Haakon, is now yours. And we could, if we wish, divide out that country amongst us, and we could defend it. What more can any conquerors do at any time? Is not this a greater possession than any you have on the fjord at home? And certain things we have got, though we have not got much gold. But these stories of gold may have been exaggerated, and it is a pity, too, that Kan and the rest of them in their great danger could not both fight and carry, which no men can do. To have come back with their lives has meant great valour, and the dead will have the reward of

Odin's welcome to great warriors.' Sweyn had the accent of greatness. They all felt his skilled wisdom and were moved by him.

'You are wise, Sweyn,' Haakon said. 'One thing remains – to take the Tower.'

'Yes,' Sweyn answered. 'We shall take the Tower this day. You will find your treasure there. Tomorrow morning the wind will moderate and we shall go forth again.' His prophetic tone uplifted them. 'This is but the beginning. Yet some day – listen to me – we may come back here – or some of you may come back here. There is fertile land for you here and homes and flocks. You will bring women with you and beasts and children. And if you will not come, then others will. We are but the warriors who go before.'

The prophecy moved them like a saga recited by a skald.

'We will take the Tower,' concluded Sweyn, 'and this night we shall sacrifice to our gods.'

They all remained silent, light flickering on blue eyes, wind on faces and hair, resolute men, chins tilted to the far look, while their minds gathered what Sweyn had said and were stirred by it. *Warriors who go before* – words for the blood which carried them to the mouth and the eyes and the brain, so that presently they all rocked on their feet and hitched their bodies in a restlessness that was pleasant and terrible.

Thord relieved himself by asking softly of his friend, what had come over Sigrid who was marching back to the longship.

'He'll be frightened Sweyn asks about the damage,' said his friend.

They suppressed their laughter. Haakon and Sweyn were walking away together. Fires were being stirred to a blaze for the cooking.

'Let us go and see,' said Thord. With an exaggerated air of conspiracy they strolled carelessly to the longship. Sigrid was leaning against the vessel, his chin on his breast. Drawing within a few paces, they bespoke him, but he did not look up. They stopped.

'What's up now, Sigrid?'

He ignored them still, then flashed a face of wrath.

'Clear out, you—!'

They were genuinely shocked.

'Freeze you, won't you clear out?' They gazed at his working face. 'Clear out!' he yelled, and lifting a stone let it fly at Thord, who avoided being brained by inches.

They were amazed.

'Clear out!' He stooped for more stones; he was beside himself; he did not know what he was doing. They retreated to a safe distance.

'Stones of Odin!' swore Thord, softly watching the fury of action that now beset Sigrid the boat-builder. He leapt over the gunnel. There was the crash of a bag of rivets thrown on the beach, the clank of iron tools, the thud of wood, and Sigrid jumped out after them. He tried his hammer on a stone which smashed asunder.

'The demons have got him!' said Thord.

Sigrid rubbed the back of a hand into his eyes, then cracked another stone and a third stone. His sight was troubling him. Thord's friend whistled softly.

'Valhalla – I know – he's weeping for his friend Skervald!'

'Icebergs of hell!' whistled Thord.

They continued to gaze at Sigrid with a certain awe. Haakon and Sweyn drew near, talking together. Thord said to them, 'I wouldn't go down there just now.'

Sweyn looked quickly at Thord. Haakon's brows netted, then both Sweyn and Haakon turned their gaze on Sigrid who was brandishing a new rib that he had made. He apparently thought it a bad rib for he smashed it on the beach, then crushed it to smithereens by heaving boulders upon it.

'Has he gone mad?' asked Haakon.

'No,' said Thord; 'he's weeping for his friend Skervald.'

'He loved him more than any woman,' said Thord's friend.

Sigrid saw them and stood still, his face appearing extraordinarily vindictive at the distance. All at once he yelled, 'How do you expect me to carpenter your bloody boat if you have no cow's hair?'

After a moment, Sweyn answered, 'We'll get you some tonight.'

'High time,' roared Sigrid, and stamped about the stones, speaking to himself, so that they overheard – 'Suit yourselves, suit yourselves, you hoaryodin bastards!'

'Let us leave him for a bit,' said Sweyn.

There was a smile on Haakon's young face as he turned away and a light in his eyes. The death of his men was secretly a terrible thing to him, but also a terrible glory. This new manhood had made him at moments a little uncertain, like one who is drunk with too great and too sudden a power. The strength of his youth surged in him with a god's ease. Sigrid's love for his friend moved him to confession as he came by Drust's cairn with Sweyn.

'I was mad, too – that time you interrupted me with Kan.'

'I knew,' said Sweyn.

'I didn't mean—'

'I meant you to mean,' said Sweyn. 'I am a man getting on in years. You are my last adventure. I must see you through.' He paused and then said in a pleasant voice, 'If you had spoken as you did twenty years ago, I'd have killed you on your feet.'

Haakon flushed.

Sweyn looked at him and smiled. 'You wonder whether I would have been able?'

Haakon appeared embarrassed.

'I like the way you look. There is a sensitive manner to your spirit. Without that you might have been a great fighter, but never a great leader – one who can increase his power and hold it, who can see what's coming and make alliances.' Sweyn spoke pleasantly, an old man to a young man. It was cunning talk, too, because it expressed his own mind and made Haakon confident.

'This is the first monument to your valour.' Sweyn put his hand on Drust's cairn. 'And these are your first slaves.' Haakon's eyes were blue light and his fairness a confusion. 'You have done well. This is only the beginning of our adventure. We do not know what the end will be. Who knows what is before us? Would you like already to go back?'

'No,' said Haakon. 'I could go on for ever.'

'Good,' said the dark Sweyn. 'But some day you will want to go back. Something or someone will call you back.'

'There is no one,' said Haakon, his brows ridging stubbornly.

'As to that I do not know, but I may have heard.'

'I know what you have heard,' said Haakon. 'I am not going back – not until I have plenty of wealth.'

'That would give you the power of being indifferent. You are right there. There may always be some final man or king to whom you may have to submit, but never submit to any woman. That's old Sweyn's advice. Take your women as they come. Don't tie yourself early. The power of a woman can be a more terrible thing than the power of any man, because it is a jealous power over his spirit. It is with him in the morning and in the evening; it is with him in the gods' night and poisons it; it can move him on to deeds that he is ashamed of before men; to secret black acts that destroy him.'

Haakon looked at the dark Sweyn, whose grizzled expression smiled strangely. Haakon looked away.

'I am wasting my words on the air. Yet some day – when you are in her dark eddy – you may remember old Sweyn's words, and backwater to the clear sea where man sings and fights and conquers. There is no other life for the warrior. Valour is your sheath, your skin, and the cool seawater about your skin, and your cool sword on your skin. Man is a naked animal and he protects his nakedness with his sword. That is the song of his manhood, the saga of his adventure. To die of sickness, to die of disease, to die in bed – pray the gods, my son, to save you from that unclean humiliation. But to go as you have lived, flashing and terrible, to be received by those like you who have gone before, that is a noble faring. You see rising before you the wisdom of a man's life. For a man's life must be whole and inviolate. Once you have seen this, seen it naked as a man's body coming up out of the sea, you will never after be divided in darkness against yourself. When your rage is upon you, you will kill first and think afterwards, if think you must. And that is just. For once you are as a

naked man come out of the sea with the sun on the sword
of your body and on the sword in your hand, then you are
a whole man and your rage will be just. But if you are not
a whole man, then your rage will be mean, and your deeds
desperate, and your mind twisting upon itself like the mind
of a woman. That is all the wisdom of living I know,' said
Sweyn.

They kept walking by the stream, and Haakon did not
wish to stop, for all that Sweyn had said was raising fire
within him, so that he could have plunged by the head into
the sea and have risen and shaken the sea from him and
exulted aloud. All that had been said was of himself. No
one else was concerned but himself – except perhaps the
flashing face of one young woman whom he triumphed
over. And when his deeds were known in many lands, then
would he triumph more than ever. And finally he would be
whole, as Sweyn said, and would die on a sword, when his
triumph would be complete, and those could mourn him
who would.

Sweyn talked of the life after death, taking Sigrid as
an example of one who did not see clearly into death.
'Because of his impatience, the gods are blurred before
him,' said Sweyn. 'When he profanes against the gods he
has a feeling of recklessness and power. It is a weakness
in him. And because of that weakness, he is perverse. He
will never be in the hall of the heroes, because he does not
possess himself whole. But he will have his place – as he has
his place with us.' Sweyn paused a moment. 'Lamenting
death like that is wrong to Skervald and wrong to the gods.
If you were to be killed, Haakon, I would grieve for you,
but not greatly. When you hear a skald tell of a hero, you
do not grieve over the hero's death: you are moved by what
he did, by his deeds, and you are then lifted into exaltation
at the thought of how Odin will receive him.'

The morning was clean and cool and valorous, and its
light was in Haakon's mind as the vision of deathless life.

'Let us turn back,' said Sweyn, in his companionable
voice. 'I have thought over things at night by myself. I
have seen strange things. Of what I have seen I may tell
you another time.'

This talk remained with Haakon during breakfast like a fire in his veins, and it uplifted him, so that though he tore at the food he got little taste of it, and was soon satisfied.

When they were at last ready, he turned at the head of his men and raised his sword. The mute sustained action sent the flame of his mind through all of them. So sudden and strong was it that no one raised a shout; but as they went on a voice broke through, and the valley rang with the shout of warriors and brothers.

Sweyn looked sideways at Haakon, then turned his eyes ahead again, well content. And if he was not as exalted as the others, yet was his satisfaction deeper and smoother, as of one going to a familiar place.

## CHAPTER SIX

GOAN and Lys were feeling the effects of the morning sun in a great weariness and desire for sleep. At the dawn, Silis had gone to rest and was lost in exhaustion. Breeta's mother was asleep in the lean-to by the side of Donan the child. Nessa lay alone, her head fallen off her arm, her mouth open, her breath threshing lightly to the ground. Her body had a tired abandon, wanton in its ease. A tethered goat, bearded, stood by her. Her colour was drained as colour drains from red under the moon. No memory of anxiety touched her forgetfulness; no stress of the defender was visible; as both anxiety and stress were visible in the face of the one-armed Erp and in the bright brow of Talorg the courteous, both of whom were aloft in the first gallery, resting beneath the sleepless Goan and Lys.

On the tongue of land beyond the burnt hall, six Northmen slept openly, while two walked up and down without speaking. They were just out of stone's throw, and commanded the fort's one door and the open space to the wood on the left. That wood presented their danger, for enemies could crawl up within bowshot; but they had all taken part in the sacking of the glen and had no real fear. Their difficulty, in fact, had been to get the enemy to stand against them anywhere. That the enemy should come back to fight was hardly to be hoped.

All the same it was a tiresome business this, and they could wish it over. Meantime it was their job to see that those inside the fort were not allowed to escape, and were given as little rest as possible. When the beards disappeared from the top for a time, one of the Northmen would approach the stone door and hammer upon it. At once heads would reappear and stones fly after him, for all missiles other than stones from the wall of the building itself had long since been exhausted.

Now, however, Goan and Lys did not withdraw their heads, but kept them bobbing here and there in their barefoot patrol, so that no hammering would come on the door and awaken the sleepers. They were going to hold out in shifts.

They were no longer afraid that their fort could be taken. They had food to last many days; grain indeed to last them months. The well never went dry, and the bank of turf would keep kindling for long enough. The door consisted of two stone slabs, one behind the other, held in position against outer stone jambs by two stone arms projecting on each side from the masonry behind. But on account of the battering the door had received in the first reckless onslaught, despite the flow of heavy and liquid missiles from overhead, it had been strengthened inside by stones loosely built up against it. In the small chamber guarding the door, his long spear across his knees, sat Drust's old henchman in a deep sleep.

The legendary men who had built this fort had certainly known something of defence, for within its small compass it held a double retreat. Should that single doorway in the twelve-foot stone wall be forced, then those within could retreat to the galleries above. The only access to these galleries was by a narrow doorway and staircase, again guarded and easily defended, and while the enemy hammered within the court they could be attacked not only from the top of the fort but also from the open windows that looked upon the inner court from each of the galleries. Indeed it would be more dangerous for the attackers inside than outside the massive circular wall.

But the attackers were going to risk it, or so Lys and Goan thought when they saw the Northmen come up the glen from the sea.

'It will be their last throw,' said Goan, brows bushy over blood-threaded eyes. Sweat runnels streaked his face, and his brown beard was grey with stone dust. Tiredness and lack of sleep irritated him savagely.

Lys cursed the blood-drinking sea-pigs, and consigned

the whole fort upon their heads. 'Heathen bloody bar-
barians,' he said, 'savages,' and spat, 'the one god freeze
them stiff!'

They gathered their stones.

'What about boiling water,' said Lys, 'to tickle them
up?'

'Hach, to hell with them,' said Goan; 'why bother?'

'We might waken the women anyway,' agreed Lys.

Goan looked at him. 'What about wakening them?
Why not?'

'Why should we?' asked Lys.

'Why shouldn't we? Can't they help?'

'Never mind them,' said Lys; 'curse it, never mind
them.'

'Why shouldn't we?' demanded Goan.

'Well, waken them yourself, if you won't let them
sleep.'

'You fool!' said Goan.

'Fool to you!' said Lys.

They glared at each other; but their irritation was really
for the Northmen, and those on the tongue of land
were awake and lively enough. Goan bounced a stone
to their feet.

But Sweyn had not prophesied lightly when he had
foretold the taking of the fort. His plan was simple enough,
and the instruments had been made ready overnight.
With their axes the Northmen had stripped some trees;
the longest and straightest they could find were lashed
together, with wedges fixed between for foot-grips, a
thick one was to be used as a battering ram. The plan
of campaign was to attack the door with the battering
ram and, when the attention of those on top was directed
entirely to repelling this, then to set up against the wall
on the opposing side the trees lashed together to form a
ladder. Once two or three men got over the top with their
swords, the rest should be easy, for there was nothing to
stop the attack downwards. One expert sword would drive
all before it. Indeed there would be nothing to drive once
those on top were accounted for. The plan could hardly
fail if ordinary caution was used, because the defenders

were a mere handful, were worn out, and could not conceivably have a thought for any part of the wall but that immediately over the one vulnerable spot, namely the doorway. That spot should be made to occupy their time furiously enough!

And it was. The sight of the long battering ram, when it appeared on the spit, drew the complete attention of the two fierce heads on top of the fort. Five helmeted men took up their places on one side, time about with five men on the other. Like trained athletes, the ten stooped, lifted the tree, and fondled it into a secure grip. In the absence of Haakon, Sweyn was in charge of the operation. And he was in no hurry. His movements were deliberate and provocative; he examined his engine as if it held inhuman powers; he spoke to the men; he looked about him; and at last stood back and shouted, 'Let her go!'

Like a ten-oared racing boat, the ram swept down on the stone door, to the cheers of the onlookers. But great as was the shock, the door held, and, as the Northmen staggered in recoil, Lys and Goan heaved their missiles like demons. The ground was already so littered and piled with stones near the doorway that it made any sort of footing precarious, and while a moving target is not easy for a stone-thrower, particularly from above, the Northmen retired, carrying two of their number, to the derisive shouts and hoarse boasts of Lys and Goan who were maddened with joy at the sight.

The two wounded were stretched out and cared for, being little more than stunned, while two new men took their place. Several shoulders ached from glancing stones, and there was rubbing and movement of numbed arms before the ram was once more held in position. There were four heads now on the fort wall. Sweyn walked round his men, unhurried as before, until he got his secret signal from his scout in the trees beyond the clearing. That meant the ladder had been successfully placed during the first charge and the men were in position upon it waiting the cover of the second charge before one after another they would go over the top.

And this time when the ram started on its race the

clamour and shouting set up by the Northmen was tremendous. Those on the fort responded even more fiercely, Lys and Goan climbing waist-high for the greater freedom to heave destruction. And some of the stones they tore from the unmortared masonry would have smashed to pulp any man careless or unfortunate enough to stop one of them.

But this second effort of the ram was more successful than the first, for one of the stone bolts was burst, and the double door sagged inwards against the loose barricade behind. The Northmen, as they staggered back, yelled their delight. Those on top answered with their most deadly hail. It was the moment for their harvest. The loins of Lys and Goan strained under their mighty efforts. 'Smash the sea-swine!' roared Goan. 'Smash them!' And Lys responded weight for weight and shout for shout, while Talorg of the bright brows looked like an avenging prophet, and Erp of the one arm dislodged stones with his stump.

And then Sweyn saw it happen. Erp's narrow bitter face jerked up and his one arm shot in the air as he disappeared backward with a wild scream. Talorg was caught as he half turned. Then Goan on the other side saw what had happened even in the same moment as he was engaged. Lys leapt to the wall top and stood in full view of those below, his back to them. He had a stone in his hands and smashed it downward; was smashing another when a swinging blade cut his legs. With a roar he leapt on the blade and disappeared. Heads bobbed, sword points flashed, Goan's head upreared as if it were tearing up the fort by the roots, and slowly sank. It was the end.

Haakon, who had been first on the ladder, now mounted the wall and raised his red sword. He stood on the edge of Valhalla. The Northmen gave their thunderous hail. Sweyn smiled and saluted with his axe while a small shiver of pride went over him. He loved the lad and would plainly love him even better in the hall of the heroes.

The Northmen outside the fort were now as delighted and excited as children. There was an intense pleasure in the mere success of the simple ruse. To have deceived so completely the wild men on top was extremely laughable.

They laughed as they stamped about. And at last as many as could crowd against the ram lifted it and gave themselves over to loud argument, some wanting to thrust at short reach and others desiring to retire the full distance in order to have the fun of the charge. The long-distance men won and, like a great centipede, the ram at last bore down, shedding legs on the way, legs that rolled over in mirth, but finally delivering a shock that broke the remaining stone bolt and freed the double door. Only two men could work on the narrow entrance and, when they had cleared it, Sweyn told them all to stand back.

Sweyn was a man who knew many ruses and thus, through his care, he avoided the spear that yet drew blood by grazing the skin of his neck. Those without saw the scuffle, but presently Sweyn waved them back with his wet blade, because he perceived that confusion was already in the inner court with Haakon and his men.

For as Haakon had led over the top, so he led round the galleries and down the stairs and leapt first into the inner court, his dripping sword before him, his face a flame – and encountered Nessa and stood still. Her back was to the wall, the fingers of her right hand clutched the hair of the goat's forehead, her head was up, her chest panting, her face so vivid that its searching flash of fear was sunfire to his crude flame. They stared at each other. Haakon's breath, which had choked in his breast, came hissing through his nostrils. A boy could have got at him in that instant and killed him. His men leapt past. Breeta's mother, hiding with the child Donan, gave a dreadful scream that rose to a screeching frenzy as the sword pierced her and pierced the child. Still Haakon stared at Nessa; then suddenly he broke from her in a fury of blind action, and just stopped short of wantonly killing one of his own men who was about to do violence to a defiant Silis. He roared as if he had gone berserk. Then he swung round again – and met Nessa's eyes across the whole court. Sweyn came in. Haakon glared at him – laughed uncertainly – and his flesh that, before the vision of Nessa, had started trembling, calmed a trifle.

The men outside had heard the scream of Breeta's mother and grown silent, until one had turned and winked.

There were women of course! And one perfect young beauty! Haakon, if anybody, had earned her, and the wise Sweyn could have her flaming mother, whom they had all seen. Sweyn was fond of women, particularly the sort that threatened and talked! Hoaryodin! The scream probably meant that he had answered her already, driving the point well home!

There was a hush when at last those within came out. First two of the men who had climbed the wall with Haakon, then two more carrying a clamped wooden chest, obviously of weight. Every eye fell on the chest. Behind the chest came Silis, and every eye lifted from the chest to her face.

Her long green dress was swathed closely by a leather girdle studded with gold and green enamel, and the bones of her shoulders showed firmly in a body that looked spare and queenly. Her face, too, was spare, the eyes flaming between the cheekbones; and the bone of the chin was hard and smooth and the mouth firm. The blood had drained back from her skin and left it extraordinarily fair against the yellow gold of her hair. She hesitated a moment in the strong light and ran her eyes over the men. If expression at all touched them, it was hard mockery at the number of her captors and bitter despising; and such was its invisible power that it silenced them utterly.

Behind her came Nessa. Always when Nessa was vivid like this, she was most beautiful. The quick movements of her breast were clear; her panting was in the very flush of her skin. Her mouth was slightly open, and her lips red as if they were wet. And she had, too, something of the royal air of her mother, an air she might be escaping from perpetually, and achieving in the escape. But somewhere behind her lashes, her fear had a veiled assurance.

Haakon followed her. He was flushed, and a certain stern seriousness in his brows gave his eyes an extra flash. As he looked about him in this way, everyone felt it as a command and no one cheered. The mood of excitement and frolic dropped from them; each became the individual fighter, and each secretly admired Haakon for importing into the moment its spirit of greatness that left them warriors receiving a captured queen.

A certain number were told off to search the fort thoroughly and carry away the grain and other foodstuffs, while the remainder set off for the shore, Haakon and Sweyn walking together in their midst behind the two women, Silis and Nessa.

Haakon was not inclined for speech, and Sweyn saw relief come to his face when at last they were marching by the riverside. His imperious manner at the fort entrance had been half a disguise to cover his unease. He had been embarrassed because of the young woman who had upset him, and to hide his embarrassment had compelled respect for her and for her mother. Very effective! Yes, Haakon had leadership in him. They would not only have to respect him but also that which he himself respected, or upon which he had set his heart or his desire.

Very delicate indeed, these youthful fervours! Not a subject for easy discussion!

Haakon had been hit!

And she was conscious of it, the young one. Sweyn knew it by her walk, without having to remember their faces in the fort. But he could hardly point out to Haakon in his present mood how her back responded to his eyes! Behold how her whole figure spoke, down to the lifting of her heels! Yes, she was full of sorrow; true, her father had been killed by her captors, her home was ruined, herself and her mother were being led to what ignoble end, her resentment was proud and bitter. See it in her walk! Sweyn looked at Haakon and found his eyes on her bare ankles almost self-consciously, as if he were prying! And she had a neat ankle, the leg rising from it in a firm curve. And the hips too were not at all dull, and the shoulders moved, and the head was high. But not always high; sometimes drooping, so that the bare neck, round and smooth, glistened to the roots of the hair in a golden pallor.

But if Haakon would not believe him, let him but glance at the mother. A glance only, shade of Valhalla, to see what concern that body had with them. Not much, he would perceive. It was even beginning to cease hating them, to have the sexless motion of a doomed woman walking in her sleep. In this, give it its due, it was impressive. She had the air of a saga woman, and that was not produced in a couple of days. There was a history behind that body. Men's minds had been whipped by it, and it was not unacquainted with disappointments, was properly bred to the high tragic end.

When at last a man stood clear from the tortures of women, he could see them – Odin smile upon him! – as a breed to be pitied. What is there for them in the end? A woman is a walking cage. In the beginning a bird sings within her, but it too is caged, and as the song dwindles the beak and claws develop. If she does not marry, the beak and claws ingrow and stifle her. If she does marry, then they fix in the man and keep in trim by clawing up his back and reaching over his head to power. For her urge to rule is stronger than a man's. And it is without mercy or law. If the gods died, if Valhalla fell to ruins, if man ceased fighting, then would woman's paradise be on earth. This last speculation brought a dark smile to Sweyn's face, and his eyes flashed to the daring blasphemy. For, all in all, what more blissful hour in life is there than that which follows the glory of victory and, through pleasant reflection, leads the enemy captive?

Not that any of these thoughts would have meaning for Haakon. The girl was getting into his blood. His flush was not lessening. He was having love images! He looked hot!

Haakon suddenly turned his face as if conscious of his long silence and saw Sweyn's faint smile. He grew red, forgot what he was going to say, half laughed, stuttered, and begot anger behind his confusion.

'Hot today again,' said Sweyn pleasantly.

Haakon muttered, wiping his neck.

'Even the wind has heat in it,' said Sweyn; 'but it won't last.'

Tautening his brows, Haakon looked over the men in front, and over those behind.

Old grizzled Sweyn was talkative. 'The taking of the fort was the cleverest exploit I ever saw. The men could not help laughing.'

'What at?'

'The neat way you took it. They will follow you now to death.'

'Oh,' said Haakon.

They went on in silence.

Sweyn was in pleasant ease, but Haakon's eyes were now restless.

'What about this wind?' Haakon asked.

'The saying is: variable as a woman's mind. Who can say exactly what it will do?'

'I thought you said it was going to fall by morning?'

'It may fall by that time – if the gods are kind.'

'How do you mean?' But Haakon did not yet look at him.

'Have you forgotten our promise – to sacrifice tonight?'

'Sacrifice – whom?'

Sweyn heard him hold his breath and made no answer.

Haakon did not ask again – for fear. Sweyn smiled slightly. In that which had to do with the gods, Sweyn was supreme, and not even Haakon would dare question. Sweyn would be implacable there, as different from the pleasant Sweyn of the moment as night from green day. And Haakon would bow before him, for Haakon's knowledge of sacrifice was little more than the hearsay of young men gathered together. What he had done to Drust, Sweyn had foretold him on board ship he would do. In Sweyn the old unspeakable practices still lived. And even if they were shunned in these days, yet they were feared and, beyond a man's reason, believed in and never spoken of. For all gods are jealous gods, and not even Sigrid would blaspheme that which appoints the black feast of death. It was all very well pulling Odin's grey beard. Odin was a warrior. But there was the unnamable, older and more terrible than the warrior gods. And Haakon was finding, too, that with responsibility his acknowledgment of the ancient world was increasing. He wished things to be done properly. He found himself hankering after the more conservative ways, for these gave his youth full manhood, and gave his spirit self-reliance and a manner of life and death befitting the warrior.

Haakon walked in silence beside Sweyn, and the company continued its way until at last they were arrived at the crest of the river beach by Drust's grave. There Silis paused, and Haakon and Sweyn drew up, stopping all the men behind them. Those in front turned round. But no man made a step towards her.

In a moment, curiosity was worked up to an intense pitch at the sight of this remarkable woman standing blindly by her husband's grave.

She turned her head and looked at Haakon.

'Does Drust, my husband, lie here?'

He did not understand her tongue. No one understood, but Sweyn nodded gravely, returning the short yes of his own tongue, his face hard and expressionless, the eyes glittering and watchful.

Silis turned from them to the cairn, then lifted her head and stared unseeingly over the tide.

The strong bony figure with its force of personality and singleness of emotion held them all. Plainly she knew that her husband had been sacrificed on this place, and the inscrutable intention that sat in her mind fascinated them.

'Drust, my husband, my lover, you are dead.' Thus she began in the loaded voice of one repeating a great poem. She told who he was, naming his forefathers and their deeds. She might have been among her own people, uttering the widow's lament over the grave of her husband, so unconscious did she appear to be of the stranger enemies around her. Shortly she told of her own people and what they had done and the land they occupied and how into this land Drust had come. Then her voice lifted to its theme, and all the fierce love that had been crushed for years found outlet. Drust, the golden Drust, the splendid one. Their love had been like sunlight in the morning of the world, and like starlight pale with the scent of flowers. The colour and the scent came over her in a wave. Bitterness broke on its crest and cast white salt petals on the wind. Her face in its moment's ecstasy was anguished. But she was not going beyond the moment now. She was holding by Drust, holding by her husband, holding by the love which

was Drust's and hers. It was her right – their eternal right.
She was not giving it up. She was not going alone into the
realm of death. She was going to Drust. The ways of the
world might have parted them, might have poisoned silent
thought and let it twist upon itself like an adder. But she
was casting the snake now from her breast. 'I come, O
Drust,' she called, and drew her hand from the folds at her
breast. The narrow blade of the dagger glittered a moment
before them as she held it at arm's length, then with a fierce
stroke she buried it to the haft in her breast. Her head jerked
up and for still a little time she stared before her, then even
as she swayed her knees gave way and she fell upon herself
to the ground.

Nessa's scream broke the spell upon the men. She
screamed, her hands a nest of writhing fingers. She stumbled to her mother; she fell upon her knees and hid
her face.

'Remove her,' said Sweyn calmly.

Haakon caught her under the armpits. She screamed
and fought Haakon blindly. Haakon crushed her in his
arms and carried her away. She struggled against his
arms. 'Leave me!' she called. 'My mother!' came her
voice heart-rendingly. 'Mother!' Sweyn watched her being
borne away, saw the ineffective legs, the mouth that did
not bite, and there came over his face a faint hard smile.
It would take a long time for Haakon to placate her! She
would crumble in sorrow! She would grow magnificent and
hate him! She would. . . . Sweyn turned in his satire to the
dead woman, and his eyes ran over her slowly, feature by
feature. Then he bent down and stretched her out. As he
withdrew the knife, a gush of blood followed it. She had
aimed well.

There had been no false acting here. She had meant it.
And when a woman means it – only death can stop her. If
death can.

He looked up at the men who were watching him. 'Do
you think she has earned her place beside him?'

No one spoke.

'Or do you think that he should be left free of her? He
died like a warrior, and is worth a warrior's peace.'

Some of them smiled.

'I leave it to you,' said Sweyn on an odd note.

All were silent, until a voice said, 'Bury her' – the voice of Kan.

'Why?' asked Sweyn.

'Because she killed herself,' said Kan.

Sweyn saw how her manner of death had secretly moved them all. He turned to the cairn and watched them tear it apart and expose the crushed remains of Drust. They stretched Silis beside him, and Sweyn saw by the way they put the stones on her face that they would have preferred to have put soft earth there first. When the cairn was built again, Sweyn said, 'Death hasn't stopped her,' and, turning from them, walked away by himself.

## CHAPTER SEVEN

THE light was failing in the forest where Aniel wandered. In time he came to the edge of the pine belt and leaned against a trunk looking down a heather slope to where small birch trees crested the glen. The wind, though still strong, had lost its heart and was blowing in fitful waves, darkling and of the soft texture that turns the mind to rain. But, though clouds had won into the sky, they gave no sign of rain. They were firm, and moved with a high indifference. They breasted the blue seas loftily, prows swelling and turning off, the mast-high light of the evening in their sails. . . . His thought stirred to the lessening wind that would let the longships put to sea in the dawn. He stirred himself, his eyes dropping again to the birches.

The birches were like little men shrouded in green. Their sides whitened warmly where the wind blew. Their heads were cowled. The leaves were small and occasionally separated in little rifts, as beards separate or the thick coats of animals when the wind is strong.

Beyond the birches, across the glen, the bare moor rose slowly as the sea to the dark horizon line, beyond which was the darker stillness of the Grove, with its black tree stumps and charred bones. Only the Stones remained, grey and upthrust, in an isolation complete at last – and for ever. The darkness of the Grove was left with its eternal horror for the mind.

When in the middle night Breeta had walked away from him, he had crawled to a dry spot and lain there, gathering a strange relief. He was glad to be rid of her, glad to be rid of them all, glad to be rid of the Master, glad to be alone. He had got a swift new realisation of the Master's 'loneliness'. Only in this loneliness of his there had been something else, something more than the moment's perfect

release or freedom – there had been a moving malevolence.
It had been clear and bright and edged. He did not care
for the unthinkable thing he had been about to do, he shut
off even the burning Grove, felt no restriction at thought
of the Master, and could have laughed at what Breeta,
in the awful moment of full realisation, would think of
him; did indeed laugh, looking about him into the dark
moor, laughed softly within himself, within his freedom,
this new exquisite loneliness, with its subtle malevolence.
Something had come to his spirit, like the edge of a knife
dividing one thing from another, dividing all things, all
life, into two equal parts, poised and still, while his eyes
had roved, catching glimpses of things, within and without,
stars and demons, and keeping them at their distance,
most malevolently smiling; had snuggled his head into his
arms, keeping them daringly at a distance even within the
darkness of closed eyes, and, spent, had fallen asleep.

The day was far advanced when he awoke. The wind
gave the sunlight a clean barren quality so that the moor
was darker and barer than he had known it. The world
had gone empty and noiseless, and the wind searched and
hunted, not as the sky shepherd driving the full-uddered
clouds down the sun's blue pastures, but as the nameless
who are invisible, who rear and plunge with the dark
forefeet of the wind, who approach and sweep past, but
who at any moment may converge racing upon one directly,
directly, with the terrible plunging of reined-in hooves.
They are fierce and malevolent, and tear and rend and go
streaming down the unwatched places on their mad hunt.

The Red One, who is at times the Grey One, who is also
the Skygod, and who, to Gilbrude, was the All-father, does
not always know of them, for they are the old small Dark
Ones who have never been finally conquered. They are of
the night that was before the first morning of the world.
And they will endure until the final night of all the world.
The god of war and his wife are less terrible than they, while
Manannan, whose horse is swift as the cold spring wind, is a
gentle god beside them. All these gods are not so old as the
Dark Ones, and the new Sungod of whom the Master had
once told him, the young golden-haired god of the Greeks

whom it was he had really tried to paint, was but a splendid human hero against their dark malignity. At times all this came upon one, and such a time it was when Aniel awoke and found the moor bare and wind-hunted and the world beneath noiseless and void.

Usually the ecstasy of loneliness comes to one in the sunlight. But last night he had had it in the darkness, and it had been a keener experience than he had yet known, for he had caught the malignity that is at the heart of darkness itself and kept it at bay, his mind taut in its own malevolence, his sight swift and smiling.

But now as he rose in the sunlight he knew the terror of loneliness, of everything being drawn away from him in an empty world. The light was the light off whitened bones, and the Dark Ones, who rode the wind, rode past him, and he saw the wind emptying itself and there were no Dark Ones, only loneliness – the bleached horror of loneliness.

He turned to the Grove before he knew what he was doing, and went quickly. He saw great charred arms thrust up out of the moor and ran towards them. Tree stumps, the ruins where he had lived, the scorched bones of his companions . . . the loneliness of that place was the ultimate abode of horror.

The grey Stones, the Stones, rose up out of the time before the gods, before the Dark Ones, out of the loneliness before the beginning when the world was lifeless and grey as a bone.

As he fled he had every now and then to turn round, and in his haste he thus often stumbled and fell on his back. But in a moment, watching what he fled from, he was on his feet again, and when at last he got over the crest he found that his gasping was a wild sobbing and that tears were blinding his face.

At that he calmed himself and began looking about him, alert again, and then he headed for the forest. The trees and the animal life and the birds knit him together and he lay down and let Breeta come back into his mind.

At first he scoffed at her airily as though she were beside him, but soon his body became quite still and the full force of what they had been about to do to her last night came upon him.

To begin with, he grovelled before the knowledge in little violences, shutting it out. Then he stared, biting on the prongs of a pine leaf, until the knowledge began inwardly turning on itself again like a ball of snakes – and he swiftly looked outward, snicking the pine leaf from his teeth violently and smiling in an odd daring way.

Until he faced Breeta herself, the enemy, looking at her as though she were by the tree trunk in front of him, and felt superior to her and carelessly cruel. The image of her body in love made him hot, and his animosity grew overbearing and ruthless, and he was stung with the pleasure of hurting her; then withdrew, uncaring but watchful. And in a moment was scraping the ground with his toes and thinking of nothing, his skin warm from the wind and sun, his body divinely at ease.

This last was the condition of being the Master had somehow made him understand. He had been about to explain it to Breeta by the image of two animals on a bank. That was in fact the way he understood it himself. Two animals stretching themselves on a sunny bank, curling over, lying still, stretching themselves again, scraping with their toes, lazily, touching, sleeping, half awake, faintly excited, cool as two trees, dreaming watchfully; then hit by a wind of mirth, stirred by excessive ease, touching quickly, teasing, tickling, laughing, fighting, tossing, panting, and stretching again, lazily, drowsily.

Though that was only half of it, the other important half dwelling in the mind. For this picture was the true picture of loneliness, of being abstracted from the world-in-common. And the loneliness of one was intensified and made complete by the loneliness of two. For one will have often a watchful malevolent loneliness, but two will live at the centre of the circle of perfection where thought has ceased and the moment achieves the eternal.

The Master was difficult, his words were difficult, but in images he could be perceived. With the Master it was a state of being. *A state of being!* Aniel turned over and crushed his smile. But as the earth blackened under his closed eyes, Breeta's face came staring up and he jumped to his feet, petulant and violent, and started off through the forest, not caring where he went.

Late that afternoon he encountered three men. They had news to tell. They had watched the fort being taken, and the two women, Silis and Nessa, being led captive.

Aniel let the men speak, only now and then asking them a question and then saying something inwardly to himself, such as, 'So Breeta's mother has been killed as well as her father.'

And from what the men said it was clear that nothing more could be done. Their only hope, in fact, lay in the immediate departure of the Northmen. Anything that would annoy them into staying longer would mean further disaster. And a good part of the flocks had been saved. Who knew but that at any moment the Logenmen might return and capture what was left, and perhaps take hold of the land itself? When the Logenmen heard how many the Northmen had killed, would not that be likely? In this way the men spoke and Aniel listened to them.

'So you won't gather a party?' he asked, and waited coldly.

No, for even if they did kill a few Northmen, what difference would that make now? And were they not more likely to be killed themselves? After all, they were not a fighting people. All they wanted were their flocks and their children and the good times to come again. But in the end one of them said that he would try to gather a handful of young fellows, who would at least see the Northmen depart. Aniel was now waiting for that handful, though it was early yet, the adventure being timed for the middle night.

The noise of the wind in the branches covered light footfalls, and when Aniel heard himself named he turned sharply. It was the Master. Among the rough pillars he was small and alone. The sensation – of all things receding from him – confused Aniel, and the beating of his heart was loud and painful. While the Master read his mind, he looked to one side.

Then the Master sat down, for he had walked far since the night and he was tired. Aniel sat down with him and explained that he was waiting for others in order that they might see the Northmen depart. The Master sat uprightly without visible movement of breathing. There was about him something of that terror of loneliness, of the grey Stone upthrust where no life is. Aniel knew that he had come here to question and to instruct him.

Breeta entered Aniel's mind from the Master's. He saw now that all day he had not really faced the issue. He became confused, but with a gathering knot of defiance at his core.

But the Master's voice caught even that defiance, calmly observing that when defiance is complete it changes to strength, and strength to harmony, and harmony to tenderness. But one does not come to that completeness for a long time. Wisdom is squeezed out of experience. Knowledge is the honey or poison of many flowers. Had he been compelled by his desire to sacrifice to the gods?

'Yes,' answered Aniel.

*And not by his desire to sacrifice to himself?*

Aniel looked swiftly at the opaque eyes that were full upon him, and there started within him the swirling of an ineffable and terrible meaning. Coming up against those eyes was like coming up against a blank wall that advanced and passed through one, taking all privacy before it. The swirl went round within him like a widening wheel.

Within the wheel the voice spoke. There is a time when the importance of what one is about to do takes possession of the spirit. The spirit then becomes a leader and the body obeys it. As they march together their confidence grows, their importance increases; they grow and increase like the circle of a club swung round and round, or like a wheel of light expanding to the sky. Now there is no greater importance than the offering of blood. It unites the mortal to the gods in the most terrible and lasting of all compacts. And when it happens that the one that is led is of great attraction to him who leads, then he, leading, approaches in his self-denial her ecstasy of sacrifice. His importance swells upon the night. The compulsion of the gods is upon him in a deep pride. No demons can harm him, for he goes further than all demons. He is wrapped about like the hero in a hide that no weapon can pierce.

The circle of meaning whirled about Aniel, but it was not true, not all true! He had led across the moor; he had stumbled on. . . . Under a sudden muscular stress, his thought went blank and his breath came faster.

'The men were there,' blurted Aniel; 'they were in a circle, waiting for us. They received us into it. The girl was chosen. The night – the night reached over. We were caught. I did not know – I—' His mouth closed firmly; his eyes glistened.

The stress of his thought eased, as if an invisible hand went down over his face, and so knowledge was added to the grey emotionless place within him. The Master's thought had lifted and was elsewhere. It was at the shore, whither Aniel had said he was going; going to see that the Northmen depart.

Was that the only reason? Or had it been deep in Aniel's mind that they might *rescue the woman Silis and her daughter*?

Aniel's mind grew hot. The daughter, Nessa, deep in his mind, hidden . . .?

But the Master was not concerned now with Aniel's confusions; he was concerned only with what had to be done for their people.

For tragedy had come upon this place and upon them all. But that was not an end. Tragedy may kill an individual, but it does not kill a people. When a people has been broken, then the broken has to be gathered again. That was their task now. They needed leadership to gather together that which had been broken, and to start it on its way once more.

It was the new phase in destiny, and it lay ahead.

Aniel saw the bodies of the Master and himself sitting in a ring of disaster. Around them were the burnt houses, destruction, and the dead. The red seashore to the red shielings was a line through the circle, whose centre was their dead chief's ruin.

Aniel's head drooped.

Silis the woman could be a leader. Otherwise the people

had no leader. What did that mean? *Why had not the people a leader from among them?*

*This phase would reveal the people, would reveal Aniel to himself. It would throw light into the pit of their soul, his soul.*

*It was about to begin.*

In the silence that followed, the leaderlessness of the dark people was a note of fatality, high, pervasive. The Master's meaning was writ in black lines against the light. They had lost the power to produce leaders of their own. What was that which had happened compared with that which was to happen to them now?

Yet what was immediately to happen was clear. One could not change destiny in a moment. Aniel must be prepared to go to the Broad river for the son of Silis and of Drust. The son might come back with knowledge and with power, for doubtless there would be young men who would adventure much for him and for their king. Drust was well liked, and in his time gave the king gold. What other leader? There was no other leader.

'I will go,' said Aniel in a low voice.

'There is no more a home for you in the Grove. I am an old man whose time has come upon him.'

The calm remote tone affected Aniel strongly. 'Will there be no more Grove?' he asked. And then the Master spoke to Aniel of himself. He had interfered little with Aniel so that wisdom might come to him in many ways from many things. Aniel was a maker, and a maker can retreat from what evil he has done, or from what evil has come upon him, to the happy solitude of his own creation, and yet have a cunning understanding of that evil. The girl Breeta might have retreated from Aniel, but he had power over her. With the Greek god – there Aniel had even been ready to sacrifice his gods for a painted image. Beware of the painted image when it shows that true fear does not sit deep enough. To be without fear is to be without thought. The eyes lose the power of staring at truth, which is behind fold and fold, year and year, age and age. Without truth the image is trivial and of no account amongst men. All this would have come upon Aniel and he might have been a teacher for the new and difficult times ahead. Because even now he could be

alone and have pleasure in his loneliness; he could sit still
and keep the demons at a distance; he could put around
him a circle that no one might cross. The Master's mind
grew tired with its load of years, but it found it easy to be
young as Aniel and to remember, though in a ghostly way,
the fevers of the flesh.

Though the Master's face looked smooth from a distance, close at hand it was an intricate network of tiny
wrinkles, which all came to life when he smiled, however
faintly. 'Aniel, there were times when I watched over you
more than would a father or a mother.'

Aniel bowed his head. The Master had never spoken in
this personal way before. When he heard the Master move
he dared not look up. 'I will speak with you again before
I go.' Aniel watched the small figure disappear among
the trees.

Aniel got up and moved quietly down into the glen, full
of a keen joy, which had far within it a secret joy of its
own, as though within his deep love or the Master there
was a tiny core of love of himself, this reality of being Aniel
who now was loved by the Master. And as he went, his eyes
sometimes had the cunning side-flash that keeps things at
bay. And once he sat down and tore slow handfuls of moss,
and said to himself that the Master was the greatest man
who had ever lived, and thrust the moss deep into the
ground. He would die for him. Remembering how the
Master had spoken of the leading of Breeta, he twisted fresh
moss violently and thrust it into the ground and looked up
swiftly, smiling, with an odd wariness, and followed his
wary thought to his feet. He crossed the river and, when
the light had failed to its summer night, climbed the slope
of trees and came upon the fort.

Here was the beginning of ruin, of the new and difficult
times the Master had spoken of as lying into the future.
A great part of the upper wall had been pushed over so
that a mound of stones ran round the base. Stones were
everywhere. Drust's hall was gone. The enclosure wall was
in places completely levelled. The blackness of fire here,
too, and silence – that silence which suddenly to Aniel
seemed to come not from a remote past but from a remote

future, as if death were not in the beginning but in the end. The Grove was the past. Here was the future, and it was in ruins. The division of future and past held him quite still. Never before had a sense of future desolation touched him, and the vision was in a way more terrible than his vision of the bleached bone before life was.

He circled quietly to the door. Here the stones had been cleared, and after listening a moment he stooped, and trod noiselessly to the level of the inner wall. It was dark in the court, but soon objects loomed upon his eyes. The side erections had been torn down and beams leaned gauntly. The ruin of the wall was stark, but this inner ruin was malignant and held a life of its own. It was like a well of the night that demons might inhabit. The wind funnelled past him. It was suddenly cold and his skin responded with a shiver of fear. Something flapped high up, like the heavy wings of a blood bird or bat demon. Over from him on the ground a dark thing moved. Fear so weakened him that the wall came against his back. A moaning sound arose from the dark thing. It was a swaying body. The body arose. Its face under the funnel of sky light was the face of death. It came towards him with the groping deliberation of blindness from a lost mind. It came straight towards him. One hand touched him. Aniel's body, that had gone icy cold, was sinking down into the oblivion of terror, when the touch of the hand stopped it; and the jerk of the hand backward jerked his body to an intense pitch.

'Breeta!' he whispered.

'No!' she screamed, falling back.

'Breeta!'

'No!' She stumbled away. He followed. 'Breeta!' he cried. His bare foot landed on the yielding surface of a human face, and he slid and fell upon the body. It was the body of a woman, of Breeta's mother. In a moment, he was scrambling up and after the girl. 'Breeta!' he cried madly. She dodged him. 'Breeta!' He caught her. 'No!' she screamed, and her swinging fist smashed into his face. 'Breeta!' he yelled, clutching her dress and ripping it as she wrenched herself from him. 'Breeta, don't be a fool!' She was gone. He scrambled after her through the doorway, took a few steps against the empty night, cried her name once more, stood listening, but was in such a state of trembling that he stumbled to the brink of the decline and sat down.

She had revolted at him so intensely that he might have been a carrion wolf!

Keeping watch in there by her dead mother. . . .

Buried her – they could have buried her . . . that's what had flamed into his mind. Together.

A flesh destroyer . . . what he was to her seared his mind. He tore at the grass. He struck his forehead into the ground. Then stealthy sounds reached him. He lay still. Ah, she was watching, waiting! The core of his mind hardened to a smiling cruelty. He would deal with her! Slowly he turned over, quietly got up, and five young men came out of the wood towards him.

'We thought we heard some one yelling,' said one, coolly.

Aniel looked at them.

'Are there no more of you?' he asked.

'What use would more be?' came Rasg's harsh voice.

'Let us sit down,' said Aniel, still trembling, 'for we are early enough.'

'The night is going on,' said Miran, who was a thin keen hunter with the unusual dust-coloured hair.

They all sat down.

'What use would more be?' persisted Rasg.

'None, as you say,' answered Aniel.

'I didn't say,' answered Rasg.

'What do you mean?' asked Aniel.

Rasg, who could be a dour harsh fellow, was silent. What the Northmen had done was in their minds. They hated them, and time had given their own impotence a malign edge. At first there had been the disaster of the sea fight followed by escape; then the disaster of the shieling fight followed by the struggle to save what stock and humans they could. All that had occupied their minds intricately. They had fought a retreating action to save the core of their tribe. They were a pastoral rather than a fighting people. Field sports and hunting and music were their pastimes, not in a spectacular way, but here and there singly or in groups, though sometimes in the shieling season all would find themselves combining on great and memorable days of rivalry and boasting and fighting and roaring fun, yet the typical picture was that of a man fashioning something by himself and whistling a low liquid tune he only half heard, or of women working together, helped by an endless song.

When people like these have saved what they can, their minds come into play and will not give them rest. They brood. They hate. They hated the Logenmen more than the Northmen, and would some day wreak black vengeance upon them. But that could wait. It could mercilessly wait. Meanwhile here were the sea-pigs slipping away. It would have been sweet to club them in their sleep, destroy them savagely, cutting off each reeking head. The desire to destroy them grew in the mind, twisting it evilly.

This came upon Aniel from his companions. They were in that evil mood. And because Rasg knew they could do nothing, he was surly and ready for a quarrel.

When presently they set out they all walked in silence. The sky had flattened and stretched to an immense distance, with the dark night clouds islanded in a light that fused its livid blue northward in the eerie afterglow of the dead day. The evil mood came upon Aniel and islanded him from his companions. At first he felt he was not one of them, that he was carried along as a stick is carried by a deep-flowing pool, moving to the sea. They were profounder than he was; the current of their minds set more deeply within the black sea of their common mood. This feeling – of being borne along – irked him and roused a gradual hostility to Rasg in particular. But soon the increasing strength of the very hostility merged him with them. And at last what had been evil was no longer so. For the evil searched for action, craved bodies to kill and mutilate. It ran through their flesh like a lust turning the blood black.

Aniel let it flow full tide in him. His body gathered power, his thought recklessness. He remembered with a rich satisfaction the Northman he had knifed in the hag. He

remembered himself with Breeta immediately afterwards –
and the vision brought a richer satisfaction. She could hate
him as she liked, he had got her, she had surrendered.
And because that had happened, he had her! Even the
Master knew! Aniel looked at the others stealthily, and
his smile deepened inwardly. The urge of evil was a black
rich laughter. What were they brooding about, the fools!

But he found, when at last they came to the wooded
hollow, whose far brink commanded the river mouth, that
their brooding had the same core as his own. 'Sea-pigs out
of hell,' said Rasg, staring at the Northmen's camp; 'if only
we had fifty of us!' There was fire in his black eyes. There
was fire in all their eyes. Their skins were taut over their
faces. Their jaws moved clenchingly, and two of them spat
grass and oaths. A writhing twined through their muscles.
Eyried thus above the encamped beach, they looked forth,
seeing but unseen, and their impotence caught the very
exaltation of evil.

The dusk of morning was thinning to a grey light. The
long rollers pounded on the beach and ran into the river
mouth, but the wild horses had fled the sea, and only odd
manes lifted over the wrinkled mackerel waste. Upon a full
tide the longships could head for the open easily enough.
There was a small man moving about one of them now.
Behind the crest of the beach the Northmen lay asleep like
a herd of seals. On the river flat three walked up and down
in the slow easy walk of men used thus to pace in the lee of
a shed on a cold coast before a colder sea. The camp was
guarded. There was no earthly chance of taking any one
of these men by surprise. There might have been the sea
chance of landing out of sight on the windy beach beyond
the crest, of swarming up over and swooping down on the
seals and clubbing their skulls. For these men set no guard
on the sea, because they were the sea's masters.

The five with Aniel lay and watched, unable to take
their eyes off that scene. The way the three men turned
and turned fascinated them. If only they could have been
got at without rousing the lot! But there was no chance
of that. There was first of all the flat ground to the river,
then the river itself, and then the flat ground beyond on

which the three men walked and the rest slept. There was nothing to do but lie and watch and dream mad dreams of violence, including violence by the gods. They were not in the mood for praying the gods; they were in the mood to be gods themselves. Aniel's eyes, however, kept drifting around the galleys, searching out his thoughts of Silis and Nessa, particularly of Nessa, until the golden thought of Nessa penetrated the black thought of evil.

The twilight of the morning waned, and the day came clear, an increasing wind blowing away the last shadows. In this wind was a stir, a secret movement of life, an awakening that gave to the sleeping Northmen an appearance of death. The watchers saw now that what had looked like gear on the creek's slope were captives. A wriggling amongst them was like the last contortions of the dying. The same movement went through the bodies of the watchers and their eyes distended with hate.

The awakening touched one of the galleys, for movement of undoubted life was seen there. It touched Sweyn in particular as he looked after Haakon and Nessa, whose backs were the more potent for being dumb as their mouths. He had remarked their wakefulness as he had returned from the last secret rites some little time ago. Haakon appeared lost in sleep. Nessa looked at Sweyn once, full and long, and closed her eyes, chafing against her bonds in an infinitely weary manner, before half turning her head away. The effect had been complete, for what might have been appeal served to give her spirit an indescribable air of disdain. From this Sweyn knew that Haakon was feigning sleep and that the girl had power over him, to such an extent indeed that it left him powerless.

As Sweyn carefully disposed himself for sleep, he did not smile down his grizzled beard. True, he would have preferred Haakon to have taken her on the spot and have got his trouble over; but, listening to Haakon's breathing as he closed his own eyes, he knew that any such healthy violence was beyond Haakon now. Haakon was trapped; his breast was congested; the full breath that he took every now and then did not come out of innocent deeps of sleep;

and his cramped movements indicated something more than the hardness of the bed.

There was an excitement in the situation that Sweyn appreciated. He experienced the good nature of the hunter watching two animals in the toils. There was no possible rest for them. The speculation lay in merely how long it would take Haakon to break through. It was necessary, too, for Sweyn to see how he would break through. For this business of women can readily be the most treacherous element in life. If, for example, Haakon had had his will of this girl at once, then his future could have been prognosticated and assured. But he hadn't had; hadn't even touched her yet; and ignored her now.

Sweyn almost closed his eyes on Haakon and his breath came heavily through his nostrils. Haakon turned again so that his face was towards Sweyn, who observed the wakeful richness of the skin and the odd lax torment of the body. Haakon, as it were, let himself go, let himself sink – and his body floated burningly to the surface! Even the eyelids were not still, but had a quiver in them over the rich skin.

All at once the eyes opened full on Sweyn, whose breathing did not lose its heavy ease. From the twilight of his drawn lids, Sweyn saw a flame in the blue eyes that his own lashes made waver and dance. Haakon turned his eyes on Nessa. She looked back at them. Sweyn admired her ease. First she looked straight at Haakon concentratedly with all her face and all that was behind her face, and then as if aware of, but not disturbed by, what she was doing, she looked past him by no more than a hand's breadth. She made no appeal. He was not in her face at all. She was staring at something in her mind, and its tragic cast gave her features a distraught loveliness that was composed. Then she lifted her eyes and face away, chin tilting from the pure line of her throat, and her breath quivered out in a faint moan.

It was all exquisitely real. Her father had been killed; her mother had killed herself; her home was destroyed; she was a bound slave to whom anything might happen, to whom something should have happened. And she was a beauty, her youth just full, her skin spring-fresh.

Haakon stretched himself slightly, as if he had only just wakened, and half yawned. Then he carelessly made himself comfortable and went in search of rest again.

A curious torment, thought Sweyn, this of Haakon's! He could not leave her out of his sight. And yet he could do nothing with her in his sight. A difficult situation! Sweyn let his lids fall and half raised them again.

The tension increased in Haakon's body. The night had slipped away, and here was the dawn. In a few hours they must put to sea. Haakon's restlessness grew. It got beyond him. He sat up rubbing his bones yawningly. His mouth closed and held, his eyes suddenly flashing. Inaction had become intolerable and he looked at Nessa, his colour rudely deepening.

She moved slowly. In the morning light her eyes were extraordinarily clear. They wandered all round his gaze, then met it, full centre.

There was stillness for a long time. Then Haakon's breath could be heard muffled and quick as in one who had been running.

He slid to his feet and advanced against her eyes. He made no noise. She made no sound. He stooped and untied her thongs quickly, impatiently. Sweyn saw his hands trembling. He stood up again. She slowly stood beside him and looked at him. She was at his mercy, but splendidly.

Haakon became more impatient. He cast swiftly about him. Sweyn saw him hide his vast awkwardness under an eagle flash. He beckoned to her with his head. He could not speak. Sweyn watched their dumb backs. Even now, thought Sweyn, he does not know what he will do – if he knows what he wants! Sweyn gazed before him in amused speculation.

Already as a girl she was forming into the perfect wanton woman. She had all the arts. She would drive men to deathly deeds as the wind drives the sea. She would stir hate and black jealousy. And, strongest of all, she would rise to the great occasion greatly, like fire. Every gesture she had made before Haakon was acted and yet was natural. Already, at her age! Before Odin, they might have to slip

her overboard to save Haakon. She was only beginning!
Sweyn's wry speculations slid into sleep.

Sigrid, who was fashioning unnecessary ribs with a knife,
saw the two go past. Lack of sleep had lined his face and his
small eyes were bloodshot. His mouth twisted in a coarse
humour. Their passing gave this humour to the morning.
An oath or two exploded within him warmly. He wondered
if some of the men were still visiting the native women and
if these two would catch them in the act. Early in the night
the women had been inclined to yell but that had soon been
put right, while love scenes before the native men had had
an amusement all its own. Drink had been got somewhere
and for an hour or two there had been what Sigrid called
a hoaryodin time; others had dubbed it the celebration of
victory; a few had exhibited an excessive beastliness which
proved most humorous of all. There had been only three
fights and then with naked fists, though a few men, who
made pretence to the women as their sole property, had had
to be threatened with bloody death. A night bloodshot as
Sigrid's eyes as they stealthily followed Haakon and Nessa
until these two came by the crest of the slope where the
captives lay. But there were no Northmen there.

Sigrid let the lovers go and, returning to his shelter,
curled himself up and with a new ease of mind went
to sleep.

One of the captive women wailed to Nessa, who was suddenly shocked at her drained face and unclothed condition.
The other women looked tattered and dead. Haakon
turned a fierce glance on the wailing woman and elbowed
Nessa away. Nessa made no protest. The woman cried
after them, but Haakon did not understand what the
woman said.

He saw the three sentries pause and look, and his breast
filled with mad anger against them. It seemed all the
accursed world was watching this girl and himself. He
was merely wanting privacy, wanting to get away from
them, freeze them! Only brutes dragged their privacy under
your nose. His eyes swept intolerantly from them and rested
on the wooded hollow across the river. He gripped Nessa's
arm and swung her to the stream.

'He's in a hurry!' said one sentry.

'He likes a quiet place for it!' said the second.

'Thor stiffen him!' said the third.

They smiled at humanity's common measure, and admired him more than ever. After all, the previous night had gone a bit too far. Hell! They laughed, and began walking again, warmed by this sudden appearance of Haakon and his lady, filled with good nature and friendliness on account of it. Their legs braced against the earth. They began to long for the sea, and when, a little later, they thought they heard the girl scream among the trees, they chuckled and kicked the mirthful grass.

Meantime there were six pairs of eyes on top of that wooded hollow watching Haakon and Nessa approach. To these eyes there was something incredible in the scene: the early morning, the green river meadow, with the young chief of Lochlann and the daughter of Drust coming walking towards them like two figures from a legend, two lovers sent by the Dark Ones to be sacrificed not with the frank ritual of the Grove but with the unnamable ritual of the dark ages.

A slight awe touched the evil in the watching eyes. The heads of the lovers were struck by lances from the rim of the rising sun. Nor did they speak to each other, but walked side by side, faces to their doom, in a strange measured pace, that yet seemed to contain within it the thraldom of ecstasy.

Rasg drew his head back and hissed softly. All the dark heads drew back. Rasg looked at Aniel. Rasg's forehead had disappeared to a grey-brown line between hair and eyebrows. His teeth and gums, usually showing, were hidden but for a white gleam between moustache and beard. The eyes had sunk to slits beneath the ridged brows. The face was altogether intense and forked – and watchful.

Aniel met it, his eyes quite open and staring. Aniel's skin was darker than Rasg's, but also had more pallor in it. His brow was smooth and his nostrils delicate.

'Come on!' said Rasg.

Aniel did not move.

Rasg slid off. The others crawled after. Aniel followed them, and when they were come to the foot of the decline and Rasg was heading to the entrance, whispered, 'Wait!'

Rasg turned on him.

'They will come in so far,' said Aniel. There was a strange look in his eyes and something of the awful calm of the priest in his manner. A smooth acquiescence went over Rasg's expression as he watched the white quiver behind that calm.

The ground was broken about the narrow course where the water had almost dried up, and out of which great masses of fern grew. Fern also grew about scattered mossy boulders. There was a foot-track by the rocky runnel and over all a certain breadth set with slim tree trunks and foliage, but not obscured by them. They took shelter on the slope and waited.

Aniel saw the two come in, saw their breasts rising against the place. There was splendour in their pride, now that the moment had come and their wave must break. They advanced more slowly. Then Aniel saw their faces, saw their bodies, and he knew in the same moment that he had seen the final picture of all desire.

Here were the lovers of legend, beyond good and evil, beyond treachery and honesty, beyond the laws of family or tribe, splendid in bearing, alive like fire, selling all the world, father and mother and home and honour, for their love's pleasure. Nessa was beautiful, and what wanton softness there might be was killed by her air of hostility and pride, a sensitiveness that gave her features that exquisite brittle denial of the consummation they desired. Her hair was softer in its yellow than gold, her eyes were restless and flashed above her panting chest; her body was so tall that it topped his shoulder and its youth was at once slender and full.

Haakon was jointed like a warrior, broad-shouldered, open-throated, silkily bearded, with hair the colour of stacked grain swept sideways from a temple. His fairness was fairer than Nessa's, and his pent emotions gave his skin a flushed transparency, through which they could be seen. For clearly he was not used to keeping emotion in check.

Action lay in the beat of his heart. It was the root of his dreams. And now the lack of it wrapped him in a net whose strands had a paralysing strength. For this woman was a stranger and beautiful, and, however his men might think, she was to be his first woman; as he, indeed, was to be this girl's first man. His emotion flamed through his skin; it gave his flesh the beauty and force of fire; it finally enwrapped all his body and brought it to an intolerable poise.

He turned on Nessa, he looked at her. She met his look, her head thrown up, fiercely hostile and terribly expectant. He gripped her. She strained back. He crushed her. Her hands came round his neck. He staggered with her and they dropped in a crush of ferns.

Aniel stared at the rustling fern fronds, in the pallor that comes to one stricken by black magic.

Rasg's hiss at him was low and sustained. Aniel's gaze never wavered. Reason had gone from him. He was no longer himself.

The others had heard the snake-hiss, and when Rasg beckoned with his head they all started wriggling noiselessly downward. Aniel's eyes got caught by their flattened bodies converging on the bed of fern. Breath began to move painfully in his breast, to whistle in his nostrils. He was like one coming to life through a sick agony.

The dark heads lifted by the ferns. As they lifted, a dark head rose in Aniel's throat. The fern fronds were slowly parted.

Nessa's wild scream released Aniel and he bounded down to them. Haakon was staggering on his feet, having flung them from him, though blood was dripping from Rasg's blade. They watched him warily. They had him! They watched him curiously. 'Don't kill him,' shouted Aniel. They sprang at him and bore him to the ground, and would not be flung from him. Rasg smashed the haft of his knife into Haakon's forehead and stunned him.

At that Nessa flew into a torment of action. Her mouth spat redly at them. But Rasg stepped between her and Haakon's body. He half raised his knife. 'Shut up, you bitch!' he said, with such concentration of venomous meaning that she staggered back. But only for a moment.

Then she faced him – a golden fury. 'You snakes!' she
hissed. 'You black snakes!' Her words choked in her
sobbing throat. Her body twisted in its hatred of them; her
arms crossed convulsively over her breast and separated,
hands clenched. Her fury increased. Having been caught
as she was caught worked upon her. Their presence was an
outrage, unclean, filthy. A cry came out of her, and, body
swelling upward, fists rising, she swept upon Rasg.

So sudden was she, so fierce, so blazing her eyes, that
Rasg stepped back, raising his knife. But she was on him
even then. Aniel caught the knife arm and wrenched Rasg
away. 'Leave her!' he cried. Nessa, in the bodily swing,
came upon him. He repulsed her violently. She stumbled
backwards, remained for a moment glaring at him, panting,
hands hanging, then she threw herself face down beside
Haakon.

Rasg eyed Aniel who was strangely quivering. Aniel
swept his glance over all their watching eyes. He choked
his voice to steadiness. 'Down, Miran, and see if anyone's
coming!' he ordered sharply.

Rasg's look never wavered from Aniel; its knowledge was
infernal. He, Rasg, dared not touch the girl! The Northman
dared not touch her! Only Aniel might touch the girl – to
repulse her in black jealousy!

Rasg's penetration grew knife-edged. If Aniel thought
this was a little affair of his, gods around! he was mistaken.
They had captured the leader of those who had burnt out
their homes and killed their people. They had captured this
wanton bitch, daughter of their own chief! And they would
wring the last blood-drop out of their triumph!

Aniel met his eyes – and held them – and transfixed
them with a narrow cruelty. Rasg saw whither black
jealousy would drive this young druid. The contorted
situation appealed to Rasg. The malignity was pleasant
to contemplate! Appeased, his eyes cleared and he nodded
to Aniel in a grim and not unfriendly way.

Aniel went and stooped by Haakon, caught Nessa's wrist
and drew it from Haakon's throat. She swung round,
tearing her wrist away, but he pinned her down. 'Lie
still!' His tone infuriated her. 'Hold her!' he called, and

two of them fixed her arms and legs. 'Let me go!' she panted. 'Let her go,' said Aniel. She sat up, defiant but without action.

Rasg's blade had got Haakon about the shoulder. 'I did not mean to do it,' Rasg muttered. Aniel examined the wound which was bleeding freely, and felt the pulse. 'We must stop the blood.'

'Your own face is bleeding.'

Aniel ignored the remark. 'Hold the wound like that till I get some moss. Here' – he said to the others – 'take these straps off his legs and tie his ankles together. And cut a bit for his shoulder and wrists.'

Dumbly Nessa watched them, but not brokenly. Aniel passed her without a look, but as he plucked the moss his hands shook with hectic energy. Yet his face looked pale with self-possession as he trussed up Haakon coolly and firmly.

When they stood clear, Nessa got to her feet. Aniel turned to her. 'Come along,' he said.

'Where?'

'Home.'

Her breasts began to heave again. Miran returned from his scouting. 'No one coming.'

'Up with him,' commanded Aniel.

Four of them lifted Haakon and started up the water-course.

'I'm not going,' said Nessa.

'You are,' said Aniel.

'I'm not!' Her voice rose thinly. Her beauty caught a wild insane look. But before she could take the first blind step, Rasg had tripped her to the ground, choking her scream with his fist. She bit his fist. He caught her by the throat. The sight of Rasg's hands at her throat put Aniel beside himself. His calm broke into bits. 'Shut up!' he shouted at her. 'Shut up, you – you – you bitch!' he screamed and tore Rasg's hands away.

Gasping, she glared at Aniel, her face blood-choked, her eyes wide and mad but steady. 'Well then!' shouted Aniel. 'What do you think you're doing?' He became incoherent and stuttered. 'What – what – Up, come on, get up!' His excitement was dreadful. Even as she arose she kept looking at Aniel, at his face with its three runnels of blood from her nails. Then her head drooped and, turning, she saw the four men with Haakon standing still. She went towards them and the whole party proceeded from that place, emerging from the narrow valley of trees at an inland level beyond sight of the creek. There they turned their faces towards the glen, and did not halt until they had crossed the stream above the fort and come among the shelter of the trees on the other side. The halt was a short one, nor did they feel secure until they finally came into the refuge of the forest.

## CHAPTER EIGHT

THEY were now tired and hungry and prickled with sleep. Aniel found that Haakon's wound had been bleeding on the way and had great difficulty in bringing him round. When at last Haakon did open his eyes and look about him, it was with a vague strained expression as though he did not know where he was and did not greatly care. After very little effort he gave up and lapsed into unconsciousness. Aniel stopped the bleeding, padded and tied the wound carefully, and turned him over on his sound side.

'You can go to sleep too,' he said to Nessa.

She was sitting dumbly, her hands in her lap, and slowly lifted her head and looked at him. He avoided her at once, turning to his companions.

'Is it sleep first and then food – or what?'

But they were all stretched out. They needed a rest and it was agreed that after an hour or so they could arrange what next to do.

'All right,' said Aniel. 'I'm not sleepy. I'll watch.' One or two of the others offered to watch instead of him, but he said that they and not he would have to do the food-hunting, so they had better take their rest now.

They were glad to do this, for there had not been much sleep going in the last few nights. Rasg said nothing, but, when the others let themselves sink, he sat open-eyed.

'Aren't you going to sleep?' asked Aniel.

'No,' said Rasg.

'You needn't mind me,' said Aniel.

'You can sleep yourself,' said Rasg.

Aniel turned his face away to hide his swift anger. After a little, he said coolly, 'You'd better try to sleep now. You'll need your strength before the night is dead. I'll think things out.'

Rasg said nothing. There was silence. Nessa fell slowly over on her side, her back to them. Her body looked abandoned, as if she had fainted, and one hand curled over on the earth behind her hip. Haakon's wrists and ankles were still tied, and his bulk had the mute helpless appeal of a great one defeated by them and dressed for the end. This appearance of the splendid trussed body fascinated Rasg. So might a hunter who has brought down a rare animal gaze on his still incredible luck. And this animal had been fierce as well, had indeed the blood of half the tribe on his claws. Rasg's look turned on Nessa, ran slowly over the contours of her body, the bare legs, the sandalled feet, one blood-flecked ankle, the open hand behind the hip, the fallen head with its hair of that colour which was so distinguishing a feature of those whom, in certain intense and terrible moments, he hated. There was something in him so much older than they, deep as the primeval dark, out of the black earth, blind-eyed and hidden as the earth – on which the golden daylight walked. They walked on the earth's body, on his body, the body of his tribe, on those who had worked in the earth, the earth into which they poured their blood; they walked on them, the rulers, the golden conquerors, the sword-killers – the sea-swine!

Rasg lifted his eyes and stared between the grey-brown tree trunks with their blood veining, and his wordless mood bemused him, and the peace of sweet security after conquest beset him; his eyes closed and, half remembering Aniel, he grunted and fell asleep.

At that Aniel rose up into freedom. He looked about him, over their bodies, listened to their heavy breathing, got caught by Nessa's hand, and lifted his head to the high swaying sighing branches. The loneliness had an exciting magical quality. It made the blood beat faintly in his temples emphasising his weariness; it made him gulp in a spent way. There could be no doubt they were all asleep. Secretly he turned and gazed at Nessa.

His mounting excitement made him exquisitely weary. Her limp fingers folded before his eyes; her head turned over; she moved; she quietly stretched herself; she sat up

and so slowly turned her head that he could not turn his
own away.

Their eyes met; and in the instant all her face, all of her,
came blinding him, though her look was most sober, and
he broke away.

But not foolishly, still with cunning, so that he might
have been little more than naturally embarrassed before
such a captive. But the beating of his heart troubled him
and a weakness went from it flushing over his body. He
picked up a pine needle and began to chew it, staring
before him, his face hot as fire.

He sat like that for a long time, supported by the
dumb quality of endurance inherited from his people.
Then when the flush ebbed within him, and a measure
of coolness returned, he continued to see her without
looking at her directly, then flashed his dark eyes on her
half-averted face.

She was gazing before her, lost in sad reverie. Her
hands had fallen helplessly to her sides, her back was bent
slightly; but her face, although it actually drooped, had the
appearance of looking far away; then, as he watched, even
her look drooped and she stared at the earth in front of her.
Slowly her back bent till it was like a bow, her head drooped
still more, and her neck was left exposed and vulnerable.
Her knees crept up and received her forehead. The backs
of her hands lay on the ground. A faint tremoring went
over her shoulders, and she was still.

He feasted on her now until the appeal of her mute body
became insupportable. A wild desire stole over him to crawl
up and kiss her neck. A mad desire, mad, choking all the
channels of reason.

Her body was a lovely arch over her breasts. Her hidden
face had all the intimacy and humility of defeat that yet may
not be approached. Her hands, her empty hands. And her
knees caught a quiver of stress.

What he had seen of her and Haakon rushed out from
his memory like warm blood from a sluice. There had
been something terrible as fire in their beauty, their breasts
uplifted against the green hollow, their faces in that strange
look. Always she had been far enough from him for thought

of her to be impersonal and intimate as legend. And now she was here.

Here – she who had been yonder crushed in the arms of that man, the conqueror. Crushed and fondled, choked with passion. Aniel's spent body prickled with fire. He tore his eyes from her and lay back, lay over, forehead on his arms. His flesh trembled and melted into the ground. He could not lie still. His head rolled, it lay over and looked at her, meeting her eyes; for she had now clasped her knees and raised her head sideways over them in a poise that gave her an air of watching and withdrawal. But now in her look for the first time, there was an indescribable air of appeal. It was not sad, it was not provocative, it was somehow almost blind, as though her eyes that were so clear saw little. And this appeal she communicated, not by way of conspiracy, but frankly and yet unknowing. Her eyes might remove from him without altering their expression and come back as before, nor could anything pass over them except tears. He had little to do with this: he only saw it; and she no longer cared whether he saw it or not. Yet in so far as she could so forget herself, so expose herself, she trusted him.

And, O God, she was beautiful.

He held his own eyes to her until they deepened and grew hot with self-conscious light. He held them steadily until their hot storm made his vision dance.

And now, as though a first thin film of the blindness was dissolved, she recognised him. He was Aniel who had come to the Tower. She was Nessa. That did not alter their positions; it was merely a fact of memory, finding them awake among the sleepers, the two of them. She saw the expression in his eyes, and her own grew soft and something came to them like a recognising smile of tenderness – but it was weary, too, and sadly uncaring, and hopeless. She turned her head away, dropped her forehead suddenly on her knees, and little convulsive movements beset her shoulders quietly.

Aniel got up on his hands. He was going towards her now; but his body would not move. She raised her head and gazed before her. Her lashes were wet.

Aniel got to his feet. He could no longer look at her. He

stepped away noiselessly up amongst the trees. She could come if she liked. He was sick with excitement, and for one terrible moment of revulsion did not wish her to come. He leaned against a tree and slowly turned round, feeling her noiseless body coming against him.

But she was not coming. Between the trunks he saw her as before, her back to him, staring over her knees.

He had not invited her. She dared not come. But wouldn't she have dared if she had wanted? How could he know? He desired her ardently to come. What for? He was light as a wand of leaves in the wind. She would not come. The leaves writhed and rustled, weak and worthless. Worthless because their sound betrayed – what?

And he saw in a moment that he would betray anything for her; but that he would get nothing for his betrayal, nothing ever, was in the back of his mind like the vague emptiness that besets life within the first faint premonition of doom.

He leaned against the tree and gazed at her back. Nor would he move if she turned round. He would keep looking at her; he would make her come. He desired her to come, impatiently, hotly, secretly. Could he stand her coming? She did not come.

His impatience caught a cruel edge. He hated her. What a fool he was! What a fool! What on earth had come over him? He had gone suddenly mad! Mad! He would go farther into the trees. She could guess as she liked what he went into the trees for. He took a step or two away, then calmly walked back and was aware, without seeing his face, that Rasg was awake. Nessa looked round at him as at a strange intruder. She too, then, had known Rasg was awake, and, by not following him, had saved him from his own treachery!

He sat down, not looking at Rasg. He did not care for Rasg. Rasg sat up. Aniel turned his gaze on him for a moment. Rasg's eyes were black with meaning. Aniel glanced at him again as if he had not quite caught this watchfulness. It was a coolness that was overdone.

But Aniel did not care. She had not followed him into the trees because Rasg was awake. Otherwise she

would have followed him. That now was certain. She
had saved him against them. It was the sort of treasure
that restores self-confidence! *And now he would save her
from them.*

His mind cleared. Nessa became a woman within that
clearness, whom, come what might of it – or come nothing
– he would serve.

Rasg shifted his eyes from Aniel to the girl, the golden-
haired, to whom their responses might be different in
all respects except one, their eternal response to the
conqueror, the ruler.

Then Rasg shifted his eyes, and his stillness was an
impassive cruelty. In the end Aniel broke on it, asking,
'Is it time?'

'What are you going to do?'

'Get some food first – and then—'

'Why not go right on?'

'All the day, carrying him, without food?'

'Wouldn't take all day,' replied Rasg. 'Where are you
going to get food here?'

As they talked, Aniel's spirit got whipped to an edge. He
declared there was no sense in killing the body by carrying
it – *in the wrong direction.* They would get food by hunting
for it. Rasg knew some of the Finlags. Let him and one or
two others go that way. Food was scarce enough amongst
their own people. Let them carry food thither rather than
go and drain a scanty store. At last Rasg stirred the others
with a foot. He turned and looked at Aniel, at Nessa, and
at Haakon, as he went.

'He seems in a bad humour,' said Miran, who was to
stay behind with Aniel.

Aniel smiled. 'Are you hungry?'

'I am weak with hunger,' said Miran. Aniel glanced at
his pleasant face and fair hair. He began talking to him,
and shut out Nessa and Haakon, but after a time silence
fell between them. 'I'm thirsty,' said Miran.

'So am I,' said Aniel. 'You go over to the burn and then
I'll go.'

When Miran had gone, Nessa turned her face to Aniel.
At first he would not meet her look, but after a few

moments did so with a strained smile, asking, 'Are you thirsty?'

'Yes.'

'Wait till he comes back,' he said, and glanced away. She was silent.

When Aniel heard Miran returning, he spoke again, and when Miran came up said to him, 'We should have stopped by the burn. You watch him till I take her over for a drink.'

'Right,' said Miran.

Aniel and Nessa got up and walked away into the trees. She had a quiet dignity, a sorrowful air. They never spoke. They reached the place – that was the place where Leu had died. They went to the pool where Breeta and himself had drunk and kissed. Nessa got down on her knees, hands widespread, and lipped the water. He stared at her back, her neck, her head, so that when she raised her head he was confused by her nearness and got down on his own knees. They wiped their faces and she stood mutely. 'Let us sit down,' he said. 'Not there,' he added, taking her from the hump of Leu's grave.

When they were seated, no word would come into his head. She saw this and asked in a low voice, 'What are you going to do with us?'

'I don't know,' he murmured. (She looked at him, turning her face slowly.) 'It's not with me. I'm only one. I—'

'It's with you,' she said.

'No, it isn't,' he denied quickly, colour and eyes flashing upward and then avoiding her.

'You will save us,' she said.

'I? How?'

She looked at him closely and then, turning away, was silent.

'How?' he persisted.

'You know how.'

'No, I don't. He can't escape. He'll be weak for days. He couldn't walk. Do you think', he said in a satiric outburst, 'I could get these fellows to carry him back to the Northmen?'

'No,' she agreed. Then she looked at him, and he recognised in a strange almost dissolving way that she had never looked at him before. And her voice came: 'You could bring some of the Northmen here and they could carry him away.'

Her eyes held him. Their intimacy and meaning were terrible. They exposed her body and heart before him. Their appeal had a shining anguish with shadow at its core; a shadow of invitation to him and belief in him, a shadow that was veiled light. She could not expose herself more. She could only withdraw, and her forehead drooped.

'I couldn't do that,' he said breathlessly. 'I couldn't! How could I?' There was appeal in his voice, almost a touch of anguish.

'You could leave us – to find the Master,' she said quietly. She looked up and in her steady expression there was a profound pleading. 'You could,' she said, her breath quickening. 'They would believe you because – because they know it is the Master who must do – what he wants to do with us.'

There was no mistaking her meaning, no mistaking that she understood what might be their joint fate, what all of them believed would be their joint fate. In a flash he realised that she had hit on the only conceivable way out. He was to pretend to go for the Master, but actually was to go to the Northmen and lead them here! That! Sheer treachery gone mad! Before he knew what he was doing, he got up. She was beside him in a moment. She caught his hands. 'Aniel,' she pleaded, 'Aniel!' her face close to his, her breath urgent, her eyes searching.

'I can't!'

'Yes, you can!' She came upon him. In the small struggle he found himself against her, his arms round her, and, crushing for her mouth, kissed her. She kissed him back. There was a lifting violence in her. 'You can!' she kept repeating. She repeated it against his mouth, her lips crushing away against his neck. 'You can!' His head went on fire and he strained her to him recklessly, mad with delight. He tried to bear her to the ground, but all through her violence came this, 'You can!' and when they did reach the ground, her hands against his chest, she said on a final note, 'You will!'

'Yes,' he said – and stopped.

Her eyes glowed. Her gratitude – she was all lovely gratitude.

There slipped down within him a cool division. *You can* – that was her passion.

There was no passion, had never been any for a moment. In a flash the division between them was wider, because it was clearer, than it had ever been.

He looked at her. She raised her head and met his look. Before it an inscrutable thought dimmed her eyes and, in an instant, appeared to hurt her.

'I may fail,' he said. His voice was clear. 'It is very likely', he said, 'that I shall fail.' His voice had an air of judgment about it.

'You mustn't fail.'

'Let us go back.' He arose.

She was beside him. 'Aniel!'

He did not speak, but stood staring at the trees beyond Leu's grave.

Her fingers were in his shoulder. 'It's my life.'

'Is it only *your* life?'

She scanned piercingly his staring face and asked, 'Is there any other way of saving my own?'

'Oh yes,' he answered. 'You could walk away from here now.'

'And what about you?'

'I should have to walk away too.'

Neither of them moved or spoke. 'It's time we were back,' said Aniel at last. 'Come along.' His manner was sensitive, almost gentle, but there was something dumb as anger at the base of his spirit.

'Could I leave him?' she asked, and her tone had the awful illusion of frankness. Aniel's brow knitted painfully. He started walking back. As she walked beside him, she said, 'If he was not there I would go with you. But—' They walked along. She looked at him. She stopped. She touched his shoulder. Their faces were set to each other like white glass. In a voice that was clear, yet little more than a whisper, she said, 'I will do what you say.'

It was too late. He was going on now, as though his legs were beyond his control. She followed him. His going was, indeed, a decision made outside his will. It was fundamental and exposed his essence. Ever afterwards he was to remember it.

How Miran looked did not concern him as they sat down. Not but that Miran would keep his thoughts to himself. They examined Haakon. He was breathing regularly and as if in sleep. They settled down again and Aniel, stretching himself out, exhausted, closed his eyes.

The sun was overhead when Rasg and his party came back with food. They had some dried scorched meat, a cheese, and a few rounds of hard oaten bread. These were shared out, Aniel presenting Nessa with her portion. Rasg was in a much better mood, having exercised strategy with a measure of successful dealing and a minimum of violence. He had obviously terrorised one old Finlag, for they all chuckled over it now and, as one or two of them went to drink, spouts of laughter could be heard.

They were a happy group and, food consumed, stretched their limbs in goodnatured expectancy. Occasionally one would regard Nessa's back and another, observing him, would wink. Their bodies had delicate repressed movements of jocular desire. They were young enough to play a game. But Rasg had other matters on his mind. And Aniel met him in talk. Aniel, indeed, seemed to be the only one who was out of humour. In his agreeable manner there was a cold directness.

'And we all wait here?' asked Rasg.

'I am going in search of the Master,' said Aniel, 'and when I find him I shall bring him here.'

'Where is he?'

'He was with me here last night, and we were to meet here again. He is to settle this matter – and all others.' He had got up. His face was almost pale. They all looked at him and their faces were solemn. He turned from them and disappeared in the depths of the forest.

He went on walking blindly, conscious only that Nessa

was thinking he was going for the Northmen. He had said he would go. He saw now that that was impossible. It was terrible of her to expect it. But she had been fighting for her life. She had also, however, been fighting for the Northman's life.

And the Northman had killed her father, his father, half the tribe, women and children, and she was cleaving to him. What sort of woman was she? What sort? She was like a fire. A golden fire that sheathed the flesh and made it tremble. She was beyond all laws, all decency. And now that he was free of her, she was with him more than ever. The whole feeling of her body crushing against him was with him. It choked the senses to the brim leaving them mad with desire. Irritation increased in him to violence and he cracked branches against trees. For he regretted not having . . . he regretted . . . and flung the branches from him. When he threw himself on the ground and buried his face, what harried him took shape. It was that matter of his own final decision. For she had said, 'I shall do what you say.' And at that moment if he had stopped and said, 'Let us go away together,' would she have gone? Her voice had been full of understanding, low-pitched with conspiracy. She would have left the Northman to his fate and gone with him, Aniel. That was all her voice could have meant. Her breath had been thick with it. The very potency of its memory ran like a warm solvent in his flesh now.

Yet he had not faced it. He had avoided decision, avoided action. And he now knew that that was the fatal flaw in his make-up, an eternal weakness of will against the supreme moment.

She, on the other hand, could have made that supreme decision of will. The Northman could have made it. As all the great figures of legend made it. Yet apart from that one characteristic, they were no different from him; he was indeed cleverer, more intricate, than they. But they had that one thing, the supreme thing, that creates the ruler and the conqueror, the maker and the breaker of laws.

And if only the words for all this had bothered him, he might have reasoned on into calm; but reason did not touch him at all. The truth is a flash of intuition that is a flash of lightning. And sometimes the lightning is forked, and penetrates the sphere of the mind with an awful illumination.

He wandered on, making it more and more impossible to turn back to the shore and the Northmen. Sometimes he leaned against a tree, and forest animals would pass close to him, and once he saw the rare wild ponies, small beautifully shaped beasts, with long manes and tails and proud curving necks, with hooves not much larger than those of the red deer. A roe regarded him in sensitive surprise. He remained perfectly still. They stared at each other until the delicate lines and fine nostrils and lovely eyes were within him. He moved and the roe bounded off. Clearing pine needles from the earth, he drew the figure of the roe with his big toe. When it was completed his foot went out to obliterate the figure, but he drew it back. From a few yards he looked round at it.

Now he had the strange feeling of being lost. Responsibility fell from him, leaving his body light and unholy as a thing outcast, but outcast too into its own delicately revengeful freedom. He was going towards the camp, not in haste, but warily and with reserve, as a man might go who had committed a secret crime. And out of this state of mind thoughts came at intervals. And, from among these thoughts, one thought emerged complete.

Aniel drew up and stared at it. All the wood, all the world, faded away before it. It took possession of his mind and of his heart and of his lungs. It had the design which life lacked; it was more perfect than death: it illumined both.

If leadership was what the Master desired, then here it was:

*Nessa and the Northman would mate. The Northman would be their leader.*

Here at last was the light that would illumine the pit of their souls – his soul.

When he met the Master he was calm. They sat down on the ground and Aniel told him what had happened that morning, how Nessa and the Northman had come away from the shore camp to the privacy of the trees, how they had been given to each other, how they had been captured in their bed of ferns, and how they had been taken to the forest where they were now guarded by the Oorish burn. He told this quietly, as if it were an old tale.

The Master looked at him for some time. Aniel bore the scrutiny, and when he glanced up saw that the Master, though staring into his face, was no longer conscious of him.

Then the Master became conscious of him, penetrating his secret and linking it to his far thoughts on leadership.

Why do their people need leadership? In the natural play of their minds they are an affectionate people, desiring peace rather than strife. They are a dark intricate people, loving music and fun, and it is a mark of them that an old man will play with a child, and the old man will pretend to be defeated by the child, for their pretences come naturally to them and twist into many games. Out of their pretences they make stories, strange stories that hold the child's wonder and so hold their own. They also make tunes, tunes that possess the mind even more than the stories, and they start with the mother tunes to the children. These tunes and these games are never forgotten, so that in times of the greatest danger, in times of brutality and terror, in times of starvation and death, in the blood times when the wolfish mind is a black demon, even then the old tune will come in, will possess and conquer. How then can they ever lead? They cannot. At a time when a great decision has to be made, a decision to go forward, to conquer for the sake of conquering, to conquer and hold, they feel that by going forward they leave their true riches behind. And if they don't feel that, yet the instinct for that is in them and acts like a nerveless infirmity of the will. They can go forward, but it is for something that no leader could ever understand; they can endure for this strange thing; they will sacrifice themselves and die for it. But what it is they do not know, and when they have conquered and died yet they have not gone forward.

There is thus in them a profound persistence rather than a conquering or leading. And out of this persistence, that often looks no more than an intricate weakness, they see with a curious clearness. They see that the ruler does not persist but is as one passing on. There is no abiding importance in him. This is known finally at the core. But the ruler by this positive power in him lives on them and draws virtue out of them. And because it is the nature of the ruler to conquer and hold, therefore he becomes vain of his possessions and his vanity can feed only on more possessions. Now the virtue that he draws out of them also becomes his possession. So that he will have their music, and he will have their best music and their best players. And so with the other things that they make. He lives thus on the blood and the flesh of the people, and is therefore for ever less than the people, and is for ever being consumed by them – to be needed once more, or the people themselves will be broken by a greater people under a greater ruler.

The lucid happiness began to creep upon Aniel, for he now saw that the Master understood his instinctive decision not to go away with Nessa. It was a blood decision. There was a dark persistent fatality in it, like sacrificial blood poured into the earth. Once, when a little boy, he had seen a strong bearded man digging in his plot of ground that sloped from the corner of a wood. He was all alone in a quiet spring evening, with the light beginning to fade and a chill in the air. The wood was bare and wintry. The earth he had turned over was black against the grey-green grass and black against the dark trees. The man was still as a root, grasping his trenching tool, and gazing at a tufted piece of ground a little distance in front. From his shelter Aniel looked where the man was looking but could see nothing. Slowly the man moved away with his spade in his hand but presently began to circle back, and soon he was walking round and round in an ever-narrowing circle, and when at last he came to the centre of the circle he swung his spade violently and at the same moment a brown beast leapt from its lair and was struck down. It was a hare, and the man brought it back kicking in his hands. The man was doubled up a little over the hare, and every now and then looked round secretly, but did not see Aniel, who was terrified at the man's stealthy ways and at the expression on his face. When the man reached the spot where he had been digging, he got down on his knees. Once more he looked over his shoulders and Aniel saw his face. The hare was now kicking strongly. The man bent his head and bit its throat and the hare let out a terrifying squeal which ended abruptly. The man then held the hare out in his hands and doubled it over so that the blood ran from its torn throat into the furrow. Before the man could turn his head, Aniel slipped away, for he felt that if the man saw him now he would do something dreadful to him. The man's face, the still trees and the black earth in the chill dusk, he never forgot. But they were also something he could never leave. And though at greater sacrifices he himself had assisted, yet rarely had the awful potency of that first experience ever been recaptured. And now to come on newly turned earth on a chill autumn or spring evening, was to have that fascination revived in him more strongly even than at the great festivals, though at the great festivals there was fire. The clarity of that experience, of evening light against frost, was what stole upon him sometimes when the Master spoke.

The Master was now speaking to him again, and, like the man circling round the hare, he had arrived at the centre where Aniel himself lay couched.

And Aniel bowed. 'Yes, that is what I thought,' he admitted. 'For you had said to me before that we would have to have a ruler and we have no ruler amongst ourselves. I was to go to the king's court and bring home the son of Drust. But who knows how that might miscarry, or what may have happened to Drust's son? And there is Drust's daughter. And if the Northman will agree to lead us and take our ways, then as Nessa's husband he could do so. I thought chiefly of one thing, that the Northmen will come back, and next time they will come in revenge to destroy us altogether. But if this Northman said he was our leader and we were his people, and no wrong had been done to him but only honour, then he would stop them and we might have peace.'

The Master's eyes were on him. *It was a generous way to save them.* Aniel flushed.

'What will the people say?'

'They will obey you,' answered Aniel.

The Master waited.

'Whatever they say to begin with, they will accept in the end,' said Aniel. 'Because these two have behaved as they did will only give them an extra greatness. They will be not as the people are, and the people accordingly will fear and obey them. And in time the bards will make a wonder story of it. It will become a great legend.'

'Are you beginning to penetrate legend?'

'No,' said Aniel.

There was no bitter smile in his heart?

'No.'

His tone had for a moment the weariness of an old man's knowledge.

'No,' repeated Aniel.

So then there was truly greatness in their behaviour. They are of those who make their own decisions. And however we rail against them as transgressors, as betrayers, yet, because they have done what we dared not do, we recognise them as our masters.

'Yes,' said Aniel.

Aniel stirred restlessly.

He had promised the girl Nessa.

'I promised', said Aniel, his face quick with defiance, 'to go for the Northmen and to bring them to deliver her – and him.'

Why? he didn't know.

Because he could not at first take the great decision to betray his own people?

And now he regretted he had not betrayed them.

'I regret,' said Aniel.

'For the manner of greatness has come upon you at last, and you could make great decisions – and go to your doom?'

Aniel bowed his head.

'Already the legend is being born within you,' said the Master.

A cold wind searched Aniel's defiance.

Because he had not gone for the Northmen he was now doing the next best thing – he was saving them and redeeming his word in a more splendid way; so that he could go to her and say: *This I have done for you. Farewell.*

Aniel's head drooped still farther.

'You see, Aniel, whatever you do you give in to them.'

'I see.'

'And there is within you a legendary love of this. You will even love your own defeat. You will turn it to music. Your self-denial will have in it the very soul of your people. And you and your people will recount the legend of these two. And the legend will adhere to these two, and you and your people will be forgotten. Not only that, but these two themselves will have added to their greatness the gift of legend-making – your gift.'

Aniel broke through the silence. 'What, then – what am I to do?'

'Go back,' said the Master, 'and tell them to wait until I come tonight.'

Aniel got up at once and was walking away when the Master called him. Aniel found his eyes on the Master's face. All his passion ebbed out of him. There was invocation and response, and he was walking away again through a thin air and clear light. There was a curious frosted pleasure in this. Decision lay with the Master, not because the Master wished it or because he wished it, but because it was in the nature of the world ruled by the gods. In Fate there was always this awful detachment, this terrifying power, to which one ultimately bowed with relief. For Fate could remove from one the pains of fear and the torture of desire. Whatever the Master decided, that should be done, and he, Aniel, could himself lead Nessa. . . .

A shiver went over Aniel's body and his head went up and he walked as though he were leading himself. But he did not make immediately back for the Oorish burn. A desire had come upon him to see others; not to go near them or speak to them, but to look upon them with this detachment.

And first he saw a number of boys digging into a turf bank for honey. They shouted and flailed the bees with switches, and when one was stung the others yelled with laughter. The bees were Northmen and the boys would

not retreat, though often they danced round in circles,
with heads bent and hands flashing bees out of their ears.
The bees increased in number and in fury. They became
a cloud round the boys, who ultimately broke and fled,
pursued by the bees. Down in the open they counted
their stings. The moor there was a marshy green, and
sheep and cattle and goats and dogs and women could be
seen moving about. The place was a great shallow basin of
refuge, with good feeding and safe footing in dry weather.
The forest here swept backward, for they were now much
farther inland than the summer herdings, where most of the
men were at the moment repairing the huts against their
reoccupation on the departure of the Northmen. The boys'
laughter gave the scene a happy air. And the boys of course
were only temporarily defeated. They returned to the fight.
They shouted insults at the bees. They slaughtered them.
And, though repulsed once more, came back. Aniel left
them, knowing their persistence would gain the honey in
the end.

Threading the forest edge, he came on the working and
sleeping-places of the women, but he took care not to be
seen. Some old women were moving about, and three
young ones were coming directly across the glen towards
him. He realised too late that the middle one was Breeta,
and that they were about to enter the forest. He hid behind
the tree, but the girls, who were arm-linked, actually broke
on the tree and one of them, in hysteric mirth, was swung
against him. She screamed in a harsh abject way. Breeta
went ghost-white, staring at him. An old crone screeched,
'What's wrong?'

Aniel walked away, smiling and smiling to himself. After
a time he relaxed his grip and eased his chest. Breeta stared
on, however, with her black eyes and parted lips and white
face. 'Yes, it's me,' he said to this image in his mind, and
felt bitter and angry with her – and smiled as if he were
only highly amused.

Then he heard a pipe being played and approached it
with stealth. It was old Poison, with the Koorich instrument
he had stolen from the dead Leu! He looked thin, as if the
thing possessed him and would not let him rest, but kept

him playing, playing, condemned to wander for ever in the forest. At the moment he was sitting with his back to a tree fingering a terrible old tune. Some of the notes hung in the air so long that time gave up and died. But more notes came, and they strung themselves one after the other until they went round the world. In this way the world was enchanted, and even Aniel himself in a very short time was enchanted too. There was no good not being enchanted. Why bother trying not to be? Why, indeed? Life was an illusion. He leaned back against his tree and gazed at Poison, whose left shoulder was towards him, whose bearded face was in profile, and whose fingers moved up and down the slanting pipe. At first the notes had no special colour, but were merely round like bubbles, rather small bubbles. When they caught the dusky hue of evening in a wood they swelled, and their hue was the hue of life and the truth at the core of life. The notes floated now on a world dissolved into a fatal sea. The bubbles did not rise, for they were heavy and laden with the doom that is the end of one man, of all men, and of everything to the farthest boundaries. At this (for nothing could be more final) the notes caught a dark-blue colour, as if the sky had dissolved and got blown bubble after bubble upon the air. This was a lovely mockery and defiance of doom. The mind went round in its own empty dark whirl and rejoiced; not openly, but with persistence and with an intimate final knowledge that a core was being saved, a core of defiance, of secret upsurging, so that fingers and toes could draw and colour in a way that would defy all things, mock all things – and remain. Each note was a face in a wood. Each note was a secret glance. But no, the wood and the glance faded, and there were the same three notes back again. Always these three notes, laying hold of Poison and finishing him off. And no matter how he wandered from them, back he came, and back they came. While he stepped from bubble to bubble across the chasms of the world, invisibly they hung there haunting him, luring him back to them, two big notes with a small note between, like a catch in the breath or a break in the ecstasy.

But they were not too much for old Poison. They might

be tragedy, the end of all effort, sorrow in the trinity of three bubbles that, when man is beaten, he should let burst to nothing upon the air. But Poison was not beaten. On the contrary, he was inspired. It might look as if tragedy in its final aspect was an orgy of creation, a flame, a terrible flame, fire. There was a fire in Poison's head. He took the pipe from his mouth and looked at it and laughed quite silently except for two insucking notes to finish up with before putting the pipe back in his mouth. He loved the pipe. And he started again on the same old terrible tune. And he put the three notes through their tragedy now with a refreshed demoniac cunning, until he produced them so perfectly that he looked at them as they hung in the air. Then he jerked the beads of his spittle upon them, and started a new melody.

This new melody was going to deal with love pretty much as the old terrible one had dealt with doom. Aniel began to rebel. But Poison was potent and overcame Aniel, and put him into such a state of reaching after love that the high branches grew out of his hair. But whereas he could make something of tragedy and doom, of love he could make nothing. It maddened him so that he marched round within himself, and his inward arms made the whirling motions of tree-arms in a storm. This was fantastic, and he stiffened outward like the breastbone of a fowl. The bone slowly melted and ran down inside him, until all that was left was under Poison's dominion.

Poison's love knew no rules. The girl who sang the dark-red notes had given her lover everything, and he had left her; and now she desired him so much that she would betray all the rules of life and sell herself to death, if only he would come to betray her again. For what would the Pleasant Plain be without him? *Day and night*, went the three notes at the end, *night and day*.

Poison enjoyed it and loved with a tremendous love. Occasionally the notes went soaring into the air over his head, balanced on a jet of blood from the gripped heart, and aspired and tumbled there, before sinking with the jet down into the body and coming out slowly, terribly, swelling out from the pipe-end, *day and night*. When the notes rose the breast nearly burst, and cold bird-feet crept over the scalp; when they fell the chest went flat and the chin sank and life went dark as night.

But Poison himself did not give in to this night. In the midst of resignation's darkness, love is a darker demon, of unending cunning and malignancy. Poison knew about him, knew furthermore that brightness can be so bright that it looks dark or blinds to dark, as heat can find its own touch in an utter cold. So Poison made the darkness dark as eternity, hopeless as hell, knowing that the more terrible he made it the more certainly was he creating the awful brightness of love.

And a love like that is worth making. It is the only love worth making. Any other kind isn't worth a burst bubble. Not a burst bubble! He held the pipe away from his mouth and watched the spittle drip. Black demons, it was a tune – that! He hunched himself and scratched his back against the tree, acknowledging the flea as a lascivious demon. He laughed silently.

The sight was too much for Aniel. He advanced. Poison saw him and scrambled to his feet, getting paces away before he was upright. His face showed the utmost consternation and fear. He clasped the pipe against his breast. Aniel shouted to him, but he only kept backing away; and when Aniel advanced again he turned and made off with incredible speed, his bare heels pelting like flint hammers. In a few seconds he was lost.

There was a darkening in the forest. Was it the shadow flung from music or from the falling sun? The tall branches swayed and crushed without violence in a wind that was blowing as if it had forgotten how to stop. There was a reflectiveness in its sound like sighing in a breast with a hand pushing hair from a forehead. But when Aniel looked up, the light on the forehead was serene, yet concerned with its own business, and murmuring in a high otherness secretly, and passing on.

He smiled bleakly, turning towards the Oorish burn. It would be night before he arrived. But he did not hurry. The truth was that the love music was still in his heart, not the sound but the unconditional nature of it. There had been no conditions, no bargaining, in the fluted notes darkening from dark-red. And Poison with his hairy face and broad nose and big ears gloated over the fact of its rightness. Music for anything else would be for laughter (and there was such music and such laughter).

The nearness to great decision trembled again within his heart. When speaking to the Master, the clearness of such a decision had come upon him in a way that he had never before experienced. For a moment he had seen its shadowless truth. Perhaps the Master had made him see it – and then shadowed it. But he had seen it. The Master had often talked to him of glimpses. That had been one. You did not understand truth: you saw it, and its clarity gave you an assurance that was profoundly happy, cool and transparent as a well, white as a bright noon, effortless as gulls' wings. That was all the Master's teaching in the end: to see clearly. For, once one saw like that, all the world was balanced on the palm and even the gods' selves danced around the Sun. The Sun, at the centre of his circle. As the Moon was at the centre of her circle, the Moon that had her own moon seasons, governing the tides of fertility not alone in the sea.

All that had been spawned out of night, of demon and black magic and gnashing horror, only in the end could they be kept at bay by one who after years of effort won thus within the circle of his own light. As the Sun put a circle round the earth and all that it contained, so a man by his vision put a circle round himself. At the centre of this circle his spirit sat, and at the centre of his spirit was a serenity for ever watchful. Sometimes the watchfulness gave an edged joy in holding at bay the demons and even the vengeful lesser gods, and sometimes it merged with the Sun's light into pure timeless joy.

Glimpses of this Aniel had, for his knowledge was slight yet, knowledge of trees and herbs and spring water, of animals and taboos and blood, of stars and falling stars and divining, of music and images and drawing, of the past as Gilbrude had had it, with all its intricate learning and those rites that gripped the body like a fist. And the love now was a glimpse.

The evening was darkening in the forest. No other glimpse had ever affected him like this. One walked to it as to a high fatal music. And while walking so, thoughts came with stinging acuteness, for all the wonder of this subject could not be resolved. Its high decision might be glimpsed – but the thing itself affected the body.

Yet he wasn't afraid of what the Master would do to Nessa. The Master would. . . . Aniel's mind hesitated, poised intolerably. His confidence shook. For whatever the Master would do would not only be right but would have the dreadful inevitability of rightness. That awful leading of Breeta across the moor would be as nothing to the speechless leading by the Master. The despair of this rightness so affected him, its certainty springing from his fear, that he began to get the smell of burning wood in his nostrils.

He knew this was delusion, but so vivid was it that his nostrils flexed as he sniffed the air and at last he stood still, head tilted like a stag. And now for the life of him he could not get rid of it. After a few moments, however, he decided his instincts had grown so sensitive in the last hours that they were exaggerating the pine scent one always got strongly on entering the forest but which, after a little, one did not notice at all.

It was symptomatic too of his fears! He could not now be an hour from the Oorish burn, and his inner thought had been conjuring with unlawful sacrifice, as if Rasg were capable all on his own of dispatching the two captives! Truly he must be very concerned about Nessa! . . . There it was again, a distinct sniff of pine wood burning. All his flesh strung taut. He advanced more quickly. Suddenly into the forest on his right he saw the heads and ears and the long backs of wolves slinking past as if some slow invisible thing were pursuing them of which they were reluctantly afraid. Sleek brutes, with their tails down, going noiselessly. He did not like the sight of them at all. And now deer in front, not the roe of the woods, but red deer, straight-legged against him, and swinging off in their startled trotting stride, nostrils up. Where on earth had they come from? A scurry in the trees above. Lynx. One on the ground, a spotted bearded brute, its eyes slitted on him before slanting past, going down wind. All going down wind. The slow lash of the bushy stub of a tawny wildcat's tail, its bounding leap full of a writhing ruthless grace. And birds chirping and cawing. Wood pigeons flapped noisily and swung up through the openings. The stream of fear increased, and became many-tongued and many-shaped, until there advanced upon Aniel's hurrying figure a grey ghostly face that opened as he paused and dissolved into smoke. The forest was on fire.

Aniel began to run. Smoke was now among the trees in a grey-blue stealthy gloom. It filled his nostrils and irritated his throat. Animals were everywhere, the smaller ones scurrying, the larger ones startled and reluctant. Then vanishing through the gloom he saw what for a moment he thought was a fat man but must have been a bear. Or perhaps one of those flesh-eating hairy half-men of the mountain caves who had names in story. For shapes became distorted and terrifying and the smoke stung his eyes and made them water.

Yet he did not pause to ask why he was heading into this. He merely went forward with a swift impatience, as though Nessa's life depended on his getting there in time, as though her prostrate body were waiting for him to carry it away, and it was a race between himself and the flames.

He became aware that his action was a growing madness leading him to death. Smoke now came in great evil unfolding masses. The darkness was increasing. The roaring of the trees overhead was a raging sea. Swirling smoke enfolded and blinded him, warm and suffocating. He tore it from him, arms flailing, throat harsh and gasping. He drew up, head buried against it. When the swirl passed, he blinked ahead, and there before him was a great white bull, black-muzzled, black-hooved, black-eared, and black-horned, with eyes flaming red in the gloom.

To his first glance it was an apparition, a mythical creature. All the past of the Groves lived in it. Garlands and legends and power; happiness and childhood; the white bull of the gods. How much he had been told by the Master, how much he had seen, he did not know; but the

majesty of that past, or of his imagination, came upon him
in terror as the milk-white beast, with its scarred forehead
and shoulders, snorted before him and set its hooves for the
charge. Delivered over to it, he waited, his body drained of
power. A soft sickening sensation of impact beset him as
the beast started.

And it was a satisfying end for the old bull, driven out
by the younger bulls of the great white herd that roamed
the southern forest. The loss of his leadership had worked
upon him until he had refused to hang about the haunts
of his conquerors, as those had done who had led before
him. His prime had been too splendid, his dignity too
great, and so bellowing northward he had set out on his
great final trek. This hot smoke was a gathering of all the
evil pursuing forces in his wake, blinding him, and goading
him to madness. At such a moment to see Man before him
was to be presented with the chance of settling a grievance
old as time itself.

But the smoke was deceptive, Man's smoke, man the
priest, the slayer. The smoke whirled about him even as he
charged, blinding, deceiving. But no matter, he was set to
it, with his ancient power rising through his bowels and his
shoulders in the thunder onward. But there was no straight
course in that forest, and an old pine broke his neck, burst
his shoulder open, and launched him at Aniel's feet. The
earth shook; the black hooves quivered upright in the air
and fell.

The smoke grew denser; the air hotter; far away there
was a furnace roar. Aniel went towards it, possessed now,
and when he was choked, and, whirling round, fell to the
ground, he tore at the ground with his teeth and clawed at
it with his feet.

For there had been treachery, treachery, oh, there had
been treachery!

The smoke rolled past now in great convoluting masses.
It was dark as in the first reach of night. The air against the
ground had clean runnels. Aniel raised his head, his body
flat and slight in this pillared world of ghostly hurrying
smoke, of high raging sound, and the far-off roaring horror
of Fire let loose at last.

There was something in the fearsomeness of the scene about him that seemed conscious. The smoke behaved as one with bent shoulders, a hushed horrible preparing and silencing for that which was to come, long arms unfolding, fingers reaching and reaching round, enveloping and smothering. The gloom was the gloom of nightmare going far in through pillars in a monstrous Grove; but more horrible than the silence of any nightmare was this raving destruction of sound.

It got hold of Aniel. Its wild roar quivered in the flesh that the hot breath fanned. Bone-cracking, consuming, the Red Beast advanced in his roaring lust. Before it what were Nessa, himself, or any of the children of men? Nothing. Nothing. In that place of deathly preparation, panic dug its sharp small lynx-claws in Aniel's flesh. Their poison ran straight into his blood and brought him quivering to his feet. Then maddened by its fever he started running, as the animals had been running, straight down wind. Only he had now lost the first cunning of the animal and, choked and blinded, smashed into trees, lacerating himself, rolling on the ground, onwards. And as he went he heard the roar gaining on him, until at last it was within him, an immense cataract pouring down from eyes and ears, drenching him, obliterating him, but even in the blindness of obliteration he went on, his consciousness no more than a small inward eye that was itself blind, until hitting his head against a root he lay still.

Then a curious change took place in him. His lungs filled from a low pocket of air, and the small central spot of being went cold with spite. It was a reaction, intensely malignant, to the Red Beast. An animal might have achieved its ferocity but not its coldness. It was an instinctive application of the Master's teaching of holding the demons at bay.

It brought all his parts together; it gave him the cunning of an extremely economical use of his remaining resources. And as, sufficiently renewed, he went on, he bore to his right, knowing now that he could never overtake the smoke straight down wind, but might just conceivably get out of the forest altogether by thus slanting towards the glen.

Panic completely left him, and in his mind he was very little distressed. He went forward in that automatic way that is a last refinement of will. No thought of anything touched him beyond the tree against his shoulder, the ground against his hands, the hollows where he renewed his lungs. The great smoke wreaths curled about him, and once or twice his cough was so congested and hot that he thought he was coughing up bloody pieces of lung. Then he lay still. The smoke and heat seemed denser when he crawled on again. And now he could hardly breathe. For a moment fear raised its panic head. But only for a moment, and it was followed by the desire to rest for good. He no longer had any spite against the demons; he no longer cared. He only wanted to bury his head and let his senses go, for his chest and his nostrils and all his body were bitten with fire, and it would be an exquisite relief to let them be consumed utterly. A long time after that he crawled out from the trees and his face fell on the small aromatic shoots of the bog myrtle. And that odd refinement of will that had been doing all this for him eased its tension.

There is a cool sweet flavour of earth beneath the bog myrtle whose twigs pinch the face with a bruising affection. Wild flowers grow in its neighbourhood, as well as the bright purple of the heath bells, and all around the canna flags are white puffs on the wind. The tiny buds of the heather are already pink-tipped, and the ends of the hill grass are browned as if they had offered themselves to the sun. And they are all about Aniel, but beneath him is the earth out of which they came. This earth, cool and dark, out of which he has come himself, out of which all things have come and back into which all things must go, though indeed they never separate rightly from it but are as its thoughts, springing for a little into being and action, then fading back even as thoughts fade. And some are pure sun thoughts; and some are horrid thoughts of the sunless night. At his best a man is a daydream; at his worst a nightmare. More than that, what story is there to tell? Or what story to listen to, lying against the dark breast? What better than to burrow deeper a bit, to dig the hands in, to crush the face more firmly, to suck into scorched lungs the sweet dark fragrant breath? All other loving is a hectic heat, licked up like vapour. Here is love's absorption, love's final surrender.

Aniel lay in a half-troubled sleep, and when the heat of the forest fire began to scorch his body he but clung the closer, unable to drag his mouth away.

When he was forced at last to lift his face, the hot air shrivelled his lungs. Smoke was rolling over his body in dense masses, and the gloom was reddened by an infernal glow. Sheeted flame pierced the smoke and tongued the sky, as if the evening of the world had come at last and the earth was being offered up in sacrifice along with the chant of all the seas.

With face trailing among the green withies he crept away, and because of the inland sweep of the wind was soon out of the smoke and among the small birches that crested the near slope of the glen.

Here he rested again, but only for a little. The image of a river pool ravished him and he set off down the slope, going slowly, allowing his exhaustion to play with him, to let him hit softly against trees, slide on his buttocks, or roll over. At the foot he lay back, looking across the narrow green flat to the stream and the rising ground beyond.

It was sweet to lie thus in the cool dusk of the night, with the desire for rest balancing exquisitely the desire for drink. He could not care what had happened to anyone or anything. Even his thirst could wait. Through the shadow in his mind he saw shadows moving. They were on the footpath beyond the stream. For a little time longer he did not focus them, and then, in the quiet way that revelation often comes, he knew they were the Northmen.

With their helmeted heads they might have been gods. Three of them, one after the other, silently walking, their faces cast now and then towards the forest fire. They were too far away for him to distinguish features in the dusk, and yet their expression could be felt. They were avenging gods, who would not sail without their chief – or if sail they must, then not without destroying the land that dared to hold him.

So they had started with the forest, the hiding-hole of the

native savages, and set it on fire to burn them out. And now they were patrolling the pathway by the stream in order to cut off whosoever emerged alive from the furnace. Before they left this shore they were going to make very certain that their chief was beyond their aid.

The power of these men came upon Aniel, the grimness of their purpose and its ordered execution. The homely pastoral Ravens were no match for them. The Ravens were like thoughts in the back of a mind as it sets forth on some adventure. They burrowed deeper than the adventuring thought, and when the adventure was over would come up again, even as adders come up to curl in the fertilising sun. But the adventure-thought was their master and could whip them underground at will.

Aniel was taking no chances. His lungs were raw and painful and he tempered the wind to them through his nostrils. His eyes smarted and his left shoulder was sorely bruised. Blood had dried along his temples from a wound in his scalp. There was a pulsing ache in his head and a sickness in his stomach prompting to vomit. Yet amid all these things his mind floated curiously at ease. He did not fear the Northmen would find him where he lay: he simply was certain they would not find him. He could hear the great roar of the invisible fire, and now and then his head made the small involuntary motion of bowing before it, and each time he did so a shadow went down over him as if he had been indulging a religious rite.

The Northmen in such small numbers dare not abide the night. When it got as dark as it was likely to get, Aniel drank and bathed himself in the stream. Then he climbed up over the path, and passing through the scattered trees came on the edge of the moor, and there he turned round to behold the forest.

MAN HAS made many symbols for himself, but there is only one to which his hands go out of their own accord and on which his eyes dream: it is the symbol of that which flickered when he first became conscious of his difference from the beasts. It has much to do, too, with the beasts and with that early darkness, for in the primeval night he sat before it and green eyes came out from the forest and glittered and retired.

That picture has haunted him through the ages, and even to this day wild beasts avoid him if they can, slinking away as if his upright body held the red gleam hidden, was indeed itself made upright for a sheath.

And not only in the dark of the jungle, but also in the white of the icefields that start where the forests end and go beyond the plains of death into ultimate whiteness. Here green eyes never retire, but stare and glitter as they slowly slay. Green eyes of green ice that glitter through a day on which no sun sets or search for the heart in a night on which no sun rises. Wastes plained and pinnacled and barriered beyond egress, until thought itself is muffled, in the whiteness that lies more lightly than silence and suffocates more surely than strength. No god can help you here, nor magic turn the flowers of ice to colour.

And you sink down upon yourself and bow your head, and the frozen wastes stand about and watch you, near at hand and afar off; white vultures that consume without eating, terrible implacable white gods.

And you can foil them, even them! Nurse the symbol there before you, stretch your hand to its flickering tongue; and when the baffled vultures rise and in a blizzard beat upon you, build an igloo round the tongue and let the blizzard roar. Within, before its lovely yellow restlessness, you can afford to smile, and curl your back, and look behind your shoulders. . . . And so from igloo to igloo, from waste to waste, until the forests rise again.

Hands go out to a flame, and back upon the body come warmth and life. It is the first act of worship, and all other acts borrow its gesture. The dark urge of the blood runs to its channel and winds before it in a maze that holds the staring eyes asleep in the visions that are fire-reflections. For here is the Flame that lives and dances and burns and slays and can be blown out even as life is blown out, leaving the cold of death behind.

AND NOW Fire was come upon the end of its world.

Great sheets of flame leapt like banners and were torn

to nothing on the air, for greater flames to follow, to thrust beyond. They filled the horizon; they besieged the sky. They drew the wind and lashed it into fury; it bore their flaming branches far upon the night.

Terror came upon Aniel. The smoke rolled and convoluted, darkening or gleaming to a blood-dyed core. Fire like this he had never known before. Fire the companion, the servant, the divine, the magical, was gone. Here was Fire the raging God, and its majesty was terrifying and august.

Its majesty cried for submission; it drew all unto itself in sacrifice. It was so vast that life could not go on living before it. Life must submit. It would be easier for life to submit. Already there seemed to be dark bodies moving within the fire.

Aniel started inland for the summer grazings. He went at a trot, gasping out of raw lungs, feeling the need for his kind. The fire that so terrified him also drew him. He did not wish to give himself to the fire, but he had within him the sensation of rushing towards it, and crying madly and waving his arms. His throat would grow hoarse and tears would roll down his face. O Fire!

There was also, however, a wary coolness within him, thin as the invisible will, and when figures came upon him from a tree clump, he leapt and swerved. The figures were after him, heads helmeted, swords swinging. One outstripped the others. Aniel went down before him, screaming hoarsely.

The sword did not descend. Aniel lay in quivering apprehension – in intolerable apprehension. Then something about the figure drew him trembling to his feet. It was Rasg. The other four came up. Two of them also had helmets and swords.

'Come on!' commanded Rasg shortly. He turned, and they followed him to the tree clump out of which they had so swiftly emerged.

As he entered the darkness, Aniel's mouth struck a cold hanging face that gave like a ball. He smothered his scream and swung back and round. There were three heads depending from one low branch. In the darkness he felt the others watching him in cold black laughter. In hunting stray Northmen, and slaying them, they were fulfilling themselves before the terror of the forest fire. They were finding the death ecstasy in killing their enemies. Their minds rose to the raging vastness of the fire. They could not keep still, but continuously padded the earth, climbing, climbing above it to the dark peaks where the mind swirled and the surge of a sea roared through the breast and the throat bayed with a note of bronze. Aniel saw eyes glisten green before him like a beast's. They vanished. He felt Rasg beside him with such intensity that he apprehended his complete outline and the expression on his face. His skin became intolerably sensitive and expectant. There was an instant's silence within him that was a bronze shout. His flesh went cold, but not with fear. The one beside him did not speak, but waited, standing quite still, while the others continued to pad restlessly. The intimacy became unbearable.

'What happened to them?' asked Aniel.

'Who?' asked Rasg.

Aniel hated him violently, so violently that something broke in his throat like a weak laugh.

'The girl Nessa and the Northman?'

Rasg remained silent, but Aniel felt him searching, and, out of the coolness there had been in his laugh, he gathered strength. The padding had ceased. They were all listening. The great roar of the fire came in surges and the birch leaves overhead shivered and streamed.

'Why don't you answer?' demanded Aniel. He wanted to shout at him, 'What are you keeping so silent for?' Did they think he didn't know them?

Rasg did not speak. He was conscious of his strength. He was trying to break Aniel. Aniel felt him bitter and implacable. Aniel grew full of the strength of bitterness himself, and held stiffly against the silence. They stood like this for a long time. Then Rasg sent a blast of air through his nostrils.

'Tell me!' shouted Aniel, maddened at the stroke.

'They are there now,' said Rasg.

'Where?'

'There.'

They were in the fire.

Since Aniel had left Nessa she had possessed him not so much visually as emotionally or as an experience opening thought to the high decision. She now came before him so vividly, face and hair and eyes, that he could have cried out. With the pain of it he very nearly did cry out. His muscles went rigid, choking the pain; and, as the vision faded under that stress, small guttering sounds came from him.

'Don't you want to know how they're there?' asked Rasg.

What Aniel heard of the voice sickened him. He wanted to push it from him, to push them all from him. They sickened him.

'We heard the Northmen coming,' said Rasg. 'They were shouting. You could hear them a mile off.'

There was something in the fellow's voice that Aniel heard very close to him.

'We wanted to carry them away. She said no. She said – *you were with the Northmen*.'

In the silence the accusation rose full-bodied. Aniel could even see Nessa telling them at first commandingly, then fiercely, then desperately.

An icy remoteness came over him. 'Did you believe her?' he asked. His voice must have startled them.

'She told us.'

'What did you do?'

'When the others were lifting the Northman, I told her to come on. She defied me. I went to lay hold of her. She ran away, yelling to the Northmen at the top of her voice.'

'What then?'

'I went after her.'

There was silence.

'What then?' asked Aniel, blood bursting through the ice.

'I got hold of her,' said Rasg, 'and choked her.'

Hot blood drenched Aniel. He went clutching at his throat. He turned away, blind, and hit into a tree. 'You brute! You bloody brute!'

'You bloody traitor!' said Rasg, and leapt upon Aniel.

The others tore Rasg's fingers from Aniel's throat and separated them.

Aniel's voice was thick and broken. 'Let me up! The gods damn you!'

'Steady,' said Miran.

'The gods damn you!' screamed Aniel. Then he tried to control his voice and repeated with terrible meaning, 'The gods damn you!' Then he bowed his head.

'I did nothing to her except choke her,' said Rasg evilly. 'For one thing I hadn't time. The smoke was coming.'

'Shut up!' said Miran to him.

Aniel was silent. The hot surge had ebbed from his brain aud left him empty and bleak. He got up, his muscles weak and jumpy. His throat was hoarse as he spoke slowly, looking away from them to the fire. 'The Master – He was following me when the fire. . . .'

They all heard this like revelation with a note of doom. Nor did any one of them move when Aniel stumbled quietly from their midst.

He went on up the riverside. The fire away on his left was something he hardly glanced at, or again something that he gazed at with such absorption that it quickened him in no way. Presently he found himself among the men of his tribe. They had driven their stock from the forest shelter to the old summer grazings, and now were watching the fire. Some of them said that the fire would take to the moor, and burn it out to the northern sea – it was in such a dry condition. But most of them were silent, and looking around him Aniel saw swathed figures on the slope towards the shielings. They would be the women. Distinctly from them came a thin high-pitched rhythm of sound like the terror of pain being squeezed through closed nostrils. Or it was like a repressed scream, fading off into whimpering, and rising again, and fading, as the bodies swayed and swathed themselves. It had a restless effect on the men, the more reckless of whom would like to have jested before so immense a spectacle. But none dared. Looking round, Aniel saw that the fire had them in its grip even more than it had the women.

Finally, speech died and the fire flickered in all eyes and

the flames possessed them. Sometimes the flames receded to an immense distance as the sea recedes when one is standing on its edge. But in the same moment it can rise up and up, swelling to the fullness that must overwhelm and drown. Overwhelm and burn. All the emotions before the simple fire of sacrifice and cleansing were intensified a thousandfold, for here was Fire itself at last, the fire of the gods, sacrificing and cleansing the world, catching up animals and birds and men and shrivelling them to nothing in a moment as a leaf is shrivelled. Only once did Aniel's own fatal calm experience this shrivelling effect, and that was when, clearly as though it were happening before him, he saw the face and hair of Nessa shrivel and melt.

Turning from that dreadful vision, he beheld Rasg standing close by him. He watched and saw him secretly claw at his breast as if his heart had a bloody itch. Others, too, scratched their chests as if they wanted to lay hold of the heart and tear it out altogether.

They began to move now restlessly. Aniel became affected. He knew what they wanted. He began to desire it himself. It was the release of tension, the loss of the individual will in a greater will, the merging of one with another in a deep abasement; the communion which in all times has had for its symbol and release a sacrificial rite.

As the religious feeling grew, so waned any merely conscious need to propitiate the gods, for communion has within itself its own ecstasy, more potent than the fear of hell or the image of paradise, consuming these as fire consumes hurrying serpents or the beautiful shapes of trees.

Aniel turned away in a thin excitement as if small white flames were licking about him. He should not be going, he told himself. The others would be secretly watching him. But he was going; he was going away from the many to the one; to the one that was his quivering self desiring its own circle, its own tired circle. A craving was on him for this loneliness, even if it was no more than a craving for sleep, for eternal sleep, the final form of all communion.

The women had faded before the religious desire in the minds of the men. Aniel saw one or two of them start away from the earth as he advanced. Then footsteps were behind him. It was Rasg.

Aniel faced him in the pale night. There was no weakness of anger or passion in his slim body now, and when he raised his pointing hand he did so with quiet authority. 'Go back.'

Rasg hesitated, muttered thickly, and turned away.

Aniel saw the men's figures moving in and out, the darkness of the hollow below them, and, rising beyond, the raging sea of flame and flame-dyed smoke.

He turned and went on again, but presently stumbled and fell; nor did he make any effort to get up, but lay, and in his weariness began to weep. Nor did he rightly know what he was weeping for, and when his tears stopped he remained breathing quietly into the earth, his forehead on his arm.

His body hardly quivered when a hand touched him. Then the hand touched him again and crept round to feel his cheek. The hand drew back. He felt it was the hand of a witch. He turned his head and a face that had been stooping flashed away. The face receded. It looked like Breeta's face. He sat up and stared at the fire.

## CHAPTER NINE

IT was a morning of broken light and soft warmth between the Tower and the sea, but inland the sky was lost in smoke rising from the charred forest and burning moor. A great pall of gloom deepened there, shrouding the entrance to some infernal region created in the night, a grey-black depression that came upon the mind as it gazed at it, and so smothered hope that fear itself was left hardly able to crawl.

That is, if one gazed at it. Aniel did not. From the belt of trees high on the southern slope of the glen he watched men and women moving about their little houses as ants about a house that had been half destroyed.

Life was taking up its abode again; it was swarming over sorrow, weaving a future in which the herding youngsters – who were fending one or two beasts off the green strips of pasture which had hardly been touched at all – would as old men tell of what happened once upon a time on a day of days.

Aniel could see the tears in women's eyes and hear their sighs. He could listen to a man's curses as some wrecked thing came before him. But he was not downcast by them. On the contrary, he was uplifted. He could hear men's godless laughter when they gathered together, the laughter that is stolen from anger and is stronger than oaths. And light brightened in women's tears; and those who would be sorrow-stricken to the end of their days would wear their gloom as a dress about their heart's nakedness.

Fine excuses these, sufficient to dress his own buoyancy! He smiled to himself. The truth was he was alone again, and a craving had come upon him to make something. It was as though he had wandered out of a maze into an old freedom, and the glittering sea, familiar because it was empty, and the broken lights and the warm fragrant air were his secret allies. Always when he had got by himself in some unobserved place he had felt a deep delight, and his heart and his eyes and his desires had gone naked.

The sensation beset him now and his responsiveness was the more intense because of that very pall of smoke which he could glance at with a bright malevolence. And he knew that others would glance at it in that way too, though for the most part without knowing they were doing it, so deep did the loneliness of life run, deeper than hopelessness, so deep that it came up on the other side.

And in this mood the memory of Nessa had the brightness of gold. To have possessed Nessa would have been to have possessed a legend. This was so clear that it did not touch even the edge of a poignant emotion. She was now as it were opposite him and they were equal, for she was as vividly alive in legend as he was in himself. And he could keep her alive there – and would. He glanced at her and glanced away, smiling in his restlessness. Imagination has its own rape. He saw that now. Nessa had been no more meant for his flesh than a fire had been. To have had her would have been to have killed the legend. . . . Would it? By the gods, he wasn't sure! A warmth played on his face. With his knife he began hacking in the turf the solar symbols and his hand stopped only when he felt the Master approach. Nor did he look up until the Master sat beside him, and then his heart chilled, for the Master had death with him for company.

'You are ready to go, then, to the Broad River?'

'Yes,' said Aniel.

'They are settling into the glen.' The voice was clear and thin as a reed. 'I was looking at the smoke there a little while ago, and far into the years to come I saw the glen smoking again.' The tide of time had made a shell of his face, and the eyes had the bluish blindness of the smoke at which they stared. Although there was prophecy, there was no gloom in the voice. It had that clearness of acceptance which is the spirit's nobility before fate.

His time had come upon him. In some quiet place he would lie down and offer his blood. The glens and the moors and the forests were full of the blood of their people back into times so far distant that they might well seem dark to them. And yet they were not dark. To Aniel's young mind on this bright morning the far mornings of time were bright, and some of them bright as legend which is bright as gold.

Aniel's eyes glimmered.

The struggle was from night to the morning. The brightness of the mornings of the world. It was as though the Master saw all the achievements of men in their moments of inspiration.

Aniel's sadness caught at its core a secret gleam.

Aniel would bring back the young chief with his Christian religion. But he need not be hopeless about that. At the end of all religions that which is offered is always the same thing. That might be difficult, more difficult than all else to feel and to believe, and impossible for the old. But if Aniel had to satisfy his own people in the old ways, then he would do so, even if he had to do it secretly. For there was only one law in the end: the spirit has to be satisfied. In the fullness of time the Christian religion might satisfy it, for it, too, was based on blood and sacrifice. There were many religions in the world and the gods had many names. The rest was loyalty. Only of one thing were we sure, that there are dark beings, malignant and cruel; that pain and terror and disease and disaster and death overtake us. Each man was a lonely being in that battle. He had to hold the gods and demons at bay by propitiation, by sacrifice, but even more by the strength within himself. Let him be as one in his circle. Then the gods will respect him and the demons fear him, and he will know that joy which gives the only vision. Our past was in the earth, and our roots are in our past. We live for a little on the surface, drawing from our roots and sending new shoots to the Sun. The earth beneath, the sun above, and we the children of their union. That is all we know, and perhaps all we need to know to find the power that has serenity at its heart.

His secret happiness increased in Aniel, and he sat as one in a trance. He wanted the Master's voice to go on, to leave the earth, to reach the Pleasant Plain and to wander there.

The Master had sometimes spoken of a blue inland sea, of bright colours and a clear sun, as a place out of which they had wandered in the beginning of time. The Pleasant Plain was like that place for ever at its loveliest moment. But Aniel knew that the Master was speaking now only of him, Aniel, on this piece of earth, with its uncertain future. And it was in him urgently to tell the Master that he would never betray him – so urgently that he hung his head.

A hand landed on his head. The Master had never touched him before, and for a moment the cold hand burned into his head and the blood streamed from his heart. Even now the hand was not familiar, for there had always been about the Master's friendliness a withdrawn quality that must for ever leave a man to himself; yet more than all other qualities it attracts the admiration of men's minds and stirs the secret love of their hearts. For such a one you can do nothing, and therefore would do everything. Aniel watched him walk away and knew he would speak no more to any mortal, and his love grew so jealous that he would have massacred the gods to have saved him.

The trees trembled in his fierce tears; the smoke of the burning glen was a curtain on his sight; the grass came against his face and blinded him.

After a time he sat up and dried his lashes with the back of his hand. The fierceness gleamed still in his face. He put a slow circle about him with his eyes. The smoking moor, the feverish life in the valley, the glittering sea. He got up and went towards the trees.

The elation pricking at his breast had the pains of birth. Nessa had gone. The Master was gone. He was delivered to freedom. The morning of the world was empty, with its ridges waiting for his feet.

The pains eased. The gleam caught a smile at its centre. His body was buoyant and his muscles quivering quick as a cat's. He could have swung round and slashed. Amongst the trees a sound attracted his quickened senses, with the movement of a shadow on the verge of vision. Stirred unaccountably, he tiptoed swiftly. Breeta was standing behind a tree. When he looked at her she walked away. He watched her for a moment with an intense brightness.

Then he stepped quickly after her. Her dignity was not strong enough, and she broke and fled. He caught her up easily. She faced him in an angry flash.

He looked at her penetratingly, then with a small smile looked away. His expression was almost gentle in its hidden knowledge.

This so hurt her that her throat protested and her fists came up against her breast. She was like a wounded animal.

He lifted a narrow conquering expression that had the gleam of laughter at its core.

He exposed her too much. She walked away. He caught her up. She lost her head. He was all gleaming concentration and fierceness, and though she fought madly he got the better of her. When, flat on her face, she had finished sobbing, he tickled the soles of her feet. Her legs leapt with a wild astonishment and she rolled over and sat up.

He did not however meet her glaring face, but with head down, smiling shyly, poked her suddenly in the navel. She doubled up and hit him on the head.

'Breeta.'

She grew nervous, looking everywhere.

'You were following me,' he said.

She did not answer.

'I am going to the Broad River, many days from here. Will you come?'

She was trembling. 'Yes,' she said.

There was nothing legendary about Breeta. She was the dark plunge into life itself, into the life that ran with his blood and sheltered in the hollows of his bones. There was that story of two animals on a bank! He looked at her. She met his look and saw in it such an intense happiness that nothing lived outside the circle it put around them, and she was caught by it as by an enchanted snare.

# CANONGATE CLASSICS: SELECTED BACKLIST

Books listed in alphabetical order by author.

Most Canongate Classics are available at good bookshops.
If you experience difficulty in obtaining the title you want,
please contact us at 14 High Street, Edinburgh, EH1 1TE.